DEATH DINES IN

DEATH DINES IN

EDITED BY
Claudia Bishop and Dean James

BERKLEY PRIME CRIME, NEW YORK

DEATH DINES IN

A Berkley Prime Crime Book
Published by The Berkley Publishing Group
A division of Penguin Putnam, Inc.
375 Hudson Street, New York, NY 10014

Visit our website at www.penguin.com

First edition: May 2004

Library of Congress Cataloging-in-Publication Data

Death dines in / edited by Claudia Bishop and Dean James.—1st ed.
        p. cm.
    ISBN 0-425-19262-8
    1. Detective and mystery stories, American. 2. Detective and mystery stories, English. 3. Dinners and dining—Fiction. 4. Food habits—Fiction. 5. Gastronony—Fiction. 6. Cookery—Fiction. I. Bishop, Claudia, 1947-II. James, Dean (Darryl Dean)
PS374.D4D44 2004
813'.0872083559—dc22

                                                        2003063629

PRINTED IN THE UNITED STATES OF AMERICA

10   9   8   7   6   5   4   3   2   1

To lovers of mysteries and good food

Contents

Walk Right In . . .

. . . and enjoy some of our favorite new mystery stories. Dean and I got together last year at Bouchercon, one of mystery publishing's largest conventions, to talk about planning a new anthology for Berkley Prime Crime. Over a sensational meal of grilled swordfish (me) and *osso buco* (Dean), we decided that two of the best things friends can share in life are a great meal and a good mystery novel. The only way life could be better, we agreed, was if we were each curled up in our favorite reading spot at home with a writer we loved to read; light just right, perhaps a snowstorm slanging at the window, feet up, and somebody else to cook the food and clean up. We could put together an anthology to appeal to the comfort-loving reader in all of us. We could ask the writers to give us recipes so that a reader could try new food and a new writer all at the same time. We could call it . . . DEATH DINES IN!

Wow, we thought. What a great idea.

Until we started to talk about who loved what writers and why.

We both agreed on Dorothy Sayers: great characters, intricate puzzles, and who can quarrel with London as a setting? But from there on in we . . . umm . . . squabbled might be a polite way to put it. I turned pink in the face and raised my voice. Dean sat up straighter and straighter (he's a very tall guy) and his pleasant voice got quieter and quieter. We couldn't agree on *anybody*.

The waiter took away the wine bottle and didn't offer us any more.

The nicely dressed couple next to us kept casting meaningful glances in our direction.

The pianist swung into louder and louder versions of "St. Louis Woman." (We were in Austin, Texas, but he'd refused to play one more version of "Remember the Alamo.") Finally, Dean said with polite finality and an air of changing the subject, "Try some of my beef; it's great."

"No, thank you," I said, "I prefer my fish."

"And how are your entrees?" the waiter interrupted.

"Delicious!" we said simultaneously.

So it should come to no surprise to anyone that the anthology Dean and I put together represents a wide array of equally interesting, vastly diverse stories. There's Bill Moody's wry and ironic take on the simultaneous existence of the cozy and the hardboiled. Meg Chittenden takes us back to the days of the classic English village mystery—except that she sets hers on a train. Marcos Donnelley puts us in the Spanish barrios of Los Angeles, mixing religion, Hispanic culture, and a vivid amateur detective. Rhys Bowen illustrates turn-of-the-century New York so sharply that we can almost smell the air and walk the streets. There's a story here for almost everyone's taste, from Jerry Healy's tough guys to Donna Andrew's birthday party gone wrong. And for all readers, we have a marvelous story from Anne Perry that introduces a new series character, Thelonius Quade.

We planned this "menu of mysteries" with the broadest possible taste; there is at least one story that should appeal to any reader.

At least, that's what we tried do with DEATH DINES IN. And, like our response to our solicitous waiter, we hope that you find the stories herein "delicious."

—Claudia Bishop

. . . Sit Right Down

. . . It all began with Poe.

Though there are examples of crime fiction that predate Edgar Allan Poe's work, his five mystery stories are the foundation upon which much of today's mystery and detective fiction are built. Short mystery fiction in particular owes its genesis to Poe, for he was the first to use various concepts that are staples of the form. The locked-room puzzle, armchair detection, the most unlikely solution as the most obvious, a mysterious code, the laying of false clues—all these and more Poe used, and he has been imitated countless times through the years.

Poe also created the genius detective whose exploits are narrated by a less brilliant friend. Before Sherlock Holmes and Dr. Watson, there were Chevalier C. Auguste Dupin and the admiring, obtuse friend who narrated his exploits. And after Holmes and Watson came Poirot and Hastings, Wolfe and Goodwin. And so on and so on.

With the success of the Sherlock Holmes stories, mysteries in the short form flourished as never before. In the years between the two great wars of the last century, however, the novel of mystery and detection came to the fore. Thus we have the first Golden Age of the mystery novel.

Innovators appeared along the way. R. Austin Freeman wrote the first inverted mystery stories, in which the reader knows who the villain is; the suspense comes in seeing how the detective will figure it all out. Francis Iles offered readers the first inverted mystery novel in *Malice Aforethought* (1931) and followed it a year later with *Before the Fact,* better known to most mystery lovers in its cinematic form, Alfred Hitchcock's classic film, *Suspicion.* Melville Davisson Post created another variation upon the theme by writing the first historical mystery short stories. His "Uncle Abner" stories, first published in 1918, are set in pre-Civil War Virginia.

One of the great appeals of mystery fiction, for both readers and writers alike, is its enormous flexibility as a form. The venues range considerably, from the snowed-in English country house to the mean streets of Los Angeles, from a Benedictine monastery in twelfth-century England to the streets of late nineteenth-century New York. Detectives can be vampires and witches as well as police officers and suburban moms. The variations—and possibilities—seem endless.

Thus, in one collection of short mystery stories, we can sample a smorgasbord of delights, from Victorian England to the contemporary American scene, from the cozy family drama to the hard edge of crime. Sit back, relax, and dig in.

—Dean James

COCKTAILS WITH
THE CORPSE

Mary Jane Maffini

*Mary Jane Maffini is a smart, gorgeous, red-haired Canadian with the
fastest quip in the Northwest. She's won two Crime Writer's of American Arthur Ellis Awards for the short stories "Ladies Killing Circle"
and "Sign of the Times." Her fourth novel,* Lament For a Lounge
Lizard *was published in the fall of 2003.*

I don't know where that damn birdwatcher came from, but
one minute the coast was clear and the next she was strut-
ting across the lawn with her field glasses trained on the
driveway. I practically tripped over her. I'd just completed a
realignment of the surveillance cameras tucked into the
climbing roses that flanked the patio. Both had a clear view
of the elegant setting. Not that I expected a big payoff
from this location, but you never want to miss an opportunity. Our business is built on that principle. That's why we
had cameras strategically placed around the house, plus the
nifty pen cam sticking out of my front pocket, good for

close-ups. You have to love the advances in miniature wire-less technology.

The birdwatcher pointed a clawlike finger and shrieked like a seagull. I barely managed not to shriek back because if there's one thing I can't stand, it's a witness.

After four months of planning and thirty grand in investment, we'd reached the critical point in our operation. We had the perfect set-up in Witt's End: two-dozen acres of historic house and garden, gated and secure. No one was expected except me, my colleague, and our target.

This oddball was truly unwelcome. I looked around. No vehicle. My own wheels, a dun-colored Honda Accord, borrowed that morning from long-term parking at the airport, was parked in the four-car garage. I assumed the bird-woman had hiked her skinny buns down the bridle path through the woods. She hadn't triggered the security system because, of course, I'd disabled that. Wherever she'd come from, she'd been watching her feathered friends too long.

She opened her beak.

"Excuse me." She pointed towards the driveway with her walking stick. "But isn't that . . .?"

"That's right. Private property. Off limits to the public. Which would be you," I said.

"I know that. The Historical Society has been trying to get its hands on Witt's End for years, and the botanical gardens crowd is after it too," she chirped, "but I'm referring to that gentleman getting out of the lovely automobile in the driveway."

"Check the sign," I said.

"I am positive it's Charles Rutherford Graham III." She adjusted her field glasses.

"I'm positive the sign says PRIVATE PROPERTY."

"No need to be rude. I am merely asking you a question."

"And the answer is NO TRESPASSING."

"It was a civil question, Madam."

"Hit the road," I said, civilly.

Why was I surprised at her interest? Charles Rutherford Graham III was the current sensation of prime-time television. Every episode of his sleeper hit "Behind the Façade—Skeletons in the Closets of America's Great Historic Houses" got stratospheric ratings. Think "Antiques Roadshow" meets "Lives of the Rich and Famous" with a salacious hint of "Jerry Springer." Charles had a winning formula. He'd earned his Jaguar and more.

That's why we'd picked him.

"Don't you just love his wonderful English accent?" she cooed. "It gives me the shivers when he says, 'Look beyond the façade, things are not always what they appear'."

She had that right. And if today's operation went well, the great man's signature phrase was about to come back and bite him on the butt. Unless the witness got in the way.

"It gives *me* the shivers to know that trespassers will be prosecuted," I said cheerfully.

"Oh my," she trilled, "He's so elegant and affable."

I knew what he looked like. In addition to his Savile Row suit and his polished wingtips, Charles Rutherford Graham III would still have the bewitched expression he'd worn since his first, apparently random, encounter with my business partner three months earlier at an upscale soirée in the Hamptons.

Bird woman chirped, "Does this mean they'll shoot an episode here? Fabulous! Everyone will be thrilled."

That was all I needed. The whole thrilled town dashing over to get a gander at the great man. I said, "This is a visit with friends, nothing more, and definitely not your affair."

"Has there been some kind of scandal here? The Delong Witt family is so reclusive. I had no idea there'd be something to dig up. Of course, you never know."

"Do you see a television crew?"

"Oh," she said doubtfully. "No."

"Neither do I. Just a trespasser so I'll be calling the police now," I said, although I'd be the last person to call the police.

I definitely didn't want her to see Verona so I stuck my face in hers and said, "Beat it."

I wasn't worried about her identifying me. No one ever does. That's the joy of being plain, boring, and unremarkable. And now grey. Not at all like Verona.

"But who is that with him?" She pointed a gnarled finger toward the splendid blonde in the driveway.

Just the finest scam artist on two continents, I felt like saying. The woman who's responsible for separating more wealthy chumps from their huge wads of cash than anyone else. I said, "Mandy Delong Witt." What if this bird-woman might be one of the few people who would recognize the real Mandy?

She raised her field glasses again. "Really? She's always away in Tibet or India. Heavens. I expected her to be more . . . bookish."

Bookish. I loved that.

"She looks a bit flashy for him. Don't you agree?"

I didn't. Verona looked perfect. And she should, since a major chunk of our investment had gone into her hair, clothing, jewellery, and designer stiletto heels. Not to mention the outlay for Botox treatments, strategic liposuction, and the high-priced personal trainer, manicures, pedicures, and body buffing. Verona looked a hell of a lot better than the original Mandy Delong Witt, who was safely sitting with her unshaven legs crossed on the other side of the world in some forgotten bug-infested ashram. Verona looked good enough to get the suave and cultured Charles Rutherford Graham III exactly where she wanted him.

"Last chance," I said.

"You really are quite unmannerly. I must conclude it's hard for the Delong Witts to get good help these days."

I had to remind myself to stay in character after that. I whipped out my cell phone and dialed my own number. On the second ring, I said, "Yes, officer. This is Hilda Entwhistle of Witt's End and I would like to report a trespassing incident."

The birdwatcher pursed her scrawny lips. Then, speaking of unmannerly, she whirled to head for the path into the woods.

CHARLES Rutherford Graham III was having a most excellent day in what was a most excellent life. Not only was he a media phenomenon with a salary to match, but he was in love.

Who could ask for anything more?

Not me. We were on time and under budget. From the moment the apparent Mandy Delong Witt had unbent from the great man's glossy black Jaguar, her artfully highlighted, long-layered blonde hair blowing in the wind and her weensy skirt showing toned and polished legs up to here, her glossy pink smile suggested she was both amorous and impressed in equal parts.

Nothing indicated that she suspected her man Charlie occasionally left the historic homes a tad less endowed than he found them. Or that early in his career he'd rubbed shoulders with people who didn't worry about the provenance of artefacts that passed through their hands. This wasn't common knowledge. One of the benefits of our line of work is access to valuable specialized information.

Today, Charles was besotted, and who could blame him? Every time Verona extended her little pink tongue, he quivered. By the end of the weekend, poor quivering Charles would be sadder, wiser, and considerably poorer.

"What a splendid specimen," the great man said, apparently in reference to the house, although his eyes kept darting to the shapely seat of Verona's pink leather skirt. Versace, if I remembered right. The bill was firmly burned into my memory.

They both gazed up at Witt's End, a century-old pile of quarried stone, large enough to house a small town, but now occasional home to the only surviving member of the De-long Witt empire, Mandy, and her stern-faced elderly facto-tum, Nanny. That would be me, for the moment.

"I guess so." Mandy shrugged. "I never pay much atten-tion to the hideous old heap of rocks."

"Never pay attention? Really? But, Mandy darling, it's a historic gem. I've heard the artwork in Witt's End is mu-seum quality." Charles Rutherford Graham III's warm brown eyes gleamed. I hoped they gleamed with greed, al-though they could have been gleaming with lust. Either one might work for us.

Look beyond the façade, things are not always what they ap-pear. That was the great man's signature line, just before he revealed the well-kept secret of some pedigreed family. Our boy Charlie was about to find out the hard way just how true this could be.

Well, time to spring into action. I hustled my buns to get in through the French doors on the side garden and on to the front door that I threw open in welcome. Then I re-ceded discreetly off to the side. I hoped I didn't look ruffled after the encounter with the bird lady.

Verona tossed her Louis Vuitton weekend cases on the floor, lifted one groomed eyebrow, and squealed "Nanny!"

I'd had a bit of trouble with the Nanny bit, but Verona thought it made a difference, and she's got the instincts.

I reminded myself to stay in character. I managed a smile, smoothed my temporarily grey hair, and offered my hand. The great man shook it in a perfunctory fashion while pretty much looking through me. No problem. The less he remembered, the better.

If life was fair, Verona wouldn't continue to look like a Vogue cover while I got to be the poster child for the invis-ible servant class. But what the hell, in the twenty-five years since we hopped the fence and left St. Malachi's School for Wayward Girls behind, it's always been the same. Verona's in charge of sex appeal, I'm in charge of technical matters. And like they say, if it ain't broke, don't fix it.

"Six o'clock! Cocktail time, Nanny!" Verona said, gleefully. "I might mention it's a bit of an emergency."

"I'll take my bag upstairs first, darling girl," Charles said with a nice show of his favourite charm, playing more to Verona than me, "and freshen up."

"Don't be silly, Charles. Nanny will do it. If I don't have a cocktail right this minute I am going to be a cranky girl."

"We wouldn't want that," I said.

"And I hate to drink alone," she added, running her little pink tongue over her lips.

She pivoted on the polished marble floor of the great entranceway, clicking along on her Jimmy Choos. If your shoes cost six hundred dollars, I guess you would want them to click too.

"Martinis at the ready, Nanny?" she said.

"They are. I thought you'd both enjoy them outside on the Rose Patio after your long drive."

"Bombay Sapphire Gin, of course," she twiddled her toes, perhaps to show off the high-priced pedicure, perhaps just to annoy me.

"Yes." I narrowed my eyes.

"Chilled?"

"Of course."

"You have Noilly Prat?"

"Naturally."

"Just a whisper?"

I sniffed.

"Yummy," she said, shaking her booty as she made her way back toward the French doors. She turned back to Charles. "Come along darling."

The great man followed, wagging his tail, even though I

was pretty sure he couldn't wait to get his eyes on the collection of modern masters that filled the walls of the second and third floors.

"Martini first, upstairs later. Anyway, Nanny will pop your bag up to your room once she serves our perfect martinis."

The great man didn't take much convincing. I think he liked the sound of upstairs later.

"Shaken, not stirred," Verona reminded me.

It's not always easy to stay in character when Verona's around.

Charles glanced around with approval. If I did say so myself, the patio set-up looked like something from a photo shoot. The triple layers of filmy muslin over the floor-length tablecloth fluttered in the breeze. The chilled glasses glinted in the late afternoon sun. My artistry showed in the cluster of coral hybrid roses in the Lalique vase, set against the backdrop of rolling lawn and surrounding woods. Not to mention Verona looking most scenic herself. The cameras would capture it all. Our man would have a hard time denying his unauthorised presence at Witt's End after that. For sure. He could only look like a charlatan or a fool.

I hustled inside and returned with the finger foods to complete the tableau; The Crown Derby plate with the lightly warmed fig and soft goat cheese scooped onto endive leaves.

Five minutes later, I left the charming couple, sunk into the white-cushioned weather-proof settee, clinking glasses. Verona lifted the endive leaf from his fingers and ate it. "A girl needs her greens," she said, wrinkling her pretty nose.

She sure does.

What the hell, let her toy with him. He was the type she prefers in a mark. Prosperous, smug, satisfied. He was a tad less beefy than her usual target and not nearly so red-faced, but still, I could tell she was enjoying herself.

Weren't we all?

*   *   *

I hoofed it upstairs with the great man's hand-tooled tan leather weekender under one arm and Verona's cases under the other. Working out in the gym pays off when you have a need for speed. Verona had promised him the Blue Suite, re-served for the male head of the household, when there was one. Wait until he got a gander at the collection of Fabergé eggs. Not to mention the glass-fronted case of leatherbound first editions and, did I mention, the Russian icons? There was much to lust after in this room. How long could our cultural maven resist?

I checked out the man's suitcase on the off chance it con-tained something I should have been aware of, but aside from his cell phone and snazzy weekend wardrobe, nada. I took another moment to adjust the cams: one in the smoke detector, one in the clock radio, and one in the fold of the valance that topped the splendid four-poster. I wanted to make sure any acts of light-fingeredness would show to good advantage. I was checking the angle of the last camera when the first scream rose up the stairs.

CHARLES was howling in hysteria when I shot down-stairs and out to the Rose Patio. His glass lay broken near the settee. Verona, on the other hand, continued to sip her martini and frown dangerously from the cushions.

"Good grief, woman, did you not see him?" he bellowed, slipping out of his urbane persona for a second.

"Who?" I said, doing my best to stay in character and not slug the great man.

"Him!" He pointed to the flagstone floor by the base of the table.

A pair of tasselled cordovan loafers protruded from under the trendy layers of white cloth. The shoes were at an odd angle, as if the owner had been practising pliés. Something suggested the feet didn't belong to anyone still stuck in this vale of tears.

"I guess Nanny's getting slack in her household management," Verona said, tilting her pretty chin to give me a dirty look.

"Household management?" Charles said.

"Whatever," Verona said. "I am sure there's a perfectly boring explanation and it can wait. If I don't get a fresh martini down my throat I'm going to be a cranky girl."

Charles moved gingerly forward towards the feet. "Hello?" he said, bending over.

Verona stood up and stamped her Jimmy Choos. "Martini, Charles. Now."

I sure hoped she was tossing those martinis and not drinking them.

To give him credit, Charles managed to withstand the implied threat. He bent over further and tugged at the left shoe. It came off in his hand. The foot stayed still.

Whoever was under that table hadn't been there when I'd finished setting up forty-five minutes earlier. And whatever the hell was going on, it didn't fit well with our plans. It was think-fast time again. I said, "It's that idiot electrician again. What a worthless layabout. You two just go into the house and enjoy your refreshments while I sober him up and send him on his way."

"Electrician? In handmade shoes?" Charles said. "I hardly think so."

"I gather you haven't had any wiring done lately or you wouldn't be surprised," I said. "The poor fellow will be mortified if you see him like this, so you two scoot inside and I'll make sure he gets home."

"See that you do," Verona said, latching firmly onto Charles and giving him a serious yank towards the French doors. That personal trainer had paid off once again. Charles moved in spite of himself.

I dropped to my knees and raised the tablecloth. It didn't

take a doctor to figure out the man was dead and to figure out he'd been killed by a nasty blow to the head. A small stream of blood dripped from his shattered forehead.

I hate blood. It turns my stomach.

I'd never seen him before. I sat back on my heels and scratched my head. Someone had rained on our parade. But who? And why?

If it hadn't been for the blood I might have prevented Charles from wresting himself away from Verona's steely grip, rushing back and dropping to his knees on the flagstone beside me. But I was doing my damnedest not to toss my cookies. I couldn't stop him from getting a good look.

"My god, he's injured," Charles gasped.

Oh, he was way past injured. I was having a bit of trouble remaining in character. "Terrible," I murmured.

The click of expensive heels on the stone announced Verona's return. "Fine, I'll get it myself," she said.

"This is an emergency, Mandy, darling. Don't you think we should hold off on the martinis until . . .?"

"No, I don't," she said.

"We must call the paramedics. 9-1-1." He turned to me, looking frantic.

"I'm afraid it's too late for that," I said.

"You mean, he's dead," Charles squeaked.

"I'd say very dead."

"Well then, I guess there's no rush for paramedics," Verona said.

Charles gaped at her. How was he to know she was just trying to distract him so that we could deal with this serious setback? I thought she could be trying harder because there's nothing like an unexpected body to wreck a good plan.

He turned back to me. "But how do we know he's dead?"

"Any fool can tell he's bought it," Verona said, huffily.

Charles's eyes were taking on a wild look. This was a side to his new love he hadn't seen.

"Well, the police then."

"No police," Verona said.

He bleated. "But, darling, of course we must call the police. There's a body here."

"Anyone you know?" Verona said.

"What? It doesn't matter who it is. If someone dies, you call the police."

"Doesn't happen all that often," I said, taking a deep breath and getting as close as I could to the body. I turned the head so we could see. Verona leaned in. She doesn't give a crap about blood.

"Darling. Isn't that what's his name, your producer?"

Charles made a sound like a plugged drain. "Good lord, it is. It's Phil Whippet. But what can have happened to him? Do you think he tripped and hit his head on the flagstone?"

"Don't be silly," Verona said." He didn't trip. Someone killed him."

"Killed him? I don't understand."

"There's not much to understand. He's dead, we're not. Time for another drink." Verona took the opportunity to fill her martini glass to the brim.

Charles blithered, "We can't sit around drinking martinis with Phil lying there murdered right under our noses."

"I hate police," Verona said, pouting as she sank back into the settee.

"But we have no choice."

We had choices all right, but calling the police sure wasn't one of them.

"Don't you talk to me like that, Charles," Verona said. "I won't stand for it."

"Talk to you like what?" Charles said.

"I think you know," Verona said. Her left foot was swinging dangerously now. I was glad I wasn't anywhere near that shoe.

Charles said, "I am sorry if I was curt, but that is my producer lying there. I am shocked. Devastated. Who would want to kill Phil?"

Verona said, "Surely you must have felt like it?"

He goggled. "What a thing to say, Mandy!"

"Didn't you call him a grasping, underhanded, greedy, little peckerhead and say he should be squashed like a roach?"

"I never said any such thing."

"I heard you. On the phone, just the other day."

"But that was just a comment in the heat of contract negotiations. Now he's been murdered. This is horrible, beyond belief. We have to do the right thing." Charles mopped his face with his monogrammed hanky, something I was sure Emily Post would frown on.

"I guess you're right," Verona said, foot still swinging, "Everybody feels like killing someone sometime."

"Mandy! Please don't suggest that. I did *not* feel like killing Phil."

"But you did say squashed like a cockroach."

"A figure of speech. Meant playfully. He was playing hardball on the negotiation." He turned to me and bent down. "What do you think happened to him?"

"Speaking of hardball. He's been beaned on the head. Rough way to go," I said.

Verona shrugged. "Not at all playful."

She was stalling nicely while I thought as fast as I could. The main thing was that Verona and I not be anywhere near Witt's End if the police did show.

Charles said, "I have no choice. I'm calling the police now." He patted his pocket. "Where's my cell?"

Upstairs in your luggage, I thought. And a good thing too.

"Who cares?" Verona said, "Although you should since you'll be a prime suspect."

"But . . ." I could see him running that scenario through his mind.

"Imagine yourself in the supermarket. Imagine the tabloid headlines: *Society Shocker!!!! Look behind the façade of Behind the Façade.*" There'll be a picture of you looking unshaven and dissolute."

That produced a sharp intake of breath from our man.

"She's right," I said. "Let's take a few minutes and gather our thoughts."

Charles reached over and touched the body, something I'd been reluctant to do. Even so, I forced myself to lean in too. He shrieked, "He's warm. Phil is still warm. He might be alive."

"Allow me to assure you he is very dead," I said.

"But warm. That means he hasn't been dead long. And I have been with Mandy for hours. It will be obvious to the police I had nothing to do with this."

"Careful," I said. "You don't want to get blood on that Rolex."

Verona brightened, "So you're in the clear and so am I. Let's drink to alibis."

I leaned closer to him and whispered. "Look. She's been shielded from anything unpleasant all her life. You can imagine this distressing incident has thrown her right off. We certainly want her to be sensible when the police arrive."

"Yes, oh yes, we do."

"Exactly. Why don't you just take her inside, away from the martinis. I'll look after things."

He blinked, "Does that mean you'll call the police?"

I smiled. "Of course. Just stay with Mandy until she comes to grips with this tragedy."

"Thank you, you can imagine how suspicious it will look if we don't notify the authorities. A public relations disaster from my point of view."

"We all want to avoid scandal. Remember the police will never know exactly when we found him."

Relief flooded his face. "Of course. How would they know?"

"Exactly, now, if you'll please look after Mandy, I'll get on it."

The sight of his elegant backside heading into the house

gave me the boost I needed. I knew I could count on Verona to keep him occupied. While he was patting Verona's shaking shoulder, I dashed upstairs, grabbed my bag and Verona's, and deposited the cameras, quick like a bunny. Sometimes you have to cut your losses. And as Verona says, marks are like buses, there's always another one coming along shortly. I'd been careful with fingerprints but I figured I'd have to do a fast swipe, over every surface. I planned to leave a few of Charles's on the patio. In case they came in handy.

Last thing was the receiver system for our video feeds, collected from the pantry and ready to go.

Twenty minutes later, slightly breathless, I beckoned to Charles. "The police are coming. They thought it was a joke at first. I suppose they're not immune to irony."

"Irony?"

"Well, you can't keep this hidden. Which reminds me, where the police are, the media cannot be far behind."

Charles blanched, a satisfying shade of off-white.

I said, "So if I were you, I'd head upstairs and collect your bag so you can depart the minute the cops are done. I'll take over with Mandy. Sometimes she requires a firm hand."

By the time Charles had scuttled up the wide staircase, I'd cleared out the Rose Patio, tossed the stemware into a green garbage bag, followed by the dishes, and anything else that might yield a scrap of fingerprint or DNA. I carefully wiped all surfaces and yanked the cameras from the climbing roses on both sides of the patio, avoiding scratches. The cameras went into my bag with the others. Verona used the time to get the Honda from the garage and whip around to the side exit. Seconds later we were peeling down the driveway away from Witt's End. Verona took out her frustrations by pounding on the dash.

"If you insist on driving when you're upset, you should

keep your hands on the wheel at this speed," I said. "No criticism intended."

"Well that was a waste of four months' effort," she pounded.

She didn't mention the money we'd spent. She never does.

"Come on. Grab that wheel and I may have a pleasant surprise for you," I said, patting my pocket.

"What could be pleasant? With the cops on the way? And that fool ready to babble anything to them. After all our preparation for this fiasco."

"Don't say fiasco too soon. I don't think he'll babble. He won't want the world to know the role he played in taking out his producer."

"But he didn't kill the guy. I'm his alibi, remember? I know where he was."

"And you don't think that's just too much of a coincidence?"

Verona's jaw clenched but at least she held onto the steering wheel. "You mean that wretch was taking advantage of me?"

"Disgraceful as that may seem, here's what happened. His confederate did in the pesky producer at exactly the time Charles was incontrovertibly with the lovely Mandy. Why do you think he was so anxious to get the police there so quickly? To confirm the time of death. How many stops did you make on the way up here?"

"At least five. To get gas, chewing gum, coffee, look at the view. And every time he got out of the Jag and flashed his credit card like he was accepting an Emmy."

"He was counting on everyone he saw to back up his location while someone else did the dirty work. Put that together with Mandy's testimony and he'd be in the clear."

"What a disgusting, manipulative, revolting thing to do. And dishonest."

"I guess things really weren't as they appeared," I said. "Behind the façade."

"And that fat, pompous little creep never even set foot up-stairs while the cams were in place. We're left with nothing. I feel betrayed. And I didn't even get any of that fig spread. I love figs, you know I love figs."

"Not to worry. You can get all the figs you want when we're done," I said. "And more than just figs. I think we'll find what we need on this. Give me a couple of minutes." I fished out the video receiver/player from my bag and quickly worked my way through the images. Sure enough. A clear bit of the bird woman by the side of the Rose Patio doing her bit on the victim's cranium with the polished walking stick. Followed by excellent footage of Charles and Verona, obviously at home. Including the drama of discovering the body.

You just gotta love digital technology. And batteries.

"Pull over," I said.

Once she did, I passed the camera over to Verona.

"Ew. Who's she?" Verona said.

"Hired help, I'd say. Keep watching. I think we'll end up with a nice shot of Charles by the side of the body."

She said. "That doesn't prove anything."

I whipped out the pen from my pocket and squinted into the little viewfinder. "This does. We've got a close-up of him touching the late Phil."

"So what?"

"Yup, there's the time for one thing, as seen on his pricy watch. It's more than a half an hour since he found the body and even if he calls the cops, the time difference will be most damning, don't you think?"

Verona said peevishly. "I don't know if any of this would get the little creep convicted."

"Convicted?" I said. "He's no good to us convicted. And, of course, there's no way he'll go to the cops now. He'll want as much distance as he can get between himself and the late Phil."

I took out my cell phone to give the great man a call.

"Charles," I said when he picked up. No need to stay in character now. "Don't worry about the police because they aren't coming. You'll be glad about that because your alibi is long gone. And if you're looking for your hired help, check the stables, I think your accomplice will regain consciousness soon. She'll appreciate being untied. We have the murder on tape if she wants a souvenir. Plus a nice record of you, as an unauthorised visitor to Witt's End, touching the late Phil. Your Rolex shows beautifully on camera by the way. We'll be in touch to work out suitable financial transactions. We've really enjoyed going behind the façade. Oh, and Charles? Don't call us, we'll call you."

DEAN AND CLAUDIA ASK MARY JANE:

Q: *If you weren't a writer, what would you be?*
A: I'm a lapsed librarian, a bounced bookseller, and escaped public servant. I'm pretty well out of potential careers. I think I'd like to read for a living.

Q: *Will we see Verona and "Hilda" again? Claudia adores them, and so does Dean.*
A: Verona and the unnamed narrator (Hilda in this story for you two) show up from time to time in short stories. They had a good time in a nudist colony looking for blackmail targets until someone got offed. The short story was "Naked Truth" and the big question was: where did the murderer hide the weapon? They surfaced again as a pair of black-mailing nuns in "Kicking the Habit." I'd like to introduce them to the Royal Family some day. Politicians should also be wary. Also cops.

Q: *How do you know when you're writing well?*
A: If I laugh out loud. And if I scare myself. I get lots if ideas while cooking—I like to stir the pot.

AND HERE IS MJ'S RECIPE:

Cocktail Party for Two

PERFECT MARTINIS

6 ounces Bombay Sapphire Gin—seriously chilled
2 whispers of Noilly Prat Dry Vermouth—also chilled
2 chilled stemmed martini glasses
2 swirls of lemon peel

Combine in cocktail shaker.

Shake, do not stir.

Repeat as needed.

LOIS'S FIG SPREAD

4 ounce roll of soft goat cheese
4 tablespoons imported fig spread
Endive leaves

Spread goat cheese over bottom of heatproof dish.
Spread fig spread over goat cheese.

Heat at medium in microwave for 40 seconds.

Spoon onto endive leaves. Place on something valuable
and serve two immediately.

LETHAL LUNCHEON

Parnell Hall

Edgar, Shamus, and Lefty nominee Parnell Hall is the author of the Puzzle Lady crossword puzzle mysteries, the Stanley Hastings private eye novels, and the Steve Winslow courtroom dramas. An actor, screenwriter, and former private investigator, he lives in New York City. He is also charming, witty, and notoriously in demand as a toastmaster at mystery events.

"Do we really have to go?" Cora Felton whined.

Sherry Carter piloted the Toyota around a curve in the road, and glanced sideways at her aunt. "That's a silly question, Cora. We're in the car on our way to lunch. Of course we have to go."

"We could turn around."

"Aren't you hungry?"

"We could stop at the Friendly's. I could get a cheeseburger and a hot fudge sundae."

"I though you were on a diet."

"All right, I'll get a coffee Fribble. Coffee isn't fattening."

"It's coffee *ice cream.*"

"What's your point?"

"Cora, we have to go to the luncheon. You're donating a dish. It's for charity."

"But I can't cook."

"You can't do crossword puzzles, either, but that's never stopped you."

Cora Felton's sweet, grandmotherly face graced her niece's nationally syndicated crossword puzzle column.

"That's unfair," Cora protested. "Did I *want* to be the Puzzle Lady. I never wanted to be the Puzzle Lady. That was your idea."

"And a pretty good one, too. You owe your TV career to it."

Cora Felton did breakfast cereal commercials as the Puzzle Lady. The residuals paid for the house she and Sherry shared in Bakerhaven, Connecticut.

"I'm not sure it's worth it," Cora said. "When I think of all the aggravation it's caused. Like this damn luncheon."

"It's for orphans," Sherry said reprovingly. "Try not to call it a 'damn luncheon' with reporters present."

"Oh, no," Cora said. "God forbid I should able to speak my mind. What's this dish I'm supposed to have created?"

"Glad you asked. You should have the recipe, in case someone asks you for it. It's in my purse."

Cora went through Sherry's purse, came out with a recipe entitled *Cioppino: Puzzle Lady Style.*

"Cioppino? What's that?"

"Fish stew."

Cora made a face. "Then why couldn't you just *say* fish stew? Why so pretentious with all the big words?"

"You're the Puzzle Lady. You're supposed to *know* words."

"I'm supposed to know *English* words."

"Cioppino is English."

"Sounds Italian."

"It's of Italian derivation. It's still English."

"Oh, dear," Cora said, looking over the recipe. "All these ingredients. You really mix them? I have trouble making toast and jam."

"Could you try not to admit that?"

"Don't worry. I'll be at my deceptive best. So what am I supposed to do at this damn lunch? I mean at this charity luncheon to aid a worthy cause?"

"Nothing. You donate your dish. You sit down and eat."

"Sounds simple enough."

"Then you give your speech."

"Oh, hell!"

"You *are* the luncheon speaker. Or had you forgotten?"

Cora groaned. "Believe me, I've been trying."

The sign over the door of the community center read, FEED THE KIDS, INC. Cora's eyes lit up when she saw it.

"Don't you dare!" Sherry hissed as they went up the front steps.

Betty Flagstaff, co-chairman of Feed the Kids, Inc., met them at the door of the dining room. "Ah, Miss Felton," she gushed. "We're so honored that you could come."

"How could I resist?" Cora smiled. "Feed the kids ink is such a noble sentiment. When I think of some of the kids I've known in my day, well, I just wish I'd thought of it then."

Betty Flagstaff was a large woman, who either had no sense of humor, or thought it best to pretend not to notice the remark. "That's wonderful. And what have you prepared for us?"

Cora, who couldn't for the life of her remember what the dish was called, said, "My niece, Sherry, has it. May I present Sherry Carter, who was kind enough to drive me here."

"And carry the dish," Sherry said. "It's a fish stew. Cora calls it cioppino. I hope you don't mind her using the Italian derivation."

"Of course not," Betty said. "You know," she confided in Cora. "I must tell you, I'm a crossword puzzle buff myself.

And I'm not that keen on foreign words in puzzles, I hope that doesn't offend you."

"Hell, no," Cora said. "Frankly, I'm not that keen on English words, either."

"Ah, yes, of course," Betty said, with zero comprehension. "Well, if you'll just sign in there." She pointed to a long table on the side of the room behind which a formidable looking woman presided over name tags, pens, magic markers, and a guest list. "Cecily will be glad to help you."

"I'll be happy if Cecily doesn't bite my head off," Cora whispered, as she and Sherry walked over.

Cecily, however, had no such intention. On seeing Cora, the dragon lady's face dissolved into a succession of smiles, winks, and titters, each one more hideous than the last. "Ah, Miss Felton, how are you? It is such an honor to have you with us. You don't have to sign in, I will do it for you. You don't even have to print your name tag. We did it in advance."

Cecily held up a name tag with the blue outline *Hello, my name is*. The name *Cora Felton* had been printed in the middle in block capitals by some machine or other.

"You, young lady. I have you right here." Sherry watched while Cecily located "Cora Felton Guest" on the list and checked it off. "Here's a magic marker. Try to print neatly."

"This is my niece. Sherry Carter." Cora Felton beamed. "I think she should print that on the name tag instead of 'Cora Felton Guest,' don't you?"

Cecily found that enormously funny. "Now, what you *do* need to print is the name of your dish. Use one of the folded cardboards. Then we can stand it up in the buffet line."

Cora, who had forgotten what she had supposedly cooked again, said, "Sherry, could you do that for me? Sherry has such nice handwriting, and mine is atrocious."

"Of course," Cecily said. "Just put the name of the dish, and then Cora's name, so people will know who cooked it."

"In theory," Cora said under her breath.

"I beg your pardon?"

"And what do we do then?"

"Put the dish on the buffet line, and find your place at your table." Cecily consulted her chart. "You're at table ten. You'll find place cards by your plates."

"They have assigned seats," Cora groused, after she and Sherry had stowed the fish amidst a myriad of casseroles, pastas, roasts, and assorted side dishes.

"You're lucky you're not sitting on a dais," Sherry whispered back.

"Amen to that. So where's table ten?"

"The tables have stands in the middle with numbered cards on them. Do you think it might be a clue?"

Cora muttered something that couldn't possibly have been a clue in any crossword puzzle in any daily paper in the country, and pushed ahead of Sherry into the middle of the room.

The tables were round and seated eight. Most were already filled. Cora and Sherry got to theirs to find six people waiting. All were women. Some were as old as Cora. None were as young as Sherry. All were nicely, if casually, dressed in sweaters and blouses and pullovers and smocks.

The two empty plates at the table sported place cards. One read "Cora Felton." The other read "Felton Guest."

Cora and Sherry sat down and smiled at the women around them, who all began talking at once. It was impossible to hear anything, but hidden somewhere in the cacophony was the sentiment that they were happy to have, if not Sherry, at least Cora there.

When the noise had died down, a rather large woman with a triple chin seated directly across the table from Cora declared, "We *waited* for you."

The women were all wearing name tags, so Cora was able to identify the speaker as Marcy Fletcher. From that simple statement Cora was able to ascertain that waiting for her had been Marcy's idea, that none of the other women were particularly pleased about it, and that Marcy blamed Cora for making her endure their wrath.

"That was too kind, but not at all necessary," Cora said. "You must be starving. Please dig in. And perhaps someone can explain to me what this luncheon is all about."

A woman with a face flat as a pancake said, "It's for charity."

According to her name tag, the woman *was* Charity, but she didn't seem to notice the coincidence. Cora was tempted to point it out to her.

"You mean you came here without knowing what it's all about?" a henna-haired woman said. Her name was Phyllis, and she clocked in at a good two hundred and fifty pounds. "I think that's admirable."

"I think it's stupid," Wendy said. Wendy had a haughty look, and undoubtedly thought many things stupid. "Why would you want to come to something if you don't know what it is?"

"It's for *charity*," Charity insisted.

"Well, at least we can eat the salads now," whined a mousy little type with the name tag *Monica Nuthatch*. Monica wore glasses that would have been thought geeky in the fifties. What they were thought now, Cora couldn't even imagine. Monica snuffled her nose as she dug into her salad, and managed to look less like a mouse, and more like a rabbit.

"Now, now, now," said the last woman at the table, the woman seated to Cora's right. She was middle-aged, but looked younger. Her blonde hair hung to her shoulders. Her ribbed, double-knit, turtleneck sweater looked comfortably warm. She had an easy-going air about her, of a woman who is happy with herself, and completely in control. "We're delighted to have you here. If the truth be known, the women couldn't care less about their salads. They just want to eat them so they can go through the buffet line. They can't wait to see what people brought this year. We all can't. But that has nothing to do with you, because no one goes through the line until Betty gives the order." She smiled knowingly. "Betty likes giving orders.

"Oh, but here I am babbling on. And I haven't introduced myself. I'm Felicity Grant. I'm the co-chairman. I helped put together this little lunch."

"Oh, for goodness sakes, stop with the false modesty," Marcy groused. "You're proud of it, and you know it. Felicity got this project off the ground in spite of Betty. You would not *believe* the back-biting that goes on in those meetings. It's *horrible*. I swear, if it weren't for this woman nothing would get done."

"Marcy, really," Felicity said.

"Again with the false modesty. We had a dinner meeting. Well, we *almost* had a dinner meeting. Turned out we had a speaker and no hall, and whose fault was that, I ask you? Had to send the checks back, and what a job that was. Who *was* the speaker that time?"

"Marcy."

"What, I'm talking too much? We're all family here. It's not like she's a reporter or anything. I mean, you think she's gonna stick this in her next crossword puzzle?"

"I wouldn't dream of it," Cora assured her.

"Of course you wouldn't. So why make a fuss? But Betty goes ballistic if she breaks a fingernail." Marcy, while talking, had managed to wolf down her salad. "Okay, I'm done. Can we eat for chrissakes? I'm starving."

"You're the one who wanted to wait."

"And aren't you glad we did? How would it be if our guests showed up and our table was empty? Come on, come on. People are beating us on line."

That was certainly true. Betty had apparently given the order, because at least half the women in the room were scraping back their chairs.

"Please don't wait on my account," Cora said. "Go, I'll be right behind you."

That was all the invitation the women needed. As if Cora had fired a starter's gun, Marcy was up and practically bowling people over to get a place in line. Charity, mousey Monica Nuthatch, and the mountainous Phyllis were right on her heels.

"Disgraceful," Wendy said. She said it while tagging along behind.

"I wouldn't want people to think I'm not happy to be here," Cora said, "but would it be impolite not to sprint?"

"Not impolite, just imprudent," Felicity said. "Your favorite dish is apt to be gone."

"I'll risk it."

"Suit yourself." Felicity hesitated. "But if you don't mind, I had my eye on that spinach quiche."

Rather sheepishly, Felicity got up and hurried toward the line.

"And just how does this all feed children?" Cora demanded of Sherry. "It seems to me they're just feeding themselves."

"They paid to be here. I think twenty bucks a head."

"They paid to be here *and* cooked the food?"

"That's right."

"Because they like kids or because they like food?" Cora snorted. "How come we didn't pay?"

"You're the luncheon speaker."

"Oh. Right. What am I gonna say, Sherry?"

"You're gonna tell them about crossword puzzles."

"I don't *know* anything about crossword puzzles."

"It's all right. They don't care. Just tell them anecdotes about your TV career."

"What TV career? All I've done is a few commercials."

"Cora," Sherry said. "This is the fourth or fifth time we've had this conversation. Let's go see if anyone ate your fish stew."

There were nearly a hundred women ahead of them at the buffet table, but as Cora and Sherry queued up to get their trays, Betty Flagstaff swooped down on them.

"Oh, no, no, my dears," Betty clucked. "Honored guests do not wait in line. Come, come, come."

Betty plucked Cora and Sherry by the shoulders and marched them to the front of the line.

Marcy, who was still halfway back, gave Cora the fisheye as she went by.

"This is not winning us any popularity contests," Cora whispered.

"Wanna object?" Sherry whispered back.

"No. I'm tired. I wanna eat."

Cora and Sherry took trays and plates, worked their way down the buffet table. Progress was slow, as the women in front of them were taking their time choosing their dishes.

Cora loaded her plate with ravioli, pasta salad, fettuccine.

"Little heavy on the starch, don't you think?" Sherry cautioned.

"You want me to put some back?" Cora said ironically.

"You might wanna leave room on your plate."

"So I won't eat the fish stew. I can have that at home."

"I hope someone eats it," Sherry said.

She needn't have worried. By the time they got there, the fish stew was almost gone.

So was the spinach quiche. There were three pies. Two tins were empty, and the third pie was half gone.

"Damn," Cora said.

"What's the matter?"

"The spinach quiche looks good, but I don't dare take it."

"Why not?"

"Felicity wants it."

"It'll be gone by the time she gets here."

"Right. If I have a piece, she'll blame me for it being gone."

"So you're not going to have one?"

"No."

"In that case, take one and give it to her."

"I still won't have one."

"No, but you'll be doing a good deed."

"I'm not a Boy Scout. What's in it for me?"

"I'll take a piece and give it to you."

"You don't want quiche?"

"No."

"Then why don't you give your piece to her?"

"I want you to get credit for it."

"Why?"

"It will make up for giving a lousy speech."

Sherry and Cora were the first ones back to their table. Marcy came next, proudly bearing a heaping plate that could easily have fed a dozen children. The rest of the women followed with plates piled nearly as high.

Cora gave her niece a look which Sherry understood perfectly. Compared to the other servings, Cora's seemed modest indeed.

Felicity was the last one back. "Missed the quiche, damn it," she said as she sat down.

"No, you didn't." Cora presented the spinach quiche with a *ta-da* gesture. "Pardon my fingers. I haven't had a communicable disease since my fifth husband, Melvin. He was a bit wild."

Felicity was delighted to get the quiche, though somewhat put off by the comment. "It does look awfully good. Are you sure you don't want it?"

"She can have mine," Sherry said. "I'm not that big on quiche." She cocked her head ironically. "I had chicken pox in the second grade, Cora."

"Probably safe." Cora handed her quiche to Felicity, and took Sherry's.

Felicity, reassured the women were joking, accepted the quiche. For a moment conversation stopped as the women all dug in.

"Don't eat so fast," Sherry whispered out of the side of her mouth.

"Why?"

"As soon as you're done you've gotta speak."

"I'll get you for this," Cora assured her.

Sherry grinned, attacking the veal casserole.

Cora had just finished her portion of medallions of something that she narrowed down to veal, lamb, or venison, when Betty Flagstaff descended on the table with all the subtlety of a steamroller. She stepped up behind Cora and Felicity, clapped a meaty arm around each, and declared, "Is this something, or is this something?"

Cora was quick to admit that it was, indeed, something, but that wasn't enough to satisfy Betty Flagstaff, "We are so delighted that you're here, and so delighted that you're going to speak. The women just can't wait. I'm going to introduce you when they start dessert. That way there's no chance anyone will finish lunch and sneak out for a cigarette. That would never do, now, would it?"

"Certainly not," Cora said virtuously. "Well, if I'm going on, I'd better run to the Ladies."

Cora pushed back her chair, grabbed her floppy, drawstring purse, and hurried in the direction of the Women's Room.

She was in luck. No one was there. Cora whipped out a pack of cigarettes, lit one, and took a greedy drag. How anyone could eat a huge lunch like that and not finish it off with a cigarette was beyond her. It would be hard enough under normal circumstances. To have to get up and speak while going through nicotine withdrawal was out of the question.

Cora took a last drag, held her cigarette under the tap water. She threw the soggy butt in the wastebasket and sailed out the door, just as two women came in. Whether they'd be able to breathe in the smoke-filled bathroom seemed a close point, but there was nothing Cora could do about that.

Cora returned to her table just as a loud blast of feedback

attracted everyone's attention to a lectern at the front of the room where Betty Flagstaff was wrestling with a microphone.

"Oh, dear," Felicity said. "You're going to miss your tiramisu."

"My what?" Cora said.

Sherry cringed. It was no easy task keeping up the ruse that Cora was the Puzzle Lady, and not she. It would have helped if Cora had a slightly more extensive vocabulary.

"Your dessert," Felicity said, pointing to the rich confection behind Cora's plate.

There was one at each setting. The eight servings of tiramisu formed a circle in the center of the table.

"It looks obscenely delicious," Cora said.

Felicity frowned at the adverb. It occurred to Sherry there were also times she wished Cora had a *smaller* vocabulary.

Another blast of reverb quieted the room.

Betty Flagstaff, smiling the helpless smile of the electronically impaired, said, "Good afternoon, ladies. And welcome to this charity luncheon sponsored by Feed the Kids, Incorporated."

"I like 'Ink' better," Cora said.

"Shhh!" Sherry whispered.

"I'd like to thank my co-chairman, Felicity Grant, for making this afternoon possible. I may do the work, but Felicity writes the checks. I'd also like to thank our committee heads."

Betty named them. One turned out to be Marcy Fletcher, who acknowledged her applause as if it wasn't nearly enough.

"And now," Betty went on, "it gives me great pleasure to introduce our speaker for this afternoon. It is someone you all know and love, whether you can do crossword puzzles or not. If you can't, all I can say is, you're just not trying. Because I can, and I graduated in the bottom third of my class."

That self-deprecating remark drew an appreciative laugh.

"So, without further ado, allow me to present Miss Cora

Felton, the Puzzle Lady, who has come here this afternoon to explain how to construct a crossword puzzle."

Cora rose to applause, cast an I-told-you-so glance at Sherry, and marched to the lectern, wondering what excuse she would use to get out of explaining how to construct a crossword puzzle. It was not going to be easy. A blackboard had been set up to the left of the lectern. Clearly she was expected to use it.

"Good afternoon, ladies and gentlemen. There are *some* gentlemen here, aren't there?" Cora smiled. "Not that I'm looking to get married again, still one never knows."

That remark drew a warm laugh. Cora took heart, plunged ahead. "Well, I can see that I'm going to have to talk fast, because that dessert that you're digging into looks absolutely scrumptious."

Cora glanced over at her table to see if Sherry had taken note of the fact that she'd said *scrumptious* instead of *obscenely delicious,* just in time to see Felicity Grant fall face first into her aforementioned dessert.

THE cop was not happy. And who could blame him? He had a room full of two hundred women who couldn't go home until he said so.

The cop wasn't sure if he should say so. He didn't appear that adept at murders. A local chief from a small town, it was a good bet he'd never had one. His opening remark, "Did anyone see what she ate?", doubtless would have been inappropriately funny, had the women not been so traumatized.

After the ambulance had taken Felicity's body away, the cop managed to herd the seven remaining women from her table off to one side of the room. It was to them that he addressed the remarks regarding Felicity's last meal.

Of the women, only Marcy Fletcher seemed composed enough to answer questions. "She ate exactly what we ate.

No more, no less. None of us are falling over dead, now are we?"

That declaration was just insensitive enough to rouse some of the others out of their shock-induced stupor.

"That's not quite true," Charity said. "She had the piece of quiche."

The cop zeroed in on that remark. "What piece of quiche?"

Cora groaned.

"She gave her a piece of quiche," Charity said.

"Who did?" the cop demanded.

"I did," Cora said. "I gave her my piece of quiche. I assure you there was nothing sinister about it."

"You gave her your piece of quiche?" the cop said insinuatingly.

"Good interrogation technique, Chief. But I already told you I gave her my piece of quiche. Could we move on?"

"*Why* did you give her your piece of quiche?"

Cora sighed. "She said she wanted quiche. But she was near the back of the line, and the quiche was almost gone. So I took a piece for her."

"You took a piece of quiche just for her?"

"That's right."

"So you planned this in advance? You knew that you would be giving your piece of quiche to her?"

"Yes. That's why I took it."

The cop glanced around to the other women. "And no one else at the table had quiche?"

"Actually, I had quiche," Cora said.

The cop's eyebrows raised. "I thought you gave your piece of quiche to her."

"I did." Cora gestured to her niece. "But Sherry gave me her piece."

"Why?"

"I wanted quiche."

"And yet you gave your piece away."

"I gave my piece away because Felicity wanted quiche. I took Sherry's piece because *I* wanted quiche."

Cora could practically see the cop's mind whirling, processing that.

"You wanted to eat quiche, but you didn't want to eat your quiche. You wanted to eat another piece of quiche. You wanted the decedent to eat your piece."

"Oh, for God's sakes!" Marcy cried impatiently. "This is our guest of honor. She didn't come here to kill the woman who invited her with a poisoned quiche."

Sherry smiled at the misplaced modifier. She figured it was a good bet she was the only one who noticed.

The cop certainly didn't. "Maybe not," he said. "But at the moment, it's my only lead. Did anyone else give her anything to eat?"

Monica snuffled, choked back a sob. Her lip trembled. "I . . . ."

"What is it, my dear?" the cop asked.

"I . . . I think I passed the rolls," Monica blurted, and burst into tears.

Marcy threw her hands to her head in disgust. "Give me a break. So you passed the rolls. Big deal. I think you're off on the wrong foot, officer. Who said it had to be one of us?"

"I never said it had to be one of you. I'm just asking questions."

"But they're all aimed at us."

"Well, who else is there? You were the only ones at her table.

"We were the only ones *sitting* there," Marcy said.

"Did anyone else come to the table?" the cop said. "Did a waiter come around?"

"It's a buffet," Charity said. "There aren't any waiters."

"Did you really suspect a waiter?" Marcy said sarcastically.

The cop put up his hands. "Just asking. Did anyone else come around?"

"Betty," Monica blurted. She immediately flushed and turned away.

"Who?" the cop demanded.

"Betty Flagstaff," Charity explained. "The co-chairman. She came by to talk to Miss Felton."

"Miss Felton. That would be you," the cop said, pointing to Cora. "And you were seated right next to the decedent, weren't you? To pass her your quiche."

"Yes, I was," Cora said. She couldn't tell if the cop suspected her or Betty Flagstaff.

"What did the co-chairman come to talk to you about?"

"My speech."

"I see. Did she also talk to the decedent?"

"I don't recall."

"Does anyone?"

No one did.

"That's annoying," the cop said. "It would appear that she didn't, but then again we can't be sure. When she talked to you, did you get up from the table?"

"No."

"She leaned over to talk to you?"

"That's right."

"Which side? The one between you and the decedent, or the other one?"

"She leaned in between us," Cora said.

"Aha. I think I'd better have a word with Betty Flagstaff."

The co-chairman, clearly distraught, blinked through tears and tried to answer the officer's questions. Neither her recollection nor her descriptive prowess were awesome. The cop was less than thrilled with her recitation.

"You remember talking to Miss Felton?"

"Yes."

"But you don't remember talking to the decedent?"

"No."

"Could you be more forthcoming with your answers?"

"I beg your pardon?"

"Don't make me drag it out of you. Tell me what you did."

"I don't know what you want me to say. I came to tell Cora I was about to announce her as soon as we began dessert."

"You did that?"

"Yes."

"And did the decedent say anything?"

"I told you, I don't know."

"Yet you remember standing between Miss Felton and the decedent. You even put your hands on their shoulders."

Betty Flagstaff could not have looked more devastated had the policeman actually accused her of the crime. "I think so. I'm so confused. It's so awful."

"Well," the policeman concluded, sizing her up. "You have to admit, you had the opportunity. Now, I understand you and the decedent quarreled a lot."

Betty Flagstaff wilted. She sank into a chair in horror, dissolved into tears.

Cora Felton cleared her throat. "Excuse me, officer."

"Yes," he said impatiently. "What is it?"

"I want to confess."

The policeman kept his cool, but he was clearly taken aback. After a moment, when the startled gasps from the women had died down, he said, "Go right ahead. Ah, before you do, let me remind you that you have the right to remain silent, and—"

"Yes, yes," Cora said. "I know all that. Not a problem. The only thing is, if you wouldn't mind, I would prefer to make my confession in private."

"In private?" He managed to make it sound as if he'd just been propositioned.

"Keep your shirt on. You don't have to rent me a room. If we could just step off to one side."

"Yes, of course."

"Be a dear, Sherry, and stay here and see that no one tries to listen in."

Cora took the bewildered cop by the arm, dragged him off into the corner of the room.

"All right," he said. "What is it that you want to tell me? You understand, of course, that you don't have to."

"For goodness sakes," Cora said. "We're alone. You could always *say* you read me my rights, and it would be my word against yours. Who are they gonna believe, you or me?"

The cop clearly had no interest in a discussion of the merits of the Miranda system. "Yeah, yeah, right. But tell me, you wish to confess to the crime?"

"The murder? Of course not. Sorry to get your hopes up, but I didn't do it."

"Then what do you want to confess to?"

"Withholding evidence." Cora made a face. "Though I'm not really withholding evidence, I just haven't had a chance to tell you. I mean, I wouldn't wanna blurt something out in front of the other women, now, would I? So I'm not withholding a thing, and that never was my intention. I just have to confess that I happen to know something about the crime that you don't."

"Oh?" the cop said ironically. "And what is that?"

"I know who did it."

CORA Felton stood at the blackboard beside the lectern. The other women had returned to their tables. All but Betty Flagstaff, who sat in a folding chair up front. The officer stood behind her, with his hand firmly on her shoulder.

"So," Cora said. "It's time for me to earn my lunch. We have a murder to solve, and I don't think any of you ladies are going to be too happy attending these luncheons until we do. So, if you don't mind, I'd like to tell you a few things about this crime."

Cora turned to the blackboard, picked up the chalk. "I'm supposed to talk to you about words, so let's start with one."

Cora wrote on the blackboard:
MOM.
Cora turned back to the women, smiled. "There you are.
MOM. M-O-M. There are doubtless a lot of moms here;
please do not think I am accusing you of the murder. If you
stop to consider it, the idea that Felicity Grant was done in
by a hundred angry mothers isn't really going to fly. So
what's MOM all about? Well, the letters happen to stand for
something."

Cora wrote:

MOTIVE.
OPPORTUNITY.
MEANS.

"There you are. *Motive, opportunity, means*. The three elements of a murder. *Motive*: who had a reason to do it. *Opportunity*: who had the chance to it. And *means*: what was the
murder weapon, and who had access to it. How do you solve
a crime? Trust your MOM."

Cora shrugged. "So, what do we have here? The *means* is
obviously poison. We'll know more when we get the autopsy report. But it's undoubtedly poison. Poison is a
woman's weapon. There are many ways to get one's hands on
poison. No problem there.

"And what is the *motive*? Well, Felicity Grant and Betty
Flagstaff are the co-chairmen of this organization. In any situation of that nature, there is apt to be tension, resulting in
a power struggle for who is top dog. So there's your motive.
Granted, not deep. Sketchy, surfacey. But as with the means
of death, I'm sure more will come to light as soon as the police have time to look.

"That leaves *opportunity*. Did Betty Flagstaff have the opportunity to commit the crime? Absolutely. Just before
dessert, she came to the table where I was seated next to Felicity Grant, put her arms over both our shoulders, and gave

me a few instructions regarding my speech. Was that while we were still eating? Yes, it was, because we had not begun dessert. I know that for a fact, because Betty mentioned that I would begin speaking when the women began dessert.

"So, Betty Flagstaff had the opportunity. No problem there." Cora raised her finger. "Except for one thing." She smiled. "Me. I gave Felicity a piece of quiche. There are lots of witnesses. Everyone at the table saw me do it. I took my quiche, handed it to her. And she ate it. Every crumb. This casts serious doubts on the guilt of Betty Flagstaff. Why? Because, clearly, I had a much *better* opportunity."

For the first time, there was dead silence in the room. No forks scraped against plates. No glasses clinked. There was no murmur of voices. The women were dumbfounded.

"Oh, don't worry," Cora said. "I'm not accusing myself of the crime. I'm merely stating the obvious. I had the best opportunity. That is absolutely obvious. It is obvious to anyone. We lose sight of how important that is because we are used to reading mystery books in which the obvious explanation is never right. In real life it almost always is. And in real life, we embrace the obvious explanation, at least initially, because we're in shock, and our minds can't handle anything else.

"Which is what happened in this case. The women at my table are all in shock at having one of their number topple over dead. When questioned, they give the usual unhelpful answers, until one of them, Charity something-or-other, recalls me giving her my quiche. Thus prompted, the other women chime in. It is the obvious answer, and the most likely too. A stranger in their midst, someone they don't know, on whose actions they cannot rely, did something that could have resulted in the victim's death. I not only had the opportunity, but my opportunity was observed by all. All embrace it.

"All but one.

"Marcy Fletcher comes to my rescue, pooh-poohs my involvement, asks who else it might be.

"And why does she do that? Because my passing the quiche was a coincidence. An accident. I was not *supposed* to be the person with the best opportunity. That person was supposed to be Betty Flagstaff. Who of course would check with her luncheon speaker near the end of the meal. And the luncheon speaker would be sitting next to co-chairman Felicity Grant. The place cards insured that. Just as they guaranteed which tiramisu Felicity would eat, allowing the killer to poison it well in advance.

"Unfortunately, the killer was a little too eager to pin the crime on Betty Flagstaff. And why not? If you want to take over an organization, what better way than to kill one co-chairman and frame the other for the murder?"

Cora jerked her thumb at the blackboard and looked out over the dining hall. "So, what have we learned from good old MOM? Can anyone tell me who did it?"

They certainly could. Some pointed. Some, buying into Cora's classroom routine, actually raised their hands to be called on.

Cora beamed like a teacher watching her prize pupil recite, as the cop left Betty Flagstaff, marched to table number ten, and put his hands on the shoulders of Marcy Fletcher.

"Well, that wasn't so bad," Cora said driving home.

"No, not at all," Sherry said ironically. "Someone got killed, and because of the quiche you were a murder suspect, but aside from that it went great."

Cora piloted the car around a curve, cursed at an oncoming driver who had swung a little wide. She came out of the turn, stepped on the gas. "You know the best thing about it?"

"Sure. The case is solved."

Cora waved it away. "No, silly." She grinned, her trademark Puzzle Lady grin. "It didn't involve a damn crossword puzzle."

DEAN AND CLAUDIA ASK PARNELL:

Q: *You're fond of doggerel and you're pretty good at it. When did you realize scansion, rhyming, and meter were going to be an important part of your life?*
A: Isn't good doggerel an oxymoron? Anyway, I started rhyming in grade school, much to the teacher's distraction.

Q: *Do you have a sample you could share with us?*
A: Sure. "The Weasels" by Parnell Hall, age 7.

> *If the weasels had the measles*
> *And the weasels had to sneeze*
> *Then the weasels with the measles*
> *Would surely spread disease.*

Q: *Is this set to music?*
A: No, thank heaven. But at age 15 a song of mine was the fourth track on a Pete Seeger album. I loved the billing: Seeger, Gutherie, Ledbelly, Hall.

Q: *Are there any reviews of your singing voice that you would like to share with us?*
A: I've sung my songs at Bouchercons, the Edgar banquet, Left Coast Crime, Magna Cum Murder, and Malice Domestic, with varying degrees of success. But I'll never forget one dreadful performance where I forgot the lyrics, got lost, and rambled on forever—an absolute disaster. Just as I finally finished, to the relief of all concerned, Loren Estleman, at whose table I'd been sitting, called out with malicious glee, "One more time!"

Q: *Who is your preferred partner in performing? We hear you and Jerry Healy have a great act together.*
A: Jerry and I have a tradition of co-hosting the Potpourri panel at Mid-Atlantic. It's a kick. I'm also up for any panel with Joan Hess, who is responsible for The Panel From Hell,

Who Wants to be a Best-selling Author, and A Jungian Interpretation of the Mythology of Mystery Fiction, to name just a few.

AND HERE IS PARNELL'S RECIPE:

CIOPPINO:
PUZZLE LADY STYLE

1/4 cup extra-virgin olive oil
1 teaspoon crushed red pepper flakes
3 flat fillets of anchovies, drained
6 cloves garlic, crushed
1 bay leaf
2 celery stalks, chopped
1 medium onion, chopped
1/2 cup chopped green bell peppers
1 cup dry white wine
1½ cup water
1 (28-ounce) can of crushed tomatoes
1 tablespoon fresh thyme or 1 tablespoon dry thyme
1½ pounds cod or halibut, cut into 2-inch chunks
Salt and pepper
8 large shrimp, peeled and deveined
16 to 20 raw mussels, scrubbed

In a large pot over moderate heat combine oil, crushed pepper, anchovies, garlic, and bay leaf. Let anchovies melt into oil.

Add chopped celery, onion, and bell pepper. Saute a few minutes and add wine. Simmer the wine until reduced by about half. Then add water, tomatoes, and thyme. Bring sauce to boil, and reduce heat to a simmer. Simmer 10 minutes.

Season fish chunks with salt and pepper. Add fish and simmer 5 minutes. Add shrimp and mussels and cover pot. Cook 10 minutes.

Serve with crusty bread.

Serves 4.

STARK TERROR
AT TEA-TIME

Lyn Hamilton

Lyn Hamilton's wonderful archeological mysteries featuring sleuth Lara McClintoch are a favorite of readers in her native Canada and in the United States. Lyn has a quiet charm and a devilish wit. When Claudia asked her to write a story with this title, she agreed with a definite twinkle in her eye. Lyn spent several years as a fundraiser for the Toronto Opera before retiring to write full time. Her latest novel is The Magyar Venus.

My ex-wife took it rather badly the way Thad Mac-naughton died. Lara had spent six months tracking down that tea set, and for Thad to end up face down in his Lapsang Souchong the first time he used it, she took as a personal affront.

Apparently, several generations of Siamese royalty had sipped from it over a century or so, secure in the belief that any poison touching the celadon porcelain would cause it to crack. Either Thad didn't know his history nearly as well as he thought he did, or the crack appeared when he dropped it, just before he went over the side.

Word was the tea set was cursed, a notion that Lara, sensible woman that she is, pooh-poohed immediately. But unfortunate things had happened to the three previous owners, an earl of something or other in England, a French politician, and a Spanish artist of some repute. All had come to spectacularly bad ends long before their time.

That Thad would want to own a cursed tea set was not as bizarre as it sounds. He had made risk-taking his lifetime occupation. He'd started out as a stuntman in movies, then moved up the he-man pecking order to take up car racing, an occupation he'd refused to give up even after crashing and burning. He liked to scuba dive under the polar ice cap, balloon across Afghanistan, and all very publicly, with the kind of bravado that makes some men—okay, men like me—feel inadequate. He was muscular, always tanned, and had a smile that apparently left women weak at the knees. To make him even less likable, he was rich, by virtue of his marriage to Sandra Wyatt, sole heir to a mining fortune.

He was also a royal pain in the butt. He liked to say, to anyone who'd listen, that the list of his enemies was too long for him ever to remember them, but he did know who his friends were. I'd be inclined to agree with the first part of that. As for the second, all I will say is that the suspects in his murder were people he presumably considered friends, including Lara McClintoch, my ex-spouse and now business partner in an antiques business called McClintoch & Swain, and, I regret to say, me, Clive Swain.

What Lara and I were doing in that god-forsaken spot at that inopportune moment is a story in itself. Thad spent his summers on an island on the outer reaches of Georgian Bay in Lake Huron in a house built by his late father-in-law. It was a rather gothic structure, all turrets and crenellations, the kind of place you expect to find filled with bats or worse.

I won't belabor the design faults, tempting though that may be for someone of my aesthetic sensitivity. I will say it was one of the ugliest houses I have ever seen.

But Thad, for all his faults, was a very good customer, and when I phoned to tell him Lara had tracked the celadon tea set to an antiques store in Edinburgh's Old Town and would bring it back with her, Thad could hardly wait. Lara's flight was a couple of thousand miles out when he started to call.

"Tell Lara to pop up for the weekend," he insisted. "It's the last one of the season before we close the place up for the winter. We'll have a barbecue. I'll have somebody pick her up at the marina."

Just popping up for the weekend involved a three and a half hour drive north of Toronto to get to the marina, and then forty-five minutes or more in a boat. When I saw Lara's tired little face, I felt a momentary pang. Her partner, a policeman by the name of Rob Luczka, was off doing whatever Mounties do when they're not in their red outfits riding horses or standing on mountain tops bellowing "Rosemarie, I love you," so Lara was going to have to drive up on her own.

"I'll go with you," I said. It was a gesture of compassion I was to regret.

By the time we got to the marina, about five-thirty in the afternoon, the prospect of a barbecue was not looking good. This late in the season, it was already beginning to get dark, and the blackest storm clouds I have ever seen hovered on the horizon. The water was also unpleasantly choppy. The boatman, a taciturn fellow named Fred, was intent on getting us out there and making it back home before whatever those storms clouds brought with them hit.

The first raindrops, driven by an increasingly hostile wind, blasted us just as we reached the dock of the island. A couple of lucky people got on the boat which immediately turned back toward shore, leaving the two of us standing at the foot of a rather high cliff, sufficiently steep that we couldn't see the house. The only sounds were the wind, screeching gulls, and the thunk of a little rowboat straining at the rope that held it to the dock.

"How do you figure we get up there?" I said.

"Elevator," Lara said, pointing.

I couldn't believe my eyes. "You call that an elevator? Elevators are lifting devices with a roof, doors, mirrors, and bad music. That is a metal platform with a flimsy railing around it. Here, let's see if we can signal Fred to come back. We'll put the tea set on that thing and send it up while we go back to Toronto. He can mail us a check."

But Fred and his boat had already turned the corner of the island and were steaming away for the shore. "We're here now," Lara said. "Let's go."

This was one of the least pleasant elevator rides I've ever endured, cold, wet, and sick-making. It must be said that, with the exception of tropical pools with bars in the middle, I detest outdoors. Why I would be standing on this little piece of metal catching my death of cold as we inched up the incline, when I could be strolling to my neighborhood bistro for a nice meal and a bottle of red wine, was a complete mystery to me.

I wasn't much happier when we got to the top. "Good, you made it," Thad said, taking the box out of Lara's hands. "Wouldn't have wanted the ship to go down with that tea set on board." I believe I have already mentioned that Thad was a jerk. "You'll have to help yourself to a drink," he said, gesturing to a bar to one side of the room, which had a fireplace big enough for me to stand in and was decorated in what I would call a rustic version of early shopping mall. "I sent the staff home before dinner because of the storm. We'll have to fend for ourselves. You know Sandra," he said, gesturing toward a bored-looking woman flipping through a magazine. Sandra did not bother to acknowledge our presence. She was a brassy blond attired in a flowered pant suit that would look out of place anywhere but in this house built by her father—all of which lends yet more credence to my personal theory that there is a defective design gene that is passed from generation to generation. Fortunately, she and Thad hadn't managed to breed.

My gaze shifted from Sandra, whose profile was framed nicely by a particularly ghastly piece of driftwood sculpture and a furry thing with big teeth mounted on a plaque over the mantelpiece, to my ex-wife, who was, as usual, in uniform—taupe trousers and a cream blouse. In winter, the trousers are black. I'm always urging Lara to pep herself up a bit, to wear brighter colors that will show off her strawberry hair, pale eyes and skin. She apparently does not agree. While this should not be construed as a conceding of the point, I will say that in this place, her understated attire came as something of a relief.

"And this is my niece, Brigid," Thad said, putting his arm around the shoulders of a young woman and giving her a squeeze. Brigid was one of those women who at first glance look rather drab in denim overalls and white tee shirt, her blond hair in a bun, but whom any guy who is paying attention knows is a smoldering cauldron. If it weren't for the fact that I was living with Lara's best friend Moira—there were some tense moments when that happened I'll tell you—I'd be chatting up Ms. Brigid before the evening was out.

"I'm David Kilworthy, the Macnaughtons' accountant," a man said, when it became apparent Thad was not going to introduce him. Kilworthy looked to be a decent enough chap, if you were prepared to overlook the fact that he ironed his jeans. With a crease.

The scotch was top notch, though, I must say. I poured a generous one for both Lara and me, and now, settled on the sofa, drink in front of her, Lara began to unpack the treasure, one fragile piece at a time. Even the always disinterested Sandra set down her magazine long enough to have a look. It was a lovely thing, that tea set, so delicate in design and in color, that ethereal shade of green.

"It's perfect," Thad said. "Write them a check, will you, darling?" I took it that Sandra was the darling in question.

"Bring me my checkbook, will you, Brigid?" was all Sandra said, before turning back to her magazine.

"I assume the curse is included in the price," Thad said.

"Ooh, Uncle Thad!" Brigid gasped, looking very prettily alarmed.

Thad smiled at her, and gave her another squeeze. "Want to have the first sip, Brig?"

"I don't think so," she said.

"David?" Thad said, turning to his accountant, who just blushed.

"Sandra. How about you?"

Sandra yawned. "The only tea I'm interested in right now is the one that goes with g," she said. "As in g and t," she added, smiling at her own cleverness. "If someone might mix me one?"

"You've had several already," Thad said.

David sprang into action. "I'll get it," he said.

"Aren't you lucky to have David here, darling," Thad said. "I think perhaps he's enamored." I noticed that Lara was watching all this with interest.

"It may be cocktail time, but I am going to have tea," Thad announced, rooting about in a large box. "What to have?" he said. "Orange spice? Cranberry? Chai? No," he said. "Almond glory. That's the ticket." He went over to the fireplace and grasped a large black kettle that had been hanging there. "The water is already hot in anticipation of your arrival," he said. He puttered around for a while, before pouring water on the tea leaves. As he did so, the lights flickered. "It should steep for a few minutes," he said, setting it on a tray on the enormous coffee table that already held milk, sugar, lemon and a few slices of cake of some kind. "While we wait, I'll show you to your rooms."

"I'm going to change," Sandra said.

"Are we dressing for dinner?" David asked, head pivoting between Sandra and Thad.

"I have a picture in my mind of you in the nude, David," Thad said. "Terrible thought. Yes, you should definitely dress for dinner."

"I meant . . . ."

"He knows what you meant," Sandra interrupted. "You're fine as you are."

Lara and I were led down the hall behind Sandra's retreating back, and shown to two rather nice adjoining rooms in what must have been a tower of some sort. We were on the main floor, and could hear Sandra clomping above us. David was across the hall.

"This is shaping up to be a long evening," I whispered to Lara before she closed the door.

"Too long," she said. "I hope we're not stuck here tomorrow." A shutter banged as she spoke, and we both winced. "Pray for sun in the morning," she said. "Sun and Fred."

I peered out of the window of my room, but by now it was very dark. I could see, however, that this part of the house went right up to the edge of the cliff. One had a sense of hovering in space. I'm sure the view was lovely from the large deck outside my room, but right now, although I wasn't going to admit it to anyone, most especially Thad, I felt uncomfortable being that close to the edge.

When we got back to the main room, the tea set was still sitting on the coffee table. Thad came in, sniffed the pot and declared it ready. The scent of almond wafted across the room.

"Are you sure you should do this, Uncle Thad?" Brigid said. "Isn't it enough just to own it? Maybe you should just put it away for now."

"Scared, Brig?" he said. "Let's make it even more interesting. Come along, everyone," he said, picking up the tray. Dutifully we followed him up a flight of stairs, along a dark hallway, and up another short flight. We were, I believe, in the tower in which Lara and I were to sleep, but two stories up, in a large room with glass doors out on to another deck.

By now the storm was in full force. Thunder rumbled and lightning flashed across the sky. It was also pitch black. I looked at my watch to see that it was, in fact, only eight o'clock.

Thad opened the doors, and the rain came pelting in.

"What are you doing?" Sandra said irritably.

"Giving the curse a good run at me," he laughed, walking out onto the deck, which gleamed in the light of the room. It looked very slippery. By now he was holding a teacup. "Here we go, Brig," he said, making a pretend scared face, and slowly raising the cup to his lips.

"Don't, Uncle Thad! Please," Brigid implored.

"Come in. You'll get hit by lightning," David said. I swear I detected a note of hope in his voice.

Thad just laughed, and took a big slurp. Come and get me!" he yelled to the storm as he downed the cup.

He turned back to the rest of us, all huddled inside, and with his one free hand, clutched at his throat, tongue lolling, mugging outrageously. Even Brigid had to laugh at the antics. What happened next is hard to describe. We were all laughing, and he was hamming it up, at least we thought he was, but then he let go of the teacup. Lara gasped and took a few futile steps to try to catch it. Thad staggered back, and then, with a kind of gurgling sound, pitched over the railing.

We all just stood there for a minute, stunned, and then Sandra and Brigid screamed. Lara, David, and I edged across the slippery deck and gingerly looked over the edge. It was a very long way down, all the way down, in fact, to the bay. And Thad was nowhere to be seen.

"You," Lara said, pointing to Brigid. "Call the police. Get help."

The three of us ran downstairs leaving the two screeching women behind, and went outside. The tower was indeed very close to the edge of the cliff, with only a shelf of rock a few feet wide between the house and the edge. Thad was not on it. It was so dark and windy that we couldn't see much of anything, but we braved the elevator once again to get down to the water, and picked our way carefully along the shore. We went as far as we could along the bank, but still no Thad, and eventually, soaked and exhausted, and knowing in our hearts it was already too late to save him even if we could find him, we made our way back up the hill.

"I can't get through," Brigid sobbed. "My cell phone isn't working."

"Get yours, Clive," Lara ordered. She is always one to take charge.

"It won't work, either," Sandra said. "We're out too far. Nobody can get out here in this storm anyway."

David, tidy person as accountants tend to be, leaned over to pick up the cup. "Don't touch that," Lara said. "In fact, don't touch anything."

"Why?" David said. "What are you trying to say? He fell."

"Maybe," Lara said.

"You think he was poisoned?" David said, incredulously. "Surely, it was an accident. He was playing silly bugger and it backfired." My sentiments exactly, and a good thing it was, too, that Sandra had signed our check.

"I think we should just leave everything the way it is until the police get here," Lara replied.

"It's the curse," Brigid said. She looked at the tea set as if it might turn into a nest of cobras if she got near it. "We have to get rid of it."

"Let's go downstairs," Lara said.

We had just taken our seats in the living room by the fire, David and Sandra on one sofa, Brigid near me on a second, and Lara in an armchair by the fire, when the lights went out. Brigid, poor thing, screamed again.

"That's not supposed to happen," David said. "We're on a generator out here. The storm shouldn't do anything to that."

"It's the curse," Brigid repeated, sobbing away.

"I'm going to bed," Sandra said.

"That's a good idea," I said. "You mustn't give up hope, Sandra."

"Oh, I haven't," she said, and then she burst out laughing. Hysteria, perhaps. Finally she calmed herself. "I'm going to bed," she repeated.

"I'll come with you," David said. "I mean, I don't . . . ."

"They know what you mean, David. Thank you, but I can find my own bedroom, even in the dark."

"Here's a candle," Lara said. I told you she's a practical woman. She'd taken the candles off the dining room table and handed them around. "I think there's one for each of us. We should all just go to bed. In the morning, when the storm dies down, we'll get help."

Brigid grasped my arm. "Please," she said. "Please stay here with me just for a little while. I'm too scared to go to my room." Even by candlelight, I could see her lovely chest heaving, and her eyelashes glistening with tears. She was an amazingly attractive young woman.

"Of course," I said, sitting beside her on the sofa, and patting her hand.

Lara was almost to the hallway of our wing, but she turned and plunked herself down in the chair again, arms folded. With only her silhouette visible against the light of the fireplace, I could tell what she was thinking. She'd been a bit put out when I moved in with Moira, her best girl-friend, but now that she'd gotten used to the idea, she was apparently all for it, and there was no way I was going to be left alone with the nubile young Brigid. Lara can be a real prude.

For a while we could hear Sandra's footsteps above us, but then silence reigned. I think that we all must have dozed off where we sat. I know I did, because I was rudely awakened by the sound of a scream, then a crash. The candles had all died, and the fire was just embers. Lara was already moving toward the sound. I could hear footsteps coming down the hall, and David's voice saying, "What's happened?"

What had happened, it became apparent, was that either Sandra did not know her way around in the dark, despite what she'd said, or she had a secret stash of gin in her bedroom, because she had fallen down the stairs. As lightning flashed I could see her lying at the bottom of the staircase, her head at a totally unnatural angle, her eyes wide open in an expression I assumed to be stark terror. One foot was still clad in a fluffy pink mule, the other was bare. Lara, who had found another candle, knelt over her. "I think she's dead," Lara said.

"It's the curse. We're all going to die," Brigid moaned, as David fainted dead away.

So now we were four. We left David, now revived, sitting on the floor beside Sandra, pathetically holding her hand. The rest of us went back to the living room, stoked the fire, and sat back to wait out the night. I'm sure none of us intended to sleep, but before I knew it, it was light. David lay on the hall floor curled up beside Sandra, one arm flung over the corpse. Beside me on the sofa, Brigid was snoring quietly. She must have been having a nice dream, because a small smile hovered on her lips. Lara was not to be seen.

I realized I was very hungry. We had not had dinner after all, so I crept into the kitchen to find something to eat. Lara was already there. She signaled me to be quiet, and pointed to a door and a staircase that led off the kitchen. "Servants' quarters," she whispered. "Upstairs. There is a second way to the upper floors. And that," she said, pointing to a door beside the staircase, "goes down to the basement, I believe." As I watched, she turned the key in the lock of the basement door, and put the key in her pocket. "Let's go," she whispered. "Take those," she added, pointing to a pair of binoculars near the door. It was a funny time to go bird watching, but I did what I was told.

We went out the kitchen door, moved along the back of the house, and then up through a small pine forest to a large rock which looked to be the high point on the property. The bay, far below, was misty, but the storm had passed. The sky was silver gray, just before dawn, and the world seemed eerily silent after all that screaming the night before. I turned the binoculars in the general direction of the marina, and was surprised to see a little rowboat bobbing in the current quite some distance away. "I think the rowboat that was tied to the dock has broken loose in the storm," I said, passing the glasses to Lara.

"That must have been annoying," she said.

I waited. I hate it when she makes these oblique remarks that I don't understand, and I am forced to ask. I tried very hard not to. "Annoying for whom?" I said at last.

"The murderer, of course," she said. "Can you see Fred's boat?"

I scanned the horizon. "There's a boat headed this way. Please, let it be Fred."

"I would be interested in your impressions of last night," Lara said. We were some distance from the house, but still whispering. "Of the people, I mean. You saw David's reaction to Sandra's death. What do you make of that?"

"Other than that he's a wuss, you mean, passing out like that? Judging by the rather familiar sleeping position this morning, I'd say they were having an affair. It was pretty obvious last night that he was in love with her."

"I thought so too," she said. "Do you think Thad knew?"

"Probably, and he'd be more than a little worried about losing his meal ticket if he did. You're thinking they killed Thad so they could marry," I said, quite loudly.

"Sshh," Lara said.

"You think this is all about lust?"

"Lust and money. Isn't that what it's always about?"

"If it was Sandra, she certainly got her just desserts. She was practically cackling last night. But why wouldn't she just divorce him? She'd have to buy him off, but she's got buckets of money."

"Exactly," Lara said. "And Brigid?"

"Well, you can't help but notice that she fancies me. Of course you noticed. You were quite evidently staying put last night to protect my virtue. I was only trying to be fatherly," I added in an aggrieved tone. "I hope that chair of yours was extraordinarily uncomfortable."

Lara ignored my petulant comments. "Be honest with me about Brigid, please."

"Okay," I sighed. "If I am absolutely honest, I would have to say that she had a rather unhealthy interest in her uncle, not me. All that, 'oh Uncle Thad!' stuff."

"And Thad?"

"I don't think he was exactly immune to her charms. He did give her more squeezes than absolutely necessary to demonstrate avuncular affection."

"So Thad and Brigid could also have been having an affair," she said.

"I guess. She is, however, his niece. I believe that kind of thing is frowned upon in polite society. Anyway, other than demonstrating that the fleshpots of southeast Asia have nothing on this household, where does this take us?"

"I think she's his wife's niece," Lara said.

"He introduced her as his niece," I said.

"I introduce Jennifer as my daughter sometimes, but she is Rob's daughter, not mine, if we're talking blood lines."

I thought about the blond hair, the noses, the eyes, and the, shall we say, chest areas of the two women. "You're right," I said. "Her niece."

"And now, perhaps, her heir," Lara said. "No kids. No husband. Who would be next in line for all that money? What is that little door in the back of the house, by the way?"

"What door?" I said. All these nonsequiturs were irritating me. She pointed. "I would guess it is a coal chute that would lead into the basement."

"Mmm," she said. "Let's go find a place to sit in the trees over there."

"I take it you don't believe in curses," I said, as we picked out a spot where we could see but not be seen.

"Nope."

"Still, you've got to wonder. The evening a cursed tea set arrives, there is both a murder and a fatal accident, or two fatal accidents, depending on your point of view. Either way, it can't be good for our business. Word gets out."

"Yes, it does, which is why we are going to solve this thing. And there was a murder," she said.

"Okay, let me work through this. The teapot sat out on the coffee table for at least ten minutes. We were taken to our rooms while it steeped. David and Sandra were changing for dinner. I saw Brigid go upstairs too. I guess her bedroom is on the second floor. Anyone could have poisoned it. Ah ha! Almond tea! Isn't there a poison that smells like almonds?"

"Burnt almond," Lara agreed. "Cyanide."

"So is that what you think happened?"

"No," she said. "They may find cyanide in it, I don't know. But it doesn't work for me. Divorce would be the preferred option for everyone but Thad."

"David did it just because he was tired of being treated like a chump by Thad?"

"I don't think so," she said. "He's not the type."

"Brigid? What possible motive would she have?"

"I can't think of one," Lara said. "Especially if they were lovers."

"So who benefits from Thad's death?"

"You mean Sandra's," Lara said.

"Sandra's! You think there were two murders? Then, it has to be Brigid. Thad can't be a suspect, and I can't see how David could, but if Brigid really is the heir, she stands to gain a lot."

"Yes," she said.

"But assuming someone pushed Sandra down the stairs—that is what you're saying, aren't you?—who was it? David came out of the bedroom wing on the lower level, at least I think he did, and Brigid was sitting with us."

"That's right," she said.

"Hmm," I said. "It was Fred, wasn't it? He dropped us off, went out into the channel, threw the cook and maid overboard, came back, hauled himself up the cliff face with his fingernails rather than use the elevator thing that might give him away, and killed Thad and Sandra because he was tired of going back and forth from the marina."

Lara glared at me. Quite right, too. The reputation of our business was at stake here. We sat in silence for a moment, both of us looking at that horrendous house. "The tower is truly ugly, isn't it?" I said. "If they'd just left it as a tower, it would be bad enough. But they cantilevered those decks off every level, and they didn't even get the decks lined up. If they were all the same size and shape, it might look present-able, but each level up is a different shape and smaller than the one below. It looks like a christmas tree."

"Exactly my thoughts," she said. "I expect it was so that the deck above would not block the sun for the one below it. Handy, though."

Another of those annoying comments.

"What exactly are we doing sitting in the bushes on wet pine needles?" I asked. "I'm sure this is bad for our kidneys."

"We're waiting for the murderer to climb out of the coal chute," she said. "I locked the door in the kitchen and took the key, so that is the only way out of the basement, and to stay in the basement would be a mistake because Fred is al-most here, and he will be swiftly followed by the police. An-other hiding place will have to be found until a way off the island is arranged. It was supposed to be the rowboat, but as you have already pointed out, it got away."

"Of course," I said, trying to sound sage.

"After which," she continued, "we will watch to see where that new hiding place is, then we will make our way carefully back to the house and pretend nothing has happened until the police get here."

"Of course," I said again.

Then Lara nudged me and pointed. Brigid, looking carefully about her, was making her way from the kitchen door along the back of the house.

"What is she doing?" I whispered.

"I'm going to give you a really big clue, Clive," Lara said. "There was only one murder."

I waited. It wasn't a big enough clue for me.

"And only one person died."

I opened my mouth to protest, but then I looked back at the tower with its cantilevered decks. If someone knew what they were doing, and was reasonably proficient . . . . "No wonder he wanted the tea set so badly, and was so insistent it be delivered here in person!" I hissed. "This has been planned forever. The body would never be found! We're the credible witnesses. Brigid gets the money, and some time later leaves the country, they reunite in, where? Argentina or something. He has a new name, maybe a new face. He was a stuntman!"

Lara patted my arm approvingly. Then we sat and watched as Brigid pulled open the coal chute and Thad Macnaughton climbed out.

DEAN AND CLAUDIA ASK LYN:

Q: *Where are you going next?*
A: I just got back from Budapest and northern Hungary. Lara is trying to prove the authenticity of a 25,000-year-old artifact found in a cave in the Bukk Mountains. I just tagged along. Once she's got that project organized and

various murders solved, she'll be off somewhere else, I'm sure.

Q: *What kind of traveler are you? What do you pack for, say, the wilds of Kuala Lampur?*
A: I think I'm a pretty relaxed traveler, except where wardrobe is concerned. I've acquired outfits for all climates and terrain and I still don't seem to take the right thing, especially shoes. I could fill a whole suitcase with shoes. Travel to research a mystery is entirely different from any kind of travel I've done before. While everyone else is out ooh-ing and aah-ing over a sunset or a beach or a monument of some sort, I'm looking for the police station and the worst part of town.

Q: *What's the scariest thing that's ever happened to you on a trip?*
A: Losing my passport in Malta was pretty scary, but I think the scariest thing occurred when I was staying in a hotel in Italy. I won't say where, because it wouldn't be good for their business. I had a recurring nightmare several times that night in which I was walking down a set of stone steps into what I knew was a crypt where something really awful was waiting for me. I woke up at the bottom of the steps every time. The next morning, I mentioned the dream to my traveling companions, whereupon the waiter told me that the hotel had originally been the villa of a very evil man who just happened to be buried in a crypt under the lobby. My room was on the second floor over the lobby.

Q: *Good grief!! Let's move on to food. Unless you've eaten something that scary, too.*
A: I've had some wonderful meals everywhere I've traveled, but the most exotic was probably the dish I was served in the countryside in China. I had no idea what it was and when I asked there was much discussion about what the word in English would be. In the end I was told it was sea concubine.

Q: *Sea cucumber, perhaps?*
A: Yes. In soy sauce. It was a delicacy. As a general rule, I would have to say I try to avoid eating some kid's pet, such as dog, cat, and guinea pig.

Q: *Is what follows a recipe for Sea Concubine with a Terrier sauce?*
A: Not!

AND HERE IS LYN'S RECIPE:

AGATHA'S ALMOND CAKE

8 egg whites at room temperature
1/2 teaspoon salt
10 ounces ground almonds (about 3 cups)
1 1/3 cups sugar
1/2 teaspoon almond extract
1 teaspoon grated orange zest
6 tablespoons flour
1/2 teaspoon cinnamon
1/4 teaspoon nutmeg

Preheat oven to 350°F

Beat the egg whites with the salt until stiff peaks form.

Mix the ground almonds and sugar together, and then carefully fold into the egg whites a little at a time. Add the almond extract and orange zest.

Sift together the flour, cinnamon, and nutmeg, and fold into egg white mixture.

Bake in greased 9-inch spring form pan for 45 minutes, or until cake begins to pull away from the sides of the pan, and a toothpick inserted in the center comes out clean.

Serve still warm with whipped cream and sliced straw-berries or other fruit marinated in almond liqueur, or dust with icing sugar and toasted almonds, or ice with orange butter cream frosting when cool. Store cake in re-frigerator wrapped in foil.

CAFÉ CON LECHE

Marcos Donnelly

Marcos Donnelly's fiction has been praised as "utterly gripping, very funny, and very clever" by the New York Review of Science Fiction *and was lauded for its "delightful voice, comic zip, and brio" by Isaac Asimoy's Science Fiction. He has published short fiction since the early 1990s, and his first novel,* Prophets for the End of Time, *appeared in 1999. Principally a fantasy writer, Donnelly is making his debut in the mystery genre with this piece, "Café con Leche."*

The good Lord, young Pe Avista knew, the good Lord Himself, through His loving kindness and most generous grace, had provided this new storefront church for the faithful of the *Palabra de Dios* congregation. A blessed place; a big place. Bigger than their old meeting room behind the bodega off East Complin. Cooler, too, with its very own ceiling fans, three of them. Pe and the Reverend Cosadón had finished painting the kitchen just yesterday; they'd repaired and re-waxed the spacious main hall in the weeks prior, getting it ready for today's first Sunday service. Pe Avista hadn't seen the upstairs yet, but the Reverend Cosadón told him the church owned all the rooms on the second floor, too, and that they'd be fixing them up over the next month to build their own homeless shelter.

It was a miracle, Pe knew. Their own place, their own church, their own front windows and doors facing the street, all in a part of town where the Lord most needed His Gospel spread—Vincent Avenue, home to the city's largest concentration of pushers, prostitutes, pimps, and pit bulls. The perfect neighborhood. Rife with sin, ripe for salvation, and overdue for the all-redeeming, all-embracing message of God's love.

Soon. All of that, soon. Right after they'd cleared up today's more immediate problems, the problems of the murdered guy, the cops, and the young white girl who turned out to be a servant of the devil.

"ARE you ready, José?" the Reverend Cosadón asked in Spanish, his gentle voice lilting with assurance that if Pe needed more time, that would be fine. Reverend Cosadón was the only one in the church who called Pe by his given name. Most called him Pepe, the common nickname for José; his closest friends shortened that to a single syllable.

"I think I'm ready," Pe answered in English. It was the hottest Sunday yet that summer. Pe sat in the front row, and he glanced back at the packed church hall. The congregation had forty-three registered members and about two dozen occasional droppers-by. Everyone was there for today's first service in the new facilities, and they'd needed to set up additional folding chairs to accommodate the crowd. Glory to God, Pe thought, that such good attendance had never happened at the old meeting room. They'd all have suffocated within fifteen minutes.

The Reverend Cosadón waved to Manuelo Vega and

Ubaldo Martínez across the hall, and the two began playing guitar for the opening hymn. Manuelo, the church's long-term music director, set pace by picking melody on his six-string; Ubaldo, the new guitarist who'd only been in the country a few months, strummed a twelve-string, creating a rich fill that wrapped itself around the voices of the congregation. The opening song was *Vamos a Bendecir al Señor,* "Let Us Bless the Lord." It struck Pe as a strange choice for the very first song of the very first service in their brand new church. The *Palabra de Dios* congregation had over a dozen African American members; the Reverend Cosadón usually insisted that all Sunday services be conducted in English, a show of respect and inclusion. They reserved Spanish hymns for the Wednesday night all-Spanish prayer service and Bible study.

On the second verse of the hymn, the elderly and esteemed Mr. Jaime Torgas Colindres stepped solemnly from near the front door, up the middle aisle formed by the rows of folding chairs. Mr. Torgas carried an oversized tome, its cover a blazing red reminiscent of the liturgy books used by Roman Catholics. Pe knew that, because he'd been raised Catholic. Now he was a Christian. Mr. Torgas's book was not, of course, a Roman Catholic liturgy book, but a large copy of *the* Book, the only Book that mattered to the believers of this church. The Holy Bible. A large-print King James Version, if Mr. Torgas's cargo was in keeping with what Pe Avista knew to be the Reverend Cosadón's preferences.

Pe forgot his nervousness long enough to smile. Now he understood why the first hymn was in Spanish. Jaime Torgas Colindres was the reason they had a new church today. Although not a rich man, Mr. Torgas had come into a small, unexpected inheritance from an intestate uncle in Costa Rica. Millions of Costa Rican *colones* became thousands of U.S. dollars, which, in turn, became this storefront church. The Reverend Cosadón was repaying the congregation's benefactor in the only way he could: with honor, allowing the man to initiate worship at the new house of God by placing the scriptures up front. Opening with a hymn in Spanish gave homage to their donor. For in his three years in America, Mr. Torgas had been unable to master even rudimentary English, despite several attempts at ESL night courses. The man simply had no ear for a foreign tongue as difficult as English.

Mr. Torgas stepped past the podium. He set the Bible atop the table that would serve as the congregation's altar for the Lord's Supper. To Pe Avista's eyes, the sight was gloriously symbolic: that large, red book, standing out in relief against the white linen altar cloth, a strong testament to the Lord's strength and glory. Not an altar with gold chalices and patens and monstrances, the idols and tools of the Roman Catholics Pe had left behind in his youth, but an altar for real believers, focused on the very Word of God.

"Palabra de Dios," he heard Mr. Torgas say. The man gave the slightest of bows toward the Book, nothing idolatrous, of course, and returned up the aisle. His grin was huge, and his single gap of missing tooth only added to the charm of his boyish elation. It dawned on Pe that this could be one of the finest days in the old man's life. Even his tie, black and stringy, was pulled up tight to cover the fastened, topmost button of his white dress shirt. Unthinkable in this heat, but unnoticed by Mr. Torgas, it seemed, thanks to the old man's joy. He returned to his place beside his granddaughter Lucinda. The two always sat in the back row of the old meeting room, a tradition they seemed set to continue in the new church. Lucinda translated sermons and Bible readings for Mr. Torgas. She was a pretty girl, twenty-two years old, just a few years younger than Pe. Pe always listened for her translations, a background whisper accompanying each Sunday celebration.

The Reverend Cosadón moved to the podium, which made Pe remember that now he was supposed to go back to feeling gut-wrenchingly nervous. "The Lord is in this place," the Reverend proclaimed in English, "and His people praise His Name!"

"Amen, amen," agreed many congregants aloud. The Mexican, Salvadoran, and Costa Rican believers of *Palabra de Dios* church had, over time, adopted the charisma of the black members.

"We pray that the Lord bless our benefactor and friend, Jaime Torgas Colindres. His generosity has made this new beginning possible. *Oramos que el Señor bendiga a nuestro benefactor, nuestro amigo, Jaime Torgas Colindres.*"

Pe looked to the back of the hall. Lucinda Torgas beamed at her grandfather. Ronald Lake, one of the black church members, leaned across the aisle to give Jaime a cordial slap on the shoulder. The old man nodded, his face serene.

"Today," the Reverend Cosadón preached, "we look back to remember our old home, and we look forward to our future in this new House of God. How fitting, then, that this place should be a gift of the oldest member of our community, and that it should be inaugurated by the very first sermon of our new minister."

Pe Avista's stomach rumbled. *Give me your wisdom and strength, Lord.*

"Some of you have scolded me for keeping José's talents to myself for the two months since his graduation from Elim Bible Institute. And I confess that I have, as our Lord might say, kept his light hidden under my bushel basket."

Some laughs and several *Amens;* Pe took heart, realizing he had no reason to be nervous. He was among friends, people he'd known for ten years, who loved him with the love of Christ.

"I wanted to save José's first sermon for today, so we could truly thank our Lord for making all things brand new for us. We have called this young man many things—José, Pepe, simply Pe. I am blessed and proud to be the first to call him by his newest name: the Reverend Mr. Avista."

They clapped, then stood up and clapped louder when Pe

stepped to the podium and embraced the Reverend Cosadón. Why had Pe been so nervous? He was here to serve, to give them the teachings of the Lord, to start the life he'd longed for, worked for, since his conversion to a true Bible-believing faith ten years ago! Manuelo Vega and Ubaldo Martínez respectively picked and strummed guitar accompaniment to the ovation, and several in the congregation waved hands and gave glory to God in shouts of praise. Pe's heart lifted. It took a full three minutes to get everyone back into their seats.

"I preach," Pe started, "in the shadow of a great, great man." Pe's eyes fixed on the now-blushing face of Reverend Cosadón, who had taken the empty seat in the front row. "I am humbled by this reception. And in my heart, the Lord has spoken, telling me that today is the beginning of very exciting times."

The front doors of the church slammed open, the inside walls of the hall reverberated. Two men stepped in briskly, hands positioned and ready on the butts of their holstered guns. Police officers.

"*La Migra!*" someone rasped. Dozens of sets of eyes lowered to study the toes of dozens of sets of shoes. But the congregation sat with their backs to the door, and only Pe was facing forward to see that the officers were not from *La Migra,* U.S. Immigration. The two wore state police uniforms, troopers. They halted in mid-step, looking as surprised to see the church as the church was surprised to see them. Everything froze for a heartbeat, and Pe got his breathing under control.

"Um, welcome, law enforcement people," Pe said. "Please, have a seat," he added, trying to sound congenial.

The smaller of the two police officers began stammering, "We're sorry to—we thought this—Mike said, Mike told us—"

The larger officer (a *lot* larger, Pe thought, large even by white-guy standards) looked irritated, but less at a loss than his partner. His massive width of shoulders angled back toward the door. Had his hair been a little longer than stubble, Pe might have been able to guess its color. "Mike!" the huge trooper shouted toward the sidewalk, toward the street. Pe squinted at the doorway; the morning was bright, the front doors faced due east, and direct sun blurred the edges of the outside world of Vincent Avenue.

"Mike, this is *not* a restaurant," the trooper barked.

Mike's outline shadowed the sting of the sun in Pe's eyes.

The smaller cop sounded anxious. "We're not supposed to be here, Jim. Come on."

Trooper Jim ignored his partner, addressed Mike the Shadow. "You said this was a restaurant."

"Operative word being 'was,'" Pe heard Mike say. "Maybe it *was* a restaurant, now it *is* something different."

The voice sounded snotty, petulant, and it took Pe a few moments to process the sound. A high voice. A girl's voice. "Mike" was a girl.

She stepped into the hall, and Pe's vision adjusted. She had her arms crossed tightly, looking every bit the chided, miffed, beleaguered adolescent. No, she was older than adolescent. Regardless, she was a wisp of a girl. Her long, straight black hair did little to break the line of her gawky length, and only her dejected slouch kept her from looking sticklike. She wore basic denim jeans and an unadorned black tee shirt, short sleeved.

"Oh!" Mike seemed to notice the hushed, passive, *Migra*-fearing congregation for the first time. "Hi, everybody! Is this a town meeting or something?"

Why wasn't the Reverend Cosadón saying anything, doing anything? It struck Pe that he'd always assumed the Reverend was in the country legally. Was he also afraid this was a raid by *La Migra?* That made no sense.

"No, this is our church," Pe announced from his pulpit. He bolstered his voice with a tone of authority. "You're sort of interrupting. Sirs. Miss."

"A church!" the girl named Mike squealed, sounding delighted. "I always wondered what one looked like." She appraised the meeting hall, eyes sweeping south to north, ceiling to floor, kitchen to stairway. "I thought there'd be statues or something," she said.

The mammoth palm of Trooper Jim's hand settled on the girl's shoulder. "It's not a restaurant. It's not our place. You were wrong, Mike, and we're leaving."

"*Good,*" the smaller cop said. He hadn't moved from his spot near the door. "I thought maybe I was the only one who noticed that this was private property."

"Shut up, Cowles," Trooper Jim said. "Let's go, Mike."

The slim stick of a girl, almost two feet shorter than Trooper Jim, slapped the cop's hand and shoved it from her shoulder. She clomped up the aisle, grabbing one of the empty folding chairs as she came. She pointed at Pe. "This gentleman invited us to stay. He said to have a seat. I have a seat." She kept coming, right up to the podium, past it to the altar. Some scent, something warm and fruity, whiffed at Pe as she passed. It distracted him, confused him for a moment, as if anything could have added to the confusion he already felt.

She plunked the chair down in front of the altar. She sat. From the back of the hall, church member Ronald Lake must have decided enough was enough. "Look here, this is our Sunday worship service! You officers ain't from Immigration, and you got no right to disturb—"

"A man was murdered *here*," the girl Mike shouted, punctuating the assertion by slapping the altar. Pe clenched both hands in response to the volume and force of her sudden anger. "He was sitting here, typing into a palm pilot, eating a meal with yellow rice, chicken, shrimp, and mussels, and getting himself shot in the back of the head. The table cloth was white, just like this one. The blood pooled, the same spot as where that book is sitting. The same shade red as the book."

Her eyes had teared up. Pe figured he was the only one close enough to notice. Now she looked away.

The trooper named Cowles came up the aisle toward them. "I'm sorry, everyone, I'm sorry. She's upset and confused, we didn't mean to interrupt you. We didn't mean to intrude."

"I don't care if it's not a restaurant," Mike said. She was looking past Cowles, talking at Trooper Jim. "You think I like finding these things? It happened. In this spot. And for all you know, the killer's right here in the room watching us."

Her eyes widened. Cowles stopped walking toward her.

"Was that real?" Trooper Jim demanded. "Mike, was that real?"

She said nothing, but nodded once, slowly.

"Are you okay?" the huge cop asked with genuine tenderness in his voice. Pe was surprised.

Mike repeated her nod.

Cowles looked unsure. "Jim, you can't take her word every time she says—"

"Please!" Pe turned at the sound of the Reverend Cosadón's voice. The Reverend stood from his seat in the front row, finally, Lord be thanked, taking charge of this confusion.

"Let there be a little peace," the Reverend pleaded, his own face showing anything but peace. "I don't understand what you're looking for, but the young lady is right. A man was killed right there."

There were some gasps from the congregation.

"Right there, where our altar sits, "the Reverend Cosadón affirmed. "We only recently moved here. The building is now our church, but before we came, it was a restaurant."

Trooper Jim flashed Trooper Cowles a triumphant smile.

A restaurant? Pe thought. A murder? He'd known nothing about this.

Cowles' shoulders slumped. "Well, it figures," he said with

resignation. "We've had cases with missing murder weapons, missing corpses, and missing suspects. Guess we were overdue for one where the whole crime scene's missing."

"SOME ice water?" Pe asked Mike. He took a glass tumbler from the cupboard beside the sink in the *Palabra de Dios* kitchen. The air back here was still. The kitchen had no fans. The heat was oppressive.

"Do you have any coffee?" the girl asked.

Coffee. It was so warm in here that the old icebox had a veneer of condensation, and she wanted a cup of coffee. But the Reverend Cosadón had insisted Pe bring her back here to sit, to calm down, to get a drink. So Pe dug into the kitchen's still-unpacked cardboard boxes, searching for the coffee pot he'd assumed they wouldn't be needing in the scorch of August. There were a lot of boxes back here; the kitchen was spacious, and Pe realized he should have suspected that the building had once held a restaurant.

When he finally found the coffeemaker, he started setting it up on the shelf beside the sink. "My name is José Avista," he said to the girl. "Everyone calls me Pe, short for Pepe."

"Pleased to meet you." Her words sounded more like reflex than response, her voice distant and wispy.

"I'll bet you have a full name, too," Pe prompted.

She seemed to come back to herself. "Sorry. Michaela Trapp. Unwilling participant in today's investigation." She extended a hand, and when Pe shook it, he was struck by the pallor of her un-sunned skin against the deep richness his own hand. Dark on light, coffee and cream, *café con leche*. A shiver ran through him, a reaction to her touch. He pulled back, hoping his face didn't show the embarrassment he felt.

"*Con leche?*" he asked, eyes averted. He realize he'd asked that in Spanish. "With milk, I mean? Your coffee?"

"Saffron," she said. It took Pe a moment to understand

she wasn't asking for saffron in her coffee. Once more her voice sounded far away. "That's the spice that makes rice yellow, right? Saffron?"

"Sure," said Pe, "I guess."

"But it's a red spice, not yellow."

Truth be told, Pe knew almost nothing about spices, or herbs, or cooking in general. "I think it might be red."

"Bright red," she said. "Like the blood on the white altar cloth."

"There wasn't any blood on——"

"On the restaurant's tablecloth, I mean. The red on the altar is the book."

"The Bible," Pe said, happy to be back on familiar ground. "It is the Word of God, you know."

"Yeah, cool," Mike said, dismissing his comment with a wave of her hand. "So why would a red spice turn things yellow? And why would a restaurant really be a church? I'll tell you why." She looked directly in his eyes, making a point of telling him why. "Things are different from how they appear. Always."

"Yes, I see," Pe said, nodding and smiling, trying to sound calming. He was a Reverend now. It was his job to calm people, to minister to them. "You should relax," he told her. "I'm sure the police officers will straighten everything out, and then we'll know what's going on."

She laughed. Really, it was more like a single, crisp bark, a startling sound coming from such a thin girl. "That's another thing different from how it appears," she said. "Jimmy and Cowles don't solve crimes. They just hang around waiting for me to solve things. Especially when there's no body, no evidence, and no leads."

As if to confirm her assertion, the police officer named Cowles opened the door and stuck his head into the kitchen. "Are you okay now? Jim needs your help. He's taking names and arguing with people about how to spell them."

She rolled her eyes. "Yeah, all right, fine," she said, not

bothering to hide her exasperation. "Bring my coffee when Pe finishes making it."

"Sure," Cowles agreed. When she'd gone, he asked, "What did she call you? 'Pe?' I thought your priest called you José."

"He's not a *priest*," Pe said, scooping grounds into the coffee filter. "He's a minister. And I *am* José. Pe, Pe Avista. I'm a minister, too."

Officer Cowles's lips pursed, and his eyes squinted. "Ministers. They're different from priests? Okay, I think I remember hearing that somewhere. I don't follow religion too closely, see. I like sports." He smiled, looking satisfied that his love of sports explained why he didn't know about religion. "Football," he added, explaining further.

"Are you guys going to be here long?" Pe asked.

"Well, until Mike clears things up by having another vision or something."

"Vision?" Pe's interest suddenly rose. "Mike has visions?"

"Yeah, she's spiritual, like you guys. Church guys, I mean. Although she's not a Bible nut or anything like that."

"Oh, good," Pe said, trying not to react uncharitably. "And the visions she has, they're of murders and crimes? And the police use her for investigating those things?"

Cowles chuckled. "Not officially. Her brother Jimmy uses her, kind of on the side. And I don't really know if she's having visions, talking strictly. It happens whenever she says the words, 'For all you know.' Everything she says right after that turns out to be true."

Pe stared at him.

"Yeah, yeah, I know," Cowles said. "It's the weirdest thing. But after you've seen it work a couple dozen times, you start believing it."

Believing it? Pe wasn't sure what he was having more difficulty believing—that the hulking Trooper Jim could really be tiny Mike's brother, or that these cops had actually invaded their church on the whim of a psychic. An "unofficial" psychic, at that.

"For all you know," Mike had said earlier. "For all you know, the killer's right here in the room watching us."

Pe tried to stay calm, tried to sound casual. "You say Mike is spiritual. What do you mean by that? When she walked in the church, she sounded like she'd never been inside one before."

Puzzlement returned to Cowles's face. "Yeah, she doesn't do churches. It's a neo-something religion. I wanna say she's in a convent, but that's not right."

"A coven," Pe offered.

Cowles brightened. "That's the word!"

"She's a neo-pagan. A Wiccan."

"Yes, that's what she calls it. Hey, no wonder you're a minister. You've got a good handle on religious stuff."

Pe didn't answer. He stormed through the kitchen door, his fury building, and behind him Cowles was saying, "Okay, then, I'll finish making Mike's coffee."

PE Avista had graduated fourth in his class from Elim Bible Institute. He knew about Wiccans, the modern-day witches who called themselves "neo-pagans." It was a faddish faith, New Age vogue. Fad or not, though, it was evil, with satanic powers underlying it, of that Pe was certain. The Word of God was crystal clear—witches had no place among the Lord's faithful. That was God's direct command, right from the Book of Deuteronomy: "There shall not be found among you anyone that useth divination, or an enchanter, or a witch." And the prohibition wasn't just an Old Testament mandate, either. The apostle Paul's letter to the Galatians also forbade witchcraft, calling it a sin as heinous as adultery. As fornication. As drunkenness.

As sinful as anger, the Apostle Paul had said. Pe walked slower. *As murder.*

All right . . . so, why? *why* hadn't the Reverend Cosadón mentioned that there'd been a murder here? If he'd said something, Pe wouldn't have thought much about it. This was Vincent Avenue, after all. But withholding the information, that made things kind of suspicious.

Information. Pe decided he should calm down, keep his own head level, and work with facts. There weren't enough facts, so he knew his first chore should be to find some.

He didn't walk to the main hall. Instead, he turned right, and walked back to the makeshift office he and the Reverend Cosadón had assembled in the northwest room. Well, it could barely be called a room. More like a walk-in closet. But it had the phone Pe needed.

"NO, there's no 'w' in my first name," Manuelo Vega told Trooper Jim. They stood by the podium. The officer scribbled notes; the witch named Mike was beside him. Manuelo still had his six-string guitar strapped across his back.

My podium, Pe thought, mine and the Reverend Cosadón's. He didn't feel the least bit shy about walking right up to it to join them. Throughout the main hall, much of the congregation remained seated, still looking very guilty. That made sense. They hadn't been in this building as often as Pe and the Reverend Cosadón. They felt like visitors, and, with state troopers here, probably like intruders in their own new church.

"No 'w' at all?" Trooper Jim acted incredulous. " 'Mahn-WAY-loh.' "

The girl Mike intervened on Manuelo's behalf. "Surprise, Jimmy, there's no 'W' in the entire Spanish language. And it's almost like they have a different word for *everything*."

"I didn't ask you out here to be sarcastic."

"Bro, you want the brains, you take the brine." Trooper Jim didn't react to that, and she said, "Brine. You know, like salt water, or pickles? I'm using it as a clever metaphor for my acidic personality—"

"—And what can you tell me about the restaurant that

was here, Mr, Arroyas?" Trooper Jim didn't seem to want Mike's explanation.

"It's Mr. Vega, officer," Manuelo corrected him. "Like I said, I'd only eaten here twice, what with it being over on this side of town and everything, but she was right. The girl here, I mean. They served a great paella, the saffron rice with the seafood and chicken. Just hearing her describe it made me hungry. Well, except for part about the red blood on the white tablecloth. That part wasn't too appetizing."

Trooper Jim got angry. "You told me your last name is Arroyas!"

"No, you asked me for my full name, and I told you I'm Manuelo Vega Arroyas. That would make me 'Mr. Vega.' 'Mr. Arroyas' would be my mother's father, which is why I have that as my *other* last name, see?"

Trooper Jim grimaced. The girl Mike smirked. Pe interrupted. "Manuelo, you can sit down."

The trooper looked at Pe with surprise, and then took a step toward him. "I'm not done questioning this guy."

"Then question him more when the other police get here. Sit down, Manuelo."

Manuelo grinned and bobbed his head in acknowledgement. "Sure thing, Pe. I mean *Reverend* Pe. That sounds so cool."

"Other police?" Trooper Jim looked uncomfortable.

"Yes," Pe said. "The city police. You know, the *local* ones who work right here *in* the city? I called them to find out about the murder that happened here. They sounded eager to talk to any state troopers who might be conducting investigations on Vincent Avenue. They kept talking about their jurisdiction and said they'd be right over."

"You had *no* right—"

"Bonito Papada. That's the dead guy's name. Did you know that?" Trooper Jim's face showed no hint of recognition. "No," Pe said, "not even that much, huh? You're only here because this girl did some witchcraft to tell you this *used* to be a restaurant that *used* to have a dead guy in it. And now you're harassing our church, just because demons whisper things to your sister! Well, I will *not* tolerate this in our place of worship! I will not tolerate it in this *House* of *God*."

Pe wasn't sure when he'd started shouting. Everybody in the congregation stared at him.

"Sorry," he said to the church. "But she's a witch, you know. And they're using her as a psychic detective. That's why I'm angry." And anger was as bad as witchcraft. And witchcraft was as bad as murder. "*Kind* of angry," Pe clarified. It didn't make him feel any better.

"I don't care how mad it makes you," Trooper Jim managed to say through clenched teeth. "You're interfering with an investigation."

"How?" Pe demanded, astounded by his own assertiveness. "By calling in more police?"

"Yeah, Jimmy, how?" The girl Mike had moved next to Pe. She was taking his side. "He called the locals. You're just mad because they'll want to know why D Troop is here, two counties over from your legit area."

"I'll tell them it was hot pursuit," Trooper Jim said.

"Gee, that's convincing."

"Look, Mike, if you're going to help *him* instead of me—"

"I don't care if I help anybody!" Again she looked as if she was going to cry. "Just lay off this guy. He's a minister. Show some respect. For all you know, he's the one who'll help us solve this thing."

She gasped.

Trooper Jim looked at her. He looked at Pe. Then he looked at her again. "Was that real?" he asked.

Mike stared at Pe intently. Pe fought the urge to squirm.

"I'll let you know," Mike said.

Cowles, the cop in the kitchen, popped the door open and yelled out, "Coffee's ready, Mike! What do you take in it?"

"*Café con leche,*" she called back, not moving her eyes from

Pe. She took hold of his forearm, drawing him toward the kitchen. "Come talk to me where it's quiet," she said. "This place is gonna be lousy with cops soon."

"Whose fault is that?" Trooper Jim muttered.

Pe went with Mike.

BONITO Papada hadn't been a customer at *La Cocina Valenciana*. He was the owner, as well as the landlord for the three upstairs apartments. He'd been eating at one of his own tables on the night he was murdered, early in May of that same year. It was well after hours; the restaurant was closed, and he was enjoying a plate of the day's leftovers. No, the man on the phone assured Pe, the police never caught the killer. Yes, there was something about Papada having a palm pilot computer with him. No, he didn't know whether Papada'd been eating paella. Yes, everybody near the restaurant, outside on the sidewalk, upstairs in the apartments, and up the road in the two nearby bars had been interviewed by the police.

"You didn't learn all this from the city cops," Mike insisted, sipping her coffee as they talked. She'd ordered Cowles out of the room. "Cops don't answer that many questions, especially over the phone."

"I called the weekend news desk at the paper, too," Pe admitted. "You're right. The police didn't want to tell me much. Newspaper people, on the other hand . . . well, they're in the information-sharing business, I guess."

They'd been talking for ten minutes now. Well, Pe had been talking, prodded along by Mike's rapid, disconnected questions about the church, the repairs he and the Reverend had done, the move from East Complin, any number of other topics. Very little about the murder. Pe brought those details up.

"So you guys bought this place from the bereaved Papada family? The dead guy's relatives?"

Pe didn't know, and said so. The Reverend Cosadón would know, but Pe didn't mention that to Mike.

"What kind of price did you pay for the building?"

"Look," Pe said, feeling he'd said enough for the time being, "maybe it's your turn to answer questions. Wouldn't that be fair?"

To his surprise, she nodded and sat back in her chair. He hadn't expected such quick acquiescence; he thought he'd need to argue and cajole. So his first question sounded like a blurt, even to his own ears. "Why do you serve Satan?"

Her eyebrows lifted. She crossed her arms, but she was smiling. "I've never heard Jimmy called by *that* name."

Fine, the more coy she played, the more direct Pe would get. "Trooper Cowles told me you're a Wiccan. That's neopagan witchcraft, right?"

"Right," Mike agreed. "It's the religion Mom raised us in."

"Raised you in? Nobody raises their kids to practice witchcraft!" Pe felt he was still doing too much blurting, not enough talking.

"Where'd you learn that? Minister school? Look, Reverend Pepe, witchcraft isn't the scary, dark rituals you see in horror movies. We don't sacrifice virgins and babies. We don't worship Satan, since Satan is a spirit in *your* religion, not in ours. And just in case you're confused by episodes of *Sabrina* on television, our cats don't talk to us, either."

Pe had no illusions about witches being pointy-hatted hags, the stuff of Halloween. Nor did he believe Wiccans performed human sacrifices. But he let Mike talk on. He had to show her he was willing to hear her out. Otherwise, how could he expect her to listen when he told her about the salvation she could have by accepting the Lord Jesus Christ?

"Be honest, Mike," Pe said. "Isn't it at least *possible* your psychic powers come from darker forces? From spirits outside of the grace of God?"

She made that single-bark laughing noise again. "Pe Avista, I *told* you things are different from what they appear to be. Weren't you listening? I'm no psychic. I just look like one to my brother."

Now Pe felt confused. Hadn't she told him she was psychic? Well, no, she hadn't. Cowles had said that. But Pe had heard her with his own ears, hadn't he?

No, come to think of it, he hadn't.

"One day last year, Jimmy and I were at my mom's for dinner. He was going on and on about the homicide of a black guy in Livingston County. He kept spouting about how 'those people' keep killing each other, about how he needed to arrest another one of 'those people,' about 'Leroy' this and 'Toby' that, until I lost my temper. I called him a racist lout. I hollered, 'For all you know, the killer is a fat white guy named George!' He didn't think much about what I said until the next week, when he and Cowles got a tip, found the discarded gun, and arrested a white neighbor of the victim whose name happened to be George. It was a fluke, but try telling Jimmy that."

"Was George fat?" Pe asked.

"Everyone named George is fat," she asserted.

Not a psychic? Pe had convinced himself that the girl was enslaved to demons. "But your brother and Cowles make it sound like you do a lot of psychic work for them. How do you keep it up? And how would you know there'd been a murder here?"

She shrugged, showing little curiosity. "I could have seen something on the news, noticed something in the paper, read an article online, mulled facts over subconsciously until something clicks. I'm intuitive. I'm always puzzling through things, it's how my brain works. Jimmy has me trained to pop out with 'for-all-you-know' comments whenever I have an insight. The only magic involved is intuition. Otherwise I'd say, 'For all you know, there's twenty bucks under your kitchen sink, let's grab it and get some lunch.'"

Pe felt nervous again; he imagined himself inviting her

out to dinner, asking her on a date. Where had that come from? Inappropriate thoughts—it was as the Scriptures said, that temptation prowled like a lion, stalking, seeking to devour. Pe Avista reminded himself that he had only one goal, and that was to tell Mike about the salvation and grace of God so that she could be born again, be saved.

"You mentioned the Colindres guy, the one who bought the church. Tell me more."

"Mr. Torgas. Jaime Torgas Colindres. He was our benefactor. He used a small inheritance to buy us this building."

"How small? You think maybe the property value lowered because the owner got shot through the back of the head in his own restaurant? Would that save a few bucks? Or maybe, do you think, his family had to sell the place quickly, since their breadwinner was dead?"

Pe felt himself bristle. "Mr. Torgas is an old, respected man! Look, can we talk more about you? Let me be honest. I don't think that your coming here is an accident. Our Lord offers salvation to everyone, and sometimes He raises opportunities in miraculous ways. You're not here today by mistake. Everything happens for a reason."

Mike reached out her hand, bringing it close to Pe's face. For a moment, he thought she would gently cup his cheek. Instead, she cuffed his ear, hard.

He startled. It hurt. "Hey! Why'd you do that?"

"No reason," she said, walking to the kitchen door. "Which kills your theory that everything happens for one. It's ridiculous that the only skeptic in the building today is the psychic detective herself." She opened the door a crack, peering through. "Torgas Colindres is the old guy in back? Who's the hottie babe next to him?"

Pe's face warmed. "His granddaughter, Lucinda."

"Hmm. Family. They would care a great deal about the honor of their elders, wouldn't they?"

" 'They' who? You mean 'those people,' us Latinos?"

"Touché." She looked pleased with his sarcasm.

What on Earth was she getting at? Pe was going to protest that Lucinda should be left alone, but Mike was already pointing, waving, and motioning for Jaime Torgas's granddaughter to join them. After a few uncertain moments, she did.

Here she was, Pe told himself. This was the young lady he was truly attracted to. He was glad Mike had waved Lucinda into the kitchen. Now, seeing them side by side, Pe could get back to his senses, and put a stop to the silly reactions he had while talking to Mike alone.

"You're Lucinda Torgas Colindres?" Mike asked her.

"Lucinda Torgas Fontana," Lucinda said. She was demure. Pe liked that. It was a refreshing change from Mike. "My grandfather is a Torgas Colindres, but since my mother's father is a Fontana, that is my second name."

"But Reverend Avista here has only one last name."

"The longer people live in America, the more they pick up the customs. So he uses just one last name. He was born here."

"I see," Mike said, sounding pleased to have that cleared up. "We were wondering if you knew why a red spice like saffron can turn rice yellow. Do you know?"

Lucinda kept glancing at Pe, but Pe tried to control his face and his reactions. This was certainly not a proper time to show his feelings of affection for Lucinda.

"I don't know why," Lucinda confessed.

"I don't either," Mike said. "So, how do you like the new church?"

Lucinda remained cautious. "I like it very much."

"Pe did a great job patching up and painting, didn't he?"

Now Lucinda let her guard down, and smiled. "Yes, he did a wonderful job!"

"So is the Reverend Cosadón related to your grandfather?"

Lucinda's smile disappeared as quickly as it had come. "No. He is not in my family."

"Did you ever eat here? When it was a restaurant."

"No."

"But you visited once or twice when Pe and the Reverend were fixing the place up?"

None of the questions seemed intrusive. Pe saw no reason to interrupt.

"I visited six times."

"Did you help him patch the hole in the ceiling above the altar?"

Pe looked at Mike.

"No, I guess that was something he fixed when I wasn't here." Lucinda looked frightened. It was no wonder. The questions seemed random, disjointed, designed to cause imbalance. Still, Lucinda composed herself, arching her back. "The people of my church are whispering that you are a witch. Is that true?"

Pe was proud of her for asking such a direct question.

"Yup, I'm Wiccan," Mike answered. "And, hey! That's a great dress. Gorgeous. What's 'dress' in Spanish?"

"Vestido," Lucinda said.

"It ends in an 'o'? I thought Spanish words ending in 'o' were masculine."

"Um," said Lucinda. "Yes."

"See, Pepe? Things are always different from how they appear. Lucinda, I want to thank you. You've been a huge help. Send your aunt in next."

"I—" Lucinda stopped. "How can I do that? My aunt lives in Costa Rica."

"Of course she does," Mike said, as if anyone with a brain knew that. "She's there living with your uncle. That guy she married."

Mike waited. Finally, Lucinda offered, "Tío Carlos."

"Right! That's Uncle Carlos . . . Carlos . . ." Mike raised her voice at the end of the name Carlos, inviting completion.

"Carlos Martínez Lopón."

"Of Costa Rica," Mike finished, snapping her fingers. "But paella isn't a Costa Rican dish, originally. It's right from Spain. The Valencia area, right?"

Lucinda shook her head. "I . . . I don't know."

"You've been great." Mike walked her through the doorway. "Thanks ever so." Mike shut the kitchen door.

"You're very odd," Pe told her.

"Oh my gosh, Pe, she is simply *whipped* over you!" Admiration glowed in Mike's eyes. "Did you see how often she looked your way to see if her answers were right? Woo! She's *yours,* chico!"

"She only . . . no, she's reacting that way just because I'm one of ministers here." But he'd noticed Lucinda's looks, too. And Mike Trapp was a psychic. No, wait. Mike wasn't a psychic.

"Come on, she's whipped. You've only been doing the Reverend thing for about thirty minutes. You think she's just deferring to your vast experience and authority?"

"Hey." Now Pe remembered what bothered him. "How did you know there was a hole in the ceiling over the altar? You tell me you're not psychic, then you just pop out with that."

"Intuition plus deduction, Pe. Work it out. Bonito Papada is eating a delicious plate of paella. He's using a palm pilot at the same time, working on who knows what, inventory, budget, surfing porn sites. He gets shot in the back of the head. Not from *behind,* but—"

"—but from *above.*" The realization hit Pe. "Because he probably would be looking down at the moment of his death. Eating or reading the palm pilot's screen. The bullet came from *above* him, not from behind him."

Mike smiled satisfaction at him. "Through the hole you fixed. And the topside of the hole is upstairs, probably under loose floorboards in one of the apartments, where the police will be able to find gunpowder residue. Welcome to my world. When we go out to announce this, they'll think we're *both* psychics."

A few pieces fell into place for Pe. "The hole was the size of my fist. You could look through it and you could fire a gun from above."

"And I'll bet the ceiling was dark. You painted it white."

"It was brown. It took three coats."

"And since it was brown, no one noticed a small, dark hole twelve feet up. Especially since the shot seemed to be from behind, execution style."

Pe couldn't avoid the feeling that the two of them were working a miracle, solving the crime just by talking about it. Gut feeling, intuition, deduction. No psychic powers behind it at all. But it was exhilarating. It felt like magic.

"Okay, so *why* did this guy get killed?" Pe asked.

"We already figured that out. So that the Papada family would sell it, quickly and cheaply, to your church. I'll bet you guys always wanted a place in this part of town."

Pe tensed. Yes, for a couple years, he and the Reverend Cosadón had talked about moving into the Vincent Avenue neighborhood. Where the Lord was most needed. Where they could do the most good. Nothing was said about this specific building, this part of the avenue. But for years they'd dreamed of getting into a part of town most people were trying to escape.

"You think," he said, "that maybe Bonito Papada was trying to sell, trying to get out of here and into a better location, but couldn't afford to sell it for so little money?"

"So little money as what?" Mike asked. There was a strange quality to her voice, as if she were comforting him without actually using words of comfort.

"So little money as what the Reverend Cosadón could offer. As what Mr. Torgas Colindres could give us to use."

She reached out her hand, but this time there was no cuff to his ear. She touched his cheek with tenderness. "You're worried that the Reverend knew something about the murder. I don't think he did. And I certainly don't think Lucinda or her grandfather know anything about it. Intuition, again."

Pe could see no other conclusion. "You keep hinting at Mr. Torgas and his honor. You think that's behind the killing. But you also hint at the price being too high for the Reverend Cosadón to buy the church. Which is the real reason?"

"Both," Mike said, sounding certain. "Let's kill two motives with one murder. Time to settle this. We can take the long, drawn out approach by determining who rented the upstairs room used to shoot down at the landlord . . . or we can do it the quick, down-and-dirty, fake-psychic-detective way. What's your pleasure, Reverend?"

Whatever they discovered would point to someone in his church, Pe knew. So he thought it fitting use the words Christ spoke to Judas the betrayer. "What you do," he told Mike, "do it quickly."

A commotion arose in the main hall of the church. The police—the local police, Pe's police—had arrived, and Trooper Jim was having an animated discussion with two of them, presumably concerning the finer points of jurisdictional authority. To their credit, the members of the church were still seated quietly. Well, except for Ron Lake, who spoke with a third city cop in almost as loud a voice as Trooper Jim's. The Reverend Cosadón remained in his seat, passive amid the chaos. Jaime Torgas Colindres and his granddaughter whispered back and forth to each other.

"We got here just in time to make things crazier," Mike said to Pe, sounding a little too pleased about that. She led the way up toward the podium and the altar. "Quick, how do you say the word 'killer' in Spanish?"

"*El matador.*" Pe told her.

"Cool! Like the guy who fights bulls?"

"And then kills them."

"Well. There you go," Mike said.

"What are we doing now?" Pe whispered the question, since they were nearing Trooper Jim and the local cops.

"You look authoritative and stay quiet. I turn into a drama queen. People need drama from their psychics."

Right when they reached the altar, Mike spun around to face the congregation. She lifted her hands toward the ceiling, and then she shrieked. It was impossibly high-pitched. Pe was stunned, again, by the sounds that could come out of her.

"The angels have spoken to me! The angels and spirits have whispered truth in my ears!"

The screech had gotten everyone's attention.

"Help me understand their words! I merely speak for the spirits. They whisper to me, '*El matador, el matador! Se habla nombre el matador.*'"

That was really bad Spanish, Pe thought. But she still had their attention. The Reverend Cosadón even stood up. Please, no, Pe thought. My Lord and Savior, please, no.

"*El matador es . . . el matador es . . .*" Mike swayed, as if getting a message from beyond. Drama queen indeed.

"*. . . es Señor Martínez Torgas.*"

Mike fell to one knee, head bowed, breathing deeply. Her spirit possession had ended, apparently. Everyone waited. Just as Pe was about to ask aloud who in the world Mr. Martínez Torgas might be, the sound of a guitar distracted him. A guitar dropped, in haste. Pe heard several strings snap and twang.

Ubaldo the guitarist rushed past him.

Ubaldo Martínez. The new guitarist, the one who'd been in the country for just a few months.

I'm an idiot, Pe told himself. He's related to Torgas.

Any other girl would have screamed holy terror when Ubaldo grabbed her in a headlock, the tip of a very long knife blade positioned at her neck. Not Mike Trapp, though. She twisted, looked toward Pe, and said, "From how your names work, I'm betting this is Mr. Martínez. Cousin of Lucinda Torgas. Mr. Torgas's other grandkid."

Pepe watched the knife, watched Ubaldo's grip on Mike. He tried not to let his panic show. "Family honor," he said.

"Usually an admirable trait," Mike managed.

"Shut up! You both shut up!" Ubaldo looked frantic, like a trapped animal. And of course, that's exactly what he was. Even if Mike hadn't flushed him out today, further investigation would have turned up the names of former upstairs tenants, their connections to this church. There was no doubt who one of those tenants was.

"Ubaldo—"

"Don't stick up for her, Pe! She's a witch! She's ruined everything!" Ubaldo was crying, but didn't look as if he'd be letting Mike go. *"Perdone, abuelito,"* he sobbed, begging his grandfather's forgiveness. *"Lo hice pa' ud.* For you. Back home they say it is the one dream you have, to help build your church here. I didn't mean to hurt you, it was to help! A tribute to you, and to our family . . . ."

Pe chanced a look behind. The esteemed Jaime Torgas Colindres sat stone-faced, rigid. Pe had never seen such fury in the kind old man's eyes. In anyone's eyes.

Pe heard the words "hostage situation"; a local cop was speaking into a cell phone. Another was edging Trooper Jim backward, away from the pulpit. Pepe saw that fury-in-the-eyes thing again. Twice in one day.

"The Word of God says you must kill her, Ubaldo."

Ubaldo gaped. He didn't look like he understood Pe's words.

"It's true," Pe said, walking toward the altar. "She's a witch. She confessed it to me back in the kitchen. She's unrepentant, so she'll keep being a witch unless you do something about it."

Ubaldo's stayed motionless. He tightened his grip on Mike, but didn't move when Pe reached the altar.

"Don't take my word for it, Ubaldo. It's here, in *the word*." Pe opened the red King James. "Here, in the Book of Exodus. The twenty-second chapter, verse eighteen. 'Thou shalt not suffer a witch to live.'" Pe said it matter-of-factly, reasonably. "'Suffer' means 'allow.' It's right here in the Old Testament. It's a direct command. If you kill her, every Christian will understand that you had to."

Ubaldo had the empty gaze of a lost, crazed soul. "Really, Pe? It says that, really?" And the knife blade lowered the inch Pe hoped it would.

"But I prefer the New Testament," Pe said swinging the huge tome, the spine, at the side of Ubaldo's head. It connected, not really making much noise. Ubaldo spun, probably already unconscious when his face slammed into the top of the altar. That did make noise, a muffled crack. Blood from Ubaldo's nose trickled, soiling the white altar cloth.

"*Palabra de Dios,*" Pe muttered. He helped Mike up.

SUNSET came. Forms, paperwork, interviews with cops, more interviews and forms . . . the first day of Pe Avista's ministry became the longest day of his life. Mike, despite her bravado, had been in mild shock. A paramedic tended to her; she was so chilled, he wrapped her in a thin blanket. Pe took a moment to go to the kitchen and grab her more coffee. *Con leche,* of course.

"Well, I certainly enjoyed your first service," Ron Lake said, shaking Pe's hand. "I look forward to less exciting times in the future, though."

Pe remembered his first words to the congregation that morning, about the Lord speaking to his heart and saying exciting times were ahead. Did Ron take that literally? Did he think Pe had been delivering a prophecy rather than using a figure of speech? Pe decided he didn't want to know

the answer. He was afraid it would have too much in common with Mike's psychic detective routine.

"I'm out of here," he heard Mike say. "Where's Lucinda?
I wanted to say goodbye."

Pe turned to her. It wasn't a day that called for smiles,
but he gave Mike one anyway. "Lucinda's in the kitchen,
cleaning up my mess."

"Hang on to her, Rev. She's a find. And I wanted to thank
you, too. Not just for keeping me from getting killed, but
for working through the case with me. I spend most of my
days with idiots. This was a nice change of pace."

That was a compliment, Pe knew. "Sure," he said. "And
thank you. It's good to know truth, even when truth is hard."

"How's your Reverend?"

Pe sighed. "Feeling guilty. Ubaldo had been telling him
about this building for a couple months. They'd even approached Bonito Papada about a sale. A few times. So when
the price dropped because of the family's rush to sell the
place . . . well, the Reverend thinks he should have guessed
what was up. Like I said, truth is hard. So, is your brother
okay with the locals?"

"He's a hero," she said, smirking. She was awfully good
at that, Pe noticed. "He broke the case wide open, got it off
the local boards, ended the stalemate, thank goodness for
the state troopers! For years I've watched Jimmy fall in crap
and come out clean." She brought her hand to her mouth.
"Sorry. Forgot where I was."

Pe laughed. "I spend most of my days with careful talk-
ers. This was a nice change of pace."

She accepted that gracefully.

"So," Pe said, first hesitating, then deciding to ask, "how
did you know some of the other details? About what the victim was eating? Where the table was sitting when he died?"

In the fading evening and the church's weak lighting,
Mike's shadowed grin looked impish. "If I tell you all my

secrets, you'll become a psychic detective, too. I don't think I want the competition."

"You just don't want to surrender the mystique," Pe challenged. "But thanks. For everything. I wish I'd had more time. I wanted to share some of my thoughts about our faith."

"And I might've listened without sarcasm. Hey, you may get a second chance. For all you know, we'll be working together on another case before the month is out."

Pe nodded; then he realized she'd just used the "for-all-you-know" phrase. "Was that real?" he asked.

"I'll let you know," said Mike Trapp. She left.

Fifteen minutes later, Lucinda came out of the kitchen. "I'm finished," she said. She held a twenty-dollar bill out to him. "Here. I found this."

"Where?"

"In the kitchen, while I was cleaning. It was way back in the cupboard under the sink. Behind some old boxes. The boxes had a lot of water damage, so I threw them out."

Pe took the bill. It, too, had water damage. It must have been there for some time.

"For all we know," he said to Lucinda, giving her a playful smile, "this twenty dollars got under the kitchen sink by *magic*."

She giggled. "Don't be silly."

"The day's ending. Can I use it to take you to dinner?"

Lucinda's face blanched. Or maybe that had something to do with the shadows and fading light. "Yes. I'm glad you asked me. I mean, that would be very nice."

Pe called back to the church's closet-sized office, telling the Reverend Cosadón he was leaving for the evening. The old Reverend was taking the day's events hard. But that was a matter to be worked out over time. Pe Avista needed the night off.

He took Lucinda to dinner, leaving the Reverend to lock up their new Vincent Avenue House of God.

DEAN AND CLAUDIA ASK MARCOS:

Q: *Where did this recipe come from?*
A: Paella originated in southern Spain, in the general area of Valencia. It migrated to South America, where it's cooked and eaten under the open sky of the *pampas* by *vaqueros,* South American cowboys. The core of the recipe is saffron rice and meats; its specific ingredients vary from region to region, person to person. The recipe I include here is an amalgam of four or five of my favorite variations.

Q: *And is your variety any good?*
A: Well, Claudia herself has sampled this version, and she claimed to like it quite a bit. In fact, I suspect I was invited into the anthology just so she could get her hands on this recipe.

Q: *We can neither confirm nor deny that. Tell us: since this is your first experience writing a murder mystery, did you find it difficult to commit murder on paper?*
A: I've killed dozens of people in the course of my career. On paper, I mean. In this piece, I had a blast throwing together two characters who would have mutual animosity, making each irritating to the other while trying to keep either one from becoming irritating to the reader. Compared to that, killing the victim, Bonito Papada, was easy. Incidentally, that name is a Spanish translation of the name "Ken Gill," a friend of mine who suggested I should use this story to kill a real human being, maybe someone we both knew. I made it him.

Q: *Do you often weave hidden biographical elements into your fiction?*
A: Always. In a sense, even my fantasy writings are part mystery, too, since I've concealed real-life details in them that might take some biographical digging to unearth. That way, if I inexplicably become famous after I die, English Lit

students will have extra material to work with in their term papers about me.

Q: *Do you really expect that to happen?*
A: Of course I do. Everyone dies.

Q: *Um, no . . . we meant the part about becoming famous.*
A: Ah. Well, it would be nice to entertain as many people as possible. If that requires my becoming famous, it's a burden I'm willing to bear.

AND HERE IS MARCOS'S RECIPE:

PAELLA VALENCIANA

6 tablespoons extra virgin olive oil
1 pound raw shimp, peeled and deveined
4 chicken drumsticks
pinch of cayenne pepper
pinch of salt and pepper
1 cup chopped onion
4 garlic cloves, minced
1 1/2 cups medium grain white rice
1 teaspoon paprika
5 cups chicken broth
1 cup dry white wine
pinch of saffron
1 pound mussels
French style green beans, cooked
about 8 ounces roasted red pepper

Use 1 medium skillet and 1 large (14 inch) frying, sauté, or paella pan with cover. Assemble, clean, prep, and chop everything before starting to cook anything. It will make your life easier.

In medium skillet, fry shrimp in 3 tablespoons of oil; remove with slotted spoon. Set aside, keeping warm.

Sprinkle cayenne, salt, and pepper on drumsticks; fry them in medium skillet for 20 minutes, covered, turning once after 10 minutes. Set aside, keeping warm.

In large pan, fry onion in 3 tablespoons oil for 3 minutes or until softened. Add garlic and fry 1 more minute.

Put rice in onion/garlic pan. Stir and fry for 1 minute, then sprinkle with paprika.

Combine chicken broth and wine. Sprinkle saffron on the rice in large pan, then pour two cups of the wine-broth mixture over the saffron rice. Stir well, bring to a boil.

You are getting nervous that this dish shouldn't stay at medium-high temperature the whole time. Buck up, you wimp. You'll boil for about 25 minutes.

When most of liquid has been absorbed, add next 2 cups of wine-broth mixture. Put the shrimp, the uncooked mussels, and the cooked green beans into the pan and stir. Keep boiling.

When liquid is almost gone, add final 2 cups of broth. Boil another 5 minutes, then reduce heat to a very low simmer. Stir once more, then nestle your chicken drumsticks into the mixture. Simmer 10 minutes.

Take the paella off the heat entirely. Cover it, and let it sit 10 more minutes before serving.

Serves 4-6. Goes great with crusty bread and a palm pilot.

ALICE AND THE AGENT
OF THE HUN

Elizabeth Foxwell

A native of New Jersey, Elizabeth Foxwell has edited or co-edited nine mystery anthologies and published several historical mystery stories, including a previous Alice and FDR story, "Come Flit By Me." A co-founder of Malice Domestic Ltd, she is a director at large of the Mystery Writers of America Board of Directors, editor of MWA's newsletter "Third Degree," and a contributing editor for Mystery Scene Magazine. She lives outside Washington, D.C.

"I am not Mata Hari, Franklin," I snapped.

It sounded like pure melodrama—or more likely, farce. I, Alice Lee Roosevelt Longworth, Theodore Roosevelt's daughter and congressman's wife, succumbing to wartime Washington hysteria to help trap a traitor. But the assistant secretary of the Navy, otherwise known as my cousin, sat where he had planted himself in my electric runabout, sans the moustache of a nickelodeon villain but grinning just as evilly.

"Of course not. You're much more handsome."

I snorted, immune to the infamous Hyde Park charm.

"But you are attending the McLeans's New Year's Eve party."

"It seemed a good way to greet 1918. But not if it means spying on Evalyn." Evalyn, the down-to-earth daughter of a Colorado mine owner, was married to Ned McLean, owner of the *Washington Post* and none too sober at the best of times.

"No, not Evalyn. It's a German agent, or agents. The McLeans's parties have coincided too often with enemy reports on our ship movements—most troubling with all the German submarine activity. I can't attend; I'm too conspicuous."

"Meaning Eleanor wouldn't let you play secret agent."

He scowled, which meant that I was right. "You, on the other hand—"

It made sense—although I would hardly admit it and feed Franklin's invincible ego. There was nothing to excite attention about The Gadfly's usual appearance at the McLeans's. "So what would I do, chief? Eat any coded cables that I find?"

"Keep your eyes and ears open and report anything unusual to me. Isn't that what you do best?"

I gave him a withering look and considered. Lately the press had been grumbling about my lackluster contribution to the war effort. Franklin could set it about that I was working secretly for the government. That certainly would be more glamorous than selling Liberty Loan bonds, rolling bandages, or washing teacups in a Red Cross canteen. "Very well."

"How very patriotic of you, Alice." Franklin's smile widened, and I knew that he knew precisely why I had agreed, the rat.

"You're fortunate that the dinner isn't next week, when Father is due."

We both shuddered at the narrow escape. Our former

president would have hidden in the potted plants, badgered potential accomplices, and probably shot the suspected spies. He liked that sort of thing.

"Well, I should dash home and dress if you want me to arrive on time."

He clambered down from the car and paused. "Alice." The dying sunlight glinted off his pince-nez.

"What?"

"Don't forget your gun."

"Really, Franklin." I retied my veil under my chin, flung the ends over my shoulder, and started the runabout. "One never wears silk with firearms."

BY the time I had finished one circuit of Evalyn's endearingly vulgar mansion, I was extremely irritated.

Not that she provided an inferior party. In marked contrast to the wartime austerity of other local occasions, the drink flowed, the long tables in the dining room glittered with silver and crystal, and every light blazed from the chandeliers. My husband had accompanied me but soon disappeared with Ned; I could only guess that they were insensible under the aspidistra somewhere. Ned had been listing at a good forty-five-degree angle when I arrived.

No, I was irritated because ferreting out spies was more difficult than I imagined. No one was obligingly whistling *Deutschland über alles* or praising the Kaiser. What's more, a reporter, a rabbitty-looking, bespectacled fellow by the name of Samuel Perkins, had attached himself to me.

"Don't you have a wife to annoy?" I finally said, after his third attempt to discover if my friend Bernie Baruch was a spy.

"I'm on my own," he said, his pencil checking in midspate over his pad. "You may be my ticket off the society pages, Mrs. Longworth. Will Colonel Roosevelt challenge President Wilson in the next election?"

I produced a Mona Lisa smile and repressed the impulse to lift my floor-length gray silk and kick him in the shin. But more favorable ink would not be earned by fisticuffs, however tempting, and discretion really was the better part of valor, for I found that Perkins had been assigned to my table. Although seating at class-conscious Washington occasions was based on rank so that one often was placed next to the same people over and over, the leech—er, reporter—came from one of New York's finest families.

Our companions were no different in either position or gnat-like annoyance. Alexander Chase, the man across from me, was somewhere between age ninety and nine hundred, one of those irascible, venerable banking figures in fusty evening dress who dribble soup into their beards and fall asleep frequently at the table. He apparently had not forgotten Father's trust-busting past; he glared at me whenever he remembered that I was there.

On his left was Clara Winthrop, whose green gown was so deeply cut that the whole of Dupont Circle could see her somewhat fleshy charms. Clara drove perfectly satisfactory roadsters off of piers on wagers and gadded about with escorts whose only common characteristics were a fat wallet and the mental capacity of a pomegranate (although I suspected the pomegranate had the advantage). She also wore so much silver jewelry that she clanked like a medieval knight.

Next to Clara, Perkins was conversing with a sallow girl whose small head was tortured by piles of overdressed raven hair. I recognized her as Susan Cartwright, a newly launched debutante of eighteen—and lucky not to sink, I reflected, taking in her nervous smile, rounded shoulders, and black velvet that sagged on her thin, gawky frame.

My stepmother once remarked that when I am bored, my face swells up so that my eyes disappear. By the end of this meal, I expected to resemble a hippopotamus.

Over the consommé, the gloom lifted a little. On my right a square-jawed lieutenant in a smart naval uniform turned from the woman on his other side and smiled at me. He resembled a Viking—all blond, blue-eyed ruggedness with an attractive dash of cynicism—and introduced himself as David Muller.

"Muller?" My ears pricked up. "Isn't that German?"

His features creased in amusement. "Dutch, actually—the same as you, Mrs. Longworth. Weren't you once linked to the Prussian prince?"

"Touché, Lieutenant."

"Muller," he corrected, a little sharply. "Just Muller."

"*Doctor* Muller," grumbled Chase, with the air of referring to a social disease.

"You're scarcely old enough to remember that episode," I said to Muller. "You've been talking to Franklin."

"I believe Mr. Roosevelt did mention something of the sort, yes."

"Mr. Roosevelt is an old hen."

"He does like to hear himself cluck," he agreed, and I chuckled.

"Roosevelt," muttered Mr. Chase. "Bolshevik. Meddling busybody."

"Please, Great Uncle Alex," murmured Miss Cartwright, with a worried glance at me. So she was related to the old coot. At lease she had better manners.

I waved an indifferent hand. "Sticks and stones, you know. Besides, Mr. Chase—*which* meddling busybody do you mean? There are so many in my family."

Chase choked on a roll, and Muller, lips twitching, pushed a glass of water at him. "Steady, cousin."

Chase gulped then scowled at Muller. "Be quiet, boy. Get a medical degree and your head inflates like any other quack. And you—" He jabbed a finger at Miss Cartwright. "Confine yourself to nabbin' a rich husband instead of do-gooding. Only chance you'll have."

Clara giggled, and poor Miss Cartwright looked as if she wished the floor would swallow her up. Chase sniffed suspiciously at the green beans. "What's in that?" he demanded of the rigid waiter.

Clara patted Chase's hand, jangling the heavy charm bracelet on her wrist. "Don't fret yourself, Uncle Alex. You have to consider your heart."

I glanced at Perkins. "Don't tell me you're related to him too."

"Godson," he said, attacking his salad as if it would bite back, and Chase snorted, fumbling with his watch.

"Thank God you're not of my blood. Scandal-mongering whelp."

An unmistakable reference to Perkins's occupation, I thought as the reporter stiffened, and not far off the mark, really. Clara jumped into the uncomfortable pause and said, "I'm not a relative either, Alice. Dear Uncle Alex was Daddy's business partner."

"Until he lost his nerve," huffed Chase. "One ship sunk and he acquires scruples."

A fork clattered. Perkins, ashen-faced, emerged from under the table, muttering an apology.

"What have you been doing lately, Clara?" I inquired, helping myself to filet of beef from the proffered platter and wondering if I should fling it at the disagreeable Mr. Chase. "Driving off the Coney Island Pier?"

Muller broke into a spasm of coughing. "No," Clara answered, leaning forward in uncomprehending concern as he took refuge in his napkin. I fully expected a breast to pop out and land squarely in Muller's potatoes. "I've been in Middleburg."

"Never thought you cared much for the hunt country."

"It has its—diversions." She smiled at Chase and patted his hand again. A suspicion formed in my mind. An old man marrying a younger woman was not a new scenario, and Clara had demonstrated a predilection for a healthy bank balance, if not a decided lack of taste.

"Ridiculous," he muttered. "Bobbing around on horseback

and betting on which nag won't go lame. Imbecilic exercise."

At least horseflesh was a fairly neutral subject that my companions seized like a life preserver. Chase subsided for the moment, glowering. As the discussion moved to the best trainers and owners, I resolved to talk to Evalyn immediately about her idea of congenial seating arrangements.

The arrival of dessert was greeted with wide smiles and at our table with decided relief. Tipsy pudding, which resembled English trifle, contained a key ingredient that cheered guests subjected to meatless, sugarless, and otherless wartime fare: sherry. Lots and lots of sherry.

Chase slipped in his chair, head lolling—probably exhausted from all the vitriol he'd been spouting—and my companions visibly relaxed. Perkins asked Muller about the reaction to women serving in the Navy, Miss Cartwright contributed some surprisingly spirited support, and Clara sniffed that the women's uniforms made them look masculine. I declined dessert and a part in the discussion, too preoccupied with my next move in spy-catching.

Chase slid gently down in his chair and landed face first in the tipsy pudding.

EVALYN'S dark eyes telegraphed frantically from the end of the table. "Do something, do something, DO SOMETHING!"

I elbowed the flapping, ineffectual Clara out of the way and tipped Chase's head back. A sticky mixture of whipped cream, custard, and nuts smeared his pouchy face—a decided improvement—yet he did not stir.

"Poor Mr. Chase is exhausted," I cooed, mopping at the mess, and jerked my head at Muller. Perkins also leaped up as if shot, and together we managed to tidy Chase up. Amid sympathetic murmurs and Muller's ruder whispers about prescribing a polo mallet against Chase's suppertime slumbers, we half-led, half-dragged Chase from the room and into the book-choked library.

"Weighs a ton," panted Perkins.

"Must be his money belt," answered Muller. Grunting, they deposited him on the settee and loosened his clothing. Suddenly Chase began to cough, then choke, flailing, and Muller whacked him on the back several times. Yet Chase continued to wheeze, turning purple, eyes bulging. "Something must be lodged," the doctor muttered, groping in Chase's mouth. Chase gasped again, and Muller pounded on his chest. "Breathe, you old buzzard," he swore, pumping on Chase's chest and blowing into his mouth. But something about the old man's sudden stillness told me the outcome, and I did not need the doctor's sharp shake of the head at Perkins's query, "Is he all right?"

Perkins looked blank. "Choked?" I asked.

"I couldn't feel any obstruction. Tongue's swollen, though; he could've bitten it." Muller's strong shoulders slumped. Kneeling at his side I laid my handkerchief over Chase's face, then began to rummage through the dead man's pockets.

"What are you doing, Mrs. Longworth?" Perkins asked, eyebrows nearly disappearing into his scalp.

I held up a pill case. "What's in this?"

Muller took it and examined the contents. "Digitalis. For the heart."

"Clara said something at the table about his heart. Could he have forgotten to take it?"

"Easily." It was Perkins who answered, still rooted to one spot. "He's been slipping more and more. But he never would admit it in a thousand years."

Muller nodded in agreement, and I had to admit that it did sound characteristic of Chase. I asked Perkins to fetch Evalyn and when he left, continued to turn out the dead man's pockets.

"Is it your habit to loot corpses?" Muller inquired, folding his arms as he watched me.

"I'm merely examining possible evidence. My, what a lot of junk he did carry about." Spreading them out on the desk, I surveyed a pile of odds and ends: two rabbit's feet, handkerchief, cigarette case, lighter, wallet, watch and chain dangling with silver fobs, pieces of string, card case.

"I don't have to tell you that Alex was eccentric. And what evidence? If he did not take his medication, then his heart conked out."

"Or is it meant to look that way? Consider the possibilities. What's your cousin's worth?"

"Several million, I believe. Don't know about insurance . . . ."

"There you are. A plethora of possibilities."

"Am I one?"

"Of course. I wouldn't want you to feel left out."

His perfect teeth flashed as Evalyn entered with Perkins, stopping short at the sight of Chase. I drew her to one side and explained I had one or two ideas I wanted to explore, none of which included explaining to her other guests about Chase's demise. Evalyn quickly saw the advantages of discretion over a full-scale rampage to the hospital by hysterical guests screaming about poisoning and promised to herd them into the ballroom and away from the library. At my request she duly produced our waiter, a lanky towhead by the name of Carl.

Perkins pounced, his rabbitty reporter's nose twitching. "A Hun!"

Carl looked bored. "Swedish. From Minnesota."

Good God—was there *anyone* German on the premises?

"You're not in the Army," Perkins observed, still bristling with suspicion.

"Flat feet, sir." Carl's gaze swept over Perkins, as if to ask why the reporter was not in uniform. I cleared my throat hastily and asked if Chase had been served the same dishes as everyone else. Carl nodded.

"And no one except the staff and the cook were near the food?"

"That's right, ma'am. Cook don't much like interferin' noses in her kitchen."

Neither would Evalyn, I thought; too much risk of other hostesses learning her cook's secrets. "And were you acquainted with Mr. Chase?"

"Just as one of Mrs. McLean's guests. Mr. Chase wasn't one for natterin' with the staff."

"Did he complain about the food?"

"Wouldn't be Mr. Chase if he didn't grumble," the waiter answered frankly and fairly accurately. "Besides, he usually ate every scrap 'cept maybe Waldorf salad, but heaps of folks don't cotton to it, so I never paid no mind."

I thanked him and asked him to fetch Clara and Miss Cartwright.

"Gathering the suspects?" murmured Muller in my ear.

I ignored his cheekiness, too absorbed in mulling over the dinner menu. The women duly appeared, and Clara uttered a little shriek and collapsed when she spotted Chase's recumbent form on the settee. Muller moved to revive her, and I drew Miss Cartwright aside.

"Please call me Susan," she offered shyly. "Miss Cartwright sounds like my old governess."

"Very well, Susan. Who benefits from your great uncle's will?"

She turned startled eyes on me, soft and brown as a hunted doe's. "Why—me, I suppose. He stopped talking to my father, and his only child died on the *Lusitania,* poor thing."

"What did he mean by your do-gooding?"

Her hands fluttered in her lap. "I've been—helping out." She thrust out her chin as if expecting to be hit. "At the YWCA."

Muller, rejoining us, gave a low whistle; clearly little Susan had been leading a secret life as a canteen and welfare worker. "I must introduce you to my cousin Eleanor," I said, suppressing a yawn. "You have something in common." I turned to Muller. "What about you?"

"He's only a second cousin," Susan blurted out and bit her lip when Muller glanced at her.

"You heard his views on physicians," he said.

"Did you mind?"

He shrugged. "At one time, when he rescinded his promise to pay for my education. Thus the indentured servitude of the uniform."

"You don't want to serve your country, Muller?"

He refused the bait of the implied white feather. "I prefer to have a choice."

"But he did, Mrs. Longworth," supplied the helpful Susan. "Great Uncle Alex demanded that he go into banking. He refused."

"Admirable," I answered, "if short-sighted."

Susan bridled but Muller squeezed her arm as if to forestall her. "It's true enough, Susie," he said.

She blushed, and I realized that the girl was in love with him. It was in her defense of him, every word she uttered designed to show that Dr. David Muller had no motive for killing Alexander Chase.

But although I liked him, too, he had the know-how to dispatch Chase and more than enough motive. Muller had been forced into the Navy because of Chase's withdrawal of support. How far would discontent take him? To the Germans? And wasn't it just like Franklin to dump a charming potential spy in his department right into my lap?

"What about—?" I indicated Perkins, trying to shake off uneasy speculations and intrusive ideas about throttling Franklin.

Susan tore her attention from Muller. "When David refused to become a banker, Great Uncle Alex turned to Sam. But since he joined the paper he was cut off without a penny, I'm afraid."

She would have all the pennies, I realized, and so would Muller if he married her. That was a tidy package: revenge for disinheritance plus his cousin's money. Was he ignorant of her feelings, or counting on them?

But Perkins the reporter might be in worse financial straits than Muller the doctor and so pursue Susan. Might have a better chance too, I thought—Perkins's bespeckled visage was less alarming than Muller's Nordic radiance.

And what of Susan herself? I looked at her. Awkward; unsure, certainly, but did the gauche exterior mask a more sinister core? Much confidence can be gleaned from a fortune, and a fortune never humiliates a girl in public.

Then there was Clara. I considered her as she sidled over to the desk, then tripped. She hardly had the brains to walk, let alone mastermind a murder. And if she had matrimonial aspirations, surely Chase alive meant more to her than Chase dead—unless he had some hold over her.

"Sit down, everyone," I said. As they settled themselves, I crossed to the desk where Chase's belongings lay. I picked up the watch and chain, weighing them in my palm.

Submarines, Franklin had said . . . .

"Ladies and gentlemen," I began. "I ask you to consider submarines. Hidden from view, yet lethal. And other things that are concealed that also destroy.

"Alexander Chase was nothing if not cantankerous and critical, so it was perfectly natural to disregard the never-ending flow of his disfavor. But what if he had one condition that was legitimate? You may recall that he asked Carl what was in the green beans." I looked at Muller. "What if a certain food was literally poison to him?"

Muller snapped his fingers. "The swollen tongue, the respiratory distress—of course!"

"But—can that really happen?" Susan breathed.

"Absolutely," Muller replied. "Fatal to certain people."

"But—green beans?" She looked doubtful. "He's eaten them on hundreds and hundreds of occasions."

"Not the beans," I said. "You mustn't be so literal. You

should consider what is frequently served *with* green beans, in Waldorf salad—any number of dishes, including tipsy pudding." My gaze swept the group, now gratifyingly attentive in their leather club chairs. "Nuts."

"There's no need to be rude," muttered the inevitably slow Clara. I sighed.

"Almonds, Clara, pecans—in this case I think walnuts. Alexander Chase had a fatal encounter with nuts."

"But—why?" Susan asked.

"Remember that Chase resented my father's trust-busting efforts that reduced his investments," I said. "Clearly, amassing a fortune was a major occupation for him. I think he was engaged in profiteering with the enemy. I think he was passing naval secrets to the Germans."

They all exclaimed, and Perkins protested, "But he was ancient!"

"Oh, I don't think he was skulking in damp alleys. He was too smart to publicly associate with men known to the government as German sympathizers. I think he had help." Holding the watch, I grasped one of the cylinder-like silver fobs on the chain and twisted it. It came apart, revealing a slip of paper inside. I looked at the spy.

"You have interesting taste in jewelry, Clara."

She bolted, bracelet clanging like a clarion, and darted around the half-open door. We crowded after her. "Out of the way!" cried a young voice behind me, scattering us like a flock of pigeons. Clara's feet abruptly flew up in the air, and she crashed to the floor in a tangle of green skirts and curses. Muller began to check for broken bones, and I turned to see what had caused this phenomenon.

Susan Cartwright clutched the Persian carpet runner, which she had clearly yanked from under Clara's feet. She was very pink, her heavy hair liberated in the excitement from its burden of pins—quite becomingly, I thought.

"Well done," I said, and her color deepened. But her eyes were fixed somewhere beyond my shoulder, and I turned.

Muller had straightened up, his expression was as rapt as hers, as if he had been clobbered by an express train.

Clara jerked as if to flee again; I sat on her, disregarding her yelps. "Muller," I said firmly, and he started, then shook himself, like a dog emerging from a lake.

"How did she manage it?"

"The messages were given to her in silver charms, probably at hunt meetings and horse races where there are plenty of people about. Then she just added another charm to the bracelet; who would notice a new one in all that jumble? She would pass it to Chase at one of these functions, and he'd put it on his watch chain like a fob—we saw him do it tonight, after she patted his hand."

"Why would she turn spy?" asked Perkins, scribbling furiously in his notebook.

Clara squeaked as if to answer, and I shifted my weight so she had to stop for breath. "I expect Chase was holding the markers for her debts and blackmailing her; she does like to gamble."

Clara squawked, more or less in confirmation.

"You are so clever, Mrs. Longworth," Susan murmured.

Really, the child was perceptive.

Perkins's pencil was worn nearly down to the nub. "And why did she kill him?"

Clara lurched again, this time more violently. I nestled my evening bag cozily against her ribs, and she subsided. "I think, Muller, now would be a good time to summon assistance."

"Oh. Yes. Yes, of course. Will you be all right, Mrs. L.?"

I settled myself more comfortably, ignoring the outraged spluttering beneath me, and powdered my nose. "Perfectly."

OUT on the first floor landing my cigarette smoke curled, and I contemplated the stained glass roof of Evalyn's reception hall with some satisfaction. The resentful Clara had been bundled off into the capable hands of some very large and appreciative officers in naval intelligence. A call to one of Evalyn's veritable armada of doctors had resulted in the unobtrusive removal of Chase's body. The party was in full swing in the fourth-floor ballroom, although I fully expected Ned and my husband were reeling about the roof garden. There were certainly some odd shadows flitting across the stained glass.

Yet there was a footstep. "Please sit down," I said.

"So Clara Winthrop murdered him."

"Passed government secrets to Chase—yes. Killed him—no."

There was dead silence.

"He didn't eat the tipsy pudding," I remarked. "Oh, he fell into it, of course, but I don't think that would be enough to finish him. I shoved Clara away when it happened. It was only someone at close quarters who could push enough nuts into his mouth. Someone trained to observe personal habits—including what one does and does not eat."

The silence was almost eerie, and I felt vague pricklings of unease.

"Chase said, 'One ship sunk, and he acquires scruples.'" I continued, stubbing out my cigarette with every appearance of carelessness. "I think the ship he was referring to was the *Lusitania*. After she was torpedoed, the battle lines were more clearly drawn for some. Others, like Chase, didn't care as long as money was to be made." I watched my companion, slipping my fingers into my bag. "And if Chase was dealing regularly with the Germans, he would have known they would sink her. Who was on board, Mr. Perkins?"

"He knew," Perkins spat. "He knew and he let her go."

"Her," I repeated, then remembered what Susan had said. "His daughter?"

"We loved each other. She'd promised to marry me. She was defying him."

"Convenient—and profitable—for you," I noted.

"I signed a paper renouncing all claim to her money. But Alex considered a reporter lower than dirt."

Shock rippled through me. "Are you saying that he killed his own child to prevent her marriage to you?"

"To 'save' her," he confirmed bitterly. "Really to control her to the end. I denied what he'd done—couldn't believe it—then he said what he did tonight with that sneer, and I knew beyond all doubt. I lost my head."

There was a pause, as if Perkins realized that he had just confessed, then he made a sudden, convulsive movement.

"I wouldn't," I said conversationally. "It would be a pity to riddle this undeniably smart evening bag with bullet holes, but I will do it if I must. I am an excellent marksman, Mr. Perkins."

"No doubt, Mrs. Longworth." He relaxed. "So—what now?"

"Chase was a murderer and a traitor with a known heart problem. My cousin Franklin has nabbed his spy in Clara Winthrop. And you have your ticket off the society pages." I had a sudden vision of black water, rows and rows of faces stiff and still. "The Irish Sea has claimed enough victims."

"You are very generous."

"Hardly," I said cooly. "I think that, should any interesting information come your way in the future, you would be delighted to share it with Franklin. Otherwise, my ill-regulated tongue could find itself prattling away to just anyone."

"You are a devil, Mrs. Longworth."

"My father's daughter, Mr. Perkins. There is a difference." I rose to my feet. "Now—shall we go to the ballroom and rejoin Muller and Susan? At midnight Evalyn will lower a staggeringly patriotic red, white, and blue electric-light sign, which I simply must ridicule. After all," I added, tucking my gun-stuffed evening bag under my arm, "I have a reputation for frivolity to uphold."

DEAN AND CLAUDIA ASK BETH:

Q: *You obviously love mysteries and all that surrounds them. What started your passion?*
A: My start and inspiration in mysterydom can be explained in two far-from-simple words: Barbara Mertz. Little did I know that my undergradute interview of this remarkable and energetic phenomenon would lead to involvement in the mystery convention Malice Domestic and a seismatic shift in my career. I've been triply blessed by her example, her encouragement, and her friendship.

Q: *Do you have any advice for new writers?*
A: I can't emphasize enough the need to do homework. Although mystery authors are often the most generous and supportive people on the planet, new writers must be acutely aware of the intense demands on the time of more seasoned writers. Do not rely solely on the Internet; do old-fashioned research. Read the industry publications, note carefully the names of editors and agents of your favorite mystery writers, talk to booksellers, join the professional groups such as MWA and Sister-in-Crime, hang out at a mystery convention or two. To make that sale, equip yourself to understand and take the pulse of this always-fascinating, multi-faceted genre.

AND HERE IS BETH'S RECIPE:

TIPSY PUDDING

Tipsy pudding, a form of English trifle, was said to be one of George Washington's favorite desserts. Marietta Minnigerode Andrews mentions in her book *My Studio Window: Sketches of the Pageant of Washington Life* (1928) that she was served tipsy pudding by Addie Daniels at a World War I-era luncheon—an especially ironic occurrence as Daniels's husband, Secretary of the Navy Josephus Daniels, had banned alcohol on Navy ships.

2 cups hot milk
1/2 cup sugar
1/8 teaspoon salt
2 eggs, beaten
2 tablespoons flour
3 tablespoons sherry
8 ounces of heavy cream, whipped
1 pound cake
Chopped nuts for garnish

In top of double boiler, heat milk. Combine sugar, salt, and beaten eggs. Take a small amount of hot milk and stir flour into it until smooth. Combine egg mixture with hot milk and place over boiling water. Add flour mixture. Stir frequently until it starts to thicken. Cool.

Add sherry, stirring well. Whip cream until peaks form. Stir cream into custard. Alternate custard with layers of pound cake cut into small pieces, starting with cake and ending with custard. Chill a minimum of 1 hour before serving. Garnish with chopped nuts.

WAITING FOR GATEAU

(With apologies to Samuel Beckett)

Claudia Bishop

Claudia Bishop writes the Hemlock Falls series, mystery novels featuring Quill and Meg Quilliam, amateur detectives who run the Inn at Hemlock Falls. She is always surprised when people describe her as a long-haired blonde with a smiling face, since she thinks she looks like Sherlock Holmes. This story introduces two new characters of whom she is extremely fond: Dr. and Mrs. MacKenzie.

He's rude, he's drunk, and he's vulgar. He should be hung by the heels and forced to listen to Jerry "Springer and his ilk until his hairy ears fall off." I set my glass of Australian Shiraz (sufficiently ashy, but not at all complex) on the tabletop and folded my napkin neatly. "And someone should take his cell phone and stuff it up his nose."

"You betcha, sweetie," Madeline said approvingly. My spouse patted her full lips delicately and laid her napkin beside my own.

The tabletop was bird's eye maple; the napkin heavy

linen; the dining room of the remote inn where Madeline and I had come for a long weekend luxuriously quiet due to deep pile carpeting, plaster walls, and the heavy timber construction of two hundred years ago.

Or rather, the dining room had been quiet—until the arrival of a big, fat, drunken slob with a cell phone.

He'd come into the restaurant some moments before, accompanied by the maitre d' and a large woman with dyed black hair and dull, shifty eyes. The maitre d' had seated them between a pleasant-looking couple with a sleeping baby and two females who bore the unmistakable stripe of the academic. "Young professors," I had said instructively to Madeline. "It's something about the clothes, I believe. Female professors are prone to wear long skirts of colors found in the muddier parts of the Mississippi." I narrowed my eyes. "And indeed, it looks as if Mississippi mud has splashed on the skirt of the younger one. Note the tunics made from beige string. The earrings hacked from chunks of rock. That, and naturally graying hair, free of any artificial dye. Quite professorial." I smoothed my mustache. "A mere matter of deduction, my dear."

"Weren't both of them at your lecture yesterday?" Madeline asked innocently. She tore at a piece of the inn's excellent bread with her strong white teeth. "The younger, cuter one asked that question about nineteenth-century methods of treating colic."

"Ah, yes," I said, with a slight blush. "I recall that, now."

It does not do to forget how acute my wife can be.

At any rate, the big slob and his companion had been seated with the deft efficiency that had made our own luncheon such a pleasure. He bellowed, like the Cyclops, for more wine. He made rude noises about the special entrée of the day (Cod Quilliam with a Molasses Coulis). He threw his burning cigarette into his water glass when the waiter discreetly informed him of New York State's ban against smoking in public areas.

A shrill series of beeps (the opening measures of *Rondo
alla Turca!*) caused him to pat frantically at his suit jacket
and withdraw a bright purple cell phone. His preliminary
shouts into this repellent fruit of twenty-first-century technology were initially invective-free, but his language rapidly
degraded in direct proportion to the escalating argument.

Hence my wish to have the drunken bum hung by his
hairy ears.

To be quite accurate, I should say that I assumed he was
drunk. I may have been precipitate. These days, four-letter
words in a world-class restaurant may not indicate a loosening of civility due to inebriation. And his physical state may
not have signaled intoxication, either. I peered at the bozo
with a clinician's eye, and then looked at Madeline over the
rim of my spectacles. "Were he a horse, the unnatural red of
his sclera, the sticky tracks of sweat on the folds of his fat
neck, and the rapidity of his inspiration would have led me
to recommend a tranquilizer to forestall a cardiac event sec-
ondary to panic. But he is not a horse." I took another sip of
the Shiraz and sighed. "The physiology of *homo erectus* is a
mystery to me, whereas the physiology of *equidae* is not. I
decline to speculate further."

"Not *homo sapiens,*" Madeline said, who after fifteen
years of connubial propinquity knows me well, "but *homo
erectus,* huh? So you think he's pre-human. You're so cyni-
cal, cupcake. And as far as you declining to speculate—the
only time you've declined to speculate was when you didn't
sell the energy stocks when I told you to. THAT was the
time you should have declined to speculate. Other than
that, you speculate all over the place. All the time." Her
tone held no animosity. It rarely does. "Maybe he isn't drunk
at all. Just rude. Or scared." She turned slightly in her chair.
The man's imprecations had subsided to a belligerent mutter. He seemed to have trouble remaining upright in
his chair. He took a large, unseemly gulp of what seemed to
be port and wiped the back of his mouth with his free

hand. The other kept his cell phone mashed to one thick ear. "Nope. He's drunk, sweetie. As a skunk."

"A fact which an experienced wait staff should have noticed," I said, without reproof. "I might have seated him nearer the kitchen, amongst the empty tables there, had I been the maitre d'."

"But you're a noticing old geezer," Madeline said affectionately. "You always have been."

Our young waitress appeared at my elbow and began to remove the detritus of our meal. Properly. From the left. She had neither nametag nor outlandish costume, and had not offered to name her first-born after one or both of us— as I occasionally expect the wait staff in more egalitarian establishments to do. I liked the Inn at Hemlock Falls more and more.

"Would you care for coffee? Or perhaps some fruit?" she asked.

"No, thank you, Kathleen," Madeline smiled warmly.

Madeline always discovers the name of the wait staff. Or the field of study of a gas station attendant working her way through college. Or the numbers and gender of an airline steward's progeny. She says I married her for this. I did not. Women understand very little. I married her because she is like a swan's-down pillow. "I think I would like to try some of the chocolate gateau. I saw a review of your restaurant in last month's issue of *L'Aperitif*. It mentioned Gateau Quilliam in particular."

"That's a terrific choice, Mrs. Mackenzie," Kathleen beamed. "It's Maitre Quilliam's own recipe. You'd love it. If we had it. Which we don't. Maitre Quilliam is off for the weekend. She and her sister have gone to New York for a few days and we have a chef temping in the kitchen. Meg, I mean Maitre Quilliam, has trained the chef herself, of course. But only she has the recipe for the dessert. We do have an excellent sorbet au chocolot, though. Would you care to try that?"

"I would. And to heck with the diet." Madeline patted her pillowy midriff. She is forever trying to reduce the swan's-down to whipcord. Fortunately, she has not succeeded. "And decaf for you, Austin."

Madeline is forever trying to reduce my intake of supposedly toxic substances, too. She has not succeeded in that, either.

"An espresso," I said firmly. "A double. With a twist of lemon peel, if you please."

"Crap!" the drunken fellow roared into the cell phone. "Screw you and the horse you rode in on!"

Either the venom or the volume woke the sleeping child. It began to wail. Loudly. Piercingly. Its screeching was unpleasantly reminiscent of the appalling version of *Rondo alla Turca* that had signaled the phone call. The child's fair-haired mother picked it up, slung it over her shoulder, blushed rose pink and made mommy noises.

"Oh, dear." This from the more slender academic to the right of the obnoxious slob. She leaned forward, tapped the man on the arm and said with an authority that must have kept many an obstreperous student in line, "I'd appreciate it you'd take your call outside, sir."

The fat slob's response was a rude finger gesture familiar to automobile drivers everywhere. Her friend gasped in indignation. I myself half-rose to my feet, restrained only by my wife's mild but admonitory eye. (Years of wrestling calves from the wombs of recalcitrant heifers, of restraining colts alarmed by the proximity of castration pincers, have strengthened my upper body to a satisfactory degree. Neither Madeline nor I have any fear for my physical safety. Under any circumstances.) The father of the squalling baby scowled, and said, "Look here." The baby itself screamed with redoubled fury.

"Shut up!" he shouted back.

"Uh, Daryl?" The woman with the badly dyed hair patted at the beet-faced man rather tentatively. Daryl shook her off, dropped the cell phone, grabbed the baby from its startled mother and roared, "Aaagh!" He pivoted, both hands firmly around the baby's middle, and thrust it at the equally startled female professor. "Go ahead, kid. Scream your head off. Think the cell phone's noisy? Get a load of this! Come on, kid. Let 'er rip!"

But the baby—intrigued perhaps, by the novelty of being suspended in mid-air—failed to "let 'er rip" and gurgled happily instead. The younger professor lunged for the baby, and knocked over the wine glass from which Daryl had been swigging. Daryl glared at the mess, glared at the baby, handed the baby back to its astonished mother, and sat down. He shouted for more (bleeping) wine and demanded that it be attached to the young academic's bill .

Madeline and I have frequently observed that true character emerges only in crisis. The Quilliam sisters—for it was their Inn to which Madeline and I had come for our restorative weekend after my lecture on bovine back fat at Cornell—clearly had the character necessary for the success of the finer-quality hotels and resorts: discretion, unyielding integrity, diplomacy. Even in their absence, the staff behaved promptly and with tact. Daryl and Mrs. Daryl were evicted without incident in the middle of chewing the excellent special, primarily through the silent efforts of a large, muscular gardener the maitre d' called Mike. (He demonstrated a chokehold that would have been quite useful in getting irritable thoroughbreds calm enough to dose with colic medication. Had I not retired from active practice some years ago, I would have inquired further.) The smashed wine glasses were cleared with dispatch and the table reset with a clean cloth. Order was restored.

Madeline and I finished our coffee and sorbet without incident, and left the pleasant dining room for a nap before we resumed our exploration of the village of Hemlock Falls.

I awoke some sixty minutes after retiring, alone in the comfortable bed. The charming young receptionist had assigned us to the Provençal suite. The blue and yellow material on the spread, the drapes, and the cushioned armchair before the cobblestone fireplace were indeed reminiscent of that lovely part of the world. The bed itself was placed directly across from a double set of French doors. Propped as I was against the pillows. I could see the green waterfall that gave the inn and village its name, flowing away like anything. Refreshed by this glimpse, and my nap, I yawned, stretched, swung my feet to the floor, and set out to find my wife.

Descending the circular staircase to the foyer, I waved cheerily to that same receptionist.

"Hello, Dr. Mackenzie," she said.

"Hello to you, young Dina."

Madeline's omnipresent interest in her fellows had led us to know this about Dina: she is a graduate student at my own alma mater, nearby Cornell University; she has worked for Meg and Sarah Quilliam for some years whilst pursuing her studies; and she has the brashness common to the twenty-something generation. Yes, Madeline is frequently mistaken for my daughter, but only the young and the rude make allusion to the difference in our ages. Dina's artless observation that age didn't matter because I was a "sweet old dink" confirmed what does not need confirming: a great deal of civility has been lost in these vulgarian times.

"Are you looking for Mrs. Mackenzie?"

"I am, Dina."

"She's in the kitchen with Deputy Sheriff Kiddermeister." Dina's big brown eyes blinked owlishly behind her round glasses. "I'm afraid she's found a body."

This was alarming news. Although I may say that Dina took it within stride, further confirmation that the Misses Quilliam ran a superior inn. No emotionally undisciplined staff at the Inn at Hemlock Falls!

Dina directed me to the kitchen: back through the dining room where we had lunched, through the swinging doors, and into a very pleasing space of large ovens, stainless steel refrigerators, stone flooring and another cobblestone fireplace. Madeline was seated at a long counter, back straight, long legs crossed, chatting up the deputy. (More assumptions, I'm afraid! Although the young man was dressed in a gray uniform with a shiny badge affixed to the shirt, and had a holstered .38 Colt on his hip, he could not have been more than seventeen years old. His bright blond hair contrasted oddly with his blushing face. I suppose a village as remote as Hemlock Falls has trouble recruiting adults.) I dodged a bunch of hanging herbs, several hanging copper sauté pans, and enveloped my wife's hands in my own. "My dear!" I said.

"Hey, sweetie," Madeline responded. "You know that horrible man with the cell phone?" She drew one plump but shapely hand horizontally across her throat. "Dead as a doornail. Right by the gazebo with the sweet peas around the bottom."

I gazed at her, awash with misgivings. "His throat was cut?"

"Nossir," the youngster said. "Mighta been a heart attack."

I drew in a breath of relief. Murder would have been a blot on our projected weekend.

"Then again, it might not of been a heart attack. Maddy, maybe your dad would like to sit down. It's gotta be a bit of a shock, sir."

I drew my eyebrows together.

"Dr. Mackenzie is my hubby, Dave," Madeline said.

I frowned at her. She knows how I much I dislike that particular locution. "Hubby" indeed.

Deputy Sheriff Kiddermeister's face blushed pinker than before. "You're a doctor?" he said eagerly. "Maybe you could take a look at the body, sir. Our usual doc, Doc Bishop, is off in New York with Meg and her sister Quill. So's Sheriff McHale."

"I am not that kind of . . . . I paused. I must confess, I

was more than concerned by this sudden death. And after all, the unlucky Daryl had behaved in an animal-like way. I snorted a bit with laughter. Ha-ha on this young deputy when he discovered I was a retired veterinarian! (More to the point—'Dave' was it? 'Maddy,' was it? I might teach that young man a thing or two about getting on a first name basis with my wife so quickly.)

"Now, Austin," Madeline said. "Don't get cranky, dear."

"Lead me to the corpse, young man."

We proceeded single file through the small crowd of curious sous chefs, dishwashers, and potboys, and out the back door. It was a glorious day. The sun shone bright in a cloudless sky. The waterfall burbled away like anything. A small cloud of flies was already gathered about the unfortunate Daryl, contorted beneath a spray of Sweet Adeline sweet peas at the base of the gazebo. His wife (Assumptions, again! Although she did wear a dull gold band on the fourth finger of her left hand) slumped in the grass nearby.

Deputy Dave drew a small disposable camera from his shirt pocket and began to snap pictures of the body *in situ*.

I, of course, am familiar with autopsy procedures. How often in the past have I been called to the scene of similar tragedies: a Black Angus bull felled mysteriously in his prime; a sleek racehorse broken upon the rigors of the track; a beloved dog crushed beneath the wheels of a carelessly driven car. (Although I must admit, for those of us who love animals as I do, the death of one of God's blameless creatures disturbs one far more than the death of such as Daryl. But still, bodies are an affecting sight. It is true; a light goes out. Forever.)

I knelt in the soft grass and peeled back an eyelid. I reviewed what I knew of the signs of mortis: timor mortis, the time of death; rigor mortis, the stage of death; livor mortis, the color of death. "He has been dead at least half an hour,"

I said after attempting to manipulate the stiffened limbs and checking the corpse for blood pooling. "And he fell here. I should say the body has not been moved. To know more, I shall have to examine the interior. If I might send for a set of scalpels, I can perform a field autopsy, if you wish."

Deputy Dave paled. "Ah. Nossir. I just wasn't sure if we should transport the body without doing a full forensics exam of the site. If you think it's murder, I'll have to call the Staties."

"You're right of course, deputy. No need to cut him open in the field. This man weighs no more than two hundred and fifty pounds. The three of us should be able to get him into an automobile. My wife and I are quite strong. From thence we can transport him to your local emergency room. I will perform the autopsy there."

"Well, sir. Thank you. But I've already put a call into the EMTs. They'll be here stat."

Jargon. Acronyms. Chunk by chunk our language is being eviscerated. I gave Daryl's belly a regretful pat. I've never autopsied a human being. I would have liked the chance to try. I rose to my feet. Madeline, with her keen eye and ear for the despair of others, sat in the grass next to Mrs. Daryl. The women were holding hands. Madeline is swan's-down.

"Sir?"

"Yes, deputy."

"About calling in the state troopers. Should we?"

"Do you mean, is it murder?" I gazed down at the flaccid remains. The face was flushed—more than the sun and the man's consumption of alcohol would allow. Foam had settled in corners of the lips. The sclerae of the eyes were suffused with red. "My guess, deputy, is that this man has sustained a sudden, fatal, cardiac event." I pursed my lips. "Was he helped to his doom via an outside agency? Or was the combination of flab, choler, overindulgence in alcohol, the heat, and nicotine sufficient to kill him? That I cannot say at this point. But if you care to wait while I fetch my scalpels . . ."

"That's just fine, sir," Deputy Dave said hastily. He removed his hat, scratched his head vigorously, and said, "Nuts. Rats. Heck."

". . . had a heart mumble mumble." A leaden voice broke the momentary silence. Mrs. Daryl chewed at her lower lip. Madeline patted her back soothingly.

Deputy Dave jammed his hat back on his head. "Ma' am?"

"Mrs. Aronson just said that her husband had some kind of a heart attack last year." Madeline gave Mrs. Aronson a last, brisk pat and rose majestically to her feet. Madeline is tall and well-formed and resembles nothing so much as the *Winged Victory of Samothrace*—with a head, of course. Her dark brown hair glinted with hidden gold in the June sunlight. Her deep blue eyes, (hidden by a large pair of sunglasses, but I know that color better than my own) transfixed Deputy Dave. "You aren't going to leave the poor man out here? In the heat? How long do you think it'll take for these flies to settle in real well? Dr. Mackenzie has just diagnosed a possible cardiac event and Mrs. Aronson has verified that he had a warning shot last year and totally ignored it."

"A warning shot?" asked Deputy Dave.

"A heart attack! And get his body someplace cooler." She paused. "Get a move on, Dave!"

Deputy Dave got a move on.

"I really want to try Gateau Quilliam, sweetie," Madeline said wistfully, some hours later. "Can't we wait here until what's-her-name, Meg, comes back? If I hadn't read about the dessert in *L'Aperitif,* we could have settled for the Marriott. It's a lot cheaper."

"Perhaps the promise of the gateau is what this weekend is all about, my dear. And not the gateau itself." I patted her knee. We were seated on the flagstone patio outside that part of the inn called the Tavern Bar. I sipped at cassis and soda; Madeline had asked for dark beer. She drank her Guinness and frowned. She is not fond of my occasional excursions into obloquy. "So are we going to stay?"

I gazed out over the serene prospect. The ambulance had come and gone, bearing the late Mr. Daryl Aronson to a cooler place. Apparently, a routine autopsy would be performed when the coroner returned to work on Monday. The Quilliams, along with Sheriff Myles McHale, were due back from their sojourn in New York also on Monday. One of the dubious benefits of retirement is the time one has to peruse the national press; I was well aware of the sisters' reputation as amateur detectives. And even more aware of Mr. McHale's expertise in investigation, which had reached across the pond to several foreign countries. And I had a strong surmise what the routine autopsy would reveal. I would have been certain had Mr. Aronson been a horse.

Had Mr. Aronson been a member of the genus *equidae,* I would have said that he had been poisoned by a low dose of strychnine. The lividity of his skin, the viscosity of his mucous membranes, the lack of the almost infinitesimal brown specks that betokened fly eggs, told me death had been recent. And yet, his limbs were stiffened. The smile on his face was not, as the poet would have it, a smile of content. It was a rictus if I'd ever seen one, which I have. On numerous occasions. That, and the purple blue of his lips suggested the ingestion of a small amount of strychnine an hour or so earlier. In his food or wine, perhaps. And it had probably been contained within a bolus of some kind, so that the effect would have not been immediate. Once in his stomach and on its labyrinthine way through his intestines, the strychnine had precipitated a myocardial infarction as soon as the bolus had dissolved.

Murder is not common in the universe of veterinary science. Excitement is not common in the universe of retired veterinarians, either, excepting, of course, the connubial delights provided with satisfying regularity by my beloved. And Austin Mackenzie is not one to back away from a challenge. I smoothed my mustache. "Yes, my dear. I believe we should stay here. For the nonce, as it were."

"The nonce?" Madeline wrinkled her brow prettily. "Who cares about the nonce? The dessert. That's what I want to stay here for."

"The repellent Mr. Aronson was murdered," I said.

Madeline jerked upright, rather as if she had inadvertently grabbed an electric fence. "You're kidding me!"

I lowered my tones, lest we be overheard. "And I intend to investigate."

Madeline glanced from left to right, then leaned in to my ear. Her full breasts swelled appealingly beneath her loose muslin blouse. "That's fabulous, sweetie!" she whispered. "What do we do first?"

I considered this for a long moment. "I'm not at all certain."

"I'll tell you something about poor Myrna . . ."

"Myrna?"

"Mrs. Aronson. They've only been married a year or so, Austin. And he was just horrible to her. Horrible. He never let her see her family. He's never even *met* her family. And I'll bet he beat her. He was just an awful person." She closed her warm hand upon mine. "Every so often, I remember just how lucky I am, sweetie. So I'll tell you what we should do first. We should talk to the widow. Everybody knows family kills each other first."

The syntax was a little muddled, but then, Madeline's sometimes is. Her reasoning is intuitive rather than ratiocinative. At any rate, I got the gist. "I agree."

"And I'll tell you what we should do after that. Look for the weapon." Her long lashes swept the curve of her cheek and then flew up. Those deep blue eyes looked into mine. "How did he die, Austin?"

I explained.

"Wow! So he was poisoned." Madeline's eyes widened and she wriggled her eyebrows. She calls this "bugging" her eyes out. It signifies amazement. "And opportunity? I mean, that's what the detectives on *Law and Order* always get asked by the prosecutors—we have to establish means, motive, and opportunity."

"It could only have been at lunch, I'm afraid. Which limits the pool of suspects, of course." I cleared my throat and sipped my cassis, necessary preparation for the rather lengthy summary which the listing of the relevant facts required.

"The murderer was either the waitress, the family to the left of him, or the ladies to the right of him," Madeline said, unconsciously imitating one of my favorite poets (and consciously forestalling what in rare moments of irritation she calls my blabber). "I guess we can rule out the baby. Okay. Here's what we do. You find the wine glass and the remains of his lunch. And I'll talk to the widow. I'm going to find out if any of the others at lunch had a link to Daryl. We'll meet back here at . . ." she consulted her watch, "five o'clock. That gives us each an hour. We'll pool the preliminary info and take it from there."

"The kitchen staff would have thrown out the lunch by now," I protested.

"Check the dumpster. He had the cod and the thingummy potatoes."

"The Potatoes Duchesse."

"Whatever. Anyhow, we have to get that food and busted wine glass, Austin. It's evidence."

I sighed. "Very well. I'll check the dumpster."

"We'll leave separately." Madeline said. "Just in case."

I did not ask her just in case of what. Frequently it is better not to inquire too closely into Madeline's thought processes.

Saturday afternoon in June at the Tavern Bar in Hemlock Falls attracts a fair number of citizens. The French doors that opened to the patio were flung wide. The joint, as they say, was hopping. There appeared to be a fair number of tourists (notable for sunburn and irritable children) in addition to the folk of the town. All of them turned and looked as Madeline rose from our table, went into the bar, and floated across the floor. She disappeared down the hall that led to the foyer. She is a lovely woman, and in her long light summer dress, resembled nothing so much as a sloop in full sail.

The entire bar fell silent as she left.

I sighed, signed for our drinks, and slipped across the verdant lawn. On our perambulations to the gorge that morning, I had noted that the kitchen lies directly to the rear of the Tavern Bar (although it is only accessible from the inside by going down the hall, crossing the foyer, and from thence to the dining room). I strolled around the corner of the great, sprawling building, hands carelessly clasped behind my back, looking as if I were merely out for an admiring stroll.

There was much to admire. The Inn at Hemlock Falls is constructed of warm cobblestone and brick mellowed by the years. The sound of the waterfall is a constant, pleasing susurration in one's ears. Thus disguised as a gentleman out for an instructive stroll, I soon found myself in front of the dumpsters.

I had forgotten an important fact about dumpsters. They are approximately five feet high from brim to bottom. I am five foot nine. I peered into the depths. There were, alas, no green garbage bags neatly labeled "remains of Aronson entrée." On the other hand, there weren't many bags in the dumpster at all. Perhaps four large ones. There must have been a trash pick up prior to lunch.

I have no particular objection to rummaging in garbage. In the course of my large animal practice, I have been in many places less fastidious persons would find intolerable.

(Meg Quilliam's leftovers would be far less objectionable than finding oneself hip deep in pig manure!) There was, however, an access issue. How was I to get in?

Bless Chef Quilliam for her insistence on fresh eggs and milk. Several sturdy wooden crates labeled 'Hemlock Falls Dairy' were neatly stacked to one side of the dumpster. I placed one on top of the other, climbed on top, swung my legs over the edge and dropped agilely in.

I uncovered the evidence in the third bag. The shattered glass had been rolled into plastic wrap, a safety precaution of which I thoroughly approved. I set the roll aside. Several persons, however, seemed to have ordered the Potatoes Duchesse. I segregated the potatoes into the remains of some waxed paper and set that aside as well. Red stains from the remains of his port, happily, distinguished Aronson's cod. I wrapped the evidence in a portion of the green plastic garbage bag and tucked it under my arm. Victory was assured.

As I prepared to leave, I realized something I had not known before. It is not possible to exit a dumpster without the support offered by a stepladder or a pile of dairy crates. I looked around the cavernous bin. No one had seen fit to place a stepladder in the dumpster. And the crates on the other side were impossible to retrieve.

I counted to ten. I inhaled deeply, several times. Then I piled the three remaining garbage bags one on top of the other and stood on them.

This did not give me sufficient height to gain purchase on the edge.

I grasped the edge of the dumpster with both hands and leapt into the air and banged my chin.

I stepped back, raised one leg to the level of my ear and scraped futilely at the edge with the side of my shoe.

Stymied.

I cleared my throat, filled my lungs, and bellowed "HALLOO!" in tones which have successfully called the cows home in barns from here to Topeka.

No one showed up.

I crossed my arms on my chest and brooded.

The breeze was mild and from the southwest. The sounds of the inn were carried upon it. I could hear the tinkle of glassware, the hum of voices, the clack and clatter of persons eating and drinking in blithe ignorance of my plight. If the wind shifted to the northeast, the bellow of my halloo would fly in the proper direction.

I raised my finger and tested the breeze. I did not think it would shift any time soon.

I gazed over the edge at the crates, which remained frustratingly out of reach. I looked up at the sky, which remained annoyingly blue, and over the edge of the dumpster to the waterfall, whose burble was becoming increasingly offensive to my ear.

In the end, I just waited. Someone would be coming out to dump more garbage. At the rate that the fatheads in the Tavern Bar were swilling food and drink, it should be soon.

It was not soon. It was, in fact, a damned long while, and by the time the sound of footsteps smote my ear I have to confess my patience was a bit thin.

"Sweetie!" Madeline's blue eyes gazed at me over the edge of the damned thing. "Are you all right? What are you doing in there?"

Several replies occurred to me. Waiting for a bus? Performing a feline hysterectomy? Preparing a response to the ignoramus who had questioned my research methods at yesterday's lecture?

I forbore to reply at all.

Madeline's eyes flew to the bump on my chin. "You're hurt!" she cried. "Oh goodness! Oh, dear! I'm going for help. No. Wait." Her eyes narrowed purposefully and she tensed for action. She drew her skirts up to her waist. "Don't move a muscle, darling. You might be bleeding somewhere. I'm coming in."

So we both would be stuck in this dumpster? I settled on

the truth. "I am not injured, Madeline. I am constrained by my inability to gain any purchase on the walls of this dumpster."

Madeline blinked. "You mean you're stuck?"

"I am stuck."

"You're stuck in the dumpster?"

This repetition was meaningless, but I carried on. "I am stuck in the dumpster."

I was wrong. The repetition was not meaningless, not to Madeline, at any rate. Her face was pink and there was the suspicion of a tear in her eye. "Ha-ha-ha," she said. "Oh ha-ha-ha-ha!" And when she regained a sufficiency of oxygen, she repeated the obvious: "You got stuck in the dumpster. YOU got stuck in the dumpster. You got STUCK! In the dumpster!" several times before she tossed in the crates so that I could get out.

I had, however, successfully retrieved the evidence. Madeline admired the remains of the Potatoes Duchesse and the cod, and we repaired to the tavern bar for a drink.

"My part of the hunt wasn't exactly a bust," Madeline said as we settled at our former table. I noted with approval that the marble top had been scrubbed clean, the linen replaced, and the small bouquet of early roses refreshed. "But it was pretty much a bust."

"A bust?"

"Couldn't find hide nor hair of the Widow Aronson, That cute little receptionist. . . ."

"Young Dina."

"She's made a hit with you, Austin."

Was that a hint of jealousy in her eye? Madeline is prone to attacks of the green-eyed monster (as, I confess, am I). I smiled to myself, and straightened a bit in my chair. "A most attractive girl," I signaled to the bear-like fellow who ran the bar. Same again, I nodded, in response to the interrogative lift of his eyebrow.

"Uh-huh. I've got to keep tabs on you every minute." She

took a deep breath. "At least you weren't hurt. I mean, when I first saw you standing there with that bump on your chin . . . ." She pressed her lips together so firmly the dimples in her cheeks came out. "And all the while it turned out that you were just st . . . ."

I cleared my throat in a definite way.

"Anyhow," Madeline said cheerily, "Myrna hasn't checked out yet. Dina thought she might be down at the police station, so I just wandered around the inn a bit while I waiting for her *and,*" Madeline took a deep, satisfied breath. "Guess what I found."

The bartender set a cassis and soda and Guinness draft in front of us. I sipped my cassis with pleasure. "I have no idea, my dear. What did you find?"

"Molasses."

I paused, my drink in mid-air.

"Molasses where molasses shouldn't be. Especially in a place like this. Molasses under the empty tables in the far corner. You remember when Daryl first came into the dining room? How the maitre d' plunked him and Myrna right between the devil and the deep blue sea?"

"Myrna and him," I corrected gently. "And I'm afraid I don't quite . . . ."

"It's a *metaphor,* Austin. You know, like between a rock and a hard place. The guys with the baby might have done it, or the geeky ladies in the gunny sacks might of done it and the poor slob didn't have a chance once he sat where he sat."

I blinked rapidly several times. Experience told me it was not the cassis that was the cause of my light-headedness, nor was it the appealing proximity of Madeline's soft, smooth skin. There is one thing I have learned in my years with Madeline: as confusing as her style of communication may be on occasion, she is one smart cookie. "Whomever wished to murder the poor fellow intended him to sit there."

"Got it in one, Austin. So I asked the guy . . . ."

"Which guy?"

"The maitre-whosis, who else? When did he notice the molasses? And he said . . . ."

"It was the ladies from Cornell."

"Austin!" Madeline smacked me on the shoulder. It was an affectionate smack, but she is remarkably fit and packs, as they say, quite a punch. I rubbed my clavicle. "If I am not mistaken, he sat them at those tables first. Am I correct?"

"Yeah! Dina said at first the professors asked to be seated next to Table Seven, which was where Daryl had made a reservation, but somebody else was sitting there when they walked in. They sat at the other table first. . . ."

"And they complained about the sticky floor and asked to be moved. They spilled the molasses, probably on purpose," I added.

Madeline took a long gulp of her beer. If I hadn't known better, I would have said she was sulky. "I bet you don't know *why* it was molasses. I mean, who comes to a dining room carrying molasses?"

I patted her hand. "What better substance in which to suspend the strychnine than molasses? And where better to obtain strychnine than the veterinary school at Cornell, where it is still used in the treatment of horses?" I sighed, heavily. "Of course, it was the younger of the two women. The one who leaped up to assist the unfortunate baby. She had ample opportunity to drop the molasses ball into the cod. A matter of deduction, my dear."

"And you saw the molasses on her skirt," Madeline said. "Only you thought it was part of the general Mississippi-mud effect. Well, ha ha on you. I did, too. Only I knew it was a stain and not on purpose. We both solved the case, Austin." She smacked my clavicle again. "And don't you forget it."

So we called the unfortunate Deputy Dave, who was most distressed that he had not "secured" the crime scene, as I believe the expression is. And he was quite annoyed when I presented him with the shreds of the cod and the Potatoes

Duchesse. I had, he said crossly, broken the chain of evidence. But Professor Belloc, for such was the murderess's name, confessed immediately and was hauled off to pokey.

Professor Belloc's fate remains in the hands of the justice system of the State of New York. There were mitigating circumstances, I believe. Myrna Aronson was Professor Belloc's older sister, and subsequent investigations by the authorities revealed that Daryl was indeed a bestial husband.

I sincerely hope the Professor has an adroit attorney. She deserves one. I, myself, offered to testify on her behalf. The cell phone and the cigarette thrown into the wine glass should be sufficient reason for leniency.

Our weekend was over late Sunday afternoon, and the Quilliams had not returned. And Madeline longed for the gateau, which remained, like Godot, unavailable. But we had been away from home too long; our dogs and our horses called us. We never met the famous chef and her artist sister. One day, we shall have to return to Hemlock Falls and do so.

DEAN ASKS CLAUDIA:

Q: *This is your second time out as an anthology editor. (Claudia edited* Death Dines at 8:30 *with Nick DiChario in 2002.) Why did you do it again?*
A: I'd rather read other people's fiction than write my own stuff. I hate writing my own stuff. I'm never surprised by whom the murderer is.

Q: *Why did you choose Dr. and Mrs. Mackenzie as characters for this short story? Are you getting bored with Meg and Quill?*
A: You know, I'm never bored with Meg and Quill. When I work on a Hemlock Falls novel, I have the distinct sense that if I turned around very quickly, I'll see them sitting next to me. I'd sooner get rid of my best friend or my cranky

little sister. And I didn't really choose the Mackenzies. They wouldn't go away until I wrote about them. Madeline showed up first. She's been hanging around for a couple of years, but I couldn't get her into a story. I decided to marry her off a few months ago—and Austin walked right in and took over. And then I had something to work with.

Q: *Do you ever run out of ideas for murders?*
A: Nope. Scary, isn't it?

AND HERE IS CLAUDIA'S RECIPE:

THE WORLD'S BEST CHOCOLATE CHIP COOKIES

These are Madeline's favorite chocolate chip cookies. They are part of how she keeps her voluptuous figure.

> *2–2³⁄4 cups flour*
> *1 cup salted butter, at room temperature*
> *3/4 cup brown sugar, packed*
> *3/4 cup white sugar*
> *2 large eggs*
> *1 pound miniature semi-sweet chips*
> *2 cups chopped walnuts*
> *2 cups shredded coconut*
> *1 tablespoon vanilla extract*
> *3/4 teaspoon baking soda*
> *3/4 teaspoon baking powder*

Mix all ingredients in a bowl, using an electric beater. Beat until light and fluffy. Then add 1 cup flour and beat. Add a second cup of flour and beat. Then add a little more flour—perhaps as much as 3/4 of a cup, until dough is sticky and dense. You will have to mix it in with a wooden spoon.

Add a pound of miniature semi-sweet chocolate chips, 2 cups of chopped walnuts and 2 cups of shredded coconut. Mix well. Drop by huge spoonfuls onto greased cookie sheet and bake at 375°F for about 15 minutes.

ALL IN THE FAMILY

Dean James

Dean James is the author of a popular series of vampire–detective nov–els. A scholar, Dean holds a Ph.D. in Medieval History and manages the popular Murder By The Book mystery bookstore in Houston, Texas. Dean is a well–known figure at mystery conventions.

Great-Uncle Elwood never ate fish.

For a long time, all of us thought that this was sim-ply more evidence of his many and varied eccentricities. Great-Uncle Elwood also insisted on wearing only brown shoes, carrying an umbrella with him everywhere no matter what the weather was like, and eating corn at least once a day.

As we discovered, however, Great-Uncle Elwood had a perfectly good reason for not eating fish, though none of us ever understood the brown shoes, the umbrella, or the corn.

Great-Uncle Elwood was allergic to fish. To be precise, he was allergic to shellfish of any kind. When you're as wealthy as he was, you can insist that no fish ever be brought into the house, no matter who else might crave the taste. No money of his would ever be spent on fish, goldarnit! The Barminster family just got used to it.

The great irony in all of this lay in the fact that the Barminster family fortune began in a fish cannery in Maine. Over the years, as the family moved farther south, to settle eventually in Houston, Texas, the fortune got diversified and grew to a staggering size. But it was fish money to begin with, and I believe Great-Uncle Elwood still owned a bit of that original fish cannery.

Great-Uncle Elwood probably also still had at least seventy-five cents out of every dollar he had ever made. He could be generous to less fortunate members of the Barminster clan, when it suited him, but the trick was always to make it seem like Great-Uncle Elwood's idea to part with money.

Over the years we had all managed to winkle gifts out of his tight fist. My elder, and only, brother Bob got enough to go to law school, and I managed to get enough to make it through college without having to work three part-time jobs every semester. Cousin Elwoodine, so named by her conniving parents in a blatant (and mostly unsuccessful) attempt to curry favor, eventually worked her namesake to get enough dough to open her own business. After a strong start, though, I hear that her flower shop is struggling.

As long as you were planning to do something sensible with the money, Great-Uncle Elwood wasn't too hard to sell on the idea. Education and business sense were two things he respected above all others. He didn't have much of the former, but he had heaps of the latter. If I had been smart, I would have chosen some other career, and I might have managed a few more gifts through the years. But Great-Uncle Elwood was suspicious of anything he called "artsy-fartsy," and a writer of novels fell rather sadly into that category.

I had managed to scrape out a decent enough living, though in comparison to my big brother Bob, the corporate lawyer, I was a failure. He had a big house in one of the best residential areas in Houston, drove an expensive car, smoked expensive cigars, and had a lifestyle any single man would envy. He has occasionally helped me out, because he takes his duties as a big brother seriously. I put up with the lectures that come with the help, because what are you going to do? Can't look a gift horse in the mouth, as they say.

I had been staying with Great-Uncle Elwood for a bit over a week when the calendar approached the one really significant day in the Barminster family schedule. Great-Uncle Elwood was about to turn eighty, and family tradition demanded that everyone show up for a big dinner celebration. Since I hadn't seen most of the family in quite some time, not counting brother Bob, I was looking forward to the reunion. I was especially looking forward to the little schemes various relatives would try to get money out of Great-Uncle Elwood. With the notable exception of myself, the Barminsters were not known for their imaginations, but when it came to begging for money, they usually outdid themselves.

The clan began gathering on Saturday, the day of the birthday celebration. I had come along ten days before, when Great-Uncle Elwood's housekeeper, a much put-upon woman, had left in a huff. She would eventually come back, Great-Uncle Elwood would apologize, and all would be well again for a year, until the next time the poor woman wanted some time off. Great-Uncle Elwood didn't set much store on vacation time, you see. It was their little way of each getting what he or she wanted.

One of the junior Barminsters usually stepped into the breach, and more often than not, I was the junior Barminster who did. Not having had much luck lately selling anything, I needed a temporary haven, and I really didn't mind waiting on the old boy hand and foot for a few weeks. Being appreciative of good service, he usually paid me enough to swallow my pride.

Elwoodine and her two thoroughly obnoxious offspring

were the first to arrive that morning. Elway, her son, was nineteen and fancied himself as the next Springsteen, but without the least bit of talent, sad to say. Deena, the daughter, was two years younger and far brighter, but she was going through one of those repulsive stages favored by girls her age. Dressed all in black, with black lipstick, eye shadow, and so on, she looked more like a carrion crow than the moderately attractive child she had been last time I saw her.

Elwoodine was thin as the proverbial rail, with new lines about her eyes and mouth, making her look more pinched than ever. "Things not going well at the flower shop?" I asked with sympathy as I helped her carry her bags up to the bedroom assigned to her.

She groaned as she collapsed onto the bed. "If I don't come up with some money real soon, I'll have to file for bankruptcy."

"That bad, huh?" I sat down on a chair and regarded her.

"Yep, that bad. And asking Elwood for help is out of the question. He's bailed me out twice, and the last time I asked, he made it pretty clear that he wouldn't help any more. Oh, God, what am I going to do?" She began sniffling.

"There must be some way out of it, other than bankruptcy," I said, trying to sound soothing. Elwoodine was hopeless as a businesswoman, that was the problem. She was born to be a rich man's wife, but she was no better judge of men than she was of business schemes. Her husband had decamped years ago, leaving her with the two children and numerous debts. Marrying a rich man would solve all her problems, but most potential suitors headed for the hills, once they had a small dose of Elway and Deena.

"Elwood is my only hope," she said gloomily. "Which means I have none whatsoever." She sat up. "He might leave me something in his will, but he'll live to be a hundred just to spite me, I'm sure."

I shrugged. "You never know. He's getting a bit frail. He's not as durable as you might think."

Elwoodine rubbed her nose and stared at me. "Yeah, right. He's a tough old coot, and he'll be around for years to come. Just to spite us all, like I said."

We sat in silence for a moment. I should be getting back downstairs, because there was still a lot to do to get ready for the evening revelry.

"You've been here for awhile, haven't you?" Elwoodine asked. At my nod, she continued. "You were always a snoopy kind of kid, so I know you must have been poking around. Have you seen the latest version of the will?"

Great-Uncle Elwood loved making new wills; it was one of his favorite forms of entertainment. Not that he ever shared the contents with any of us, mind you. He rather liked to keep his little jokes private.

I cleared my throat. She knew me a little too well to believe any protestations of innocence. "I may have seen something," I admitted.

"Come on, give," Elwoodine said, her tone very urgent.

"You won't leave me alone until I tell you, I know. You were always a pushy kind of kid, weren't you?" I smiled at her.

She didn't find that amusing. She just sat and glared at me.

"Oh, what the hell," I said, giving in. "Let's just put it this way, if Elwood popped off in the next few days, you wouldn't have anything to worry about." I sighed. "Whereas I will still have to sing for my supper."

Elwoodine didn't waste any time on sympathy for me. In addition to being a pushy kid, she had also been selfish. She hadn't changed.

I stood up. "You could at least help out in the kitchen since you got here early enough. I'm not going to do all the cooking today. Besides, you know how Elwood likes to see us all working together like one big happy family."

She snorted. "Don't get your knickers in a knot, dear cousin. I'm not going to do anything to make him change his will in the next day or two. I'll be down in a few minutes to help you."

As I left her, she was looking considerably less pinched. In fact, she looked downright cheerful. Well, bully for her, I thought sourly.

Big brother Bob was the next to arrive. When I had admitted him into the house, he swept me up in a hug. "Hey there, little guy, how's it going?"

He literally *was* my big brother, outweighing me by about fifty pounds and standing about half a foot taller. He was a Barminster through and through, while I took after our mother's side of the family. French peasant stock, small and squat. *C'est la vie.*

"Put me down. Bob," I said, after patting him on the back. He set me down.

"How's Elwood?" he asked.

"Doing just fine, for someone about to turn eighty."

"Glad to hear it," Bob said. And he truly was. Bob, the only one of us who never needed money from Elwood anymore, was genuinely fond of the old guy. In his turn, Elwood was inordinately proud of Bob and was constantly holding him up as a model Barminster. It was to barf, sometimes.

"You're in your usual room," I told him. "Need any help with your bags?"

"Nah," Bob said, hefting them both in one beefy hand. "I've got to take care of some business, but I'll be done in about an hour. What say we have a talk and catch up on things?"

"If I can tear myself away," I said wryly, "it's a date." Responding to Bob's puzzled look, I explained. "Mrs. Seton is off on her annual huff, so yours truly is filling in for now."

Bob stared at me a moment. Then he shook his head. "Why didn't you ask me for help? You didn't have to do this. I know you hate it."

I shrugged. "It's no big deal, and Elwood usually comes up to scratch."

"Okay, little guy," he said, heading up the stairs. "I guess you know best."

I stared after him for a moment. I wondered if he realized how much I hated being called "little guy." Probably not. He's been calling me that for nearly forty years.

I was in the kitchen washing some vegetables for tonight's dinner when the doorbell rang for the third time that day. After wiping my hands on a cloth, I headed for the front door. Elwoodine had yet to appear to help, and I was feeling more than a bit annoyed.

I opened the door to my cousin Jasmine Meadowflower. She had been christened Elaine Barminster, but having joined a radical lesbian faery group in her teens, she had eschewed her patriarchal name ever since. She clumped in, wearing her usual heavy work boots, jeans, and flannel shirt. She might as well have the word "dyke" tattooed across her forehead, she was so stereotypical. She even drove a pickup with a huge toolbox.

Trailing behind Jasmine was the girlfriend of the month, a waiflike creature with a toddler clamped to one hip. This did not look good. Great-Uncle Elwood was not fond of small children. Neither was I, for that matter.

"Hey, Cuz," Jasmine said. She grasped me in an awkward hug, then stepped back to introduce the girlfriend. "This is Esmerelda. And that's her son, Ricky."

"Hello, Jasmine. Hello, Esmerelda," I said. Ricky I ignored, and he returned the favor, being more interested in rooting around on his mother's chest in search of nourishment. As I watched in horrified fascination, Esmerelda lifted her top and Ricky set to with gusto.

"Um, isn't he a bit old for that?" I asked. I couldn't help myself.

Esmerelda shrugged. "Keeps him quiet."

Jasmine was beaming at both of them fondly. I had lost track of how many times she had changed partners. They all had one thing in common, however. They were usually delicate-looking creatures with a small child. Frustrated maternal instinct on Jasmine's part, I gathered. They never lasted long, because Jasmine was so possessive she soon drove them completely bonkers.

"How's Elwood?" Jasmine asked after she had brought their meager luggage inside the hallway and shut the front door.

"Just fine," I said. "What's that?" I pointed at a cooler.

Jasmine responded with a shifty glance. "Special food for Esmerelda." She cleared her throat. "She don't eat beef or chicken or pork. Only seafood." She scuffed the rug with the toe of her boot.

"Uh huh," I said. "And how are you planning to explain that to Elwood?"

"He doesn't have to know," Jasmine said defiantly. "Unless somebody rats me out, that is."

I threw up my hands. "Not me, Jasmine. I couldn't care less. But I'm not going to be cooking any of it. That's up to you and Esmerelda. I can't take the chance of contaminating Elwood's food."

"Don't worry," Jasmine said. "You won't have to dirty your lily-white hands with it." She sneered openly. She shared Elwood's attitude toward writers. "I'll take care of everything, and Elwood will never know there's any fish in the house."

Since Elwood almost never visited the kitchen, Jasmine was pretty safe. She just had to disguise the look and the smell of the fish. Elwood did have a sensitive nose.

"Fine," I said, turning away. "Just bring it along to the kitchen. You know which room is yours, I'm sure."

Muttering under her breath, Jasmine followed me to the kitchen, clutching the cooler to her considerable bosom. Esmerelda and Ricky, still dining, came right behind.

Elwoodine was just coming in to the kitchen from the back stairs when we entered. She and Jasmine air-kissed after Jasmine had deposited the cooler. Barely acknowledging the introduction to Esmerelda and Ricky, Elwoodine set to work at my direction.

Jasmine took her girlfriend and the child up the back stairs to their room and was back down again in a few minutes. She set about unloading the contents of the cooler into the refrigerator, all the time looking nervously over her shoulder.

"How's the contracting business these days?" Elwoodine asked as she chopped some onions.

Jasmine did remodeling stuff, and she used an all-female crew. Sometimes she did quite well, but most of the time she was looking for work.

"The usual," Jasmine said glumly. Elwoodine snorted.

"If you're looking for money from Elwood," I said, not bothering to hide the malice in my voice, "I'm not sure dragging Esmerelda along for the weekend was the best way to go."

Jasmine's dark look let me know what she thought of my advice. She took a plastic bag of shrimp to the sink and began to wash it.

"Be very careful with that," I told her. "You know how allergic Elwood is. And if he even sees something that looks like shrimp, he'll have a fit. That wouldn't be good for his heart."

"Don't you worry," Jasmine said. "I'll take care of it." She found a knife and a cutting board and began cutting the shrimp into tiny pieces.

Elwoodine and I left Jasmine to her preparations and concentrated on tonight's main course. I had decided to try something a little different. Elwood was not terribly adventurous when it came to trying new dishes, but I had one that I thought he would enjoy. If he liked it enough, he might give me some extra little reward.

I explained it to Elwoodine as we worked. "It's basically one big stir-fry. I got the idea from a friend," I said. "I won't cook any of it until tonight, but since there'll be about ten of us at dinner, it will take longer than usual to prepare the ingredients."

I pointed to the various containers arranged along the counter. "You can vary it in any number of ways, just by the ingredients you use. You can use either pork or chicken, cut into small strips and marinated in soy sauce. For tonight I've chosen pineapple chunks, mushrooms, onions, bean sprouts, and fresh baby spinach. Normally I'd also add some cashew pieces, but Bob is allergic to nuts."

"Sounds pretty tasty," Elwoodine said. "What are we having with it?"

Pointing to a large cooker, I said, "I'll serve it over brown rice. We'll also have a salad and some fresh corn. I thought you might want to do your special creamed corn for tonight."

Elwoodine nodded with enthusiasm. "I'll be glad to. Elwood always likes that. So what else do we need to do?"

"I've already measured out the various ingredients," I said. "We just need to chop up everything and have it ready for tonight. And you need to shuck the corn, of course."

"Dinner's at seven?" Jasmine asked.

"Yes," I said. "The rice will take about half an hour, and the rest of it will take only a few minutes in the wok. I could use some help at that point."

Jasmine and Elwoodine both agreed to help with the final preparations. To my surprise, Jasmine also agreed to hang around and help Elwoodine shuck the corn. Once I had finished what I had to do, I left them and went upstairs to take a nap before the rest of the family, elderly twin cousins, arrived for dinner.

I must have been napping for about an hour when I awoke to a tapping at my door. "Who is it?" I called groggily. "And what the hell do you want?"

The door opened, and Jasmine sidled in. She didn't apologize for waking me. Instead she plopped down on the edge of the bed and regarded me with considerable hostility.

"Well, what is it?" I said, rubbing my face, trying to wake up.

"Elwoodine told me you've seen Elwood's latest will," she said, her voice harsh. Jasmine was rarely subtle. "You always were a snoopy kid."

I forbore to remind her what a mean kid she had been. I had never appreciated the drubbings she had given me when we had been forced to play together by our oblivious parents.

"So, are you going to tell me?" she said. "Do I get anything?" She didn't bother to keep the desperation out of her face or her voice.

I regarded her with disgust.

"Well?" she said.

I shrugged. "Yes, you'll get something. You won't get it all, but you should get enough to solve your problems."

Her shoulders relaxed.

"But you'll have to wait, of course, like the rest of us," I said. "Elwood's not going to pop off, just to solve your problems for you."

Jasmine snorted at that. "He's eighty, isn't he? Someone that age could go at any moment."

"Especially when he's surrounded by so many loving members of his family."

But the irony was lost on Jasmine.

"Go away, Jasmine, and let me sleep," I said. I turned over on the bed, facing away from her. I felt her heave her bulk off the bed, then heard her stomp out of the room. At least she didn't slam the door. I drifted off into sleep again.

I couldn't have slept for very long when I again heard knocking at the door. Cursing under my breath, I sat up. "Come in," I said, disgusted. I might as well give up trying to have a nap.

"Hey, little guy," my brother Bob said from the doorway. "Did I wake you? Sorry about that. Want me to go away?"

I shook my head. "Come on in, Bob. What can I do for you?"

Bob shut the door behind him, then came over and sat on the bed beside me. He drew two cigars from his jacket pocket and handed me one. "Thanks," I said. Bob drew his cutter and lighter out of his pocket, and we proceeded to light our cigars.

"So, what's up, Bob?" I said, once we had the cigars going.

"Just wanted to check on you, little guy," he said. "If you needed money, why didn't you come to me?"

I shrugged, then blew a smoke ring at the ceiling. "I don't need you to bail me out all the time. I can look after myself, you know."

To his credit, he didn't laugh at that. "I know that, little guy. But it's been awhile since you've sold a book, hasn't it?"

I nodded. I hadn't had much luck lately, and I was afraid my agent was going to drop me if I didn't come up with something marketable pretty soon.

"You could always come to work for me," Bob said. He had offered me jobs before. He had even said I could do investigative work for him. I actually think I would have liked that, but then I would also have had to put up with being called "little guy" every day.

"I'll get by," I said.

Bob shook his head. "You're an independent cuss, I'll say that for you." He laughed. "But you don't ever have to worry. I'll always take care of my little brother." He patted me affectionately on the back.

"I know, Bob," I said, "and I appreciate that. I'll think about the job offer."

"Okay, little guy," he said, standing up. "I think I'll go and spend some time with Elwood, see how he's doing. Dinner's at seven, right?"

I nodded. Bob was the only member of the family Elwood would consent to see before dinner. Tomorrow, he would grant audiences to each of them in turn, but today, only Bob would gain entrance to the inner sanctum, his bedroom.

"See you later," I called to Bob's retreating back. The door shut softly behind him.

I finished the cigar, a very good and no doubt very expensive one, ruminating on the plot of the book I was currently working on. Around six, I went downstairs to finish preparations for dinner.

Jasmine and Elwoodine were already there. Jasmine was putting the finishing touches to the shrimp and rice dish she was preparing for her girlfriend, and Elwoodine was busy with her creamed corn. I rinsed out the rice cooker, then measured out the rice for our dinner. Once I had that cooking, I set the wok on the stove and began collecting ingredients from the refrigerator.

I directed Jasmine and Elwoodine to set the table in the dining room, and I promised to keep an eye on the corn, bubbling away on the stove. I wanted to get Elwoodine out of the room for a few minutes. She was wearing some excessively cloying perfume, and it was giving me a headache.

By the time they returned from setting the table, I had the stir fry done and ready to be ladled onto plates when the rice was done. I looked at my watch. The rice should be done in about five minutes.

My head was aching from Elwoodine's perfume. "I've got to go upstairs for my sinus medication," I informed them. "If the rice finishes before I get back, you can start putting it on the plates and ladling out the stir fry."

"Yes, sir," Jasmine said, sourly. "Your wish is our command."

I clumped up the back stairs to my room and into the bathroom. I found the bottle containing my sinus medicine and extracted a pill. Downing it with some water, I stood and tried to relax for a moment. The pill would make me drowsy a bit later, but that was a small price to pay for getting rid of my headache.

I waited a few minutes, letting my head clear, then went

back downstairs. As I entered the kitchen, Elwoodine and
Jasmine stood with their backs to me. They turned with a
start as they heard my feet hitting the tiled floor.

"Everything's ready," Jasmine said, stepping aside and
waving a hand at the counter. Ten dinner plates, with rice
and stir fry already apportioned, sat there steaming.

"Thanks," I said, my eyes narrowing slightly in suspicion. They acted like they were up to something.

"All we have to do is get the salad on the salad plates and
bring in the creamed corn," Elwoodine said, smiling, "and
we're all set."

Glancing at the kitchen clock, I noted that the time was
five minutes to seven. "And right on time, too, because we
all know how punctual Elwood always is."

"We'll take the plates out," Jasmine said, picking up two
of them, and heading for the door that led to the dining
room. "You do the salads."

Elwoodine followed her, also with two plates in hand,
and I went to the refrigerator to get the large bowl of salad I
had prepared earlier in the day. I retrieved chilled bowls
from the freezer and set about filling them with salad. By
the time Elwoodine and Jasmine had the plates of stir fry on
the table, I had the salads ready to go. I put them all on a
large tray and carried them in to the dining room. Elwoodine followed with a tureen of creamed corn. Since Elwood
would eat most of it himself, she placed it next to his place
at the table while I dispensed the salads.

Right on cue, Elwood marched into the dining room,
followed closely by Bob. Elwoodine's two delinquents-in-
training pushed ahead of the elderly twins, Martha and
Mary, who had arrived minutes before. Breathlessly the
twins babbled about the traffic which had made them almost late. Elwood paid them not the slightest attention. He
never did.

Each of us knew his or her accustomed place at the table.
Bob sat on Elwood's right, I at his left, and the rest down

the table. Jasmine's girlfriend, Esmerelda, slipped into her place at the last moment. Elwood, for once apparently in a tolerant mood, elected not to notice as he began to intone grace. I had no idea where Ricky was, nor did I care. We didn't need him complicating our dinner conversations or giving Elwood apoplexy.

As Elwood finished saying grace, he lowered himself into his chair. The rest of us remained on our feet, waiting for Bob to give the annual toast. We each dutifully raised our wine glasses, filled earlier by Bob, and drank to Elwood's health.

Then we sat down to eat. Elwood eyed the plate in front of him with some curiosity. He had always liked Chinese food, and I didn't think he would take exception to my little experiment. Quickly I explained what the ingredients were, and how it was all prepared. He turned a beaming face to me.

"Capital, dear boy, absolutely capital. I'm sure we'll all enjoy it."

With that he plunged a fork into the food and lifted a hefty portion to his mouth. He chewed for a moment, then turned to me again. "Very tasty," he said. "Very tasty indeed."

Smiling with pleasure, I tasted my own first forkful. Yes, it was good, I decided. The combination of flavors and textures was delicious.

Around the table, everyone else had dug in, seeing how pleased Elwood was with the food. I glanced down the table at Esmerelda's plate. She was far enough away, I hoped, that Elwood wouldn't notice particularly that her food looked a bit different. I shrugged. That was Jasmine's lookout, after all.

Bob was regaling Elwood with some legal story, and Elwood was forking the food in with great gusto, when all of a sudden, he began to choke. Forks clattered on to the table as we all watched in horrified fascination.

At first, we all thought he was choking on a piece of food stuck in his throat. Bob even attempted the Heimlich maneuver, but to no avail. Bob ordered me to call 911, and I did.

By the time the ambulance arrived, however, Great-Uncle Elwood was dead.

WHILE everyone else sat, stunned, around the dinner table, I went into the kitchen. Great-Uncle Elwood had eaten some of the shrimp Jasmine had brought into the house for her girlfriend, of that I had no doubt. His reaction had been that of someone who was highly allergic. Since he had a weak heart, the allergic reaction had killed him even more quickly than it might have done.

I opened the refrigerator door and looked in the compartment where Jasmine had stored the shrimp she had brought. It seemed to me that quite a bit of it was missing. More than would have been needed for just Esmerelda's dinner, I thought.

I went back to the dining room and sat down at my place. I glanced back and forth between Jasmine and Elwoodine. Their eyes glittered with excitement, and they avoided looking at each other. Perhaps they had worked together; it certainly would have been easier that way. All they had to do was mix in some finely chopped shrimp with the ingredients of the stir fry on Elwood's plate, and he would never have noticed the taste of the shrimp. The other ingredients would have masked it.

Cleverly done, I had to admit. I permitted myself a small smile. All they needed was the opportunity, and Elwoodine had created that, as I had known she would, by wearing that obnoxious perfume. If I hadn't gone upstairs to take an allergy pill, leaving them alone in the kitchen at a crucial time, I was sure they would still have managed somehow. They were both fairly desperate. And predictable.

I could just imagine how chagrined they would be when they discovered that Great-Uncle Elwood had left each of them only twenty-thousand dollars in his will. The bulk of his fortune would go to my own dear big brother Bob. They certainly wouldn't be happy with me for lying to them about the will.

In addition to being a snoopy kid, I had always been a fairly adept liar. I think they must have forgotten that. They had certainly never read one of my mystery novels, I was sure.

They would be even more chagrined when the police began nosing around. I had no doubt that Bob, astute criminal lawyer that he was, intended to have Elwood's rather suspicious death investigated. I wondered which of them would crack first under the stress of the investigation.

Bob would see that they were prosecuted for having connived at murder. Big brother Bob, who was so deathly allergic to nuts and who, I knew all too well, had designated me, his "little guy," as his sole heir. Family was important to Bob. It was a shame about the allergy to nuts. One of these days, it would be the death of him.

CLAUDIA ASKS DEAN:

Q: *You have a Ph.D. in Medieval History. Why did you choose this field?*
A: As a teenager, I "discovered" medieval England thanks to a novel called *Bond of Blood,* by Roberta Gellis. I was already interested in English history, and I found myself increasingly fascinated with the Middle Ages and with Elizabethan England. I also loved my history courses in high school. When I went off to college, it was a foregone conclusion to major in history.

Q: *When did you start reading mysteries? Who were your earliest influences?*
A: I discovered Nancy Drew the year I was ten and was immediately hooked. I started trying to find as many of the

Nancy Drew books as I could and, before long, I was reading other series like Trixie Belden, the Hardy Boys, the Dana Girls, Judy Bolton, and many others. When I was about fifteen, my Aunt Mary lent me a copy of Victoria Holt's *The Shivering Sands,* and that launched my discovery of classic romantic suspense writers like Holt, Phyllis A. Whitney, Mary Stewart, Velda Johnston, and Elizabeth Peters/Barbara Michaels. In college I began to read Agatha Christie and Ngaio Marsh and eventually I encountered Margery Allingham. Allingham and Peters are my all-time favorite writers.

Q: *What's the most fun part of writing for you?*
A: Writing that first chapter, where the possibilities are limitless, is always great fun. After that, it gets tricky.

Q: *What's the worst part of writing?*
A: Other than the pay? Seriously, the worst part is not being able to do it twenty-four hours a day. I've wanted to be a writer since I was twelve years old. I can't imagine anything better.

AND HERE IS DEAN'S RECIPE:

"WOK ON THE WILD SIDE" STIR FRY

From the kitchen of Tejas Englesmith, FRSA

8 ounces skinned chicken breast, pork loin, or beef
1/4 cup soy sauce
2 tablespoons honey
1 cup rice (3/4 cup brown rice & 1/4 cup wild rice)
3 cups water, vegetable broth, or chicken broth
1/4 cup peanut oil

1 tbsp minced garlic
approximately 1/2 cup each:
sliced mushrooms
baby spinach
pineapple, cut into chunks
bok choy, chopped
bean sprouts
onions
1/4 cup chopped cashews

Slice skinned chicken breast, pork loin, or beef thinly into bite-sized pieces. Marinate in 1/4 cup soy sauce and 2 tablespoons honey for three hours or more in a ziplock bag in the refrigerator, turning and mixing every hour or so.

Cook rice in 3 cups water, vegetable, or chicken broth.

Vegetables can vary, depending really on what you have on hand! Suggestions: mushrooms, onions (white, red, or green—or a combination), bean sprouts, baby spinach, pineapple chunks, chopped or sliced garlic, bok choy, red or green pepper, broccoli.

Heat the wok until very hot. Add peanut oil (about 1/4 cup) and toss in the meat, stirring constantly until cooked. Add the veggies and nuts; keep tossing till spinach is just limp.

Serve over rice with a salad on the side. Serves 2 to 4.

MATINEE

William Moody

Bill Moody is a big, quiet guy with a sharp eye and an enormous talent. The New York Times said of Looking for Chet Baker, Bill's fifth mystery novel: "A musician himself, Moody is a fluent writer with a good ear for dialogue, a deft and ingratiating descriptive touch, a talent for characterization and a genuine feel for the jazz world." The Los Angeles Times gave Baker a long review, concluding that, "Moody, a drummer who has toured and recorded with Maynard Ferguson, Lou Rawls and Earl, "Fatha" Hines, is one among very few authors who've . . . used literary means to bring the jazz world to life."

"Idiots. I'm dealing with idiots," said Arthur Webb. He turned to look out from his tiny cubicle office on the third floor of the humanities building. Scattered across his desk was the latest response in his attempt to market his detective novel.

The manuscript was in tatters. Several pages were missing, and others were marred with coffee stains and cigarette burns. Stapled to the title page was a form rejection and one word, hastily scribbled beneath the signature: Derivative!!! The editor had seen fit to underline the word several times, as if the exclamation marks were not enough.

Derivative? Webb was outraged. Were all the editors in New York cretins? Angrily Webb glanced at the other results of his efforts stacked on the floor near his desk. In his wildest dreams, Webb had never imagined the difficulty he would encounter in finding a publisher or agent, much less selling his manuscript. He leaned back in his chair, running his hands through his steel-gray hair. The idea had come to him full blown on a day when he was besieged by term papers and requests by students to discuss their grades before upcoming exams. Webb had been so sure it couldn't miss. How? How could they not see?

In preparation, he read, studied, and literally dissected hundreds of detective novels for style, plot, and character development until he felt sure the genre was second nature. After all, for a professor of eighteenth-century literature, who had analyzed and taught complex works for a living, had been published in the MLA Journal several times, this was child's play. Most of the books he'd read he had found derivative, and sadly lacking in any literary merit. Tough guys, wise-cracking private eyes, feminist radicals, bungling amateurs, cozy suburban murder mysteries that were no more than updated versions of Agatha Christie. It was these that were derivative. Webb's would be not only original but well-written.

How could a novel about a transgender detective who solves a murder be derivative? Webb reviewed the plot in his mind once again. A man's wife is murdered. He undergoes a sex change operation, dates the suspected killer he uncovers after an exhaustive and clever investigation and, finally, gets him (or her, Webb wasn't sure which) to admit to killing his wife. It was brilliant, topical, and executed with elegance, at least in Arthur Webb's mind.

Once underway, Webb had written with a fury, an all-consuming passion that left his colleagues and students to wonder about his sanity, and his wife, Janet, frightened and totally confused. Every hour he could spare from his schedule was spent in pursuit of the novel's completion. He found himself waking in the middle of the night to scribble some note on the plot, an incident of one of the characters, or merely some piece of description.

By end of term, exams and papers graded, the novel was ready. Webb carefully typed in the final draft on his new computer and made several photocopies—courtesy of the English Department's machine—and then, one day in June, he sat down to map out his marketing strategy. He bought a copy of a market directory of publishers and agents and studiously noted submission requirements. He clipped articles from writer's magazines, haunted the bookstores, noting which publishers bought detective novels, and finally narrowed down the field to ten.

Next, he assembled his materials, a dazzling array of padded envelopes, labels, and cardboard backing sheets, and packaged five sets of the manuscript for submission. He wrote cover letters and marched triumphantly to the post office.

Later the same night, he took his wife to his favorite restaurant, where they had a splendid dinner of seafood pasta accompanied by a superb Sonoma County Merlot. He sipped the wine and settled back, mused in anticipation, secure in the knowledge that a contract and sizable advance would soon find its way to his mailbox. Perhaps even a phone call from an editor, singing the praises of his book and inviting him to New York at his convenience. All at their expense of course. But now, alone in the spartan confines of his office, Arthur Webb's fantasies were shattered.

Two of the five had come back unopened with a brief note stating these publishers did not accept unsolicited submissions. Wrong. Webb double checked his directory and put it down to changes in editorial policy. The post office lost one copy and all that was returned was his address label.

Number four arrived in tatters—not even in the return mailer Webb had provided—but instead in a cheap manila envelope. The fifth was returned intact with a puzzling note: "Enjoyed this very much. We wish the publisher who buys it all the luck."

Why didn't they buy it then? What was wrong with these people? And now this. Derivative! The word stared back at Webb, mocking him.

Slamming his fist down on his desk, Webb stood and paced around his office. No longer trusting the U.S. Mail, careless editors, and the charlatans of the publishing world, Webb decided he would make five more copies of his masterpiece and buy a round trip ticket to New York. He, Arthur Webb, would storm the Big Apple himself, forgetting at least for the moment that he was scheduled to go to New York anyway. He frowned. There was that business with Pearson.

For a moment he let his mind slip to the other reality of his life.

Making assignments to Pearson was never pleasant. The man had this annoying air of superiority about him, although his reputation was obviously well deserved. Pearson had never failed.

He shook off these thoughts, gathered his things together, and went home to announce his decision to Janet. She thought he was having a breakdown. "You're going where?" she said.

WEBB was already in the departure lounge when he remembered. Well, remembered wasn't exactly right. What he knew was he'd forgotten something.

What, he realized with a twinge of panic, he had no idea.

He glanced around at the other waiting passengers as if they could somehow remind him of what it was he'd forgotten. His big suitcase was checked, the small carry-on bag sat on the floor in front of him. He patted the inside pocket of his blazer for his ticket and boarding pass, felt for his wallet. No, it was something else.

He listened to the public address system announcements and checked his watch. There was time to call, but whom would he call? Janet wouldn't be home yet, which was precisely why he'd booked this flight. He'd be on his way, touching down at JFK before she would get home, see that he was gone, and find the note. He could hear her voice in his head now.

"You just fly off to New York and leave me a note?" Janet would shout to the empty house.

He watched one of the attendants on the desk pick up a microphone and make the boarding announcement. Well, at least the flight was going to be on time. At least Janet hadn't come home early, at least she hadn't had him paged to argue the point once again. He looked around quickly, feeling suddenly like someone on the run, like Pearson perhaps. No, Pearson was too calm and cool to ever feel like that. God, what a way that would be to live, he thought as he made his way to the gate and surrendered his boarding pass to the smiling attendant.

As soon as they were airborne, Webb ordered a drink. He poured Scotch out of a miniature bottle, let it trickle over the ice in the plastic glass, and ate a couple of peanuts, although as usual he had trouble getting the damn bag open. Next to him, a man in a dark suit and tie was going through the contents of his briefcase, a slim aluminum thing that looked to Webb like it might be used for transporting ransom money. Webb watched him, fascinated. The man smiled briefly at Webb and eventually fished out a small hand-held calculator. "Thought I'd forgotten it," he said.

Webb nodded but ignored the man. He didn't want to talk to anyone. What? What had he forgotten? Whatever it was, there was no going back now. It nagged him, but with everything he'd planned in the last few days, he might be forgiven a slip or two, although that was not at all in character for Arthur Webb.

In what seemed like only minutes, he could feel the plane descending into New York and heard the usual announcements about seat belts, tray tables, and personal belongings.

Webb was one of the first off, as if there might be some penalty for staying on board longer. He pushed through the crush of people and looked for the sign to baggage claim when he heard the public address system.

"Arthur Webb, please pick up the white courtesy phone. Arthur Webb."

Webb stopped in his tracks at the sound of his own name, and began looking for a phone. He found a bank of courtesy phones further down the corridor and picked up one. "Arthur Webb."

"Arthur?"

"Janet?"

"That wasn't very nice, dear, just taking off like that."

Webb slapped his hand on the wall above the phone and looked at the poster of the woman who stared down at him. "Oh my God," he muttered to himself, suddenly remembering what he'd forgotten as he stared at the woman's face on the poster. It was an advertisement for a Broadway show.

"Arthur? Are you there?"

"Janet, listen to me. On the hall table is there an envelope that . . . ."

"Yes, that's why I'm calling. I thought you might need it. There's no address on it, but it's sealed with tape. Shall I open it and read . . . ."

"NO!" Webb shouted. He shuddered at the thought of Janet opening the envelope. Two other callers looked at him with raised eyebrows. "Listen to me Janet. Don't touch it, don't open it. Take it to FedEx and send it overnight to me immediately. Do you understand?"

"No need to shout, Arthur."

Webb rubbed his forehead. "Just do it, Janet. Right now before you do anything else." He quickly gave her the name of the hotel he had reserved.

"All right, Arthur, calm down. I will."

"Remember, don't open it. I'll call you later."

Webb hung up the phone and wiped the perspiration beading his forehead and headed for baggage claim.

AT the same moment Arthur Webb walked toward baggage claim, Pearson strolled through the West Village, enjoying the good weather, letting his whims take him where they would, catching the eye of a woman now and then, and glancing in shop windows.

He stopped in front of a used bookstore when a book of jazz photographs caught his eye. He took off his sunglasses, then stepped inside. A bell tinkled overhead, announcing his arrival. He nodded to the clerk who looked up as he headed for the window display. Lifting the book from an acrylic stand, he gingerly thumbed through the pages of an old collection by William Claxton, who had begun his career photographing Gerry Mulligan and Chet Baker. The book was in excellent condition. Pearson smiled and knew he had his find for the day. He opened the book to the first page and noted the penciled price and smiled again.

He started for the front desk, then paused. "Is there a cookbook section?" he asked.

The clerk nodded. "In the back on the left. It's marked."

"Thanks," Pearson said. He made his way to the back of the store and found two bottom shelves of cookbooks. He knelt down and quickly scanned the titles. His pulse quickened. Sometimes it happened like this. He ran his finger across the books and then stopped. There. A collection of recipes compiled by famous and not so famous jazz musicians. Scanning over the table of contents, his eye came to rest on a salmon recipe by vocalist Annie Ross.

"Yes," Pearson whispered to himself. He closed the book and headed back to the front where the clerk was just finishing a transaction with another customer. Pearson waited patiently, then stepped forward. "I'll take these two," he said.

The clerk noted the price of each book and glanced up at Pearson.

"Charge?"

"Cash," Pearson said.

"No haggling?" The clerk allowed himself a small smile.

"I never bargain for something I want," Pearson said, not smiling at all.

In minutes he was back out on the bustling streets of the Village. He decided to go back to his hotel and wait for Webb's call and decide whether tonight would be the Blue Note, Bradley's, or the Village Vanguard.

It was going to be an all-jazz day.

PEARSON studied the photo and looked up at Webb, "She's very pretty," he said, "Kind of a shame."

Webb gave him a bemused look, "That's not like you to be concerned." He shook his head. "Anyway, you'll be long gone. The rest of the information—schedules, hangouts, and friends—is in the envelope. There's even a copy of the script if you think that will help."

Webb had spent the afternoon haunting the front desk of

his hotel, pacing, checking every half hour for FedEx deliveries, sure Janet would have botched the sending of the envelope. He still couldn't believe he'd forgotten to bring it with him. How would he have explained that to Pearson, to his control? Pearson had flown in from who knows where and he was so expensive.

To make the trip for nothing would have cost everyone. Webb shuddered at the thought. But it had arrived. He must pick up something for Janet, perhaps have her join him, and take in a show. He suddenly became aware of Pearson looking at him.

"Sorry, what did you say?" He watched Pearson study the photo again, probably memorizing her features: cascading blonde hair, greenish eyes, and skin too smooth for a woman over forty, if the rest of Webb's information was correct, and Webb knew it was.

"Deadline. I said deadline." Pearson repeated.

"Oh, of course." Webb cleared his throat. "We'd like it ah . . . ." Webb searched for the word. "Attended to by Wednesday. There's a matinee at two. Maybe before or after that?" His eyebrows rose questioningly.

Pearson nodded and slipped the photo back in the envelope. They were in the Blue Note, one of Pearson's favorites. He took another bite of his salmon, leaning back, savoring the flavor of the mesquite grill, the seasonings, aware of Webb watching him, waiting for his answer. He took a sip of the chilled Chardonnay and nodded at Webb.

"Shouldn't be a problem. I have some business in Boston, but I have to be back on Thursday anyway, so I'd like to wrap this up as soon as possible."

Webb's sigh was audible. "Splendid," he said. "I'll pass along the word." He downed the last of his wine and put his hands on the table as if to go. He hated it that despite the fact that he had dispatched Pearson a number of times, he never knew what the man was thinking. In fact, he knew nothing about him (not even his first name) except for a phone number, and he guessed that was an untraceable cell phone. It was always a different number.

Pearson put his hand on Webb's arm. "Not yet. I want you to hear this group." He glanced toward the bandstand where a bassist was leaning over the piano, striking a key, plucking a string on his bass, tuning up, and joking with the drummer, who was attaching cymbals to the stands. "There's a new young tenor player and a pianist," Pearson said.

Webb leaned back. He had hoped to escape before the music started. Jazz was not his pleasure and Pearson always made so much about it. America's classical music, he called it.

"You know why I like jazz so much?" Pearson didn't wait for Webb's answer but simply went on. "Because it's so different from my work. These four musicians are going to choose a tune in a few minutes and, despite them all knowing and having played it many times, they won't know what they're going to do until they do it. Improvisation. I love it but I can't afford it. I have to know every move I'm going to make in advance. These guys," he waved his hand at the bandstand, "are spontaneous. It's exhilarating. Don't you agree?"

Webb considered. "Yes I suppose it can be." Before Webb could say more, the lights dimmed and a voice from the sound system filled the room. "Ladies and Gentlemen, the Blue Note is proud to present in his first New York appearance, Tyler Browne and his quartet."

The saxophonist snapped his fingers several times and then the piano, bass, and drums were playing, all lost in their own little world. The saxophonist listened for a while, then put the horn to his lips and joined them in some song Webb didn't recognize at all.

Webb watched Pearson. A slight smile creased his lips and his head nodded in time to the band, his hand lightly tapping on the table. Webb looked at his watch. He wanted to go, get back to his hotel and forget Pearson, distance himself from this place, this music, but now it was too late; he'd have to wait for intermission.

They played for nearly an hour before the saxophonist thanked the audience to enthusiastic applause and their sound was replaced by taped music. People were paying checks, getting up and starting to leave before the next set.

"Amazing," Pearson said. "He's a real talent." He turned to look at Webb. "What do you think?"

Webb was at a loss. He admitted one slow ballad had been nice, but for the most part he just didn't get it. "Well, it was, ah, very lively."

Pearson smiled. "Lively. Yes, I like that." He sipped the coffee the waitress had brought them during the music. She had slipped in so quietly, Webb had hardly noticed.

"Well, ah. The check is taken care of," Webb said. "And I really must get along. He got to his feet and stuck out his pudgy hand. "Good to see you again, Pearson. We'll have a money transfer on deposit as usual."

"You'd better," Pearson said, his eyes boring into Webb's. "Oh, by the way. How's the writing going, a detective novel isn't it?"

Webb sat down again. He didn't remember telling Pearson about it. He couldn't lie to Pearson. "Not well. It's so hard to find a publisher or an agent." He tried to avoid Pearson's eyes.

"Rejected you, huh?"

Webb shrugged. "Resoundingly. They said it was derivative." The two editors he had tried to talk to today had just blown him off, too. It was hopeless.

"Maybe it was," Pearson said. "It's a tough game. There are lots of P.I. books out there." He looked at Webb, then said, "Write something different."

"Different?" Webb couldn't imagine anything more different than his transvestite hero.

"Yeah," Pearson said. "You know the old saw. Write what you know. Write about yourself, what you do besides your teaching job." Pearson continued to look at him. "Our business," he said.

Webb stared back for a moment, light emerging in his mind. Of course.

What did he really know about sex change operations or how long they took? He'd have to know more, learn about jazz, all the details, but he knew a lot already. Pearson nodded at him, seeing that he understood.

"Think about it," Pearson said. "You already know the ending."

"Yes," Webb said, getting to his feet again. He started away, then turned back. Pearson looked at him. "Was there something else?"

"No, no, I was just wondering."

"Yes?"

"Will you see the play first? I can arrange a ticket."

Pearson thought for a moment and smiled. "Maybe. I'll let you know. I always liked Neil Simon."

"I can't believe you got tickets to this show, Arthur. And such great seats. I'm so glad you had me join you."

Webb smiled at her. "Oh, I have a few contacts." He had the program open, studying the cast list, wondering if . . . .

"Ladies and Gentlemen, due to serious illness, the part of Clarissa will be played by her understudy for this performance. Thank you for your patience and understanding."

"Oh no," Janet said. "I wonder what happened to her."

Webb smiled and leaned back in his seat as the curtain opened.

DEAN AND CLAUDIA ASK BILL:

Q: *Do you listen to jazz while you write?*
A: Yes. I usually do listen to music while I'm writing, mainly solo piano or piano trios—Bill Evans, Keith Jarrett. I also like solo classical piano, mostly Chopin.

Q: *You're a drummer. Are you playing now?*
A: I haven't been on the road in years, but I still play and record quite a lot in the Bay Area. I work mainly with a trio and a quartet and have recorded with both. There's a significant jazz scene around San Francisco and, fortunately for me, more than enough playing. In the spring and summer there is a lot of jazz featured at the wineries in the area. And I've played everywhere from a converted aircraft carrier to the San Francisco Zoo.

Q: *Are there any similarities between writing and playing?*
A: With jazz, you have the framework of the tune/melody, the chord progression, and the structure. When you solo, you don't know what you are going to do until you do it. With writing, I start with a premise, the basic mystery framework and improvise as I go. I don't outline much in advance. I'm a big advocate of the 'what if 'game, and this often causes the story to be changed as I go along. I'm often surprised at what happens. And that's not so strange as it sounds.

AND HERE IS BILL'S RECIPE:

SIMPLE SALMON
ÁLA ANNIE ROSS

2 tablespoons olive oil
6 to 8 cloves chopped garlic
4 salmon filets
2½ cups teriyaki sauce

Heat the oil, add garlic, and then place filets in shallow baking dish. Pour teriyaki sauce over the salmon and place the sautéed garlic on top. Marinate for half an hour or so. Bake at 350°F for 12 to 14 minutes.

Be prepared for sheer bliss.

THE BIRTHDAY DINNER

Donna Andrews

Donna Andrews burst onto the mystery scene a scant while ago. In a very short space of time, she's won the Agatha, (twice!) the Anthony, the Barry, and the Romantic Times *award for best first mystery novel of 1999. She also won the Lefty for funniest mystery of 1999. Her most recent publications are* Leaping Loon *and* Click Here for Murder. *Donna is as droll as her fiction, and a frequent guest at mystery conventions.*

"But Meg," Dad said. "Your Aunt Millicent hasn't poisoned anyone in years."

"That's because she hasn't been out of the slammer for years," I said. "I'm not going to her birthday dinner."

"She wasn't in the slammer this last time," Dad said. "At least, I don't think that's the right slang for a psychiatric hospital."

"Correction: she hasn't been out of the slammer and/or loony bin for years," I said. "I'm still not going."

"But someone has to go," Mother said. "Or she'll think we don't trust her."

"Well, we don't," I said.

My parents looked at each other. My father blew his nose noisily, to remind me of the cold he'd come down with three days ago, when Aunt Millicent's invitation arrived. Mother sighed and gazed reproachfully at the ice pack that apparently wasn't doing much for her sick headache.

"I suppose we'll have to," Mother said, lying back as if the mere thought were too much for her.

"Oh, all right," I said. "I'll go. But I'm taking my own food."

"She'll be insulted," Mother said.

"I'll pretend I thought it was a potluck supper," I said. "Or that I'm on a special bland diet."

"She really is a rather good cook, you know," Dad said.

"Shall I bring you a doggie bag?"

WE would have been thirteen at table if everyone originally invited had come. Instead, we were five, all women, because Aunt Millicent only poisoned men. At least, that was the theory, since her previous two poisonings had been men. After serving twenty years for poisoning her own spouse, she'd poisoned a cousin's two-timing husband and spent another five years undergoing psychiatric treatment.

I planned on eating light. Two victims wasn't much of a pattern, as far as I was concerned. For all we knew, she might have some other way of selecting her victims. People who criticized her cooking. People who salted their food before tasting it. People who chewed with their mouths open.

"That's crazy," Mother said, when I expounded my theory to her.

"And Aunt Millicent isn't?"

She seemed sane enough when she opened the door,

ushered me into her overheated parlor, and disappeared into the kitchen with the pie I'd brought. Mother had finally agreed, after a long argument, that bringing a dessert wouldn't look too suspicious. Especially if I brought Mother's famous pumpkin pie, which took three times as long to make as any normal pumpkin pie. Not that Mother ever made it, of course, but she was the one who had originally found the recipe and cajoled one relative or another into making it for every major holiday for the last thirty years.

I was the first one there, and I perched politely on a lumpy, needlepoint chair seat while mentally reviewing all the lore about poison I'd tried to absorb before coming.

"Of course," Dad rasped, as we sat in his medical library, flipping through books, "there are plenty of odorless, colorless, tasteless poisons she could use. But somehow I think Millicent will play fair."

"Play fair? She poisoned two people; just how is that playing fair?"

"It all came out at the trial, remember?" Dad said, waving the transcript in one hand as he groped for the tissue box with the other. "Her husband Jack wouldn't have died if he hadn't eaten a second helping of pie after she specifically told him not to. In less than fatal doses, strychnine produces no symptoms, and no real ill effects."

"And when she poisoned poor Heidi's husband by putting nicotine in the bourbon?"

"Which was in a locked liquor cabinet," Dad pointed out. "He'd have been in no danger whatsoever if he'd behaved himself."

"Do you mean the fact that he picked the lock and drank the bourbon without permission, or the fact that he was using Aunt Millicent's house for a rendezvous with his mistress?"

"Well, neither was a very nice thing to do."

"And that makes her poisoning him all right?"

"No, but it makes her more predictable," Dad said. "She

laid traps and they fell into them. So I think she'll play fair, as she sees it, and I don't think anyone who does likewise is in any danger."

So what constituted playing fair, I wondered, gazing at a large box of chocolate truffles that sat on the coffee table. Unopened, though. Was this a test?

I glanced down and made sure my purse flap hadn't fallen open. I didn't think Aunt Millicent would appreciate all the antidotes Dad had insisted I bring. Not that I expected them to be of any use. What were the odds that if anyone started showing signs of poisoning, I could diagnose it accurately and administer the right antidote? Especially since most of the antidotes were, themselves, poisonous. I had more faith in my cell phone and 911.

For a while, it looked as if I would be the only guest, but eventually the other three brave souls showed up. Aunt Prudence, a bluff, hearty, sixtyish widow. Cousin Dolores, a meek, soft-spoken cousin whose frizzy ash-blond hair only compounded her resemblance to a sheep. And the never-tactful Mrs. Fenniman, who was so distantly a relative that even my family might have ignored the connection if she wasn't also my mother's best friend.

"Hell's bells," Mrs. Fenniman snorted, when it became obvious that we were the only guests. "She probably calculated her dosages for a dozen people. We're goners for sure."

"Ssshhh!" Dolores hissed, glancing anxiously at the door to the kitchen, where Aunt Millicent was making more noise and taking more time than seemed reasonable for the simple chore of finding napkins.

"Now, now," Aunt Prudence said. "We must simply stick together and we'll get through this just fine."

I wondered what she meant by sticking together. Only eating what Aunt Millicent ate? That would be the sensible plan. Of course, that would be a lot easier if Aunt Millicent would sit down and eat, instead of flitting back and forth to the kitchen in search of various forgotten items. The vegetables and dip she'd put out on the coffee table went largely untouched, since she was too busy with last-minute preparations to eat any of them, and the rest of us were too busy being suspicious. It was a pre-made dip, served in the original plastic container, so I was ready to dive in when Mrs. Fenniman, studying the surface, pronounced it too smooth. By which I suppose she meant Aunt Millicent could have stirred something in and then fixed the surface. No one felt much like sampling it after that. Dolores stirred up the surface, trying to make it look as if we'd eaten some, and when that didn't work, put some in a napkin and paid a quick visit to the powder room. Aunt Prudence contented herself with munching some celery sticks, after wiping them off with her handkerchief when Aunt Millicent wasn't in the room.

"Are you sure that's quite safe?" Dolores asked.

"Nonsense; how could she possibly poison celery?" Aunt Prudence said.

"The same way you freshen it when it gets too dry," I suggested. "Just put it in a glass of cold water and let it soak up enough liquid to replump."

It took Aunt Prudence an awfully long time to finish that last piece of celery.

Eventually, Aunt Millicent chivvied us, each carrying a barely touched glass of wine, into her candlelit, tapestry-lined dining room and brought in the first course—a tureen of delicately fragrant leek soup. It actually smelled quite good, and I could tell I wasn't the only one waiting impatiently for Aunt Millicent to finish serving and take the first spoonful.

Or the only one dismayed when she leaped up and ran back into the kitchen.

"I must check on the roast!" she called over her shoulder. "Don't wait! It's best piping hot!"

We all stared down at our bowls, breathing in the undeniably delectable steam for a long minute or two. Dolores rummaged through her purse as if hunting some elusive, urgently needed item. Aunt Prudence feigned deep interest in the flower arrangement. I frowned at the tapestry-covered wall separating us from the kitchen, and managed to avoid starting when I noticed something odd. One of the horses charging stiltedly through the woods appeared to have an eye in his rump.

Should I mention this to the others?

"Oh, hell," Mrs. Fenniman finally said. "Odds are she won't do it with the soup. She'll want to watch us squirm for a few more courses."

She picked up her soup spoon and dipped it into the bowl.

We all watched raptly as Mrs. Fenniman sipped the soup and paused, looking up at the chandelier. Then she grimaced. My heart skipped a beat, and Dolores gave a tiny shriek.

"No salt," Mrs. Fenniman said, reaching for the shaker. "I know it's supposed to be bad for you, but I can't eat a damned thing without salt."

She shook enough salt into the broth to turn it into brine, while the rest of us took tentative sips of our soup and agreed that yes, it was rather flat. The salt shaker made its way around the table, though Dolores refused it with a wan smile.

"I'm told I need to cut down," she said.

And I found myself pausing with shaker in hand, wondering if there were any poisons that looked like salt. Or that were activated when combined with sodium chloride.

The hell with it, I thought. Mrs. Fenniman's probably right. Once I added a little salt, the soup was excellent, and when I thought about it, the lack of salt made it easier to tell that the soup didn't have any unusual flavors or odors. I finished mine, as did Mrs. Fenniman. We were the only ones, apart from Aunt Millicent. In the brief time she perched when she finally returned from the kitchen, she consumed hers with gusto.

Aunt Prudence, who gardened avidly, took the lead when the salads arrived, elegant little mixed green salads with a small cluster of walnuts in the center. And our choice of dressings, blue cheese and raspberry vinaigrette, though these seemed destined to languish untasted in the center of the table. Apparently nobody's diet permitted salad dressings any more.

"Hmm," Aunt Prudence said, spearing a leaf with her fork and holding it up where she could look at it over her glasses. "A great many poisonous plants resemble salad greens."

Forks fell to the table.

"This is radicchio, though," she said, popping it into her mouth and chewing with an air of relief.

The others waited until Aunt Prudence had identified the major constituents of the salad before digging in. I shrugged, and reached for the blue cheese dressing, thinking that I may as well be hanged for a sheep as a lamb. The rest watched me intently, and when I didn't keel over halfway though my salad, I could see one or two looking regretfully at the dressings.

And even more regretfully when Aunt Millicent reappeared and consumed a generous portion of the raspberry vinaigrette with her salad.

"Meg, I'm so sorry your parents couldn't come," she said, over the salad. "I did so want to thank them."

"Thank them?" I echoed, pausing with my fork halfway to my mouth. Being singled out for any reason reminded me of getting called on in class when I hadn't read the homework assignment.

"For writing me all those years," she said, with a seemingly genuine smile of gratitude. "You have no idea how much that meant to me."

In the ensuing silence, I could hear the crunch as she bit into a slice of radish.

"Well, some people are better than others at this letter writing stuff," Mrs. Fenniman said, finally.

"You were allowed to get letters?" Aunt Prudence said. "I wish I'd known."

Cousin Dolores merely whimpered faintly.

"So thoughtful. I know they would have enjoyed this evening enormously. Ah, well. Another time, perhaps."

So, did this answer my most burning question? Which, oddly enough, was not whether Aunt Millicent had put strychnine in the merlot, but why my loving parents had sent me off to face danger in their stead? Had they guessed that Aunt Millicent intended to take revenge on all the relatives who had abandoned her during her exile, and known that their kindness had given them—and by proxy, me—immunity?

Even so, wouldn't the same family loyalty that inspired all those letters ensure that Mother would do anything possible to prevent a wholesale slaughter of her relatives, however ungracious they may have been? So why wasn't she here trying to do something? And Dad, whose love of mysteries made him so happy to have a pen pal in the joint—why wasn't he here to avert a real crime?

Either they didn't anticipate any danger or, more likely, they expected me to figure out Aunt Millicent's intentions and foil them. If that was the case, I had no idea how to begin. Disappointing your parents' expectations isn't supposed to have fatal consequences.

"Have some more wine, everyone," Aunt Millicent said, as she began to circle the table, collecting our salad plates.

Cousin Dolores sighed, and I could understand why. We were probably in for another lengthy period of making polite conversation and listening to every noise in the kitchen while Aunt Millicent prepared the next course. As if we could somehow hear the telltale sound of a poison bottle being opened.

"Let me help you with that," I found myself saying. I stood up, holding my plate, and picked up Mrs. Fenniman's.

"You don't need to, dear," Aunt Millicent said.

"No, but I want to," I said. "And it's not fair, when you've gone to all the trouble of cooking, for you to do all the work."

"Well, if you insist," Aunt Millicent said. She didn't really seem put out. The others looked relieved. I suppose they thought having a pair of eyes in the kitchen made them safer. Nonsense. I assumed that Aunt Millicent's willingness to let me help meant either that she wasn't going to poison anything—that would be nice—or that whatever poison she had chosen was already in place.

I saw nothing unusual in the kitchen—apart from noticing that a convenient moth hole in the tapestry Aunt Millicent had hung over the former pass-through gave a wonderful view of the dining room. Aunt Millicent chattered away cheerfully, all the while ordering me about in the polite yet matter-of-fact manner aunts generally use.

The pork roast came out of the oven, smelling divine, and Aunt Millicent set me to carving, which seemed to eliminate the suspicion that she'd poisoned one side, or one end, or anything tricky like that. I was reassured that she came to look over my shoulder and nibbled little bits that fell off as I carved. I wasn't that thrilled with the mixed vegetables, though. They contained quite a lot of mushrooms.

Mushrooms. Dad was fond of calling them the accidental poisoner's best friend.

Then again, where would Aunt Millicent find poisonous mushrooms? It wasn't as if she could pop down to some poisoner's central warehouse that supplied them in bulk to the trade.

Not that I didn't plan to focus on my meat until she'd started on her own mushrooms.

During the main course, we guests hit on the tactic of monopolizing the conversation, never letting Aunt Millicent get a word in. She still spent an uncanny amount of time flitting out to the kitchen and picking at her food, but at least she gradually consumed enough of the contents of her own plate that we all relaxed a bit and began to nibble at ours. It took a while, though; it was pushing ten by the time she finally announced that we had pie for dessert.

I left the others discreetly checking their watches, no doubt wondering if they could plead an early bedtime, and followed Aunt Millicent back out to the kitchen. She was shifting things around in her crowded refrigerator, digging down to where she'd stashed the pie. I went over to the counter by the sink where I saw half a dozen elegant dessert plates waiting. I was about to pick them up and take them over to the table where Aunt Millicent was setting the pie when—

"Don't!"

I started, and then froze, with my hand a few inches from the stack of plates. Her voice held a note of genuine alarm.

"I use those so seldom that I always like to wash them before I use them," Aunt Millicent said, her voice calm again, as she gently moved me aside. "They get so dusty."

They looked squeaky clean to me. Aunt Millicent pulled on a pair of gloves and began washing them. Odd way of doing the dishes. Most people immerse them in a sink full of water. Or just hold them under the tap if the purpose is to rinse off dust rather than remove food debris. Aunt Millicent was squirting dish soap liberally on each plate and scrubbing them meticulously.

"This is going to take some time," Aunt Millicent said, sighing, as she finished the first plate. "I really should have done it earlier today. There are some everyday dessert plates in the cabinet just to the right of the sink. Why don't you serve the pie on those?"

I found the substitute plates and cut five pieces of pie while Aunt Millicent worked on her dishwashing.

A contact poison, I thought. She's smeared contact poison on the plates. DMSO plus cyanide or nicotine or . . . well, any number of things. But she didn't want me hurt apparently. Or maybe she changed her mind about hurting anyone. Why?

I glanced over, carefully. The darkness outside had turned

the window above the sink reflective, like a smoked mirror.
I could see that she was smiling slyly.

I pretended to be focused on the pie. So I noticed when
she picked up a plate, shifted it to her left hand, and
scratched her nose with her forefinger before slathering the
plate with soap.

By the time I finished slicing the pie and arranging the
plates on the serving tray—and I made a precise, time-
consuming job of it—she still hadn't keeled over.

There was no contact poison.

She was toying with us.

"There's whipped cream in the refrigerator, dear," she
said, removing her gloves after the last plate and placing
them beside the sink with her sponge.

She picked up the tray with the pie slices, leaving me to
follow with the whipped cream.

Everyone else sat in silence as Aunt Millicent heaped
whipped cream on the pie slices, passed them out, and flit-
ted out into the kitchen again for something.

Aunt Prudence sighed. And then she sniffed sharply. Put
her nose closer to the pie and sniffed again.

Mrs. Fenniman and Dolores did the same.

"Almonds!" Dolores whispered.

I had a hard time keeping a straight face. Yes, cyanide fa-
mously smells of almonds, as any good Agatha Christie fan
knows. So does Mother's pumpkin pie, thanks to the half
cup of Amaretto that's part of the recipe. Every one of these
ninnies had eaten Mother's pie on at least a dozen occasions.

"Don't let me forget to thank your mother for sending the
pie," Aunt Millicent said, as she bustled back to the table.

The other guests breathed audible sighs of relief at learning of the pie's presumably benign origins and picked up
their forks.

"Wasn't it lucky that I had the whipped cream!" Aunt
Millicent added, beaming.

Forks froze.

"Wonderful luck," I said, cutting off a huge forkful of pie and whipped cream and shoving it into my mouth.

Was it a trick of the light, or had she just winked at me?

Somehow, everyone managed to finish her pie. I had seconds. Everyone stared at me, aghast. Except Aunt Millicent, now openly beaming her approval.

Aunt Millicent made no objection to my helping with the dessert dishes. I could hear the other guests chattering cheerfully in the foyer. Perhaps their unusually warm farewells were inspired by relief at having survived the meal and guilt over suspecting Aunt Millicent.

Probably a good thing I wasn't leaving with them. I'd have been so tempted to spoil their relief as soon as Aunt Millicent closed the door behind us, by snapping out a reminder that not all poisons acted immediately. Some took hours or even days for the first symptoms to appear.

Of course, keeping that in mind, perhaps I should wait a few days before I started feeling too smug about having figured out Aunt Millicent's game.

"Well, I think that went off splendidly," Aunt Millicent said.

"Yes, everything tasted divine," I said. Which was true.

"Thank you, dear," she said. "Yes, quite splendidly. In fact, I was thinking perhaps I should have another dinner for all those poor people who were sick tonight. What do you think?"

Another dinner for all those cowardly souls who left the four of us to carry the ball, I thought.

"Wonderful idea," I said. "Though this time of year, it's going to be awfully hard to find a time when someone or other isn't ailing."

"Well, I don't give up easily," Aunt Millicent said. "I'll start talking to people about a date tomorrow. And Meg, I do hope you'll come back. I know you'd enjoy yourself even more next time."

Yes, there was definitely a twinkle in her eye.

"Wouldn't miss it for the world," I said.

DEAN AND CLAUDIA ASK DONNA:

Q: *Are you writing full time, now?*

A: Yes. I left my day job in 2001. Writing one series with a day job was hard enough. Writing two would have been impossible. And now I have time to do a few other things—like occasionally writing short stories.

Q: *And aren't we glad! What is your work routine like?*

A: Actually, I'm still trying out work routines, seeing what is best for me. About the only consistent thread is that they don't involve getting up early. I've never figured out why the world admires people who get up at five A.M. to work on their novels. And I use quotas. Word or page quotas, not time quotas. It's so easy to spend hours doing research and searching for the perfect word and fritter away what could have been a productive working day. Quotas keep me honest, so I set deadlines and I assign myself quotas.

Q: *How do you work out the story? Do you outline? Do you revise a good deal?*

A: I outline first. For me, the outline is a key part of my creative process. My outlines often run twenty to thirty pages and contain not just the key events and clues to the mystery but bits of dialogue that come to me while I'm working on it. And yes, I revise a lot. Luckily, the computer makes this easy.

Q: *Which comes first for you—character, plot, or setting?*

A: Well, I guess what comes first is the killer idea. This usually involves putting a character or a group of characters into a particular situation. I figure out who is killed and who did it later, as the characters and the plot emerge from the situation. I usually get the main character's voice fairly early, With my story for you and Dean, I heard the opening conversation between Meg and her father long before I had any idea what they were talking about.

AND HERE IS DONNA'S RECIPE:

MOTHER'S SINFULLY RICH PUMPKIN MOUSSE PIE

Like Meg's mother, my mom found this recipe in the *Newport Daily News Press* about thirty years ago. It's much more work than the average pumpkin pie, but the Langslow and Andrews families think it's worth the trouble.

1 9-inch pie shell, baked and cooled
1 envelope unflavored gelatin
1/2 cup praline liqueur or Amaretto
1 16-ounce can of pumpkin
4 lightly beaten egg yolks
1/2 cup packed dark brown sugar
1/2 cup granulated sugar
1/4 cup butter, melted
1 teaspoon ground cinnamon
1/2 teaspoon salt
1/4 teaspoon ground cloves
4 egg whites
1/8 teaspoon cream of tartar
3/4 cup heavy cream

Soften gelatin in liqueur. Set aside.

Heat pumpkin and all ingredients through the cloves in a saucepan over medium heat. Stir constantly until lightly boiling and slightly thickened.

Remove from heat and beat in the gelatin mixture.
Cool, but do not let harden.

Beat the egg whites, cream of tartar, and a pinch of salt
to soft peaks.

Whip heavy cream.

Fold egg whites and whipped cream into pumpkin mixture.

Pour into pie crust.

Chill until firm.

WHERE THE WILDFLOWERS BLOOM

Nick DiChario

Nick DiChario's short stories have appeared in science fiction, fantasy, and mainstream publications. He has been nominated for two Hugo Awards and a World Fantasy Award. He is Director of Programming for Writers Books, a non-profit literary center in Rochester, New York. He has taught creative writing at universities and is the Fiction Editor for HazMat Review, a literary journal. Nick's short stories have been reprinted in TheYear's Best Fantasy and Horror, The Best Alternate History Stories of the Twentieth Century, *and many others.*

Each new day, Henry hopes that he'll not have to think about it anymore. But of course he does. He thinks about it in the morning, even before he's fully awake. He thinks about it late at night as the TV flickers him into restless sleep. It's his first thought and his last thought every day, and how many millions of thoughts in-between he cannot even begin to guess. He thinks about the shame and public humiliation. He thinks about the injustice of it all, how the district attorney made him a scapegoat, and how there is nothing he can do to save himself—his job as assistant D.A., his career as a lawyer, his ruined self-image and equally ruined reputation. He thinks.

Had it happened in a small town, he might have been able to run far enough away from the publicity to live a normal life in some other small town. Had it happened in a big city like Los Angeles or New York or Chicago, where political indiscretions are a normal and even integral part of the not-so-hidden landscape, people might have believed he was set up to take a fall—he might have even gained some of the public's sympathy. But it happened in Tuscany, New York, a moderate town in every way: moderate in population and religion and government, moderate in business and education and entertainment, moderate in fashion and roadwork and garbage collection. Here in this moderate town, Henry is big news. There is no escaping his mistakes, regardless of who is to blame for them.

HENRY meets Joyce at the farm market. He bumps into her as they both reach for a summer squash that's as dark yellow as a yield sign. Her laughter catches him by surprise, maybe because it has been so long since he's noticed anyone laughing. She insists he keep the squash, but only if he agrees to buy her a cup of coffee. Standing there partially blinded by the sun, Henry doesn't know what to say, so he allows Joyce to cradle his elbow and lead him off.

They chat over coffee, but she has "a million and one chores to run" and can't linger. "Come to my restaurant this Sunday evening, seven o'clock," she says, handing him a hastily scribbled napkin-note with the name *Kyle's* written on it. Henry has heard of this restaurant. It's the hottest new place in town. "I'm closed Sunday, but drive around back and ring the service bell. I'll let you in. Do you know the address?"

"It's near the airport, isn't it?"

"Yes, only about a mile north on Grand Avenue. You can be the guinea pig for my new sweet potato soup. I've been working on the recipe for God-knows-how-long to get it just right."

"I'll be there," says Henry, surprising himself, folding the note neatly in thirds and tucking it into his wallet as if it were a winning lottery ticket.

KYLE'S Restaurant looks small from the outside, but something about its demeanor—perhaps the way it's fronted by short, sprawling maple trees with leathery red leaves, or the way it's eclipsed from behind by a gigantic, sagging linden tree—suggests depth and unexplored space. It has the sad look of a nineteenth-century home, not so much in need of repair as in need of someone to love it. The restaurant rests on the edge of a public park, where the wildflowers bloom.

Henry's finger is poised inches away from the service bell. He's not sure why he hesitates, except that he has led a life full of uncertainty, and he still hasn't learned how to change the small things that could make a difference in the way he meets the world, the things that might make him happier if he learned to give in, or give up. His timidity, he understands, has cost him dearly, lending the weight of inertia to his fraught relationship with his parents and siblings; his ruined marriage; the lousy deal he made when he bought his Toyota; the poor performance of his 401k plan. Even now, when Henry hasn't had a chance to relax and enjoy himself with a woman in months, he is daunted by the task of ringing Joyce's bell. And he's dwelling, of course. Oh, yes, he couldn't survive a day without the dwelling. A bad habit that has only gotten worse since the scandal.

"I will *not* back down," Henry insists. "I need this." Yet his finger remains frozen over the bell. He stares at the lines in his forty-five-year-old-hand. He is reminded of his father's strong hands, of the time in the park when he was just a boy and his father took him out to fly a kite. Henry was afraid to hold onto the kite string for fear of being dragged off his feet. The way the string tugged at him with hidden power, the way it disappeared into the sky, made his heart race inside his tiny chest. If he held on, he would be ripped off the face of the earth, the solid earth, that place where his feet met the ground and somehow made life possible. He refused to hang onto the kite string unless his father held on with him. "All right," his father said. "Together." It was the first time Henry heard disappointment in his father's voice, although it would not be the last.

A jet takes off from the airport, shakes the earth, and wakes Henry out of his trance. He watches the plane disappear over Tuscany Park, and then he presses his finger forward into the bell as if following the pilot's flight plan.

SHE is a lovely woman, Joyce is, although Henry is uncertain as to what that means, exactly. He has heard the term "lovely" used many times to describe women—so many times that he knows it's a cliché—but Joyce seems to fit his vague impression of it. She looks early fortyish, neither falsely beautiful nor inherently unattractive. She is lean and, when she greets him, stands straight with her chin tilted at a slight upward angle. For her date with Henry, she has chosen a black dress that follows her shape without choking it, a knee-length sleeveless that compliments her short-cropped, manila-frosted hair.

Inside, the restaurant is neat and spotlessly clean, boxier than Henry expected, with carpeting the color and texture of knotted rope. Attached to the walls are rectangular light fixtures that remind him of bullion—hollow, shiny ingots of gold. At first he thinks the restaurant smells of potpourri, but then he notices the flowers, the wildflowers, laid out beautifully in vases throughout the dining area.

Now that Henry is in among the tables and chairs, he's not nearly as nervous as he was outside. He knows nothing about Joyce other than what she revealed over coffee. She goes to the market on Saturday to buy fruits and vegetables. She is looking to lease a new car, something small and fuel-efficient with one of those hybrid engines. She works out at the gym twice a week, although it's not nearly enough to fight off her "swiftly aging metabolism." There is one soap opera she videotapes, but he can't recall which one—*General Hospital,* maybe.

Henry imagines Joyce a competent businesswoman. She has raised a conservative investment portfolio that has allowed her to indulge a fantasy and open her own restaurant. She has taken a hit in the stock market, as everyone else has these days, but she hasn't suffered nearly as much damage as the speculators. Henry could be wrong about all this, but he doesn't care. It's nice to think about someone else for a change. It gives him a quick thrill, a sudden freefall out of himself that is both real and unreal enough to create the illusion of pleasure.

"Your flowers are magnificent," he says. "They smell . . . ." He hesitates here, not wanting to say overwhelming, although it's the first word that comes to mind. The scent is so strong Henry is reminded of the harsh perfume of a funeral parlor. "They smell so fresh."

"Thank you. Do you really like them? They're wildflowers from the park."

The restaurant, Joyce tells him, is the beneficiary of scores of wildflowers that spill over from Tuscany Park— mountain laurel, mint, goldenrod, chicory, lilies, and countless others. She never really cared much about flowers until she bought the restaurant.

"The groundskeepers for the Parks Department don't mind my clipping and trimming as long as I don't stray too far from my own property, so my restaurant always has fresh flowers. I was going, to name the place Wildflowers, but . . . then . . . well . . . I changed my mind."

"Why Kyle's?" asks Henry.

"I named it after my son . . . my only son . . . my only child. Would you like to see his pictures?"

"Sure."

Joyce leads Henry into the waiting area, where she has set out several café style tables and chairs in a manner that at first appears haphazard until the feng shui kicks in.

"You must love your son very much. The room belongs to him."

What Henry means to say is the room is a shrine to him, but he doesn't want Joyce to misconstrue it as an insult. The photographs that document her son's life are as touching as they are impressive. Baby pictures, snapshots from Little League, birthday parties, a grade-school play where Kyle is wearing a bent and sloppy pair of angel's wings, a series of yearbook photos, a picture of Kyle playing glockenspiel in a marching band. He is a handsome boy, thin and long-legged with a square jaw, inherited from his mother, no doubt. His hair is sandy and his eyes teal. In some photos there is a man, but after the age of twelve or so, the man disappears, and the boy and his mother carry on without him. An ex-husband? Henry decides not to ask. All in good time, if he's lucky enough to get that far.

"This is my Kyle," Joyce says, her voice full of music.

"He's a fine-looking boy. You must be very proud of him."

"Oh, yes. He means the world to me. Can I get you some tea?"

"That sounds great," Henry fibs. He's never been much of a tea drinker, but he's not about to say no to anything Joyce has to offer.

THEY sit together at one of the tables, and Joyce says, "This used to be a tavern before I bought the place, but I won't serve alcoholic beverages—I don't believe in drinking and driving."

Henry admires her principles, but he doesn't know how long the restaurant will last if Joyce refuses to serve alcohol. He decides to avoid the topic and concentrate on his tea. It's quite good. Henry finds it smooth and nicely hot with a potent flavor, spicy in a way that reminds him of Indian delicacies. To his surprise, he takes comfort in those first few refined sips as he sits with Joyce in the empty restaurant. After a time she brings out the sweet potato soup. Henry is surprised at how strong and rich he finds the flavor, and how thick and pulpy the soup is, a sweet puree that doesn't so much assault the taste buds as it does tease them.

He takes comfort in the wildflowers surrounding them. He takes comfort in Joyce herself, who talks so generously about her son's interests in school—a private school, St. Thomas Aquinas—his accomplishments on the soccer field, his recent trip to Ireland where he visited Dublin and Galway and Cork and kissed the Blarney Stone, and his favorite music that she promptly slips into the CD player.

Henry wants Joyce to keep talking because he has become prosaic since the scandal and hates the sound of his own voice. Joyce is such a giving woman, he decides, so open and honest, the sort of woman who could and should and would love a man like Henry, poor misunderstood Henry. The sort of woman he needs in his life after a wife who bore witness to so many of his failures. Henry, also to his surprise, likes the music. He finds it strangely soothing.

"R. Carlos Nakai," Joyce says. "He's Native American. Lakota. He plays a wooden flute that he made out of red cedar. The sound is . . . I don't know . . . haunting . . . mysterious, don't you think?"

"Yes. It's not at all what I expected. Most teenagers like head-banging rock'n roll, don't they?"

"Kyle isn't like most teens. He's an individual. I raised him to be strong-willed."

"You're a good mother."

"Don't be silly. You don't even know me. If I were a good

mother I could protect him from . . . well . . . I could protect him. Do you have children?"

"No. My ex-wife and I tried, but it didn't happen for us."

Henry isn't sure why he tells Joyce such a personal detail
about his marriage, something he hasn't even told his family. Maybe because Joyce has made him feel safe and here
they are, after all, sitting in this room that belongs to Kyle,
a room that seems—strangely, inexplicably—to demand an
honest accounting.

"Is that why the marriage broke up?" she asks.

Henry shrugs and immediately regrets it, thinking he's
betrayed a lack of interest in his own fate, a sentiment closer
to the truth than he cares to admit. "No. We were together
for almost twenty years. Things began to break down when I
was going through some difficulties on the job, when she
couldn't handle the pressure, the public . . . the public . . . ."

"Humiliation," adds Joyce.

So there it is, everything out on the table. Henry was
hoping to avoid this conversation for a while longer. But
perhaps it's better this way. Now he won't have to guess how
much Joyce knows and when to tell her what she doesn't
know. If his past is going to ruin their relationship, better to
do it immediately, before boyish optimism kicks in.

"How much do you know?" Henry asks.

"What I've read in the newspapers and heard on TV.
Same as most people, I suppose."

"How much do you want to know?"

"How much do you want to tell me?"

Needless fencing, Henry tells himself. Move on, or she'll
think you have something to hide.

"I'm not stringing for the newspapers, Henry, if that's
what you're worried about. I didn't invite you here to get a
story."

"I never thought that." Although he should have. The
press has hounded him for months, cornered him in his
driveway, at the movies, in the supermarket, pumping gas,

at the Dunkin' Donuts drive-thru . . . . "I'll be glad to tell you everything."

And he does.

He tells her about the day the D.A. came into his office and slammed the door behind him and said, "You're fired." How he stood in front of Henry, leaning threateningly forward, accusing him of "failing to prosecute." Henry remembers the D.A.'s hands gripping the edge of the desk—small, powerful hands—although Henry didn't make the connection then, he makes it now—hands so much like his father's.

"I warned you about the time limits months ago," Henry told the D.A., a tremor in his voice that was equal parts anger and fear. "I told you how understaffed we were and how we'd lose some cases to timely prosecution if we didn't get help taking them to trial. I gave you a list of over a hundred arrests that would be thrown out if we didn't start working them immediately. How can you—"

"I don't have time to listen to your excuses," the D.A. said. "I have a press conference scheduled in ten minutes. Timely trials are *your* responsibility. When was the last time you read your job description? I'm going to have to answer for this publicly, but I'm pointing the finger at *you*." And the finger did point, so close to Henry's nose that he could see the tiny hairs on the D.A.'s index finger standing on end. "If I were you, I'd get out of the building before the press conference is over. The journalists will be hunting you down."

He tells Joyce all of this, and more. He tells her the way he felt. Victimized, violated, angry, bitter, helpless, depressed. Somehow things got away from him, he tells her. His life became a runaway construction project, a job he miscalculated and grossly underbid. To fix things he required more labor, heavier equipment, better materials, and no one was willing to cut him a break on his over-extended resources.

There is something cathartic in the telling, something that reminds him of his childhood confessions to Father Wesley, when he thought there was a God and forgiveness was an inalienable right of all blessed Catholics. As he tells her the story, he notices Joyce wringing her hands. They are lean hands, her fingernails short and unpolished. He's not sure why he's suddenly thinking so much about hands. He glances down at his own as if the answer might be there, but he finds nothing special in them, only the hands that let go of the kite string all those years ago, the hands that let go of his job, his wife, his life, the hands that have become so accustomed to letting go he can't remember the last time they held onto anything.

"I was the perfect sucker for the D.A. He could blame me and get rid of his caseload at the same time. By waiting until it was too late to prosecute, he cleared his backlog in an afternoon without having to extend his budget. I'd say it was the worst day of my life, except that I've relived it every day since."

"I'm so sorry all this had to happen, Henry."

"I used to believe in justice; I dedicated my life to it; but I've come to realize there's no such thing."

"Don't shun God's wisdom."

There is kindness in Joyce's tone, compassion that goes just far enough to annoy Henry. He wants her to be angry for him, with him, but she is not. And the mention of God concerns him. He lost faith in God a long time ago. It doesn't bode well for their future if she's fond of quoting the Bible.

So instead of getting into it, Henry decides to change direction and rave about her soup. This prompts Joyce to bring him another bowl. As Henry sips the soup, Joyce walks over to a photograph of her son and brushes its platinum frame, as gently as if she were stroking the throat of an injured sparrow.

"All humans have certain rights, rights that come from their equal and common nature. That's what St. Thomas

Aquinas says. Justice is a *debitum,* it's owed to people, it's a natural right, and a natural right follows a rational nature. That's what Kyle says."

Something has shifted in Joyce's manner, or perhaps in the way Henry perceives her. She is looking at her son's picture, listening to the eerie sound of the Lakota flute on Kyle's favorite CD—the hollow, perfect song of an owl—as if it's speaking directly to her, and Henry has become a distraction. There is a disconcerting puissance in her calm.

"My son loves St. Thomas Aquinas. Strange for a young man to have a hero like that these days, don't you think?"

Yes, true, Henry wants to say, but when he tries to speak his lips feel oddly torpid, and the words don't quite break the surface of conversation. Henry's heart flutters. He drops his spoon into the soup bowl, and it lands with an odd thud, too loud and slowly resonant to be real.

"Human freedom and human rationality are linked," Joyce says. "A free person has dominion over his acts and has a responsibility to claim them, don't you agree? That's why animals don't have rights. They have no control over their actions. God made them simply to act, not to reason. We have to be better than the animals. We have to recognize justice and demand *debitum* when and where it's due. People have rights to just and moral laws, Henry, and when those laws are violated, the virtuous society must teach virtue. Don't you agree?"

Henry doesn't know if he agrees. Joyce has lost him somewhere in her logic. He can't seem to think straight. He can't speak. The numbness in his lips has reached back into his face. His jaw is stiff. Again the heart flutter. A cold sweat.

"My son agrees," says Joyce. "My son . . . how can I say this? My son has a justice owed to him, and someone must pay, and since a person is ordered by nature to give another his due, it's my responsibility to collect that debt."

What are you talking about? thinks Henry. *And why can't I ask you? Why can't I form the words?*

Joyce sways to the flute music. Once again she runs her fingers over the platinum frame that contains her son.

"This is Kyle's senior picture. Shortly after it was taken, a drunk driver in one of those giant sports utility vehicles ran a red light, jumped a curb, and killed him. My son was rammed into the side of a construction barrier, crushed, broken to bits, except for his face—his beautiful face—isn't that strange? You would have thought him asleep in his coffin, if you didn't know that underneath his clothes every single bone in his body was pulverized. There wasn't an organ left in him, not one, and he was hoping to donate those organs when he died—that's the kind of boy my son is, always thinking of others, such a good boy, such a special boy, my Kyle."

Henry tries to stand, gets halfway out of his chair before his legs give out. He reaches for the table, but there is no strength in his arms. When he falls, he does not feel the ground against him or the gravity that holds him to it.

"The man was charged with DWI, but he never went to trial because you, Henry, you failed to prosecute on time. I'm sure you've guessed what that means by now. I'm sorry that it has to be this way. I'll have to kill the others, too, of course. The man who drove the SUV. He's free now, walking the streets. We can't have that, can we? And I'll have to kill the D.A. after hearing your story. I hadn't planned on that, but if what you say is true, then he must be punished as well."

Henry would like to say he's sorry, but he can't. He'd like to go back and change things, make things right, but it's too late. He feels as if he's being poured down a funnel. There are forces swirling around him, and he is completely at their mercy. He can't move anything now except his hands—how marvelously ironic. He's fairly certain it's the soup that has poisoned him; although it might have been the tea. It doesn't matter. He's been poisoned for a long time anyway, hasn't he?

Joyce steps to the window and glances out at the fading sunset. "It will be dark soon. I'll bury you out back near the park, where the wildflowers bloom. The groundskeepers don't mind my digging around out there. They won't find the overturned earth unusual. Then I'll drive your car to the airport and leave it in long-term parking. I'll enjoy the walk back. It's a nice evening for a stroll. It'll be awhile before anyone notices your car has been abandoned. When they finally do, the police will figure you've run away. Why not? Wouldn't anyone in your situation?"

"And who will punish you?" Henry asks. He has no idea how he manages to get the words out, how they move so quickly from his mind past his lips, but he's certain they are his final words. A cold, numb death is moving in.

The numbness reminds him of when he tried to become an alcoholic. It was after the scandal hit the papers, after his wife moved out. Henry tried going out to bars, but he was still too recognizable, so he bought bottles of wine and vodka and got drunk at home, night after night, hoping to achieve blackouts and memory loss. He would get dizzy and sick to his stomach. He would watch his bedroom spin and he'd vomit. The next morning, alas, he would remember all of it. He was a lousy drunk, just like he was a lousy everything else. Henry couldn't do anything right or wrong of his own free will. He always needed help or hindrance to succeed or fail. He was a burden even to himself. All he wanted to accomplish with the drinking was to take control of his life, even if that meant nothing more than self-destruction. Eventually he gave it up. He didn't have the stamina for it. He wasn't a natural. The numbness, he decided, was just another kind of pain, a gentle torture.

Joyce steps away from the window and kneels beside him. "Dear Henry," she says, in a voice that falls somewhere between a whisper and a dream. Her hands move to touch his face, but he can't feel the contact. "Who will punish me?

I've already been punished. Don't you see that? I've already been punished more than you will ever know."

Henry thinks about the time he went to New York City and found a *Zagat* someone left on a bench at the train station. He was on his way to a fancy hotel on Madison Avenue for a seminar, but on a whim he flipped the book open to a random page, pointed at a restaurant, and asked the cabby to drive him there for dinner. The restaurant, Lespinasse, was at the St. Regis Hotel, where he feasted on a decadent French meal fit for a king. It cost him a king's ransom, too, but he didn't care. It was the only time he could remember being spontaneous about anything.

What a dull and careful life I've led, thinks Henry. He has chalked each moment of his mediocre existence onto a blackboard so that it could be easily erased, so that it would leave no permanent impression. Wiping the slate clean, he understands, is no tragedy. It's a blessing, a kindness, a mercy. Thank you, Joyce, dear sweet thoughtful, philosophical, lovable, blackhearted, vengeful Joyce. Thank you for euthanizing this pathetic little creature.

Henry sees the string then, the kite string, and he reaches out to grab hold of it. He feels it pull against his grip, feels it tug. This time he holds on. This time he allows it to carry him off the face of the earth, the solid ground, that place where life has been made impossible. He knows that if he holds on just a bit longer he won't have to worry about anything anymore—the disgrace, the public humiliation, the injustice of it all. It feels good, finally, to hold onto something and at the same time let it go. It seems to Henry that this is the secret to life, and he's not in the least bit disappointed to learn it only when he's dying. To learn it at all, Henry realizes, is a gift.

The music plays on—Kyle's favorite music—the low moan of an Lakota flute that fades ever so softly into a meaningless memory.

DEAN AND CLAUDIA ASK NICK:

Q: *How do ideas for short stories come to you? Quickly? Or do they ripen over time?*
A: I think the best short stories come in a snapshot. A writer, like a good photographer, needs to see something special in the mundane. And recognize the best snapshots when they present themselves. Alfred Hitchcock once said, "Drama is life with the dull bits cut out." So you take a picture of life and develop the film in the private darkroom of the writer's imagination. Maybe that sounds a bit spooky. I hope not. It's really a very natural process, although not necessarily a simple one. It takes a combination of awareness, inspiration, honesty, patience, and dogged determination to get things done.

Q: *Most of your other work falls into the category of magical realism. Do the conventions of the mystery story present any unique challenges?*
A: Each individual story presents its own unique challenges, regardless of genre, and I don't like to dwell too heavily upon conventions. An addiction to form and function will kill an idea faster than a dyspeptic editor. There is a quote I've always found helpful, though, whenever I am writing any kind of story. John Gardner said, "There is no great art without a certain strangeness." I like that. It reminds me that a writer needs to be different. Personal and unafraid. The real challenge for any writer, after all, is to connect emotionally as well as intellectually to readers, and sometimes that takes a bit of daring. Otherwise you and your audience get stuck with little more than an exercise in craft.

Q: *Wow. So, where did your recipe come from?*
A: This one is a combination of experimentation and dumb luck.

AND HERE IS NICK'S RECIPE:

SWEET POTATO SOUP

1 tablespoon of vegetable oil
1 large chopped onion
2 large stalks of chopped celery
2–4 teaspoons of Indian spices or Italian seasonings (to taste) and a pinch of salt and pepper
1 large can of diced tomatoes
6 ounces of green beans cut into bite-size pieces
4 (or 5) cups of vegetable broth
1 cup apple juice
2 (or 3) large sweet potatoes, peeled and diced
2 large carrots, sliced thin

Warm up the oil in a soup pot over medium-high heat.

Sauté onion, celery, Indian spices, salt, and pepper for about 5 minutes or until your veggies are tender.

Stir in tomatoes with broth, carrots, sweet potatoes, green beans, and juice.

Bring to a boil. Reduce heat to low and simmer, stirring occasionally, for about a half hour.

Prep time and cook time altogether runs about an hour. Makes approximately six servings. Enjoy! It's a hearty soup, loaded with vitamins, and this recipe is not fatal.

THE PROOF OF THE PUDDING

A Molly Murphy Story

Rhys Bowen

Rhys Bowen is an elegant Englishwoman and winner of both the Agatha and the Herodotus Award for Best Historical Novel. Her popular Constable Evans series is a favorite world wide. We asked her for a story featuring her new series character, Molly Murphy.

N*ew York, 1901*
       I had certainly not intended to work at Christmas. In fact, I was looking forward to my first Christmas in New York City. It would be a real celebration, unlike the dismal affairs at home in Ireland, with my father slumped drunk in front of the fire by midday and the rest of us tiptoeing around so we didn't wake him. So I would have turned down the job, if I hadn't read the signature on the letter. Samuel T. Wilcox, esquire.

*   *   *

I had only been in New York for less than a year, but even I knew about Sam Wilcox. He was an important figure in New York politics, outspoken opponent of Tammany Hall corruption, currently a state senator but clearly with his sights set on higher things.

The letter was short and to the point. He had a matter of the uttermost delicacy that he wished to discuss and would I present myself at his house at 59 Fifth Avenue. Naturally I was intrigued. A matter of the uttermost delicacy? From what I had read of Sam Wilcox, he saw himself as a champion of moral rectitude. Christmas was only four days away but my curiosity got the better of me. Besides, it was a mere hop, skip, and jump from my own humble abode on Patchin Place. Unlike the rest of New York gentry, he had not moved uptown to a more fashionable address near the park, but kept the family home on what used to be the swank part of Fifth Avenue. I put on my business suit, attempted to tuck my flyaway hair beneath my one presentable hat, and set out for Fifth Avenue.

It had snowed the night before and the streets were piled with mounds of gray, mud-spattered slush. Little boys with brooms were earning pennies at every corner by sweeping the crossings clean. I turned up my collar against the bitter wind and hurried toward Fifth Avenue. Fifty-nine was a solid brick building in a row of once fashionable homes. I knocked and was admitted by a crisply starched maid.

After my card had been presented, I was led to a gloomy gentleman's study at the rear of the house—all leather and books, with the lingering smell of pipe tobacco. Mr. Wilcox rose from his desk to shake my hand.

"So good of you to come at this busy time of year, Miss Murphy."

He was a larger-than-life figure with impressive whiskers and a heavy gold watch chain draped across an ample paunch. He leaned toward me confidentially. "I understand that you are an investigator, Miss Murphy. I have a matter I need investigated—with the uttermost discretion."

Those words usually preceded a divorce investigation. Surely that champion of morality didn't suspect his wife of infidelity? I nodded and waited for him to proceed.

"I suspect that one of our servants has been stealing from us." His voice had dropped to a low murmur. "I want you to find out which one."

"Stealing? What kind of theft are we talking about, Mr. Wilcox?"

"Odds and ends, Miss Murphy. A little Dresden shepherdess—one of a pair. A silver vase. A couple of pieces of my wife's jewelry—in fact, the kind of items a servant might take without their being noticed immediately."

"You're sure it is the work of a servant and not of an outside burglar?"

He leaned closer to me. "The work of an amateur, not a professional, Miss Murphy. When the silver vase was taken from the cabinet, a more valuable tankard was left untouched. If a burglar was going to take the Dresden shepherdess, why not take the pair? And my wife's jewelry—it was minor pieces when she possesses some fine rubies and emeralds."

"When did she notice they were missing?"

He sighed and drummed his fingers on the leather-topped desk. "That is the problem, Miss Murphy. My wife is a good woman, a fine mother to our son, but is, I'm afraid, a complete scatterbrain. She shows no interest in running the household. We only discovered the jewelry missing when I mentioned I had not seen her wearing a particular jade brooch for some time and she went to put it on for me. I had quizzed her previously about various knickknacks that seemed to have vanished. She seemed oblivious to their existence, Miss Murphy." He glanced around again, even though the door was closed. "She was a dancer in London when I married her, you know. A lovely little thing, lighter than air. I had hoped she would grow to be an asset to me in my political career." He sighed again.

"So you suspect one of your servants," I said, bringing back the conversation to safer ground. "How many servants do you have?"

"The usual number," he said carelessly. "An English butler—Soames. He's been with us only a year, but he came with the highest references and has proved most satisfactory. Then we have two footmen, two parlor maids, a housemaid, cook and scullery maid, then my wife has her personal maid and the child has his nurse. Oh, and the groom and coachman of course."

"And of those, is there anyone you might suspect more than the others?"

"We can rule out the coachman and groom," he said. "They don't come into the house. And the cook and the scullery maid never venture beyond the kitchen. The footmen would never enter my wife's dressing room. My wife's maid and the nurse would only enter the drawing room when summoned."

"So it would seem that only the parlor maids and the housemaid have full access to the house—apart from the butler, in spite of his references."

"I suppose any of them could have done it. One doesn't exactly notice servants, you know."

"If you give me a full description of the missing objects, I can do the rounds of all the pawn shops in the city. That should give us a good start."

"I have another suggestion," he said. "My wife always has a big party on Christmas Eve. We take on extra help on such occasions, making a perfect opportunity for you to observe firsthand, Miss Murphy."

I had looked forward to decorating my own tree on Christmas Eve, but this case was too good to turn down. If I were successful, I'd never lack for clients again.

"Very well. I'll take on the case. You will let your wife

know that you are hiring me, I trust. And if you can write out those descriptions, I'll get started straight away."

"Excellent." He took a piece of paper, scribbled with a frown of concentration on his face then got to his feet. "We'll expect you on the morning of Christmas Eve then." He handed me the sheet of paper. "You don't happen to have any experience as a servant?"

"As a matter of fact, I do," I said. "Another case I was working on once." Plus a lifetime of waiting on ungrateful males, I added silently.

"Couldn't be better. I'm delighted you called, Miss Murphy. It may be wiser if you exit through the servant's door so that no suspicions are aroused." He was about to open the door when another thought occurred to me.

"There is no one else who is frequently in the house and should be considered, is there? One of your wife's close friends?"

He looked horrified. "My dear Miss Murphy, we mix in only the highest social circles. My wife's friends could all afford to buy their own Dresden shepherdesses."

"Of course. I was only thinking that women often travel with their personal maids," I said hastily.

"Let's start with our own servants," he said. "Easiest access first." His hand was on the door handle, then he paused with a thoughtful look on his face. "Although now that you mention it, there is that Sergei fellow."

"Sergei?"

"My wife is currently having her portrait painted. He's a young Russian—Sergei Balenkov. Have you heard of him? Apparently he's all the rage these days. Studied in Paris before he came here. Can't see that he's anything special myself but Clara had her heart set on it so they're upstairs in the morning room at this very moment."

"But a visiting painter could hardly wander around helping himself to your ornaments, could he?" I said. "Your wife would know if he left the room."

"Of course she would, and the amount of money this fellow is making from his paintings these days, he wouldn't need to swipe the odd shepherdess. You should see him, Miss Murphy. Dresses like a dandy, dines at all the best households, and yet he still has the manners of a peasant, which he was until recently. Can't stand the fellow myself. But you'll see him on Christmas Eve. Clara has invited him to the party."

I left through the servant's entrance and started immediately to visit pawn shops in the area. I hadn't realized until I began this quest just how many pawn shops there were in the city. Two days of fruitless searching turned up nothing. Then, when I was becoming completely discouraged, I happened upon a small shop near Battery Park and spied a Dresden shepherdess in the window. The elderly proprietor insisted he kept no names. All business was done with numbered tickets. All he could tell me was that the piece had been brought in by a young lady with an accent. When I asked him what kind of accent, he shrugged and said he wasn't sure. Just that she had been hard to understand.

I invented a story of the piece having been pawned by mistake, paid for it and looked forward to returning it to its owner. Then, the next morning, I presented myself, bright and early, at the Fifth Avenue address, servant's entrance.

"It was most irregular of the master to hire extra help without going through me." The English butler stared at me with the haughty distaste only butlers can achieve. "I can't think what made him act that way."

"I've no idea, sir. I was just told to be here, and here I am." I gazed at the ground, suitably humble.

He looked as if he'd like to question me further but dispatched me to Mrs. Donovan in the kitchen. Mrs. D. was an old Irishwoman, round and fat, and at this moment was very flustered. "Don't go dropping that pudding, girl," she was shouting as I came in, while the scullery maid staggered across the room with the largest pudding basin I had ever seen. "And who might you be?" She eyed me with suspicion as I told her.

"I won't say no to an extra pair of hands," she said. "All those potatoes need peeling."

I wasn't going to be doing much detecting if I was stuck in the kitchen peeling potatoes all day. "I run my own domestic agency and I wasn't hired to be a skivvy," I said, matching her stare.

"Miss hoity-toity," she sniffed. "Very well then. You can take those bread rolls up to the dining room while Kathleen does the potatoes."

"So they're going to have a full dinner as well as a party, are they?" I asked.

The scullery maid grinned. "They have sixteen to a sit-down dinner and then they go to the drawing room and play party games. And you should see who their guests are—Astors, Vanderbilts—all the swank families."

"No business of yours who the guests are, Kathleen," Mrs. Donovan snapped. "You just get started on those potatoes, and don't forget to remind me when the pudding should go on. That size will need at least four hours of steaming."

"Is that a real Christmas pudding?" I asked. "I didn't know they were eaten in America."

"Not normally, they're not. We always have one, on account of Mrs. Wilcox wanting to be reminded of home. Now get along upstairs with you, there's work to be done."

I carried the rolls upstairs and found the dining room a hive of activity. The footmen and one of the parlor maids were laying the table, while one other maid was giving the silver a final polish. They looked up suspiciously as I came in.

"I'm Molly, the extra help the master ordered. Here are the rolls. Just tell me what needs doing."

"You can give Eileen a hand with those candlesticks," one of the footmen said.

I went to work, listening and asking the occasional innocent question. By the time the room was ready I knew that three of the maids were native born Americans, as were both footmen—thus ruling out strange accents. The other maid was a timid little thing who hardly said a word and came from England. She didn't seem daring enough for our thief. But then the strange accent could belong to a fence and not to anyone who worked here.

We had just finished when Mrs. Wilcox herself swept in, wearing a fur trimmed white cape. Her face was flushed and her eyes were very bright as if she'd just come in from the cold. "I just want to check that everything is perfect before my hairdresser arrives," she said in a voice that still bore traces of a Scottish accent. "Tell Soames I have the seating plan here, so he can have someone write the place cards." Her eye fell on me. "Who are you, girl?"

"Extra help hired for the occasion, madam." I dropped a curtsey. "Molly's my name. I'm told I have an elegant hand and I'll be happy to do your place cards for you."

"Excellent." She gave me a beaming smile. She was still very beautiful and looked so young. "Now let me look at the table. Very nice." She walked around it, then froze at the far end. "Some of these glasses have spots on them."

"Surely not, madam." Soames had materialized in the doorway.

"I distinctly see a spot, Mr. Soames. How fortunate that I caught it in time. Anya, take this glass, and this one too, and have them washed again."

I heard a gasp as the glasses were given to a pretty dark girl who hovered behind Mrs. Wilcox. The girl curtseyed and fled from the room as Soames said, "Madam, the glasses are my province, and that is not a job for your maid."

"But Anya is so quick and so willing," she said, "and I know how busy you are today." She swept from the room, leaving Soames staring after her. So much for the mistress who was unaware of what was going on around her and left the management of her servants to her husband!

I was given the place cards and sat at the table to write

them. Anya returned with the glasses. "There," she said. "Not a spot to be seen."

I glanced up as she spoke. For a moment I thought she was French, but then I wasn't sure. "You're Mrs. Wilcox's maid, are you?" I asked. "Where do you come from—I can't quite place your accent."

She smiled. "I was born in Russia but my family has to flee to Paris when I am seven years old. So now I speak Russian and French."

"Ah." I went back to my work. A strange accent, and a girl who was quick and nimble and who took on jobs not normally assigned to personal maids. I had my suspect at last. When I got a chance, I'd like to search Anya's room.

Of course, I didn't get a chance to do anything that afternoon. By the time the guests arrived I was wearing a starched white apron and was assigned to the tray of hot mince pies in the drawing room, in a good position to observe. Mr. Wilcox was at his expansively genial best. Mrs. Wilcox was decidedly nervous, her fingers playing with the long jade beads around her neck as the guests were announced. When I heard some of the great names, I could see why. I stood, invisible as they came in—Astors and Vanderbilts as predicted. Then the young Russian painter. He was good looking in a dark, haunted way, but certainly not dressed like a dandy as Mr. Wilcox had hinted. He wore a plain black suit and white silk cravat, and was clearly ill at ease as he shook hands with his hostess. "So glad you could come," Mrs. Wilcox murmured absently, already looking past him to the next guest. "Do have some mulled wine to take off the chill."

"So kind." He bowed and moved away.

I wondered why she had asked him until I heard her say to the next guest, "Yes, that is Sergei Balenkov. He's painting me now. Isn't he wonderful? Has he done you yet?" Sergei was obviously Mrs. Wilcox's trump card in the status game.

I went up to him with the mince pies and he wolfed down three, much to the amusement of two watching ladies, both of whom were adorned with diamonds.

"My dear, so animal, don't you think?" I heard one of them mutter.

"But you have to admit he has a certain charm, and he paints divinely."

Mr. Wilcox's loud politician's voice drowned out the conversation, something about the importance of religion and the family being lost in these fast and loose times.

"God, is that man a bore," one of my ladies muttered. "If you stuck holly in him, he'd pop, like a balloon."

"I see Letitia managed to get herself invited," the other tugged at her friend's sleeve as a scrawny older woman, dressed in the fashion of maybe ten years ago, came into the room, eyeing the company through her lorgnette.

"She always does, my dear. In fact, for somebody who was left destitute by a scoundrel of a husband, she fares remarkably well, wouldn't you say?"

"Naturally. She never eats at home." She stepped forward as the older woman approached. "Letitia, darling. How delightful to see you."

As the older woman held out her arms to be embraced, I noticed the sparkle of large rings on her fingers. Clearly the destitute Letitia had not been forced to sell her jewelry. I moved off with my tray, watching Mr. Balenkov move warily, like a panther, around the room. Something had just occurred to me. He had studied in Paris and the maid Anya was also a Russian, from Paris. Two lithe and sharp foreigners working together, maybe?

A bell summoned the company to dinner. I took up my position with the other servants behind the table as the first course was brought in—sherried beef consommé, followed by a lobster salad, steamed white fish in parsley sauce, then roast goose with all the trimmings. Soames supervised the pouring of a different wine for each course. I was assigned to the corner where Mrs. Wilcox sat at the foot of the table with a distinguished gentleman on either side of her. Then came the Letitia person, her eyes darting like a bird as she listened to the conversations around her, and to her right the Russian painter, who was still clearly uncomfortable about which cutlery to use. He hadn't drunk his soup from the side of his spoon, for example, and had slurped, making Letitia give him a haughty stare through her lorgnette.

Then, at last the Christmas pudding was brought in—a giant football carried, flaming, on a platter, surrounded by holly. Suitable applause from the guests.

"Take care how you eat this, ladies and gentlemen," Mr. Wilcox boomed. "Be warned. Eat it cautiously or you'll choke to death."

"What nonsense you talk, Sam," Mrs. Wilcox said, laughing nervously. "Just because I follow the tradition of putting silver charms in the pudding, he always makes this big fuss. If you find a charm, it means something, so keep it and we'll all predict our futures afterward."

"What fun," one of the grand ladies said. "Last year I was supposed to inherit wealth, but I seem to remember I gave my charm to Letitia because I already had inherited as much as I needed."

"And I have not fared at all badly, thanks in part to you, Kitty dear." Letitia smiled.

There was laughter as the pudding was cut and served, then another exclamation as the first silver charm was discovered. Suddenly Sergei Balenkov jerked upright, clutching at his throat and fell forward onto the table.

"He's choking, somebody do something," Letitia screamed.

Hands grabbed at him and somebody thumped him on the back, but it was no good. His body convulsed a couple of times, then he collapsed, his face flushed bright red.

Mrs. Wilcox had risen to her feet. "No!" she screamed. "No!" She ran to the stricken man and shook him. His body slumped forward again, this time knocking over glasses so that a red stain spread across the white cloth. "Someone get a doctor!" she exclaimed.

Mr. Wilcox's booming voice echoed down the table. "I warned you about this, Clara. Don't say I didn't warn you."

"Don't be so heartless, Sam. She's in shock. She needs brandy." One of the bejeweled women rushed to Clara's side.

But Clara Wilcox had already mastered herself. "I'm alright, Kitty. We should move everybody out of this room. It's too horrible to think about. Soames, brandy in the drawing room, please. Come, Kitty. Come, everyone." She turned to me and the other maid who stood beside me. "Clear up this mess before the doctor comes."

The other girl grabbed glasses and loaded them onto a tray. I stood staring at the corpse, trying to take in what I had seen. "Come on, don't stand there," the girl snapped. "Give me a hand. I don't like to move him, but we should take off the cloth before all that wine ruins the polish."

Cautiously I lifted the dead man and laid him back in his chair. We had barely mopped up the last of the spilled wine and whisked away the cloth when the doctor arrived, dressed, like the guests had been, in elegant evening attire.

"Choked to death, I understand, poor fellow," he said as Soames showed him into the room. "Very well—you want a death certificate, I suppose, then I can get back to my own party."

As he took out a fountain pen from his pocket I tapped his arm. "A word first please, if you don't mind, doctor."

He looked at me curiously but followed me as I drew him away from the servants who still lurked in the doorway. "There's something not right about this, doctor. I'm not satisfied that he did choke to death."

"Oh, and you're competent to make a diagnosis yourself, are you?"

I ignored the sarcasm. "I used to swim underwater when I was a girl and I could hold my breath for a good minute. This man died almost instantly. If he had been choking, wouldn't he be fighting for air for at least that length of time?"

"Unless his panic brought on a heart attack," the doctor said.

"There was also a strange smell about him."

Now the doctor was paying attention to me. "What kind of smell?"

"I'm not quite sure how to describe it. Bitter. . . ."

He didn't even wait for me to finish the sentence, but went over to the body. He examined it, then nodded and beckoned me. "You're right," he muttered and went to close the door, pushing out the other servants. "There is nothing blocking the throat and I caught a hint of the smell you detected. Bitter almonds." He leaned closer to me. "That means only one thing. Poisoning by cyanide. And the flushed skin would be consistent with that diagnosis. I suppose we should summon the police, although Sam Wilcox is an important man and a good friend. I wouldn't want to involve him in scandal unless strictly necessary."

"Maybe I could be of assistance." I saw his look of skepticism. "I am really a private investigator, working undercover here."

His eyebrow rose. "You were brought here? Foul play was predicted then?"

"Nothing like this. I was here to catch a thief."

"Ah. Then this may have been a falling out among thieves."

I shook my head. "Thieves would not choose an elegant dinner party at which to kill each other. This was designed to appear an accident." As I said it, I remembered Mr. Wilcox shouting out his warning about the pudding. Had he planned this—if so, why? He made it clear that he didn't like the young man, but he hardly knew him well enough to want to kill him.

"It has been my observation that the motives for murder

are always the most basic human emotions," the doctor said. "Fear, revenge, jealousy—"

As he said the word I froze. Was that why Mr. Wilcox did not like Sergei Balenkov? He feared his wife was attracted to the young Russian? But why choose a dinner party when all his friends were present? There were assassins aplenty for hire in the back streets of New York and plenty of chances for a quick knife in a dark alley. And surely Mrs. Wilcox gave him no reason to be jealous. She had appeared quite indifferent to the young man, as he was to her, brushing past her to get at the mince pies this evening.

"What I don't understand," the doctor said, "was how the cyanide was in the pudding. Surely it was cut at the table and everyone received a slice."

My brain was rapidly putting together more pieces of the puzzle. "I don't think it was in the pudding," I said. "I suspect the wine glass. A different wine was served with each course and the Madeira had just been poured. Tell me, doctor, is cyanide colorless and could it lurk unnoticed in the bottom of an empty wine glass?"

He nodded. "Possibly."

"Then you should instruct the servants to collect the wine glasses before they are washed, and for safety's sake, the tablecloth too."

"Very well," he said.

"And I think you should ask Mr. and Mrs. Wilcox to step into this room with Mrs. Wilcox's maid Anya."

He opened his mouth, then shut it again. "You seem a remarkably forceful young woman," he said. "I hope you know what you are doing."

Holy Mother of God so do I, I thought. I had done some investigating, it was true, but I had never attempted anything like this, especially not dealing with such powerful members of New York society. Mr. Wilcox and Mrs. Wilcox appeared as summoned, together with Anya the maid, whose eyes darted nervously at the stripped table and the slumped figure beside it.

"Now what's this all about, Peterson?" Mr. Wilcox demanded. "The damned fellow ate too greedily and choked himself. All we needed was a signed death certificate."

"Ah, but he didn't choke himself, Wilcox," the doctor said. "He was poisoned, and the young lady here, who I understand is an investigator brought here by you, seems to know who might be responsible."

I heard a gasp from one or both of the women.

"My name is Molly Murphy. I was brought here by Mr. Wilcox," I said as their eyes turned to me, "because he suspected that one of his servants was stealing from him. He gave me a description of the objects stolen and I traced one of them to a pawn shop. The person who deposited it was a young lady with a strange accent—maybe like yours, Anya. Then, when I found out that you and Sergei Balenkov both were Russians who had lived in Paris, I was even more interested. Did you have some scheme going between you? Were you secret lovers? But maybe Sergei's thoughts had turned elsewhere and you wanted revenge? You seized your chance when Mrs. Wilcox sent you to replace a couple of glasses with spots on them. You made sure one of those glasses was in Sergei's place, didn't you?"

The girl had gone very white. "No," she said, shaking her head. "It is not true. Sergei and I—we were lovers once, I admit, but I would not kill him. I adored him."

"Hell has no fury like a woman scorned," Mr. Wilcox said. "Well done, Miss Murphy, for solving it with so little fuss." He grabbed the girl and dragged her to the door. "Have her held and send for the police immediately, Soames," he commanded.

I glanced at him. He had a satisfied look on his face.

"You can't take Anya!" Mrs. Wilcox stepped forward. "How could she poison the pudding? It's ridiculous."

"It wasn't the pudding. It is most probable that the poison was in the wine," the doctor said.

"No!" the girl screamed as she was dragged away. "Let go of me! I did nothing. I am innocent, I swear. Tell them, madam."

But Mrs. Wilcox just closed her eyes in pain as her servant was taken away. I looked from one face to the other. Clearly this wasn't going as I had hoped.

Other members of the dinner party had come out to witness the girl being dragged away, imploring the Blessed Virgin to help her.

"What is going on?" one of the gentlemen demanded. "Did you say poison? In the wine glass?"

"I'm afraid so," Sam Wilcox said. "The Russian maid."

Letitia gave a little cry and pushed her way through the crowd. "I can't stay in this house another minute," she said. "It's all too shocking. I've made up my mind—I'm leaving for the continent on the next boat. I am through with New York forever. Soames—get me a cab."

"I think I'm going to faint," Mrs. Wilcox said. "This has all been too much for me."

"I'll make you up a sleeping draught, Mrs. Wilcox," the doctor said as she grasped at her husband's arm. "Go and lie down now."

A few minutes later I took a glass containing the sleeping mixture up to her room and tapped on the door. She was staring out of the window, her hands clutching the velvet drapes.

"The sleeping draught, madam," I said, as I put it on the bedside table. She nodded and waved me away.

I joined her at the window. "So the police are taking her away," I said. "Poor Anya. Is she to die for a crime she didn't commit?"

"What do you mean?" she demanded.

"Anya wouldn't have killed the man she loved at a society dinner party. It had to be someone who had no other choice. Someone who took the appalling risk of making murder look like an accident. One of you wanted Sergei dead."

She winced as if I'd slapped her and I realized I had suspected the wrong person. No wonder I hadn't extracted a confession out of Sam Wilcox. I remembered how she had come into the dining room and demanded the glasses be replaced, when her husband insisted she showed no interest in the running of the house.

"Did Sergei spurn your advances, Mrs. Wilcox?" I asked. "Was that why you killed him?"

"You stupid girl," she snapped. "Go away and take your wild fantasies with you." Her accent had become decidedly Scottish now.

My brain was racing like an express train. Then I remembered her hopeless cry, the way she had shaken Sergei's lifeless body. She was right. I was being stupid. They had taken great pains to avoid any contact in the drawing room, in case they had betrayed themselves—in case somebody else was watching.

"You loved him, didn't you?" I asked softly. "You never intended him to be the victim." As I spoke, I saw the whole scene replayed in my mind, Sergei shoveling in Christmas pudding with the manners of a peasant and then reaching out his left hand to grab a glass of wine. "And there was no thief, was there? You pawned all those things yourself—things you hoped your husband wouldn't notice. Because you had no money of your own and you had to pay your blackmailer to keep quiet about your love affair with Sergei."

She gave a tired sigh and turned away from the window. "She threatened to tell the whole world. The scandal would have wrecked Sam's political future."

"You didn't love Sergei enough to run away with him?"

"How could I have left my son?" she demanded. "I loved Sergei, but I love my darling child too. Sam would never have let me take the boy. We were content to meet in secret, but she spoiled it all."

"Letitia?" I asked. The destitute woman who nevertheless seemed to live quite well. The one who watched and listened and picked up tidbits of scandal at every party she went to. The one who had fled when she realized whose wine glass Sergei had drunk from.

Clara Wilcox nodded. "Letitia."

"So you invited her here, knowing that your husband always made a big fuss about choking on the charms in the pudding—the perfect opportunity, in fact."

She nodded again. "I don't know how the glasses got mixed up."

"But they didn't," I said. "I was watching Sergei. He had little experience of dining in high society. He was confused by the table setting and he took the glass from the wrong side—Letitia's glass. An easy mistake with so many courses and so many different glasses."

"Yes," she said. "An easy mistake. He was so ill at ease in society. I should never have made him come tonight. I should never have . . ." Her body was convulsed in sobs.

"So what will you do now?" I asked. "You surely can't let Anya take the blame for your crime."

She sat on the edge of her bed and composed her face. "I'll do the right thing. There is a pen and paper in the top of my desk, Miss Murphy. I will write a full confession. Then I'll drink the sleeping draught the doctor so kindly prepared for me."

I looked at her strangely. "It will only put you to sleep for a short while," I said.

"But I happen to have a couple more pills in my bathroom," she said. "Three should be enough, don't you think?"

"You don't need to sacrifice yourself." I grasped her hand. "A jury might not convict you, especially if you told the whole story. The worry from being blackmailed drove you out of your mind. Any jury would understand that . . ."

She shook her head and looked up with a tired smile. "It doesn't matter any longer, and I wouldn't do anything to bring shame to Samuel. He doesn't deserve it. You can leave me now, Miss Murphy, and please tell my husband that I am sleeping."

I stared at her long and hard. "Very well," I said.

Tears stung in my eyes as I came down the stairs. What would I have done in her place, trapped between losing her lover or her son, and wrecking her husband's good name? Not killed anybody, that's for sure, I decided as I stepped out into the crisp night air. Midnight was chiming at Grace Church on Broadway. It was Christmas Day.

DEAN AND CLAUDIA ASK RHYS:

Q: *You've had a great success with the Constable Evans stories. What prompted you to write about Molly Murphy?*
A: I started the Molly Murphy books because I was dying to write a strong, feisty first person female voice. Also, much as I love writing the Constable Evans books, there are certain crimes that will never happen in North Wales. I was fascinated by Ellis Island and also by the wonderful melting pot that was New York in 1901. It was a place where anything could happen and often did!

Q: *You aren't going to stop writing the Evans stories! Evan forbid!*
A: I've been asked this question so often! I enjoy the Constable Evans books and intend to alternate between the two series. I find that writing in two such different voices keeps me fresh for both.

Q: *Do you spend a lot of time on research?*
A: I spend too much time on research. *Murphy's Law* took place mainly on Ellis Island, so that research was fairly simple. After Molly stepped ashore in Manhattan, I realized what I had gotten myself into. I do a lot of reading for several months before I start writing, I also visit New York and see everything for myself. After I started the book, I found

there are still things to be looked up on every page. Fortunately, I have built up a great reference library by this time. I've started the fourth Molly Murphy.

AND HERE IS RHY'S RECIPE:

TRADITIONAL BRITISH CHRISTMAS PUDDING

This recipe makes one large pudding or, if you prefer, two smaller puddings. It should be made at least one month in advance to allow the flavors to develop.

4 ounces currants

4 ounces sultana raisins

4 ounces raisins

1/2 ounce crystallized ginger, chopped

1/2 cup grated tart apple

1/2 ounce chopped prunes

1/2 orange with juice and zest

1/2 lemon with juice and zest

1½ tablespoons soft brown sugar

4 tablespoons Guinness

4 tablespoons ale

2 tablespoons brandy

2 tablespoons sweet sherry

2 eggs

2 tablespoons milk

1/2 cup flour

3 tablespoons mixed spices: cinnamomn, ginger, and ground cloves

1 teaspoon salt

1/2 ounce ground almonds

1½ cup fresh breadcrumbs

4 ounces shredded suet

Mix fruit with sugar in large bowl; add alcohol. Marinate in the refrigerator 24 hours. Beat eggs and milk together. Add fruit mixture. Add remaining ingredients and mix. Cover and refrigerate for five to seven days. Spoon into covered pudding basin. Cover securely with plastic wrap, then tin foil, then lid. If basin has no lid, cover with pudding cloth and tie securely. Steam in a saucepan for 4 to 5 hours. (To steam, put a small plate in a large pot of water, and place basin on top of that. Water should come to the lip of the basin. Watch that the water doesn't boil down). Remove pudding. Cool. Cover with fresh, greaseproof paper to allow the pudding to mature. Before serving, steam pudding again for three hours. Turn onto hot dish, sprinkle with sugar, pour warm brandy over it, and flame carefully.

FOOD FOR THOUGHT

Jeremiah Healy

Jeremiah Healy is a graduate of Rutgers College and Harvard Law School. He is the creator of two popular series. One is the John Francis Cuddy private investigator novels (for which he has received the Shamus Award for Best Novel and six other nominations) and short stories (for which he's received seven Shamus nominations). The other series is the Mairead O' Clare legal–thriller novels under his pseudonym of "Terry Devane." Healy is a former president of the Private Eye Writers of America and is the current president of the International Association of Crime Writers, an organization with 1,000 members in 22 different countries.

"This guy slays me," said Angelo "Toots" Marino from the living room. "But somebody please explain it, huh? Why would the Weather Channel in fucking Key West hire a Swedish guy to talk for them?"

Emptying the dishwasher, Tawny Marino clenched her

teeth. How many times did she have to hear her husband repeat that same, stupid question?

"I dunno, Boss," from Al, his skinny, acne-scarred driver with the bad teeth, sitting next to Toots. "It's a puzzle to me, too."

"Honey," said Tawny, trying to look toward but not at her husband, spread like human onion dip all over the Barcalounger in front of the condo's big-screen television. "Like I told you last time you asked, it's not the Weather Channel. It's the National Weather Service, here in the Keys. And that voice isn't Swedish."

"But listen to the guy. He says, 'The bay waters becoming a slight chop' and 'the winds was from the north.' I mean, you were the college girl and all, but that's not good English, am I right?"

"You're right, Boss," said Al, beginning to look like he was about to pick his nose.

Tawny moved her lower jaw around to keep from screaming, because if she started, she was afraid she'd never stop. "Honey, it's not a real person. Look at the screen. They show the January community announcements for the Keys, not anybody's face. It's just a computer voice."

"How can it be a computer voice? Every time he says 'mostly cloudy,' he goes down on that last part, like he's real sorry he has to tell the tourists it's not gonna be the kind of day the brochures hyped them for. As if I could care about the fucking sunshine."

"Boss, the doctors're all saying now it's not so good for you anyways."

Tawny tried one last time, the triumph of hope over experience. "Honey, it's a computer voice from the National Weather Service. They make all the phonetic sounds by typing characters on a keyboard."

"Why would they do that?"

"Because," Tawny trying to keep the growing edge out of

her voice, "it would drive any sane person stark, raving mad to have to say the same things about the weather covering a very small area every ten minutes for twenty-four hours a day, seven days a week."

"I don't get that," said Toots, using his right big toe to scratch the part of his suet-like left calf that stuck out from under the circus-tent Bermuda shorts, both feet covered by sheer black socks. "I mean, I watch the show three, four hours a day easy, and I don't go fucking crazy."

No, thought Tawny, you don't. You just drive your wife there.

Then she envisioned how she'd be "driven crazy" in a far more enjoyable way.

Check the watch. Another whole hour yet?

Closing the dishwasher door, Tawny decided to arrive a little early. "Well, I'm going out for lunch, then some shopping."

Toots looked up at her. From under his eyebrows, like they were window shades pulled halfway down. "You need money?"

Toots wouldn't let her have a credit card. He'd say, "Something I learned from the first cop I ever bribed: cash and carry." Just one of her husband's many clichés, like "food for thought," or "three's the charm."

Though his worst, by far, was "maybe we should turn in a little early tonight."

Tawny fought the gag reflex that always resulted from that one. Toots Marino, the pig-flesh word-smith.

He now said, "What, am I talking to my bride or myself here?"

Tawny pushed the bad image from her mind. "Sorry, Honey. I've got plenty of money, thanks."

"You want Al to drive you, carry anything?"

Al glanced over to his "boss."

"Nope," said Tawny, as lightly as possible. "And you guys can have the car. I think I'll just walk, get some exercise."

"Get some for me, too," from Toots, grinning. "But, hey, don't stuff yourself at one of them chi-chi gourmet joints, all right? Nina's coming in on the four o'clock plane, and she's cooking us a real meal tonight."

His sister, one of those black-haired—and noticeably mustached—Italian women who came out of the womb married to her family. To the point that she had an apartment over the "family" business back home and even a snowbird condo directly above theirs down here. On the other hand, Nina really was a sorceress in the kitchen, though given the diabetes she supposedly found out about two months before, they hadn't seen her in Key West yet this season to sample those talents.

And no surprise, about the diabetes, anyway. The woman probably had ten pounds on her brother, and that put her into the Orca class.

As Tawny Marino got her favorite sunhat—a Cuban straw thing she'd picked up at one of the outdoor stalls near Schooner Wharf—she heard Al say, "I dunno, Boss. The guy definitely sounds Swedish to me, too."

AS always, Tawny breathed a sigh of relief as she closed the condo's front door behind her. Like she was sealing off a leaking compartment in a sinking ship.

Taking the elevator down to the ground floor (because of the hurricane surges in the beachfront complex, the whole building was up on stilts, which at least provided covered parking), Tawny tried to decide for the hundredth time whether Toots having Al drive them down to Key West every December in the Cadillac was just Toots being cheap—as usual—or Toots trying to control her in a way he couldn't during the nicer months back north, where she had her own car. It was just a Mazda Miata, and even then Toots didn't want to go for anything foreign that wasn't Italian.

Damn, but it would be fun to have it with you now.

Tawny walked across the complex's open-air parking lot and toward the swimming pool. Even at a distance, she could see a couple of middle-aged women standing in the shallow end, holding their arms out, trying to get birthing butterflies to land on a finger, dry their wings. Most of the people were snowbirds like Toots and Tawny, but the ones at the pool were already tanned and healthy looking, if not exactly svelte, given the amounts of alcohol and fried foods most everybody consumed. A tee shirt Tawny had seen downtown on Duval Street read, "KEY WEST: A DRINKING TOWN WITH A FISHING PROBLEM," and she thought that pretty much summed the place up. But it could be fun, if Toots ever wanted to do anything besides get a couple of the boys together from back home, go out on the charter boat to kill innocent fish or play a little pinochle, then nightcap at one of the "titty bars," watch the young ponies strip and dance around chrome poles and mirrors.

Tawny grunted out a laugh. Like you used to.

In fact, that was how she'd met Toots in the first place, thirteen years before, in a club up north. Like a lot of the other "exotic dancers," Tawny was working her way through college, but unlike most of them, she hadn't had any kids yet. And it was an okay job, too: she had high, firm breasts, and not too big a butt, so her tips were good. The dancing was fun, great exercise and effective advertising for the real money that came from the "private dances" in the back room. Tawny had figured then that as long as she could "make the bank"—for her, earning at least five hundred a night—she'd dance her four shifts per week forever.

Until the night Toots came into the club with his "crew."

Tawny could tell she'd caught his eye right away. And sure enough, he paid her the twenty bucks a song for private dances, though with all the other girls in the back room with their customers, too, it was really less "private" and more "individual" dancing.

And then, getting ready to leave that night, he'd tipped Tawny a hundred, which definitely caught her eye.

When Toots came in the next night, and the next, she got to know him a little. Oh, the guy was street, not college material, but "Toots" was also kind of cute, even to the nickname. And just pudgy back then, with a decent hairline before the stupid transplant that looked as though somebody'd stapled four-hair clumps into his scalp like rows of cornstalks.

And, most important of all, three months after they started going out, he'd wanted to marry her, not just play "hide the salami." And pamper her, which nobody Tawny had ever dated before had the money to do.

So she'd tied the knot with the guy. And within a few years, Tawny looked forward to the nights Toots would go out with the guys to the clubs, because that would mean she wouldn't have to wear a blonde or black wig over her natural—well, "highlighted" a little—auburn hair, and try to do him like a contortionist in a way he wanted that they hadn't tried before.

Okay, admit it: many's the night you wish he'd just not come home, period.

But no such luck. And no prospects for Tawny at the complex, either, brought home again as she was actually passing the pool. Every time a guy more her own age tried an admiring glance—like now, that cute one with the military build and short hair on the corner lounge—somebody would always nudge him—and there she goes, that old bat from the second floor—tell him who Tawny was and just how "off-limits" he'd better think of her as being.

Which just meant she had to . . . "recreate" elsewhere.

A small smile.

Tawny would never be so stupid as to fool around back north. Too many of her husband's crew would be in the area, spot her Miata parked outside the wrong motel—which would be any motel that wasn't sponsoring a "ladies lunch" or a "fashion show." And even then, Al or another like him might be sent out, "just to keep an eye on you, make sure nobody tries nothing."

God, you made this bed, but who'd have ever guessed you'd have to lie in it for thirteen years?

No, back then, Tawny saw only the nice car, and his apparent generosity at the restaurants. She didn't see the downside of the "family" stuff—both business and personal—or pay much attention to the fact that every meal they ever ate out together was Italian. Every opera, Italian. Every everything, Italian.

Tawny shook her head as she pushed the button that slid open the pedestrian gate on the side of the complex that couldn't be seen from either of their condo unit's two balconies. Just to be safe, though, she started in-town toward the shopping streets, not cross-town.

To where Jared lived.

LICK and nibble. Nibble and lick. Nibble, nibble—oh, a little bite, yes, right there, right . . . there!—and now lick, lick, lick, LICK—Oh, God, Ohmigod.

"OHMIGOD!"

"Ah, that's right," said Jared in his velvety voice, "that's the way." Tawny's torso collapsed back on the bed, having nearly done a stomach crunch as Jared's tongue, lips, and teeth had worked their ultimate magic. Her skin felt as though it had been attached to tiny electrodes at a million different points, little after-shocks still erupting in all the right places.

Jared pulled himself up to her while—as always—wiping his mouth with a hand towel next to them on his brass bed before kissing her so deeply, it was as though he'd already entered her down there.

As he did now, filling her and beginning to gently stroke, lots of travel, like a locomotive touching every wall of a train tunnel. After which he would rock her for what seemed like hours . . . to the state where . . . Tawny just wanted him . . . to hammer her until they both exploded, as she had once already.

NOW Tawny lay alone in the brass bed, under the clean top sheet that still smelled of both Jared and whatever fabric softener he used. She could hear the guy in his bathroom, showering "afterward" as always, too, before he'd let her take him into her mouth for "Round Three."

Tawny had met Jared at a "casual-dress" charity function sponsored by Mangoes on Duval Street, one of the island's many "chi-chi gourmet" restaurants Toots hated so much. First thing Tawny noticed about Jared—well, maybe the fifth thing, after his curly blond hair, blue eyes, clefted chin, and ripped biceps—was how polite he was, offering to get her a drink, even thinking to bring a napkin under it.

So polite, in fact, that she figured he might be gay. Which now made her laugh. Seven years ago, the first time Toots and she did go out partying on Duval, her husband said, "This town is full of fags," loud enough so everybody around them, gays included, could hear. When they got home that night, he also said, "There's no action in this town, so you're safe enough."

Which made Tawny laugh again, even now. No action, huh? Well, there hadn't been a someone every season, but the next year she'd met an airline pilot—Craig—on one of the "sunset" booze cruises Toots would let her take alone. Of course, Tawny never told Craig that her husband happened to be in a certain line of work, and as a pilot, he happened to be flexible—in his flight schedule, if not his . . . joystick. They'd had a great time for nearly the whole season, until a promotion came up in Denver that Craig just couldn't turn down. Too bad, but a few years after him she had a young artist—Robert—a truly sweet kid without much experience who had an erection you could slam a door on and not hurt very much. Robert was also a quick study, though, and they trysted like rabbits at his small apartment for almost two months before he decided to attend art school in Seattle.

But nobody had been like Jared. Not ever.

He owned a beautifully restored cigar-maker's house on a quiet street, one of those small, two-story cottages with the pointed roofs. The renovator had insulated the top floor, so it was cozy rather than cramped, and could be heated—important for Key West in January, when the day-time temperature could dip down into the fifties.

Although Jared could always make her feel warm. And wet.

In addition to his courtesy and courtesan abilities, though, most important of all was that he made her actually think. Not the stupid small talk Tawny would hear around Toots, like, "Hey, Phil, the vig on that loan to the Gambellos for their warehouse thing: was it two percent a week or three?" Or, "How's your grandmother's agita, Dom?" Or, "Al, you got to get in touch with Larry, see does he want to come down for a week in the sun after doing that shithead edging into our territory from the colored neighborhood."

Larry—a pale, hairy hitman. Dom—the paunchy, raunchy charter-boat captain down here who laundered money for Toots and still lived with his grandmother. And Al—the driver and Toots's first friend from kindergarten. All cut from the same cloth, and not a functioning intellect among them.

But Jared had gone through law school, made a ton of money protecting the environment in Montana by getting the courts to order the polluters and the despoilers to pay his legal fees so all the foundations and citizens' groups he helped wouldn't have to. And he talked with her about things: explaining why some cases had to be brought in state, not federal court; rules of evidence on what witnesses could and couldn't say; even a case he once argued in the

Supreme Court of the United States, a photo of him on the steps outside it after he'd won.

Unfortunately, though, no experience in divorce work.

Not that it mattered, really. Toots's sister, Nina, might have been married to her family since birth, but Toots had made it very clear that there were never any divorces in his world. No, it was "'til death do us part."

Which had gotten Tawny thinking. She might be able to just run away from her husband, but she'd have to go somewhere he wouldn't expect, and that someplace would have to be a pretty shitty place. And even then, she'd have to earn her own way again.

Tawny sat up in bed, let the sheet slide down. Her breasts were still nice and high at age thirty-four, but she was packing ten more pounds around the hips and butt than she'd had during her dancing days, and she couldn't really picture anybody offering her a job in her old line of work. Also, it'd take just one guy from Toots's crew—or one guy from another one in another city—to spot her and call her husband as a professional courtesy. And that risk ruled out waitressing, bartending, anything public.

All of which added up to a very simple conclusion: Angelo "Toots" Marino would have to die.

Tawny had figured going into the marriage that her husband wouldn't change radically. But now that he had, she kept herself sane by predicting that he was slowly killing himself. The calories and fat in the food Nina fed Toots back north and sometimes down here, the resultant blimping, the reluctance to exercise. With luck, he'd just keel over fighting a marlin on the boat or playing a perfect hand in pinochle.

Or, as Toots so often bragged, "die in the saddle."

Tawny had heard of such things. One of the girls in the first club she ever worked had a guy Toots's age suffer a coronary halfway through an "escort date," slump right down on top of her, his heart bursting and his bowels letting go as all the muscles went slack. The only problem with that scenario was, Toots had gotten so fat, Tawny was the one who had to do all the work. On top, her tendons and ligaments almost separating like the wishbone on a turkey as she tried to straddle him on her knees. Or from above, his front to Tawny's back, her quadriceps and triceps screaming at her as she tried to keep bouncing up and down on his member without squashing his jewels.

No, Toots wasn't going to die soon on his own. Which meant Tawny was going to have to help him a little more directly.

But, married to a connected mobster, every killer she knew worked for her husband. And Toots wasn't a big enough player for another family to whack him in order to help themselves.

Originally, Tawny had thought Jared might agree to do Toots with her, but she'd quickly learned that was out of the question. The guy wasn't just polite to her and supportive of charities. Jared had an "Official Philosophy of Key West" bumper sticker on his car ("ALL PEOPLE ARE EQUAL MEMBERS OF OUR ONE HUMAN FAMILY"), and he'd even look down before taking a step on the sidewalk, make sure not to crush an ant. Or see tourists on the street, speaking foreign languages while holding maps, and go over to them, ask if he could help.

Tawny sighed, then rolled onto her side as she heard the shower go off in the bathroom. And she pictured her "dreamboat" coming through the doorway, back to her.

Jared. Older than Tawny by only a couple of years, but with tight buns from tennis and killer abs from the health club and just overall healthiness, sexuality, and optimism. He was the only thing that made her life bearable, and any time with him was like a great "dream." Only Jared told her he'd never leave Key West, at least not for the winter months.

Then Tawny smiled. On the other hand, what could be more natural—for a young widow, devastated by her husband's untimely death—to bravely grieve in the tropical paradise where they'd found their truest happiness?

As the bathroom door opened—and she took Jared in before . . . well, taking him in—Tawny Marino decided Toots had to die.

The only remaining questions were how and when.

AFTER they finished Round Three, Jared got dressed, saying he had to leave or be late for a board of directors meeting at a foundation that tried to help the city's homeless. As Tawny brushed her teeth, rinsed that gummy taste from her mouth before showering herself, she glanced out the high, small bathroom window. There was Jared, on the opposite side of the street, pointing to a roadmap that some heavy—but at least not yet utterly obese—blonde had spread out on the hood of a four-door compact car. Their backs were toward her, but a guy Tawny assumed was the husband leaned out the driver's side window with a big camera in front of his face, and Jared turned a little so the guy could snap a photo of him helping his wife.

Damn the board meeting, if Jared could help somebody, make them feel better.

Spitting out the toothpaste, and the last of Jared, into the sink, Tawny turned away for her shower.

AS she walked back to the condo, Key West's many loose chickens barely staying out of her way, Tawny could feel the after-glow of her afternoon sliding into the toilet of her evening. First there'd be the round of drinks on the seaside balcony, and the endless "catching up" on the trivia of what Nina had been through with the diabetes, and which cousin was maybe getting engaged, and whether a member of somebody's crew might finally be eligible for parole. Then a second round of drinks, and more trivia: about their season so far, and how many bad meals had passed through Toots without his sister there to make the kind of food his wife couldn't. Finally, if Tawny was lucky, drinks would be followed by enough chianti classico and poisonous courses of cholesterol that Toots wouldn't want any kind of sex that night.

This man has to be killed, even if you have to poison him your—

Tawny stopped dead in her tracks, nearly getting run over by a woman dressed in a flannel shirt and baggy jeans, riding a huge tricycle on the sidewalk, some kind of little lap dog riding in the front basket. But Tawny thought it would have been worth getting hit by the bike, just so long as she'd gotten hit like that by inspiration as well.

Toots was always after her to cook for them herself, but Tawny had never felt much desire to spend hours in the kitchen, only to be told that none of her dishes was "like Nina can make it." There had to be food classes on the island, though, and enough information on poisons in books at the library on Fleming Street. Not to take one out, of course; that'd be stupid. But who would know if the grieving widow, a few days before her husband died, had just sort of skimmed through that kind of book, all by herself at a secluded table?

Tawny started walking again, but couldn't get the possibility out of her mind. There'd have to be poisons that didn't taste so bad. She was pretty sure one of them even had a flavor like almonds. Or maybe another would be completely tasteless, even untraceable once the stuff did its job.

Tawny was positive there were TV shows now about police investigating crime scenes and doctors doing autopsies on what killed the dead person. Maybe she could watch them, too, find a poison that couldn't be detected. Or even just something that would weaken Toots's heart, so he'd go naturally, out on the boat or playing pinochle.

Or—poetic justice—watching some tight hard body shake her booty at him in one of his "titty bars."

Feeling a spring in her step for the first time in a long while during a walk home, Tawny Marino smiled so broadly her face actually hurt a little as she used a gate key to slip back into the condo complex, after an afternoon of shopping without finding a single thing to wear.

"HEY, where you been?"

From the front door of the condo unit, Tawny could see Toots, in a Jimmy Buffett "Parrothead" shirt that clashed with the color of his shorts, craning his neck from the balcony to hear her answer his question.

She said, "I went looking for a new bathing suit, but I didn't see any I liked."

Toots took a swig of amber liquid from a tumbler in hand. "Meaning nothing that wouldn't make your ass look big, right?"

Tawny didn't hear Al's usual yes-man laugh, so he was probably out on a frolic of his own. But she did hear Nina giggling at her brother's "joke." As if "mustache momma" didn't live in a glass house on that one.

Only when Tawny reached the balcony, she was actually surprised.

Her sister-in-law had dropped at least five dress sizes. She wouldn't be a fashion model any time soon, but it allowed Tawny to pay her a sincere compliment that, for a change, didn't have anything to do with the woman's cooking.

"Nina, you look terrific."

"Thanks, thanks," standing up from the patio furniture on their balcony. "This diabetes, it meant I had to lose weight, and I got to tell you, I feel a lot better, too."

Toots said, "Doctors told her she can't eat some of her best dishes no more, but that don't mean you can't still cook for your brother and his bride, am I right?"

"Right, right."

Tawny remembered Nina's tendency to always say things

twice, but, therefore focusing on her mouth, Tawny also noticed the black mustache was gone.

Electrolysis? Actually shaving? Or maybe simply wanting to look a little better overall, now that she'd gone back to being just heavyset?

Whatever. Tawny, happy for herself thanks to the poison idea, decided to be happy for Nina, too. "So, what's on the menu tonight?"

TAWNY had to admit: it wasn't so much a dinner for three as a banquet for ten. But she wasn't complaining.

First, the antipasto of fresh vegetables and sharp cheeses on sesame crackers.

Toots said, "Nina brought a lot of the spices for the rest of the meal down here with her on the plane. They made her unpack everything at the airport, the new rules on account of the fucking terrorists."

"Right, right. They asked me, was I going to open up my own store in Key West?"

Toots and his sister both laughed. Tawny smiled politely, then noticed the second course was liver paté on long, rounded rolls that just happened to be about the size of Jared's erect member. Taking one into her mouth reminded her of the afternoon she'd spent with him, and Tawny felt herself getting a little wet below the belt.

She said, "This paté is terrific."

Nina nodded. "I used one of the special spices on that."

Toots took a bite of his. Chewing with his mouth open, he said, "You recognize what it is?"

Given her earlier take on the roll, Tawny almost laughed. "No." To avoid having to watch her husband's food roll around on his tongue, she turned to Nina. "But I'd love for you to show me how to use it."

Toots did laugh. "Hey, that'd mean you'd actually have to walk into the fucking kitchen, you know?"

Perfect opening, so take it. "Actually, I've been thinking about trying to learn how to cook, maybe even enroll in a class on it."

Toots didn't laugh this time, but he did grin. "What, Nina's cooking's finally inspiring you?"

"Yeah."

Nina seemed to blush.

Toots said, "Well, wait 'til you taste the pasta sauce. Talk about special."

Which was when Tawny noticed that Nina hadn't progressed past the veggies and cheese course. "You're not eating any of your own pate?"

More blushing. "The diabetes. Doctors say I can't have it, or most of my sauces anymore."

Toots said, "So, you eat your pasta plain, or with a little butter melted on it, like grandpa Marino did. And he lived to be—what, ninety-five?"

"Ninety-six, I think."

"See, what'd I tell you?"

The pasta course was terrific, too, the meat in it a little chewy, like maybe it was cubed chicken thighs. But Tawny didn't think it wise to over-do her own newly found interest in cooking by asking what Nina had used.

Tawny did think of something wise that maybe Toots's grandfather from the old country might have said: you've planted the seed. Now, let it grow.

As Nina cleared the plates—chef and busboy, both—she said, "We've got osso buco next."

Tawny pictured the veal shank, one of Nina's best recipes, the way she braised it with some kind of marinade.

This cooking jag might even be enjoyable. Pick up a few pointers from your sister-in-law, make some incredible meals exactly to your taste. Though you'll really have to burn them off if you're going to stay up with Jared.

After the entree dishes were cleared, Nina brought out a tiramisu for dessert. Pre-dinner drinks were always on the balcony, weather permitting. But post-dinner drinks were always at the dining room table. Toots and Nina both had some grappa, a real expensive one that Tawny knew her husband bought by the case. However, even the pricey grappas she'd tried tasted to her like goat-sweat poured over a saddle and drained into bottles, so Tawny rose and walked to the wetbar for her usual brandy.

Behind her, Toots said, "That's the best fucking meal I've had since we been down here."

"Oh, thanks, thanks."

"But I think after the grappa here, my bride and I are gonna turn in a little early."

Fighting her gag reflex, Tawny shuddered and poured herself a double, both to make dessert last a little longer and to brace herself for what was to . . . come.

TAWNY lingered in their master suite's bathroom, too, checking herself in the mirror for any bruising from her session with Jared, in case Toots noticed one and asked what she did to herself, "you clumsy broad." But no, Jared was as gentle as he was capable, giving her pleasure—incredible pleasure—without leaving any marks.

"Hey, you almost done in there or what?"

"Just about," said Tawny before swishing some Fresh Breath Listerine in her mouth to help kill the eventual flavor and dabbing a little perfume under each nostril to deal with the smell of him down there. A masseuse at a spa once told Tawny that fat people were the worst to work on, because they didn't always wash themselves well, given their folds of fat. Tawny had told the woman, "Yeah, well, on that score, you're in the frying pan, and I'm in the fire."

From the other room, Toots said, "What do I have to do, fucking come in there and drag you out?"

Tawny thought, Tomorrow: the library for sure.

She left the bathroom to see Toots lying on his back, far

side of the bed, naked and looking like a beached whale. However, on the near pillow there was what appeared to be a folded roadmap on top of a box about a foot square and high, with an envelope sticking out underneath the cardboard.

Tawny said, "We taking a trip?"

"It's kind of a present."

Present?

Tawny crossed to the bed and read from the front of the map. " 'Florida, including details of all its Keys.' " She looked at her husband. "You want to drive up toward Miami tomorrow?"

"Open the box first."

Tawny lifted the lid, then reached through the tissue paper to find a blond wig.

Shit, he wants kinky again tonight. Marilyn Monroe time, with him as that dead baseball player, Joe DiMaggio.

Toots said, "The present's more in the envelope."

Which is when it finally hit her: A car. He's gone and bought you a car for down here, and the "keys" to the "Keys" are in the envelope. And the blonde wig probably means he thinks you'd look good wearing it . . .

In the wind. Of course: a convertible!

Toots made a growling noise. "Open the fucking envelope, you don't mind."

Tawny yanked the thing out, but it didn't feel right for car keys. When she undid the flap, a small packet of what seemed to be Polaroid photos bound by a rubber band tumbled out and face-down onto the comforter.

Toots said, "Look at them, in order."

Tawny looked at him instead. "What the hell kind of present is photos?"

"First one first."

Sighing as loudly as she could, make the point of how stupid this all was, Tawny flipped the packet over and slid off the rubber band. The top photo—a Polaroid, like she thought—showed . . . .

What in the . . .? Jared, smiling and standing next to Nina, in a blond wig.

The blond wig.

Toots said, "My sister didn't come in on the four o'clock plane. She came in on the noon one, with Larry. While you were having your 'nooner' with the lawyer."

Larry, the . . . hitman?

Her hands shaking, Tawny flipped to the next photo. Jared, a terrified look on his face, in the back seat of a car, a pale and hairy hand holding a gun to his temple. "No . . . no . . . ."

"Your pilot was bad enough, but I tried to be a gentleman about that. I figure one bad step, anybody can make it. I had a little talk with the guy, found out you didn't tell him who I was. So I made the suggestion that 'Craig' might like another city better, and he got his company to send him there."

Denver.

Tawny dropped the second picture. The third photo showed Jared, walking ahead of the camera but with his head turned back to the lens. He was even more terrified— if that was possible—lots of sand and raggedy bushes around. "Honey, no . . . . No, you didn't."

"Your 'artiste,' he was just a kid. I told 'Robert' that going back to school as far away from here as they had one would be a real good idea."

The fourth Polaroid—God, no!—Jared, on his knees in the sand, facial features distorted, the tears flowing down his cheeks from eyes squinched shut, the pale, hairy hand with the gun at his temple again.

"But your lawyer?" Toots levered up on the comforter using his elbow. "Well, I'm always saying three's the charm, right?"

Tawny began crying, too. She turned to the fifth picture: Jared, lying on the ground, eyes open but at different angles, the pale, hairy hand now with a . . . saw in it?

"We figured it'd be too much of a risk to butcher him all

the way, age the meat right, so we just went with the liver and his wang."

Tawny felt her stomach twist.

Toots waved his hand toward the window. "Out on the boat, Dom and Al are feeding the rest of 'Jared' to the sharks. In bite-size chunks."

"What . . . ." Tawny tried to swallow, couldn't. "What are you . . . ?"

"The pate on the rolls there, and the pasta sauce? I figured you might like tasting the guy, one last time."

Tawny clamped her hand to her mouth and ran toward the bathroom, knowing she wouldn't make the toilet before—

Toots said, "And this has to be the last time. Ever. Because any more guys, and it's your last time, too."

Even over her retching, Tawny Marino could hear her husband saying, "Food for thought, am I right? Food for thought."

CLAUDIA AND DEAN ASK JERRY:

Q: *In a jocular mood, you'll call yourself a right-wing sociopath. Just what IS a right-wing sociopath?*
A: I think a "right-wing sociopath" is someone who believes in using deadly force regardless of society's laws, because he or she also believes that his or her sense of "justice" is more valid. Accordingly, I know a number of law enforcement officers, military commanders, and law professors (all of which I've been) who are "sociopathic" in that they make up their own rules to live by, regardless of society's. Many fictional private investigators and real-life organized crime figures also fit this mold.

Q: *What similarities do you find between practicing law and writing crime fiction?*
A: Practicing law and writing mysteries have many things in

common. As a trial attorney, the principle similarity for me is structure. A trial attorney pictures the end of the trial—the jury coming back in his or her client's favor. Then the attorney "backsteps" from there, all the way to the client first coming into the lawyer's office with the problem. As a novelist, I picture the confrontation scene between the hero and the killer, then backstep through the chapters to the initial one.

Q: *Who do you want to be in your next life?*
A: If reincarnated, I'd love to be John D. Macdonald: he got to live in Fort Lauderdale year-round, while I'm here for "just" three months.

AND HERE IS JERRY'S RECIPE:

RIGHT-WING SOCIOPATH CHILI

2 onions, chopped
4 slices of bacon, chopped
5 or 6 chopped cloves garlic
a couple of tablespoons of olive oil
2 pounds ground beef
16-ounce can of chopped tomatoes
12-ounce can of dark red kidney beans
12-ounce can of white Navy beans
12-ounce can of black beans
one large chopped green pepper
1/2 cup chili con carne seasoning
chopped onions
grated cheddar cheese

Fry onions, bacon, and garlic in oil. Add ground beef and brown well.

Add beans, tomatoes, seasoning and green pepper to ground beef. Simmer for an hour or two. Top with chopped onions and grated cheddar cheese.

THE SPIRIT OF WASHINGTON

Meg Chittenden

Meg Chittenden is small, silver-haired and sexy. Her short story "Noir Life" won an Anthony and she's the recipient of the Pacific Northwest Writers Achievment Award for enhancing the stature of Northwest Literature. She's written more than one hundred short stories and articles, and thirty-six books, including the popular Charlie Plato novels. Her latest novel, More Than You Know, *appeared in September of 2003.*

Esther was counting grapes. Audibly. As usual. Even though they were in public, on the luxurious Spirit of Washington dinner train. Even though she knew how much it embarrassed him. She was a scrawny brown wren of a woman, but her voice was anything but birdlike.

Harold sneaked a glance at the table across the aisle. On this side the tables seated only two people, on the other side they seated six. None of the three men and three women at the neighboring table seemed to be paying any attention to Esther's penetrating voice.

They would hardly notice him, either, of course. A big, bald, middle-aged man, a close relative to Walter Mitty, the Born Loser, not to mention Mr. Milquetoast, was invisible to tall, beautiful Scandinavian types like them.

Not that he resented them for it. Far from it. Considering the way Esther carried on, he welcomed their indifference. He just wished he was one of them. He formed a little bubble in his mind where he looked like one of the men—tall, blond, handsome, with wonderful teeth—being gazed at with love and admiration by one of the tall, blonde, beautiful women.

All of the seats in this Spirit of Washington car were full, he noted as the bubble popped. And judging by the crowd that had boarded the train at the charming depot in Renton, the same was true of the other cars. He was surprised. It was October, after all. And cold out. Dark, too. But inside, all was festive with bright lights and crisp white tablecloths. Hot pink napkins and happy people.

"Forty-four," Esther concluded, scowling.

"You only need fifteen grapes," Harold pointed out. She'd told him so enough times.

"These are little champagne grapes. It takes at least three times the usual amount to make a complete fruit portion."

"But they are so tiny. Surely one less wouldn't make a difference. By your reckoning, it would only be a third of a grape."

Esther was looking around for their waitress, a lovely, fair young lady with rosy cheeks. Peter Paul Rubens, the Flemish artist, would have adored painting that nice round waitress. Harold would have adored painting her. Though she'd have to have numbers stuck all over her to do so.

"I need a few more grapes," Esther told the waitress. "It's all right for me to have a few over the correct number, but not under."

Kari—as her nametag identified her—looked understandably confused.

Harold squirmed in his seat. "Please," he said. He strove always to be polite, to counteract Esther's rudeness.

Kari agreed good-naturedly to bring more grapes.

"And ask the driver to stop all this side to side movement," Esther added as the young woman turned away. "It's going to upset my digestive system."

"I don't think there's much he can do about it," Kari said with a grin. "After all, that's what trains do."

She had evidently concluded that she was joking. What a concept! Harold thought. He wondered, not for the first time, why Esther had agreed to come. His boss had given him a gift certificate for the dinner train in lieu of a bonus.

"Was she being impertinent?" Esther queried after Kari walked away, her lovely hips swaying with the movement of the train.

"Not at all," Harold said. "I thought she was very pleasant about it. She's right, you know. Trains always do rock a bit."

Esther quelled this defense with The Look. Stronger men than Harold had been known to quail at The Look.

Evidently satisfied that he had been sufficiently disciplined, Esther turned her attention to the cutlery. It was perfectly clean, but she polished it up with the spotless napkin just the same.

"The vinaigrette's delicious," Harold ventured. "Poppy seed, perhaps?"

"I'm quite sure it has sugar in it," Esther said. "I shall ask the waitress to bring me a fresh salad without the dressing."

There was no pleasing her when it came to food, unless she had prepared it herself. First of all, each food group had to have enough content to qualify as a proper serving. This didn't apply only to grapes; a fruit portion consisted of a quarter cup of raisins; six dried apricots; one whole banana, and so on, throughout out the entire FDA-recommended food pyramid.

She always made sure she had the correct serving of

organic sweet potatoes—she never ate white potatoes—of whole wheat bread, steel cut oatmeal, green, yellow, orange, and red vegetables, legumes.

After twelve years of marriage to Esther the food freak, Harold was still not sure what legumes were. Even salad veggies had to be measured, not to avoid eating too much, but to make sure there was enough to make a nutritious serving. On rare, wonderful occasions, Harold was allowed to eat range-fed chicken or cold-water fish, but never red meat. Health and nutrition magazines were Esther's bibles. It was her declared intent to live forever. And apparently she planned for Harold to live forever, too.

Harold had no objections to healthy food; even though sometimes he longed for a loaded-with-everything quarter-pounder with the kind of yearning other men might feel for sex. He'd given up longing for that years ago! A few lunch times he'd sneaked into a McDonald's near his office, but Esther could smell hamburger on his breath the second he closed the front door of their condo behind him, even if she was in the bathroom with the door closed.

Speaking of bathrooms . . . .

"Excuse me," he said, standing up. "I need to take a little journey."

Esther didn't like people to talk about restrooms, or toilets, or potties.

"In the middle of dinner?"

"A man has needs, Esther."

She sighed and recited her usual litany: "Be sure to wash your hands, before and after. Use paper towels to lift the seat and open he door, be sure to put the lid down before you flush—you don't want to release all those germs into the atmosphere."

Sometimes Harold deliberately avoided washing his hands, or else bravely left the lid up and turned all the germs loose to create havoc. Silly bit of rebellion, but it made him feel he still had control of some of his own bodily functions.

The restroom was occupied. Story of his life.

He waited, noting idly that one of the train's exit doors was next to the restroom. Its large handles looked fairly easy to open, though he doubted a child could manage it. A man could, of course.

Entertaining another mini-fantasy, he saw himself opening that door, jumping out, falling, falling, falling into oblivion. Peaceful oblivion. Nobody would notice; the area wasn't overlooked by any of the passengers in this car or the next one. This car was some distance back from the kitchen. If he could time the act just right, when nobody was serving anything, to use this particular restroom . . . .

The fantasy bubble burst as the bathroom door opened. It was a fantasy he'd called up frequently, in various guises, especially during those increasingly frequent times when he wasn't sure he could bear another day with Esther.

Divorce her, Harry, the man in the next cubicle had advised when he'd risked an after-work beer with him and found his tongue uncharacteristically loosened.

But his colleague didn't know Esther. It didn't matter what he wanted to do, she found a way to thwart him. Always. She'd be sure to convince the judge or whoever decided such things that he wasn't capable of making decisions. Somehow she'd manage to make him lose his job. He'd be sent to a mental institution and she'd get the house and the furniture and the small nest egg he'd managed to put away. At the end of the day, he'd find himself sitting in some homeless shelter, or sitting on a street corner with a knitted hat pulled over his ears, holding onto a sign that said: Will Work For Food.

He'd even fantasized a time or two about killing her.

He was afraid. She'd come back as a querulous ghost and haunt him forever.

"You took long enough," Esther snapped when he returned to his place.

"I had to wait," he explained.

She handed him a plastic bottle of instant anti-bacterial hand gel. (Kills Germs In 60 Seconds!)

"But I've already . . . ." he didn't bother finishing the sentence.

The gel was strong smelling. One of the blond men across the aisle glanced at him, frowning slightly.

Sighing, he noticed that Esther had a new salad, sans vinaigrette. His own empty salad plate had been removed. A plate of vegetables had been left in its place.

"What's this?" he asked, attempting a joke. "It sure doesn't look like prime rib." He could almost taste the wonderful rich beef flavor as the smell of it wafted through the train.

Esther gave him The Look.

He glanced over at the next table. The six beautiful people were all eating prime rib, with what appeared to be a wild rice pilaf on the side, plus some good-looking breads with a plate of little bowls holding various spreads.

They were all laughing and talking at once, even while they ate. Esther didn't think people should talk while they ate. It was uncouth, she said. As the train clacked along beside Lake Washington, and he dutifully ate his vegetables, he stared at the black and white photograph of the Seattle Space Needle at the end of the car and thought how much fun a man could have being uncouth once in a while.

A male voice above Harold's head interrupted his reverie. A PA system, he realized, after briefly fearing it was God about to chew him out for thinking uncouth thoughts.

But instead, it was someone making an announcement that the train was about to cross over the Wilburton trestle, which was the longest timber trestle extant in the state of Washington. It was 102 feet high and had been built in 1891, the voice said.

Sometimes Harold felt as if he had been built in 1891. And he'd been traveling downhill ever since.

He looked down through the dark to where the lights

shone on a road far below. Next to the road was a kind of ravine filled with trees; there's where he should have jumped. Perhaps if the man hadn't come out of the restroom when he did, he might have been at peace, now. He wondered if the laughing beautiful people at the next table would have noticed that he was gone. Probably not. Undoubtedly not.

For some reason, he found himself glancing at his watch.

Before the train pulled into its destination—the Columbia Winery in Woodinville, Kari the waitress came around to take their orders for the dessert to be served on the return trip to Renton. When Harold's mouth opened eagerly to ask for the Chocolate Paradise, Esther forestalled him by saying firmly that they would have ice water instead of dessert.

She didn't even give him the option of settling for the apple crisp.

Kari looked at Harold with sympathy as he closed his mouth. That was kind of her, but he didn't want a lovely Rubenesque young woman looking at him with sympathy. He had seen sympathy on too many faces, too many times.

He looked at his watch again as the train slowed to a stop.

Unsurprisingly, Esther didn't want to go on the winery tour, or into the tasting room where the passengers were quickly lining up at the bar and the handsome young male waiters were bustling about. As it was dark and cold outside, however, she did agree to step into the warm, brightly lit building.

The beautiful people were toasting one another with each different wine, saying "Cheers!" and "Down the hatch!" Harold felt like a child with his nose pressed to a toyshop window. He felt like that often, forever on the outside looking in.

"Why on earth did you agree to come?" he asked Esther as they returned to their seats on the train and she complained about how cold she was. "You knew you wouldn't have a good time, why didn't you just say no?"

She gave him The Look, but answered readily enough.

"They wouldn't let me return the certificate, they told me it wasn't redeemable for cash."

"You actually asked them?"

She looked at him as if he were the village idiot. "Of course I asked them."

Something clicked in his head. Afterward, he wasn't sure if Esther's statement was the trigger, or whether it was the question one of the neighboring table's beautiful women asked Kari that introduced him to the new fantasy. An infinitely better fantasy than his last one.

"Is this train as old as the Wilburton trestle?" the beautiful woman asked as the train started up again.

Harold found himself checking the time again. Just to estimate the time it would take to get back to Renton.

"Not that old," Kari said. "All of the cars have been restored, of course, but the oldest date back to the thirties, others to the fifties."

"I guess you don't have a ghost then," the woman said, pouting charmingly.

Her companions laughed. "Trust Olivia to want ghosts with her ride," one of the men said, smiling fondly.

Olivia. What a lovely name, Harold thought.

Kari gave a mock shiver. "No ghost, no." She smiled. "Though of course, it is getting close to Halloween, so who knows who or what might come aboard."

The beautiful people laughed again.

Esther made the sound *tsk* with her tongue. She always seemed to hate it when people laughed. Harold couldn't remember when he had last laughed.

A moment later, Esther stood up, giving the strained little smile she trotted out on rare occasions. "I'm going to make that little journey," she muttered.

The fantasy that had been shimmering in the back of Harold's imagination came suddenly rushing to the fore, filling Harold with so much electrical energy that he sprang to his feet, startling himself as much as his wife. "I'll come with you," he offered. "You'll need a hand to steady you against the train's rocking motion. Almost fell a couple of times myself. Can't have you hurting yourself."

She grudgingly allowed him to hold her elbow as she made her way down the aisle and around the divider to the restroom. Glancing around as she pushed the door open, Harold saw that there was nobody in sight. *Carpe the moment,* a voice said above his head. Not the PA system this time. Had to be God.

He stepped forward, following her in, cutting off her automatic rejection by saying, "Oops, that was quite a bump."

Then he closed and locked the door.

"What on earth are you doing?" Esther demanded.

For one second, she looked genuinely puzzled as he turned to face her, then his hands found her throat and her expression blanked out as she struggled to breathe and was finally, blessedly, unable to.

It was just a matter, then, of waiting and checking the time on his watch, looking out of the small window to make sure he'd pick the right time to open he door, He was pretty sure everyone would be busily eating their chocolate paradise or apple crisp about then.

Sure enough, when he stuck his head out, there was no one in sight. For once, fate was smiling upon him. Hauling his lifeless wife out with him, he wrestled her around to the exit door.

He was afraid someone might notice the draft but no one showed up when he hauled the door open and shoved Esther out with his foot. Bracing himself, he watched her body drop, catching sight of the light and trees he had seen before, and something else. Something that hadn't been there when he last looked, something he had noticed only a bare second before he had slammed and locked the door.

A moment later, he was back into the restroom, washing his hands symbolically rather than out of necessity.

Returning to his seat, he signaled Kari, making sure first

that he wouldn't sound out of breath. "Am I too late to order some Chocolate Paradise?" he asked.

"Not at all, sir." She glanced along the car, "For your wife, too?"

He shook his head. "She's having some problems with her digestive system."

Kari nodded sympathetically, with a gleam of understanding in her eyes. "I'll get it to you right away, sir."

"And a glass of Chardonnay, perhaps?" he suggested.

As his adrenaline level returned slowly to normal, he turned to look at his reflection in the dark window and realized that what he had seen below had been something very similar. Lights shining on a face, looking up, looking at him.

He sighed deeply. It wouldn't take long for whomever it was to summon the police. Everybody carried cell phones nowadays. Nobody was going to believe that the bruises on Esther's throat were due to an accidental fall, especially when he hadn't reported an accidental fall. Oh, he'd had some idea of suggesting that she'd mistaken the outer door for the door to the restroom, but who would have believed him?

A few minutes later, as he lifted the glass Kari had brought him, a miracle occurred, driving his gloomy thought away: Olivia, the beautiful Olivia, caught his eye and raised her glass. "Cheers," she said, before returning to her companions.

A glow of warmth surrounded Harold. The toast was a sign that he had done the right thing, he decided happily. No matter that the police would probably be waiting when the train pulled into he station, no matter that he would go to jail and then to prison. Esther would not be there to nag him. He would be alone, majestically alone. Even if he were sentenced to death, he would know that for one glorious moment in time, he'd have a chance to behave like a true man. The master of his fate. The captain of his soul.

And with any luck at all, if Esther did come back as a ghost, she would haunt the Spirit of Washington instead of him.

He wished he could tell Olivia.

DEAN AND CLAUDIA ASK MEG:

Q: *You physically visit the places you write about and imagine the story line as you 'walk' the story through. Did you ride on the Spirit of Washington for this story?*
A: Yes. It was wonderful! I took the Spirit of Washington Dinner Train from Renton in Washington to the Columbia Winery. It's very luxurious, beautifully decorated and extremely comfortable. The food is gourmet and the service exceptional. And the story came together while I was on the train. I have this semi-mystical idea that stories wait for me in the most interesting places in the world. I just have to go there and find them.

Q: *Do you have a 'first reader'? Do you belong to a writer's group?*
A: No and no. My agent is my first reader. I did belong to a writer's group when I started out, but that, was a while ago.

Q: *Do people really mistake you for Rhys Bowen, even though she's tall, elegant, and British and you're short, cute and American?*
A: First of all, I'm not short. I'm petite. And Rhys is barely three and one half inches taller than I. I do not call that tall! Also, I'm as elegant as she is. I have seven blazers in my wardrobe. We are both of dual nationality: British and American. But she sounds more Brit than I do. She's from the posh South and I'm from the blue-collar north. She has an English husband and writes about a Welshman and an Irishman, and I have an American husband and write about

American characters. As for being cute . . . . people call me cute. I'm not cute. I'm sexy!

Q: *Hooray!*

AND HERE IS MEG'S RECIPE:

MRS. TEMPLE'S POPPYSEED VINAIGRETTE DRESSING

(WITH THANKS TO THE FOLKS

AT THE SPIRIT OF WASHINGTON TRAIN)

3/4 cup sugar
1 1/2 tablespoons onion juice
1 cup vegetable oil
1 teaspoon salt
1 1/2 teaspoons poppyseeds
1/3 cup cider vinegar
1 teaspoon dry mustard

Mix all ingredients except the poppyseeds and oil in the blender. Add oil gradually while continuing to blend. Stir in poppyseeds and chill.

On the train, this is served with crisp romaine lettuce tossed with grapefruit sections and topped with toasted almonds. It is garnished with red onions marinated in red wine vinegar and honey.

SING FOR YOUR SUPPER

Don Bruns

Don Bruns is a charmer—a musician and a producer, he is the author of two novels, Jamaica Blue *and* Barbados Heat. *Sue Grafton says of Don's work: "Sex, drugs, rock and roll, and murder. What more could a reader want?" Lee Child finds Don's work "a bright, fresh, dead-on writer with a great new voice."*

"So who else gave up a medical career to become a rock star?" Sever watched D.R. Mosely as he bit into the shrimp, dripping with a spicy garlic lemon butter sauce.

Mosely wiped his chin with a red cloth napkin and slowly chewed. "You're the writer, the rock historian. You should know. Jan Berry was in med school when Jan and Dean first had a hit. I think Al Jardine of the Beach Boys was in dental school. I'm sure there were others."

"I can't believe this is your last show."

"I can't believe I've lasted this long with that son of

a bitch. I can't handle him any more, Mick. Jimmy is out of control."

Sever sopped up the sauce with a piece of French bread. "And this is all because of the ownership of the songs?"

"Twenty-six top ten hits. Do you know how much those are worth? Hell, we could sell that catalog for millions. Tens of millions. I wrote them! He owned the band and put his name along with mine on every one. I want them back."

"And he refuses to give up his rights?"

"No. Last night he said he might give up the fight . . . if, if I pay him two million dollars."

"And?"

"I'm thinking about it. It would be a small price to pay in the long run."

"You'll pack the hall tonight. The rumor on the street is that this is the end."

D.R. pulled on his Dixie long neck beer. "Mick, you've been writing about rock and roll longer than I've been performing. You know that groups like ours don't last long. Hell, twenty years? I'll miss it, but I won't miss Jimmy Dog."

The brunette approached the table, her eyes darting between Sever and D.R. "Excuse me. I really don't mean to interrupt, but you are . . . I mean, are you, well of course. You're D.R. Mosely from Rapid Fire."

Mosely smiled. "And you're that little brunette girl from . . . ?"

She laughed. "I thought so. That long blond hair and all. Jay and I," she motioned to the booth with her thumb, "we're going to your show tonight. I just knew it was you. Can I have your autograph?"

She offered a piece of paper and D.R. signed it with a flourish. She walked away grinning from ear to ear.

"So if Jimmy will agree to back off the song rights, what else is the problem?"

"I haven't got four hours to tell you. First of all, there's his wife, Ladonna. Mick, she is a first-class bitch. Our version of Yoko. 'Jimmy's not getting his share of this, and Jimmy would be better off without that, and Jimmy this and' . . . I'm going crazy!"

"I've met her."

"Then you know."

"She looks out for Jimmy."

"She prepares this white fish stew backstage every night on a hot plate, a couple of hours before we go on. Stinks to high heaven and Jimmy wolfs it down claiming it gives him extra energy. After a while the whole band is ready to hurl."

"Doesn't sound pleasant."

"Then, he's got allergies. Every kind of allergy known to man. And there are pills, powders, and lotions loaded on the dressing room table. And he's complaining about somebody smoking, or someone's cologne, or who knows what else."

Sever smiled. "You studied medicine. Does he really have all those problems?"

"Who knows? Ladonna lays out all this crap and he's popping all these pills and . . . ."

"D.R., settle down. You'll have a stroke."

"I'm sorry, Mick." He picked up another shrimp with his fingers and dipped it into the tangy liquid. "They add Worcestershire sauce. Nobody makes barbecued shrimp like Rosie."

Sever had one final shrimp from the overflowing bowl, and finished with another piece of French bread. "I've got to go, D.R. I've got the Rolling Stone article to do and I want to talk to your manager and maybe get a couple quotes from Jimmy and the rest of the band before you do your sound check."

"I'll see you there, man. Last show. We should kick ass tonight."

Sever paid the tab and walked into the hot, humid south Florida night. Climbing into his rental he saw D.R. coming out the door with a white bag in his hand. He waved at the singer and headed toward the arena.

THE sound technician worked in the middle of the floor, the mixing board spread out before him like a cockpit in a 747. He listened as the roadies talked into the microphones.

"Testing, testing, one two three four, one two three four."

He moved a slide and made a calculation on his laptop. Rapid Fire's manager stood off to the side talking to Sever.

"Do you believe this, Mick?" Mike Trump scratched his head. "I've managed this band since they formed and now they're going to give up on a career that covers twenty years. Hell, Jagger and Richards have put up with each other longer than that. Seems a shame."

"Seems like you're going to be out of a job."

"Yeah. Somebody should take Jimmy Dog out and shake some sense into him. You know what I'm sayin'? He and that self-centered bitch he's married to. If it wasn't for Jimmy, the band would go on forever."

"He's that bad?"

"Nobody can stand him, Mick. And because of him a lot of people are going to be looking for work."

Trump gave a thumbs up to the engineer and headed toward the stage. Sever followed.

"So why don't you fire him?"

"You know why. He owns the name Rapid Fire. It's his band, and he seems to think the songs are his, too."

"D.R. says he may be willing to move off that point. For two million dollars."

"Do you think Ladonna would settle for a measly two million? Ah, who cares. If they break up, it's no longer my concern." Trump stomped up the steps to the stage and disappeared behind the stacks of amplifiers, his bitterness lingering behind.

*   *   *

"LET'S give a huge Fort Lauderdale welcome to Rapid Fire!" The announcer's voice faded as the smoke poured from the stage. Jimmy Dog hit a power chord that swelled until it shook the seats full of screaming fans. The drummer started on the small toms and quickly ran down the eight drums with a rapid roll until he hit the lowest one. Kicking in with his double bass drums, he started a frenetic beat that thundered from the speakers and reverberated through the auditorium. The keyboards and bass followed suit, and D.R. walked through the cloud of smoke, whipping back his long blond hair. He grabbed the microphone from the stand, took a wide stance and let loose, his gravely voice showing signs of twenty road-weary years.

"Whatever you think that you know, you don't know nothin' at all. Make up a story, the fame and the glory, from your lofty perch you will fall . . . ."

Four men in black tee shirts stood at floor level, ready to repel the hordes of women who usually tried to crowd the stage. The audience was on its feet, fans punching their fists in the air and shouting the lyrics to the early hit, "Crawl."

"You've got to crawl, before you can walk, you've got to crawl, before you can talk, you've got to crawl, crawl into your hole . . . come on and do like I told you, CRAWL!"

D.R. nodded at Jimmy, waiting for the wail of his solo. Jimmy took a step forward, his hands in the air, reaching for his throat, clawing at his neck as if trying to tear the skin off. His face turned a raging red and he stumbled, catching himself, stumbling again and going to his knees. For a moment he looked into the sea of bodies swaying with the beat. Then he collapsed, face down on the cold, hard surface of the stage.

The music sputtered and the crowd screamed even louder. This was a whole new act, one they'd never seen before. Sever watched from stage left as D.R. bent down and turned Jimmy over. The guitar player's eyes were wide open, his tongue hanging from his mouth. It was obvious that the last guitar solo had been played. Jimmy Dog was dead.

THE detective took notes on a pad of paper. Several uniformed officers stood guard, protecting the scene. The grotesque body had been removed, and Sever, Trump, D.R., and Ladonna sat on folding chairs in a semicircle. Ladonna's legs were crossed, the tight leather pants hugging her long limbs.

"You say he had allergies?"

Ladonna, her steely eyes staring into the face of the detective, nodded. "He has a number of allergies. Why?"

"It appears he choked."

Trump stood up and walked to the lip of the stage, staring into the empty arena. "Could happen to anyone."

"No," the detective frowned. "His throat was swollen shut. There was no way to get any air."

"Sergeant!" The uniformed policeman approached him. "We found what you thought we might." In his gloved hand he held out a white paper bag.

"Open it up." The detective walked over and looked inside. "Shrimp." He sniffed. "With garlic butter, lemon, and some other spices."

Sever glanced at D.R. The singer's face was drained of color, almost an ashen gray.

"Mr. Mosely, you studied medicine didn't you?"

D.R. shook his head.

"When we called the hospital a short time ago, the preliminary report was that Jimmy died from a shellfish allergy. Know anything about shellfish allergies?"

D.R. stared at the floor.

"Let me help you. Someone allergic to shellfish can have a respiratory condition. Within a couple of hours of exposure, the throat can swell up, constricting the breathing process. Within minutes, the allergic person could be dead."

"I didn't give Jimmy any shrimp. Hell, if he was allergic, he wouldn't have eaten it anyway." Now the color was back and the fire was in D.R.'s eyes.

"Sir," the policeman motioned to the detective. "Back here."

They all walked back to the dressing room area. "We found this." He pointed to a white ceramic bowl with a murky liquid in the bottom. "Smells like fish."

Ladonna gave him a sad smile. Sever saw tears in the corner of her eyes. "It's the fish stew I made for Jimmy just before the show. He wasn't allergic to fish. Just shellfish." She reached for the bowl.

"No, no. We've got to check it out first. My guess is that there is some shrimp in the mixture. Someone who knew Jimmy was allergic decided to put him to the test."

Trump spun around and pointed to D.R. "There's your suspect. D.R. has been feuding with Jimmy for the last two years. And, he's got about twenty million dollars worth of reasons to get rid of him. Jimmy was threatening to sue for half interest in all of Rapid Fire's songs."

"And," the detective picked up the pace, "it's possible D.R. Mosely knew Jimmy was allergic to shellfish. What did you have for dinner tonight, Mr. Mosely?"

"Those shrimp." His gaze wandered to the white bag. "And yes, I brought home the doggy bag."

"You could save us a lot of aggravation if you'd confess now. It seems we've got the motive and very possibly the weapon."

Sever looked at the players. "Detective, I think you're overlooking another possibility. I talked to Mike Trump briefly before the show and he admitted that the band would be better off without Jimmy Dog. Trump was worried about losing his job, and he told me the band could go on forever if Jimmy was out of the way."

"Did you say that?" The detective looked accusingly at Trump.

"I did. And it's all true. But I certainly didn't kill Jimmy."

Sever gave him a half smile. "You're certainly quick to lay blame on someone else."

"Come on." Trump said. "D.R. brought the shrimp back with him. He wanted Jimmy out of the way and he knew Jimmy was allergic to shellfish. It all fits."

"Except that D.R. was close to striking a deal with Jimmy on the songs. He was considering just buying him out. Right, D.R.?"

The detective smelled the bowl. "Who had anything to gain by Jimmy's death? D.R., because he could have the songs free and clear? Mike, because the band could stay together? But I doubt Mike knew Jimmy had the shellfish allergy."

"I didn't. I really had no idea." Trump stared daggers at D.R.

Ladonna took a final look around the dressing room, her gaze resting on the powders, pills, and lotions that belonged to her recently departed husband. "Lieutenant, can I go? It's been a very long evening." She rubbed her forehead, the large diamond on her finger prominently displayed.

"I think you're missing one of the main suspects, Lieutenant." Sever walked behind Ladonna. "Jimmy was ready to settle the song dispute for two million dollars and then D.R. was going to break up the band."

"And?"

"And, it would have actually been a drop in income for Jimmy Dog and Ladonna. I don't think Ladonna was willing to give up the chance for half of twenty million dollars."

The detective tapped his fingers on the dressing room table. "So what do you suggest?"

"I think Ladonna saw D.R.'s doggy bag and decided to take advantage of the situation. She knew Jimmy was allergic to shellfish and just about everything else on this earth. She made the fish stew, and she put some of the shrimp in the dish. She knew D.R. would be the suspect."

Ladonna spun around, breathing fire. "I loved my husband. D.R. wanted him out of the way and saw an easy way to do it!"

"No." D.R. pointed his finger at the lady. "With Jimmy out of the way, you could continue legal action to retain interest in my songs. You knew Jimmy was going to roll over and you couldn't stand that. You've always been in this for yourself, and you thought if I was convicted for his murder you could claim twenty million dollars of songs for yourself."

"Grease holds fingerprint's very well. I know we'll find D.R.'s prints on this bag. But if we were to find your fingerprints," the detective motioned to Ladonna, "then . . . ."

"Rapid Fire was his band." She was screaming. "He got no respect. Those damned songs would never have been worth a penny if it wasn't for this band. We deserved more money and more credit than anyone ever gave us, and God knows I put up with the whiney, sniveling weasel for longer than I ever should have. I deserve a hell of a lot more. Do you hear me?"

The detective motioned to the closest uniformed policeman. He quietly walked over to Ladonna.

"He was going to walk away from twenty million dollars. Do you hear me? Twenty million dollars. I won't do that. I deserve a share of that for just putting up with all this crap."

The policeman quietly took her wrists and snapped the handcuffs around them, being careful not to scratch the four-carat diamond and gold tennis bracelet on her left arm.

"No, it's not fair. It's not fair." They led her away.

"Damn. Damn." D.R. paced the floor. "Those were great shrimp, but I don't know if they were worth all that."

"I'm sorry about what I said." Trump seemed subdued. "Do you want to consider going on the with the band?"

D.R. smiled. "No. No, Mike, I don't. I'm going to take some of that money and open up a little restaurant down in the Keys. And I'm going to feature barbecued shrimp the way Rosie makes it. And the one dish that will not be on the menu is fish stew. I won't allow it."

He motioned to Sever and the two of them walked out of the building.

"Got enough for your story, Mick?"

Sever looked back at the auditorium. "Hell, I've got enough for a book."

DEAN AND CLAUDIA ASK DON:

Q: *Your first novel was published about the same time we asked you for "Sing For Your Supper." How was the experience?*
A: It was, well, novel. And since this is a culinary story I've given you, I should tell this tale: a lady approached me at a mystery conference and said, "Excuse me. Would you mind signing my book?" I said, "Lady! That's what makes this all worthwhile! Hell, if you *read* the book, I'll come home and cook for you!"

Q: *You've a real love for music. Who are your partners in musical crime in the mystery world?*
A: Music! Aaah, music. The whole world revolves around music. (And so does "Sing For Your Supper.") Parnell Hall plays guitar and we're going to work on some tunes together. And I put together a CD called *Last Flight Out* and it made the charts.

Q: *It did?*
A: Well, in the Netherlands, sure. BUT IT MADE THE CHARTS!

Q: *What would you like your legacy to be, musical one?*
A: I love to tell stories. In songs, in books. One's legacy should be that of a role model. . . . But since I've lived a less

than exemplary life, I'll tell stories of heroes and villains, thieves and thugs, princes and paupers . . ."

Q: *Ah, Don?*
A: . . . saints and sinners. Oh. Right. Well, I wrote a song about a father and a son that best describes the legacy of a storyteller:
My father dies a pauper
Not a penny to his name
And as the man who is his son
I celebrate his fame.
He made all mankind richer
With the stories that he told.
Money didn't matter. It was the stories that were gold.

AND HERE IS DON'S RECIPE:

BARBECUED SHRIMP
(ROSIE'S RECIPE)

If you're allergic to shellfish, stay away!

> 3 pounds large shrimp unpeeled
> cayenne pepper
> black pepper
> garlic powder
> 4 sticks of butter
> 1/3 cup Worcestershire sauce
> Juice of two lemons
> 1/4 teaspoon Tabasco sauce
> two teaspoons salt

Wash and drain the shrimp. Sprinkle generously with pepper and garlic and place in a glass dish. Heat ingredients for sauce in a 4-cup measure on high for 2 minutes. Pour over shrimp and cover with wax paper. Cook in microwave on high for 12 minutes, stirring once or twice during cooking time until all shrimp are pink and tender. Add salt and let stand for 3 minutes. Serve plenty of French bread for dipping into hot butter sauce. Also serve with cold, long-neck beer.

LICENSED TO KOI

A Midnight Louie Adventure

Carole Nelson Douglas

♦   ♦   ♦

"A man had commissioned him to get this fish
and he was to receive ten centavos for it
because the man wanted to poison a cat."

—JOHN STEINBECK AND EDWARD F. RICKETTS
IN *SEA OF CORTEZ*

Carole Nelson Douglas calls herself a literary chameleon. She's written more than forty novels in various genres: mystery, science fiction, women's fiction and fantasy. A former journalist, Carole has been short-listed or won more than fifty writing awards. She currently writes the Irene Adler novels, the only woman to ever outwit Sherlock Holmes. The latest, Femme Fatale, *is set in New York City. Las Vegas is the setting for most of the Midnight Louie mysteries. Louie's latest adventure is* Cat in a Neon Nightmare.

I am stretched out in the shade near the pool area of the Crystal Phoenix Hotel and Casino, the most elegant establishment in Las Vegas. Filling up my view like an aquarium window is the hotel's koi pond, actually the private hobby of the hotel head cuisine artiste, Chef Song.

I should explain that Asian chefs and Asian cuisine are the

In thing in Las Vegas, given that the Chinese and Japanese are the world's most fervent and, luckily, wealthy gamblers.

And then there was that large Chinese labor pool at loose ends a century and a half back when the transcontinental railroad had been punched across the nation's wild West like push pins in a Chamber of Commerce bulletin board today. Plus, given the sizzling climate of the Mojave Desert, folks eat up spicy food of all regions and nationalities . . . south-of-the-border salsa and chiles hot enough to blister your eyeballs, sweet and torrid Indian chutneys and toe-curling curries, and, of course, tear-producing Szechuan fare and Chinese mustard. From the Japanese we get more refined temptations, like the raw seafood they call sushi, which has been right up my alley since I was a wee homeless kit.

So me, I go for koi, those plump, shiny, fifteen-inch-long piscine taste treats. Or I did when I was unofficial house detective for the Phoenix and kept an office by this very pond. I know every fin that flutters in these lily-pad-laden waters. I used to dip into these gold reserves every so often in the old days, for what are koi but very fancy goldfish, and no less tasty than their more common cousins, the lowly carp.

Many's the time that Chef Song caught me in the commission of a mid-afternoon koi dip and pursued me with his awesome cleaver that can mince onions read-through-thin.

I am too old and dignified for that game nowadays. Besides, I have since made a live-in arrangement with a little doll who has her own co-op off the Strip: she sees that I am supplied with enough shrimp, oysters, lobster, and scallops to keep me from indulging in deep-pond fishing for good.

Now I can regard these large, pricey, scaled swimmers with a cool connoisseur's eye. They are indeed worth watching. As they school they form a living collage of porcelain white-and-blue, onyx black, cinnabar red, and other artsy Asian palettes.

So I am dozing, no more desiring some instant sushi than a fallen-away Catholic craves a Friday fish, when I flick an irritated ear at a tinkle of falling water. I am used to the musical mutters of fountains in Las Vegas, but Chef Song's koi pond has no such accoutrement . . . it might disturb his precious *poisson*.

My sea-green eyes flash wide open just in time to see a boot heel disappear around a lush stand of calla lilies, trailed by a suspicious fall of fat wet drops.

I rise, shake out my best black suit coat, and amble to the koi pond's decorative stone edging. There I bend myself to the task of counting . . . not noses. Say . . . um, jaws. In counting the not-noses that always crowd the pond edge for handouts when any shadow lingers there, sure enough, I find that one of the twenty-eight koi is missing: a rare long-finned dragon carp that Chef Song had recently imported from a Japanese breeder. (Okay, so I have become something of an expert on the fine points of my former prey. Many a reformed gambler still plays church bingo.)

I back up, puzzled, my bare footpads leaving neat, damp prints on the concrete.

"Louie!" a furious voice shouts behind me.

Chef Song has caught me in a compromising position, although this time I am utterly innocent. The best course is a quick retreat. I charge past him before he can lift his cleaver to throwing height.

Although I am big for my breed, to most of the world at large I am taken for a wiry little guy born to blend into the shadows and dark carpets everywhere.

I trot hot on the heels of some tourist couple heading back into the hotel, slipping through the door into the icy interior air-conditioning. My ears are immediately assaulted by the raucous metal clangor of gambling devices. My sleek form is lost against the dark, busily patterned carpeting underlying the gaming tables. I follow the water drops and their definitely fishy odor all the way to the main elevator bank.

Whoever has managed to cop a koi and leave Midnight

Louie no out but copping a plea for a crime he did not commit will regret the day he, or she, exceeded the fishing limit at the Crystal Phoenix pond, which is zero.

Fugu is the only delicacy that cannot be served to the emperor and his family.

Before I trouble to sniff out which elevator bore the missing koi and its keeper to the hotel's upper regions, I decide I should know more about what might be going on here.

I have, in the pursuit of my profession, interrogated some pretty fishy characters, but they all wore hide, fur, or feathers. Midnight Louie, P.I., has never attempted to communicate with fish, and they, frankly, were not much inclined to stick around and chew the kelp with a dude of my ilk, since we are natural enemies going back to the dinosaur days, practically.

In this case I decide an ear to the ground is better than wet whiskers! So I wander the many public areas of the Crystal Phoenix, pausing at the shoe shine stand in the shopping arcade, queuing up unnoticed alongside the tourists at the ticket booth, ankling down the line to the front desk, and hunkering under the concierge's desk, where I finally hit pay dirt, or at least whiff something fishy going on.

"I am so sorry," she is telling a disappointed couple, "the Cinnabar Restaurant and Lacquer Lounge are closed to the public tonight. We have an international gathering of chefs serving a special fugu dinner."

Well, *mugu my tapian*! I cannot imagine what fugu is, unless it is a new variety of that so-called library paste masquerading as health food, tofu. If so, my Miss Temple is very likely to be soon shoveling it atop my Free-to-be-Feline curds of dry, army-green kibble. I may have to reconsider my life of koi.

"Fugu?" The lady tourist obligingly pursues the interrogation for me. "What is fugu?"

"It's that poisonous puffer fish, honey," her better half answers. "People die from eating it all the time."

"No, sir." The concierge is sounding a trifle desperate, as if she sees rumors of food poisoning racing around the casino floor even now. "These specialized fugu chefs are *licensed* to prepare and cook the fish and know how to carve out the poisonous parts. It is a sublime delicacy in Asia. A dinner like this is not only a rarity in the U.S., but costs five hundred dollars a head."

Is that a fugu head, I wonder, or a diner head?

"This event," she goes on, "is like a World Tournament of Poker. You may purchase seats to witness the dinner. Drinks will be served from the Lacquer Lounge."

"And how much a head goes for attending that?" the husband asks, a man after my own heart.

"Seventy-five dollars. The fugu are shipped live, with their mouths sewn shut, as they have very sharp teeth and might damage each other in shipment. Then they are fileted in full view and cooked and served in various dishes."

Right now my sympathies are with the fish for a change. Sewn shut! Granted, I would not like to joist such a mouthful of armament, but the poor devils are facing a fate worse than death: capture, mutilation, international export, and death by flaying and fileting. What we lower species have to go through to please the jaded tastes of the so-called higher ones!

Why was a koi removed from the koi pond? Money and lives are at stake in the fugu dinner planned for tonight—and the Crystal Phoenix's reputation—if someone can't hold his or her fugu. Already the programme has been manipulated for some sinister purpose.

I had better crash this upscale fish fry, or someone might die. At the least I stand a chance of clearing myself in Chef Song's eyes, which are all too accurate with a cleaver. And I owe a lot to the Crystal Phoenix and its owners for providing a home away from home before I found safe haven with my Miss Temple.

> "If blowfish weren't so poisonous, they might not be
> so popular."
>
> —KIICHI KITAHARA, OWNER, BLOWFISH MUSEUM,
> OSAKA, JAPAN

I need not wait for an invitation to this fishy affair, luckily, nor must I pay one penny for admission. I return to the elevator bank, find the one where the scent of fish has dripped into a pungent puddle, and wait behind a cigarette cylinder until a crowd gathers. Then I slip aboard alongside a woman wearing one of those ubiquitous and fashionable long, black skirts.

The restaurant and lounge are atop the hotel and have a floor to themselves. My elevator mates chatter about the upcoming event as we speed upward to our dinner date with potential death.

I hear the word "fugu" until it is coming out of my ears, which is probably better than it coming out of any other orifice. I also learn some chilling facts from the enthusiasts who consult their brochures in my undetected presence.

"Oooh," coos Long Black Skirt, her toes curling in her clog sandals. "A hundred people a year die from fugu poisoning. I'm glad we're just drinking and watching tonight."

"Eating the stuff is the Russian roulette of the gourmet set," a man answers her. "Although I'm told that, even safely prepared, the fish gives a tingly sort of high."

"Well, sure," says a portly man wearing Nike high-top sneakers. "And it's legal as long as the chef is licensed to cook, *if* you're a high roller who can bankroll an expensive freak show like this."

"I heard several celebrities will be dining," Long Black Skirt says. "Anybody know exactly who?"

Names start flying high over my head. I recognize several.

"It should be a duel of the titans," High-top Sneakers says. Whew, do *they* whiff at my nose level! "Monte Flynn, who owns the Mid-Strip hotel consortium, is coming. So is his arch-rival, the entertainment mogul Wynn Scofield. Those two guys are battling to build the biggest chain of hotel-casinos in Vegas. That's why the dinner is on neutral ground. The Crystal Phoenix is one of the few independent hotels left in town."

I fluff my ruff with pride that goes unnoticed. I began my investigative career here at the Phoenix, and my little doll, Miss Temple Barr, has their public relations contract. (This public relations is not as naughty as it sounds, but involves blowing the establishment's horn on an orchestral scale.)

Ummm, speaking of "scales," my tummy is rumbling already. It will take all my self-control to concentrate on the case at an all-fish dinner . . . that and the knowledge that not only are these alien imported fugu poisonous, but that someone is already playing around with the main attractions on the menu.

I cannot for the life of me figure out why someone would nick a koi from the hotel pond on just this night. Whatever that indicates, it means no good to someone, not to mention to the abducted koi.

It does tickle my tonsils to think that I might have a paw in rescuing one of my archenemy's precious koi from a fate worse than fugu. Chef Song would loathe having to give me credit for anything but irritation.

The elevator is lilting to a smooth stop, so I concentrate on blending in with the fortunately fashionable black that is evening wear, and exit the elevator unnoticed.

Once I scurry into a dim area of the hall, I hie farther down and around to my chosen entrance: the kitchen. These Las Vegas kitchens are as noisy and crowded as subway stations. Here I am likely to be overlooked if I can keep my shadowy form from being trampled by a stir-fry of chefs in full furor.

Music to my ears! The cymbal clash of stainless steel pot

lids. The mellifluous arias of hysterical chefs, enhanced this time by a minor Asian undertone, a beat driven by flying feet, rolling steel food carts, and falling tidbits. It is as if I am sitting under the yum-yum tree as particles of shrimp fall into my eager mitts.

But I am not here for the appetizers. I dart from rolling cart to rolling cart, my fur already frizzed from the steam heat suffocating the place.

Chef Song stands amid the chaos, a conductor with a cleaver, waving it forcefully in every direction.

My eyes remain on the floor, searching for boot-heels.

Unfortunately, boots are high fashion these days, even for women. Chef Song is ordering the fugu-licensed chefs each to their own stainless steel island. There are three, each serving two diners, each preparing the fugu's accompaniments, looking up only to call each other's names.

But where is the literal main course?

At last, atop an unused stove top, I spy a large fish tank with seaweed-choked, murky water. Spiny, shadowy forms eel past the glass. Of course I must leap up and investigate. I press my face against the glass and find myself snout to snub-nose with a dull-scaled finster a world away from the technicolor koi. This dude resembles a cross between a piranha and a really porky porcupine. Just as I register its presence, it swells up even more to emphasize its wicked spines and bares a wide jaw lined with needle-sharp teeth. Piranha is obviously the dominant flavor of the mouth here! I do not relish a mouth-to-mouth session with this razor-lipped dude, anyway. I could end up with a staple-gunned schnozzola. Maybe he is imported muscle, who knows?

I jump down onto the nearest stepping stone: a covered bucket, nearly dislodging the cover and creating the sort of noise that would draw unwanted attention to myself.

Fortunately, fast footwork allows me to land, reinstall the cover on the bucket and observe the scene a wiser and more stable dude.

I pause to interpret the hiss and spit of conversation in the kitchen and glean these facts. The Fugu Three are fierce rivals: one man, Huang, is Chinese; the other, Takamoto, Japanese; and the third fugu chef is of the female persuasion. She is a petite little doll like my resident redhead, Miss Temple Barr, but has long, spidery dark locks. When Takamoto commandeers the communal rice bowl, she leaps like a crouching tiger to procure her fair share.

As she races to defend her turf, I cannot help but notice that she is wearing Cuban-heeled black ankle boots. *Très chic*. *Très* suspicious.

Unfortunately, both Huang and Takamoto are similarly shod, though in somewhat larger sizes. I gasp. (One would think I was a perishing fish.) Even Chef Song wears similar footwear. Are humans all *sheep* these days? Sam Spade never had to put up with cloned clues.

At least I have seen the Cast du Kitchen: my own uneasy fellow koi-admirer, Chef Song of the Crystal Phoenix; the Chinese and Japanese rivals in cooking and carving fugu: Huang and Takamoto, and the oddity in the Asian triad, the China doll with the *kung fu* moves who goes by the American appellation of Chris.

Chef Song supervises them all. He is a man of nearly sixty, and a bit portly, as all chefs tend to become, but his hair is as shiny and black as wet, ripe olives, as my own formal coat, in fact, when it is freshly laved.

As for the fish, what can I say? Most naked fish are pale and flaccid and distressingly alike once their scales and heads are removed. These are still spined and mobile. I suspect that blowfish, a.k.a. puffer fish, are unique in having skin, not scales.

The licensed chefs, busy preparing the foods that will accompany the infamous fish, ignore their main courses in motion, as does everyone in the kitchen but yours truly. The sound of chopping vegetables is so frantic that the chefs seem to be juggling their implements rather than using them. In fact, one blade so sharp it would sing off-key were it possessed of vocal cords whistles through the steamy air . . . and with a startling *thwack* impales the butcher block cutting board right beside Miss Chris's elbow.

She does not even wince, but bares an irritated grimace. "If the Honorable Huang and Takamoto would concentrate on carving their bok choy rather than their rivals, we would serve these meals on time."

Apologies are profuse, but Miss Chris is too busy dicing some ugly rootlike thing to much notice.

I take this for my cue to slip into the dining arena . . . I mean, *area* . . . to study the six recipients of our chef's ceaseless labors.

> "I feel sorry when I kill fugu because
> they close their eyes and make a noise
> that sounds like they are crying."
>
> —Japanese chef

The restaurant's usual seating format has been reconfigured. Tiers of small round bistro tables circle like multiple wagon trains around a central space occupied by one long table. This produces the effect more of an operating theater than a dining room. Indeed, the spotlights that illuminate the long white cloth and the colorful figures gathered around it underline my ghoulish comparison.

Beyond the spotlights dimness prevails, both in terms of illumination and mentally, in my estimation. Nothing is so oblivious as a bunch of humans intent on watching a show. One could pick his nose without being noticed.

I ease among the audience who are all intent on the scene below. At first I think a wide-vision TV screen is suspended over and just behind the diners, who sit in one long line, not opposite each other. Then I see that it is a mirror, for the rears of their heads are unfortunately visible at the bottom, and none too attractive. I can sympathize. I find it very hard to wash behind my ears myself, and there is this one cowlick that I could use a large bovine tongue to flatten properly. Bad hair days are an intra-species problem.

OF course this event is not all about me, so I make myself low and soundless and virtually invisible as I settle near an aisle so I can still see the goings on below.

A woman with a mike is prowling among the first tier of watchers settled behind the beverage of their choice.

"Ladies and gentlemen," she greets the darkness that surrounds the illuminated tabletop. She is a tall, striking woman with thick tortoiseshell-colored hair (sometimes called "frosted"). She wears a pantsuit that mimics a gentleman's black tie and tails, and carries a portable microphone.

"What we will witness tonight is the first charity fundraising event based on the ancient Asian art of fugu eating. Fugu is native to Asian waters, and has been consumed in China for thousands of years and Japan for hundreds. This is fugu's first Las Vegas engagement. Each of our six guests has paid five hundred dollars for the dinner. You have paid to watch it. But I announce tonight that each of our fugu-happy celebrities is also donating fifty thousand dollars to FRAA, the Foundation to Research Allergic Ailments."

Well, hurrah for FRAA! Our hostess steps aside to introduce the generous experimenters, that is to say . . . the fugu-eaters.

Monte Flynn and Wyatt Scofield, the hoteliers, are hailed. Both are well-fed fellows in their mid-fifties in sleek black evening dress with thinning fur on top.

"I hope," says Flynn with a bow and a nasty smile to Scofield, "that your dinner agrees with you better than the outcome of our last bidding war for the Oasis Hotel and Casino."

"I *let* you lose that deal, Monte . . . by letting you win it,"

Scofield responds. "That property will bury you in red ink."

"Not when I finish the makeover, Wyatt."

"The makeover will finish your cash flow."

They remind me of Siamese fighting fish, except that both are still grinning like, excuse me, Cheshire cats. (I am not sure what a Cheshire cat is, but I know that it is renowned for its well-displayed ivories that would no doubt make a fugu with unbuttoned lips envious.)

"Now, gentlemen," our hostess interrupts. "Your business rivalry is legendary, but here you'll be competing only for generosity." She turns to the audience. "These two gentleman have a side bet: whoever eats the most of his all-fugu dinner will 'win' another fifty thousand for the foundation from the loser."

Wild applause and whistling from *much* too close to my vicinity. My ears flatten, affected by both the racket and by what's at stake. This side bet encourages Las Vegas's two biggest moguls to gobble down as much of the devil fish as they can. Given their competitive natures and rivalry, they could well fugu themselves to death if even a scintilla of tainted organ is left in the filets.

Such is the faith in modern science, or culinary precision, that no one besides me seems to notice that this event is a nice setup for "accidental" homicide.

Not the hostess. She has moved on to introduce a portly old gentleman. Call him the deep-sea grouper of the crew.

"And here," she says, resting a set of crimson-varnished claws on his formally clad shoulder, "is our next diner."

He has to be a Hollywood type, I guess, as the brightest spotlight swivels to bathe his position with enough downlight to force a confession in an interrogation room. But Hollywood types are used to bright lights, and only Hollywood-type guys wear funny formal white shirts with little stand-up collars, no tie. Then I recognize him. Aye, aye, sir!

"Kirk James, ladies and gentlemen," the hostess trumpets

like an elephant or a game show host, "chief gourmand on the televised and wildly popular *Iron Chef* competitions!"

James waves uplifted fork and knife like orb and scepter, nodding to the crowd so enthusiastically that I fear that his toupee will immigrate to another head, hopefully not mine. My cowlick isn't *that* bad.

"Thank you, thank you." James quiets the applause while patting his expansive grouper belly. "At least I'm assured that I have too much . . . er, stature, to O.D. on fugu."

While everybody is laughing at this self-deprecatory reference to his weight, the hostess has paused behind the sole female diner.

"And from her one-woman show at the Rio Hotel, we have here Rita Norelle. I hope a fugu dinner won't clog up those famous vocal cords of yours."

"No problem," Miss Rita says. "I understand that the divine fugu opens up the senses, rather than shuts them down."

She is a lengthy eel of a lady visibly struggling not to kiss her forties goodbye. Speaking of cords, they are all visible in her neck and she has a chest bony enough to use as a xylophone. I, myself, prefer zoftig ladies in full-length furs, but recognize that Miss Rita is the desired human type who photographs well.

I have also heard that she has made several trips to rehab for substance abuse, and you can bet it wasn't catnip, so I am not sure she should be sampling the apparently addictive, as well as dangerous, fugu.

I also remember that she is the former fling of Monte Flynn and that their parting of the ways included a public shouting match with high-priced lawyers as referees.

No wonder she is seated two chairs down from him. I do not like the way her bony fist clutches her dinner fork either. She looks as primed to spear a live person as a dead fish. A big time angler like me notices these things.

Three more celebrity diners remain unintroduced. I can

hardly wait to ID them, and the hostess is joanie-on-the-spot.

"Also, from the Hyena Hutch, that stand-up stand-up comedian and champion charity fund-raiser, Rango Williams!"

Applause stops the intro cold. Rango is the most off-the-wall of comedy acts, a man of color who can range from 'hood jokes and off-color rap numbers to sophisticated satire and suave footwork. Call him a barracuda in a Clown Fish suit. He headlines at the Raviera, Wyatt Scofield's latest high-profile performance club. I remember hearing that Scofield "stole" him from Flynn.

Hmmm. Only in Las Vegas is stealing a guy's lead act as bad as walking off with his significant other.

It strikes me the four diners so far would have reason to hope that one or more of the others will choke on a fish bone tonight, or gag on an overlooked and undercooked fugu liver.

"Of course we all know and love 'Cirque du Lune,' but we seldom meet the faces behind the makeup and the marvelous acrobatics. I present the astounding contortionist, Eland."

This is an elfin man, who even in a white turtleneck shirt seems as exotic, fey, and fragile as a sea-horse. When announced he spins somehow and ends up balancing on the chair-top, regarding us through the basket-weave of his elbows and knees. I suspect he speaks with his body rather than his tongue. How nice to know that the vain celebrity chatter at the table will be reduced by one.

"And finally," the hostess breathes into the microphone as if impersonating a tropical storm, "our sixth celebrity diner, action film star . . . Dag Heuer!"

Five-foot-ten of solid muscle wearing a black tie stands up, and the length of the part that goes around his neck would serve as a belt for Shamu, the killer whale. A black belt.

"Thank you, folks." Dag Heuer's Teutonic accent makes you want to salute something. "I will be Bach."

Why would anybody want to, these days, I wonder in some amazement. It's all rock 'n' roll nowadays anyway. I just do not see this man in some boring historical bio pic, even if he has the accent for it.

Heuer sits down while everybody holds their breaths to make sure the chair doesn't break. *Aha!* I remember now! He is rumored to be running for governor of Nevada, but he is ultra conservative politically. He would not look favorably on expanding the hotel gambling empires, divas who do drugs, comics who aim barbs at the NRA, mute contortionists one can never quite pin down, or even *Iron Chef* celebrities who get more residuals than he ever will.

I settle onto my haunches, safely hidden by the floor-length black table cloth that swathes all the bistro tables around me.

Our hostess lowers her voice to the reverential hush used by commentators for televised championship golf games.

"Ladies and gentlemen, fugu is a rare and unusual fish beyond its delicious and deadly taste. It has no scales, yet is the only fish with eyes that can close. It is also a friend to humankind and is the centerpiece of its own Genome Project at Cambridge University." Here she baldly reads from a paper in her free hand. "Its genome shares the same vertebrate blueprint as the human genome, a commonality that has been preserved in both species over the four hundred and fifty *million* years since our species diverged. Yet the fugu genome sequence is seven times shorter. This allows scientists to study gene sequences and regulatory elements much more simply."

While she takes a breath, Rango jumps in.

"Hell, I am not going to eat this fish. I am going to marry it!"

"They do look like something I *almost* married," Rita adds with a stabbing glare at Monte Flynn.

"No fish is *my* ancestor," Dag Heuer says, scowling.

I could not agree more. The great white shark is not really a fish.

I must say that I am beginning to wonder how many millions of years I was devouring when I partook of Chef Song's koi in my salad days.

The hostess hastens to less controversial waters. "And tonight, we have had three specially licensed Asian chefs flown in for the occasion who will serve our six guests. These cooks have taken intensive courses and written exams. All have served extensive apprenticeships before serving fugu to diners.

"This will be an all-fugu meal: hors d'oeuvres, fish-and-rice soup, sashimi, and stew. The chefs have been busy in the kitchen preparing the trappings, but the main event will happen here, before your very eyes. Each chef will prepare two fugu, removing the highly toxic ovaries, skin, intestines, muscles, and livers from the fish. Even touching these deadly organs can cause symptoms. The poison is tetrodotoxin, and the amount of it in a single fugu could kill thirty men." Oohing from the audience. "A few grains of powdered tetrodotoxin sufficient to cover the head of a pin could kill a man." Ahs from the audience. Nothing gets 'em like mayhem.

"You make it sound like women are immune," Rita Norelle quips.

"I was using the universal reference," the hostess says.

"Not in my universe," Rita snaps back, glancing acidly at Monte Flynn. "Some men are way too used to thinking they are the only ones who matter." She makes a point of linking elbows with Wyatt Scofield, who sits between Rio Rita and her former flame.

"What matters *here* and *now*," the hostess says emphatically, taking control, "is that we have a doctor and nurse standing by in case any of our diners show the slightest reaction."

At this the white lab coated, surgical-masked, latex-gloved

pair step out from the door to the kitchen, looking like well-starched ghosts. I recall seeing latex gloves on all three fugu chefs as well.

"What would a slight reaction be? Hangnail? Or coma?" Rango Williams sounds jocular, but also edgy.

"Respiratory difficulty, I imagine," Monte Flynn suggests. He sounds like he'd like to give Rita a dose of respiratory difficulty.

"A tingle on the tongue," Scofield adds, cuddling up to Rita with relish. "Dizziness, weakness, constriction, collapse, and respiratory paralysis. Fugu is twelve hundred and fifty times more potent than cyanide."

"Whew!" Rita fans herself rather ineffectively with her chopsticks. "And no scent of bitter almonds to warn the victim."

"Then at least," Monte Flynn says, leaning around Scofield, "I won't have to suffer your perfume again."

"Here come the chefs," the hostess announces in loud desperation.

Indeed they do, all attired in white aprons and traditional Western chefs' caps, an idiotic headgear even for an idiotic species, if you ask me.

"The honorable Huang, Takamoto, and Chrysanthemum."

All the chefs bow as named. I bow back, unnoticed, at the enchanting Chrysanthemum. No common garden variety "Chris," after all! I always had an eye for the ladies and they always eye me back.

Each chef is bearing a tray with two of the unfortunate Fish of the Day, which fortunately have closed their eyes and breathed . . . gasped . . . their last offstage in the kitchen.

A side table is being loaded with serving dishes and rice.

Each chef steps to the dining table, lays the platter before two of the diners and begins the rapid and delicate art of opening the fish and removing the fatal organs. The audience watches the process in the suspended mirror. The liver is removed with a great flourish and deposited in the bowl used for the other toxic parts. The fins are removed, put into a bowl borne by an assistant and fried at the preparation table.

During all this the hostess whispers the procedures over the microphone. "The fried fins will be dipped in hot sake and presented to the diners first. This is called Fugu Hire-zake in Japanese."

Fugu hara-kiri, if you ask me! That hot saki stuff will kill you!

While our celebrity diners are sucking down the floating fins with various expressions—stoic, grim, and devil-may-care—I watch the chefs.

These are knife-work masters as they delicately remove the fugu skin in one piece, then take pliers—yes, my friend, ordinary pliers—to despike the skin. I wonder in what culinary treasure they will use those spikes! *Ick.*

"The despiked skin," our hostess whispers reverentially, "is cut up into a salad known as Yubiki and dressed with a soy and vinegar blend called Ponzu."

The audience gasps and cries out, as they see in concert the three chefs behead the six fugu. A bowl collects these and an assistant carries them off, eyes closed.

The chefs swiftly filet the bodies and cut them into pieces for the various courses, returning to the preparation table to work without the benefit of mirrors. Now it has come down to ordinary cooking.

I do not believe that I will ever drape a claw in the Crystal Phoenix koi pond again. I have lost my taste for wild game and must admit that I only ate koi in the old days because I was homeless and starving. And then, later, because I could.

> "The taste of fugu is incomparable.
> If you eat it three or four times, you are enslaved. . . .
> Anyone who declines it for fear of death
> is really a pitiable person."

—KITAOJI ROSANJIN, POTTER AND GOURMET

And so the parade begins. The saki cups are taken away, the hors d'oeuvres arrive, followed by soup, sashimi, and stew.

Eland is not only supple with the chopsticks, but he eats with his feet. And here I have been castigated in the past for that very habit! That very . . . feat, in fact. (I myself was extremely acrobatic from birth, although I have never tried to eat with chopsticks.)

Soup is sipped, not spooned in Asian culture, and all the diners seemed to have overcome the cultural shock of bumping lips with fried fins swimming in saki.

The way a couple diners at this table feel about each other, namely Miss Rita and Mr. Flynn, bumping lips with a fugu, dead or alive, is preferable to doing it with former human partners.

I myself am a nose-to-nose kind of guy.

I watch the hotel honchos chow down fugu like sharks scarfing guppies.

Kirk James is wasting no time eating, either, and rolls his expressive eyes as he experiences, or pretends to experience, the vaunted "tingle."

Eland eats slowly and delicately. Miss Rita eats very little, but one look at her angular figure says why. Dag Heuer eats as if it was an order, methodically but with little gusto.

And Rango Williams makes a pantomime of suspicion dueling with lust for the entire dinner. Somehow he has palmed one of the decapitated fugu heads and produces it between the soup and the sashimi, proclaiming, "Alas, poor Genome, I knew it well, in my bones, you might say. Or its bones."

The audience has gone from rapt to rustling, to whispering and giggling nervously.

Nothing has happened. Relief and disappointment joust for dominance, as these emotions do in me. I suspected foul play. To have things turn out otherwise is somehow . . . insulting.

The only suspense left is which mogul will gobble down

more of the dinner and win fifty thou off the other. Gluttony for charity.

And then I stiffen. No, I did not sample any fugu in the kitchen! I notice an oddity in the tableau before my eyes. One of the diners is moving slowly, looking . . . disoriented. Maybe tingly. Dizzy.

A good stainless steel fork falls from loosening fingers, clattering into unused chopsticks.

A head nods on its neck, then wobbles from side to side. Eyes open wide. Then shut. The diner mews like a dying fugu and slides slowly out of the chair, behind the falling white curtain of the tablecloth, out of sight.

All this I see step by step, yet with the blinding speed of my inborn predator's eye. I am bounding out of my blind, chasing victim, not prey, drawing all eyes away from the big picture to the snapshot of sudden death flashing in a lethal second at its dead center.

I am atop the table, howling and pacing. I can only spy the danger. I cannot administer to it.

"Good grief," the hostess's voice growls over the sound system. "Who let that cat in?"

Nobody cares about me, for the medical team is rushing to the fallen diner, slinging the chair out of the way, bending to tend the victim.

The mirror above shows their white backs laboring, shows them pawing at the downed body, administering CPR. The doctor lifts up his theatrically masked face, shouts for 911, an ambulance, EMTs.

Cell phones burst into flower all over the audience, but the diners remain standing in their places, shocked and pale. The chefs stand at attention in front of the preparation table, eyeing each other.

The nurse rises, her surgical mask dangling at her throat. She was the first to attend the victim. I saw her head bowed over, those fish-pale unlipsticked lips giving CPR.

"Too late. She's dead," the nurse announces.

The doctor stands up shortly, eyeing the chefs. "I've never seen a toxin act so fast and so fatally. Even tainted fugu requires a few minutes before its effects are felt. What have you done?"

Now that everyone has stood up, I see the victim's face. And, of course, the entire audience has inferred the identity from the position at the table that is so suddenly vacant.

Rita Norelle, songstress, will sing no more.

All eyes fixate on the dish of fugu stew sitting at her place instead of her.

All eyes then turn to the trio of chefs.

An unnamed, unknown assistant standing by steps forward.

"They were at each other's throats in the kitchen all night," he says. "Chefs are spoiled prima donnas, even the best of them, but these three—I thought they were going to poison each other before their fugu were even dead and ready to do the job."

"Then why poison a guest?" Chef Song, standing in the door from the kitchen, speaks. "Arrow aimed at the house next door seldom lands in the arboretum."

Ye gods, he is sounding like some dime-store Charlie Chan. Someone must put a stop to this.

"Yo," says Dag Heuer. "All the better to discredit the other chef. It was Takamoto who served Rita and Rango. So Huang, here, or the deceptively cute Miss Chrysanthemum did the job. You notice they are Chinese and Takamoto is Japanese. This whole set-up is according to Japanese custom, and I bet the Chinese were pissed about that. The Chinese and Japanese have been at each other's throats for centuries."

Well, I cannot stand to have my little doll Miss Chrysanthemum accused of murder most fishy. I cannot stand to have anyone accused of something that plainly is not the case. But how can a mute little guy that everyone overlooks even though he has blown the whistle on the death, mutely, lead these dumb horses to water they do not want to drink?

I glance at Eland, who has curled into an impossibly tight ball of denial. He is no help in the present situation, but he is an inspiration.

I must, by nature, *show* not tell.

So I settle down at Miss Rita's deserted dish and proceed to gobble down all the fugu I can find amidst the rice.

Hmmm, a dry, delicate flavor, presenting as a murky blend of pond scum and fish kibble.

People are shrieking all over the place.

"Stop that cat!" "He'll kill himself!" "Poor kitty!" "Stupid feline!" "Louie, stop or you die!"

That last order was from Chef Song and he actually sounds a tad concerned. But the thing is, I do not stop, and I do not die. This is what I must show this knee-jerk crowd so ready to blame a dead fish and a trio of chefs for a murder they did not commit.

By now I am full up with fugu and the hullabaloo has died down. People are shoving the other diners' plates toward me and I attack them with the same gusto, devouring only the fish and showing no sign of giving up the ghost.

I do belch once, loudly, in the impressive silence.

"It is not the fish," Chef Song proclaims.

He walks over to watch me in some awe. I enjoy the moment, although I notice out of the corner of my eye that he is toting his ever-present cleaver.

"If it is not the fish—?" The hostess articulates what everyone is thinking, only she unconsciously speaks into the mike.

I have everyone's attention, but I do not know what to do next. This place will be swarming with emergency and police personnel in minutes and I need to finger the killer before the crime scene is all fugued up. I could yowl at the perpetrator, or leap up and claw the hell of the perp, but by now everyone here is convinced I am a crazy sort of cat acting on creature instinct.

Including my new-found friend, Chef Song.

He narrows his eyes at me. "I know this cat. He is notorious around the hotel for a great fondness for fish. He is an aficionado, as they say, for the koi fish in my personal pond. He has evaded me for years, but now he flaunts his appetite here, in public. Bird may change his feathers, but the beak still drinks of the same water."

Oy, pretty soon Chef Song will be calling me his Number One Son. Enough of aphorisms and some incisive conclusions, please.

Chef Song bends near to prod the few fish flakes I have left on Miss Rita's plate. The fish flakes I have intentionally left on Miss Rita's plate.

He lifts his fingers to his nose, sniffs, frowns. "This is not fugu, this is koi. *My* koi! Someone has substituted one of my koi for a fugu!"

Fee, fie, fo, fum, I smell the blood of a koi-killing murderer about to be undone.

"Not us," the chefs say in chorus.

"Who brought you the fish?" Chef Song demands.

"The . . . one of the . . . your assistants," Huang says. The other chefs nod.

"Which one?" Chef Song's fingers tighten on his cleaver.

For once I am not worried.

The chefs consult each other silently. "They all look alike," Takamoto says, shrugging helplessly.

Miss Chrysanthemum nods. "We were bent over our work tables. I glimpsed only a white apron and a platter, and my two fish were in front of me."

The two other chefs nod. Preparing a fugu dinner requires the focused concentration of a surgeon.

By now the other diners are milling around, aware that murder was afin.

"Wait a minute," says Rango Williams. "You are telling

me that someone switched a nonpoisonous koi for the real fugu? Why?"

"Yeah," Dag Heuer says. "She should be as fine as an AK-47 right now. Maybe a little well-oiled from the saki, but . . . not poisoned. Maybe it was a heart attack."

Everybody is frowning, because of course his points are logical, but they do not take into account the truly diabolical method at work. I am convinced that fugu killed the lady, but the fish did not.

What to do? Everybody is ignoring me again, as usual. While sometimes I appreciate my natural undercover abilities, sometimes they drive me crazy.

So . . . I might as well live up to my reputation and—

I leap up from the snow-white tablecloth with a snarl, a rather sated snarl, I am afraid, and lunge at my suspect.

My razor-sharp shivs snag in an article of clothing, which I rip right off.

Chef's hats are silly, but hats in general are an elementary piece of clothing that can totally alter a face.

Everyone at the table stares at my de-cap-itated victim. Only Wyatt Scofield gasps in recognition.

"Myrna!"

Blond hair spills like golden koi scales onto white-coated shoulders. With the mask around her throat resembling a clumsy ascot, the "nurse's" identity is clear to the one man who matters. Her lover.

"She was making up to you, even before tonight," Myrna accuses in white-hot rage.

"She was just flirtatious, darling."

"Don't 'darling' me! Sixteen years together and I never asked for a ring. But the moment she left Flynn you were hot to have her, just because it would irritate him. You never thought about what would irritate me. We are not hotels, Wyatt. This is not a Monopoly game."

I could point out that it *is* a game of Clue, but of course I cannot, will not, speak to the lower species.

"Then," Chef Song asks, gazing down at the body of Rita Norelle, "how did she die, if not from fugu?"

A calm sonorous voice answers. Eland has untangled himself into a slight modest man with very sad eyes.

"It was fugu, a concentrated powder of fugu. I saw the nurse's gloved fingers push into Rita's mouth during the efforts to revive her. Check the glove. I imagine Rita's saki had a mickey in it, to bring on the condition that required intervention. What career did Myrna have before you became her, er, sponsor, Mr. Scofield?"

"Magician's assistant at the Oasis," he answers, and can say no more.

"If you saw her," Chef Song asks the contortionist, "why did you not say something sooner?"

Eland eyes me, as one professional to another. We do not interrupt each other's acts. He twists into a pretzel of withdrawal. His voice seems to come from another part of his anatomy than his head entirely. Rather like the Cheshire cat disappearing into only a smile in *Alice in Wonderland*.

"I was not sure until the cat revealed her face, and Mr. Scofield revealed a motive."

At the words "the cat" all eyes turn to me.

But I am not there.

I have slipped to the floor and eeled my way out, heading home.

> *I cannot see her tonight.*
> *I have to give her up.*
> *So I will eat fugu.*

I stumble home, feeling fine, but a little bloated. A lot bloated. I have not had a whole koi for some time and have forgotten how rich it was.

While I walk off the evening's excitement, I savor a secret triumph. With a murderer identified, no one inquired why a koi in fugu skin was served to the victim. It was, in fact, a mistake, is all I can figure out. Hey, things happen, even to mess up a murder plot.

This much I know:

When I jumped down from the fugu tank, I dislodged the cover of a bucket. Inside I glimpsed the golden glimmer of koi. That's when I suspected that a switch would be made, and it was easy enough to sniff out my favorite fish once atop the table.

But how did the real koi get there? Each chef served two diners: Huang, the two hoteliers; Takamoto, Miss Rita and Mr. Kirk James; the lithe Chrysanthemum, Rango Williams and Eland. One diner was, to put it bluntly, chicken.

Either Miss Norelle or Mr. James had bribed Takamoto to serve a faux fugu, one that could not possibly be toxic. I'm guessing it was Mr. James, because he had both a macho and culinary reputation at stake.

It was the real murderer's luck that the faux fugu, the fish that couldn't be toxic, Chef Song's prized long-finned dragon carp, was accidentally switched in serving the cut-up fish portions for the actual dinner.

Miss Myrna was counting on the fugu Miss Rita ate getting the blame. Even if I had not figured out the switch and intervened, a toxicology report would have found the actual koi in front of her innocent of even a trace tingle of tetrodotoxin. That would have forced authorities to look further. Maybe they would have tumbled to Miss Myrna's scheme, maybe not.

The fact is that Midnight Louie got there first and delivered the goods. The fact is that I also ate the goods to draw attention to the substitution and the fact that Miss Rita's supposed fugu couldn't have killed anyone, that none of the fugu at the table was at fault.

And incidentally, I enjoyed Chef Song's stolen koi to the max. After all, it was already dead meat.

Except now, I realize that I outdid myself.

I have to hoist myself and my koi up the palm tree trunk to the second floor balcony, then spring the French doors open and stagger in, ready for a long wash and a short nap.

My Miss Temple is stretched out on the living room sofa reading a cookbook, which is suspiciously unusual for her. She spots me anyway as I try to slink past her.

"Louie!" She is upright, the book tossed aside.

It is flattering to be the idol of my mistress's eye but right now I just want to flop over on the floor and digest undisturbed.

"You poor thing! You've been out all day and half the night."

She hops to her feet. She is nothing if not a bouncy little thing, rather like the Energizer bunny, only in red, not pink.

"Louie, come here to the kitchen. Look what I've got in your bowl."

I do not need to look. My bowl is always piled with those camouflage yellow-green feline health pellets called Free-to-be-Feline. I never eat that stuff, only the goodies Miss Temple ladles on top to coax me into eating it. Usually that is something fresh and fattening.

I waddle over to look, just to be polite.

Arghgh!

"Louie! Don't turn your nose up at half a filet of fresh sole amandine. I brought a doggy bag home from the restaurant just for you. And I never even used any lemon on the part I saved for you."

Normally I would dig right in, "doggy" bag or not. But tonight . . .

Fugu-ed about it!

DEAN AND MARY ASK CAROLE:

Q: *Louie's favorite writer seems to be Damon Runyon. Has he ever thought about writing a feline version of* Guys and Dolls?
A: He's already played Sam Spade in a short story, "The Maltese Double Cross," so Louie would relish getting into something more theatrical. He does sing, after a fashion, but I don't know how good his dancing is. Louie's a ham, though. In his short stories, he's gone claw-to-claw with H.P. Lovecraft's übermonster Cthulu and he's had past-life adventures in ancient Egypt and Victorian London. His mystery series documents his sideline as a TV spokescat for a brand of cat food.

Q: *Did Louie ever audition for* Cats? *What happened?*
A: He didn't take direction well.

Q: *In addition to your role as Louie's amanuensis, you write a broad range of other fiction. Your prose is striking for the richness and sensuality of the descriptions. Are you conscious of being visually inspired?*
A: I'm definitely a "see" person. The odd thing about visual input for me is that it must be immediate. It doesn't linger. I visited Paris in 1994 to research an Irene Adler novel, then didn't resume the series until 2000. I have photos, of course, but all the sharp, sensual memories are gone. I may have to go back.

Q: *Poor you!*
A: It's a tough life. I'm drawn to extremes and dramatic setting; I like to describe both beauty and ugliness in terms of scents, colors, and textures: Palaces and slag heaps.

AND HERE IS CAROLE'S RECIPE:

Midnight Louie is a domestic cat, but he neither cooks nor cleans, though he does clean up a plate pretty well. This recipe, which is totally non-toxic, is often used at Halloween, which happens to be Louie's birthday.

MIDNIGHT LOUIE'S KITTY LITTER BIRTHDAY CAKE

1 18¹/₄-ounce package German chocolate cake mix
1 18¹/₄-ounce package white cake mix
2 3¹/₂-ounce packages instant vanilla pudding mix
1 12-ounce package vanilla sandwich cookies
3 drops green food coloring
1 12-ounce package Tootsie Rolls

Prepare cake mixes and bake according to package directions (any size pan, but it should be rectangular).

Prepare pudding according to package directions and chill until ready to assemble.

Crumble sandwich cookies in small batches in a food processor, scraping often. Set aside all but 1/4 cup. To the 1/4 cup add a few drops of green food coloring and mix.

When cakes are cooled to room temperature, crumble them into a large bowl. Toss with 1/2 of the remaining cookie crumbs, and the chilled pudding. You probably won't need all of the pudding, you want the cake to be just moist, not soggy.

Put half of the unwrapped tootsie rolls in the microwave until almost melted. Scrape them on top of the cake and sprinkle lightly with some of the green cookie crumbs. Heat the remaining tootsie rolls until pliable and shape as before. Spread all but one randomly over top of cake mixture. Sprinkle with any remaining cookie crumbs. Hang the remaining tootsie roll over side of litter box and sprinkle with a few green cookie crumbs. Serve with the pooper scooper for a gross Halloween dessert.*

*Note: Miss Carole already uses slotted metal spatulas for home litter duties, so that is an acceptable substitute for an actual pooper scooper and so much more elegant than plastic.   —ML

SING A SONG OF SIXPENCE

Anne Perry

Anne Perry's Victorian mysteries featuring Thomas and Charlotte Pitt and William Monk set the standard for historical mysteries. She is a charming and gracious presence on the rare occasions she leaves her home. This story introduces a new series with the intriguing detective, Theolonius Quade.

"My dear, how lovely to see you. You are so welcome!" Cicely Blantyre said warmly as she swept down the stairs past the glittering Christmas tree and hugged Lady Vespasia Cumming-Gould. It was Christmas Eve, 1864, and the house was decked in every room with boughs of pine and holly, garlands and wreaths twined with berries and ribbons, and, of course, candles everywhere. "I'm so glad you could come." She said it with great intensity, and Vespasia noted that in spite of her beautiful gown with its enormous skirts, she looked very pale.

"It was kind of you to ask me, how could I not wish to

come?" Vespasia returned. It was at least partly true. Since her husband's death a few years ago she had often spent Christmas away from home, but she had sensed in Cicely's invitation a certain urgency, almost an appeal. "How are you? How is Harold?" She referred to Cicely's husband, actually a man she deeply disliked.

"Oh, he's in excellent health," Cicely said without expression. "Do come into the withdrawing room and meet our other guests." And, turning around quickly, she led the way across the inlaid wooden floor, past the holly-trimmed portraits of her husband's ancestors, to the double doors. She threw them open. "Lady Vespasia has arrived," she announced. Actually, of course, Vespasia had arrived an hour or so previously, and her maid had unpacked her clothes and she had changed from her travelling habit into a gown of a rich purplish blue, and was thoroughly warm again after the chill of first a railway carriage, and then a coach through the snow-painted country lanes out to Nine Elms Manor.

The withdrawing room was also festooned with velvet, greenery, and ribbons. Harold Blantyre was standing in front of the roaring fire, effectively blocking it from the other guests who sat or stood around it. He was a broad man with a ruddy complexion and curly hair now thinning a little. To his left his sister Zelda sat on the sofa, her red skirts arranged artfully around her, her bold face full of curiosity. She was nearly twenty years younger than he, but under his protection and resenting every minute of it, except for the social position and very comfortable means it provided.

Cicely introduced Vespasia. Behind Zelda stood Charles Doland, a handsome man of roughly her age, one hand resting on the back of the sofa near her shoulder. The woman opposite was apparently his sister, Delphinium Stephenson, known as Finnie, and the tall, sandy-haired man with her was her husband Robert.

The only other person present seemed oddly out of place. He was in his forties, slender, with a gentle, ascetic face of great sensitivity, and one had to look at him a moment or two longer to see the humour in his eyes, the delicacy of his mouth.

Vespasia was accustomed to being looked at, even now in her middle age she still had that beauty which had made her famous throughout England, but she felt a moment of pleasure to be regarded with such warmth.

"Justice Thelonius Quade," Cicely introduced him.

"How do you do, Mr. Quade," Vespasia inclined her head, then spoke to each of the rest of them. They all made polite conversation about the season, the weather, hopes and fears for the turning year.

Vespasia found the chatter pleasant, but not interesting. Charles Doland was clearly courting Zelda and the match was in no way extraordinary enough to be worth observing, except that Zelda was over thirty, and therefore unusually late in marrying. There must be some story behind that, but it could be a number of things.

"Miserable business," Stephenson was saying, regarding the current civil war in America. "Tragedy."

"Brought it on themselves," Harold Blantyre replied tersely.

Cicely winced. "Robert's sister is married to an American, Harold," she said quietly.

"Why do you mention that?" he asked, eyebrows raised. "Do you think I should moderate my opinion because of it? Or are you trying to embarrass me?"

Cicely blushed, her eyes downcast. "Of course not, Harold. I . . . ." She did not know how to finish.

In that one exchange Vespasia learned all she had feared. She longed to be able to defend Cicely, but she knew perfectly well that to anger him might only cause him to take his revenge later, when there was no one to come to Cicely's help.

It was Thelonius Quade who spoke. "I am afraid I am at a loss, Mr. Blantyre. Forgive my ignorance. I did not know you had influence in the tragic war in America. I'm sure the last thing any of us wish to do is remind you of error. We are all at fault from time to time."

Vespasia's liking for him dated from that moment. She looked from his gentle, highly intelligent face to Blantyre's reddening cheeks and very obvious anger.

"I have no part in it whatever!" he said between his teeth. "You misunderstand me, Mr. Quade. I was speaking only of hospitality."

Quade's face ironed out in understanding. "Oh, I see. You were referring only to the discourtesy of slighting a guest. Of course. Excuse me."

Zelda made quite a show of hiding a smile.

Finnie Stephenson looked uncomfortable.

Cicely stared into the fire, but she too was smiling.

Vespasia looked at Quade and saw him colour very faintly as if he were aware of her approval.

Doland made some harmless remark, totally altering the subject, and Zelda laughed and added her agreement. The moment eased.

VESPASIA decided to go for a walk in the garden before afternoon tea. Two years ago when she had been here she had admired the area just beyond the terrace. It was enclosed by hedges, a space about fifty feet square with arches and pergolas, smothered in white roses, small single flowers, dozens to a head, so the effect when they were in bloom was like a wave breaking in foam high over the trellises. Every other flower was white as well: white lilac with a heady perfume, white daisies, lilies, tulips, shrubs with white blossom. It was a place of remarkable peace, an island from the rest of the world where anxieties, even griefs, could be set aside.

Now, of course, everything was white with the snow, but the summer memories would linger.

She took her coat and gloves and boots, and went outside alone. The air was sharp, but it was perfectly still, and she found it a pleasure to cross the terrace to the gravel path and go under the arch towards the white garden.

She reached it and stopped in dismay, certain at first that she had somehow become lost. The whole area was flat grass with croquet hoops set out to form a course. She turned back to see if she had come the wrong way, too far, or not far enough, but the arch she had come through was exactly as she had remembered it. The hedges were the same. It took years for a hedge to grow to this height, thick and perfectly clipped. It could not be new in two and a half years. It would barely have been new in twenty! There was not a flowering shrub or tree to be seen, the cherries, the lilies, all the roses were gone. The arbour where she had sat in the summer, surrounded by white petals, had been torn up. There was not even anything left to mask the burial places of Cicely's beloved dogs.

With a feeling of bewildering loss she turned away and walked back towards the house. Suddenly the air which had exhilarated her on the way out was cold, chilling her flesh.

DINNER was a nightmare. The food was excellent as it always was in the Blantyre house. Cicely excelled in both knowledge and art, and actually spoke in great detail to her cook, even supervising now and then. The dining room was decorated to perfection, and of course the servants were above reproach. The male guests wore formal black, the women were arrayed in gorgeous colours, silk gleamed, taffeta rustled, jewels sparkled in hair, at ears, throats, and wrists. Pale skin was flawless. The air of misery and tension cast a pall over everything.

"I hear the younger Miss Faulds is to be married," Finnie observed, spearing her fork into a roasted potato.

Zelda grasped her implements so tightly she shot her peas onto the tablecloth. Everyone affected not to notice.

"How nice for her," Cicely said vaguely. "I hope she'll be happy."

"Why shouldn't she be?" Harold demanded. "It's what she wants, isn't it?"

"Many of us receive what we wish for," Vespasia said very clearly. "And then find that we neither knew its nature, nor our own, well enough to have foreseen the reality of it."

Harold smiled with a twist to his lips. "If you mean that society demands we marry, and it turns out to give us at least as much grief as pleasure, then you are certainly correct."

"I meant rather more that we ask for things without being prepared to pay the price they require," she corrected.

"Is marriage so terribly expensive, Lady Vespasia?" Doland asked dubiously.

Zelda skewered another potato as if it were a long-standing personal enemy.

"Partnerships always cost," Vespasia smiled at him. "In thought and self discipline, and a certain sacrifice of one's own interests and habits."

Cicely took a deep breath, and let it out silently.

"If it costs so dear, I wonder so many women go to such desperate lengths to accomplish it," Harold observed sarcastically. He did not look at Zelda, but he smiled to himself with undisguised amusement.

"So do I," Cicely responded suddenly. "It seems we do not learn either from observation or experience."

Harold's smile vanished. "As Lady Vespasia said, my dear, it requires self discipline and a degree of sacrifice of one's own selfish interests and habits. You should listen to her. She appears to be a wise woman, suitably aware of her station in life."

Cicely blushed scarlet. Everyone else suddenly found their dinner plates totally absorbing. Even Vespasia was aghast.

Except Thelonius Quade. He assumed a judicial air. "I thought 'partnership' was the word Lady Vespasia used?" he said innocently. "That suggests contributions from both parties."

Finnie Stephenson giggled nervously. Her husband cleared his throat and glared at her.

Vespasia smiled at Thelonius Quade.

The meal proceeded in a similar unhappy vein until mercifully it was interrupted at about nine o'clock by the sound of music outside the window, and lanterns glowing in the darkness, shedding warm light over the snow.

"Carollers!" Cicely said with evident pleasure. She rose to her feet, flicking her skirts straight, and went to the door, as if delighted to escape.

Vespasia wished she could do the same, then decided that indeed she could.

"How charming," she agreed, and followed Cicely into the hall. The great front door stood open and the butler was listening happily to several adults and half a dozen children singing "Come all ye Merry Gentlemen" with more enthusiasm than ability.

A small maid staggered out from the kitchen carrying a huge bowl of mulled wine, and another followed her with a tray of glasses and a ladle.

"Wassail!" she said cheerfully. "Merry Christmas!"

The singing came to an abrupt end and amid much jollity the drinks were handed out, along with chocolates and gingerbread and small bags of nuts.

Cicely was very busy, absorbing herself with passing around the gifts. Not once did she look directly at Vespasia. The hall was full of warmth and the mellow light of candles, but all that Vespasia could think of was the flat light of the late afternoon in what had once been the white garden. What had happened to it? It was inconceivable that Cicely had destroyed it herself. It had been her place of retreat, a memorial to those creatures she had loved, solitude and beauty she had both built and nurtured. It could only be some natural disaster such as storms or a blight, or else the hand of man.

Cicely bade the carol singers happy Christmas, then as the door closed behind them, thanked the servants. Bracing herself she started back towards the withdrawing room.

"What happened to it?" Vespasia asked as they walked together.

Cicely hesitated as if to pretend she did not know what Vespasia meant, but her eyes filled with tears. "I went to visit my sister. When I returned he had had it all dug up," she said in a whisper. "He hasn't even played croquet since then. I don't think I have ever hated anyone so much."

They reached the door.

Cicely stopped. "I don't think I can face going back in there and being polite . . . not just yet. I'll go into the kitchen and make sure the pudding is exactly right. We don't put the threepences in until tonight, you know. I haven't even wrapped them up . . ." she stopped. She was staring at Vespasia defiantly, her face white. "Silver threepences," she repeated. "I always wrap them in little pieces of coloured muslin. Make sure nobody swallows one . . . by mistake. . . ." Then without waiting for Vespasia to respond she turned with a rustle of skirts and almost ran across the hall to the baize door through to the kitchens.

Vespasia stood at the door. She heard raised voices. She turned the handle and pushed, and instantly there was silence. Zelda stared at her, her face flushed, eyes brilliant. Charles Doland looked embarrassed. The Stephensons both shifted from foot to foot, Finnie flicking her skirts as if she had just brushed past something and disarranged them.

Harold Blantyre's face was set in granite lines of absolute decision.

"Are the carollers going to come in?" Thelonius Quade enquired.

"I'm afraid they have sung three songs and are rather full of wassail now," Vespasia replied, closing the door behind her. She could not look at Harold and keep from her face the fury she felt over the destruction of the garden.

"Wanting something for nothing," Harold said dismissively. "Cicely should have more sense than to indulge them."

"I disagree," Vespasia was blunt. "It is a charming custom, and a little kindness is good for both giver and receiver." She made it a statement.

"Your good nature is famous," Harold said with dubious sincerity.

"Nonsense," she retorted. "I am famous for several things, wit, money, and in my time, beauty—never for my good nature." She smiled dazzlingly as she said it. "Cicely, on the other hand, is widely admired for her gentleness, her generosity, and her artistic talent, perfectly displayed in her creation of gardens, such as the white garden at the far side of the terrace. It is quite the best feature of the entire estate."

"I haven't seen it," Thelonius Quade said with interest. "Would you do me the honour of showing it to me tomorrow?"

"Of course," Vespasia replied. "You will be amazed."

"Where is Cicely?" Zelda asked, her voice thick in her throat.

"She has gone to make sure the Christmas pudding is perfect for tomorrow," Vespasia replied.

"Good heavens!" Zelda affected incredulity. "Does she think the cook is incompetent?"

"Of course not," Harold snapped. "She simply likes to fuss. Interfering in the kitchen and getting in the cook's way is no doubt easier than entertaining her guests in the withdrawing room."

"I'm sure it must be pleasanter," Vespasia said. "Actually she went to make sure the silver threepences were appropriately wrapped in muslin."

"Muslin?" Harold repeated the word. "Whatever for?"

"To make sure no one swallows one accidentally," she explained. "They are very small, after all."

"I don't know why she bothers." He turned away.

"Because it is fun," Vespasia told him. "It gives surprise and pleasure."

He looked back at her, his eyes wide as if sudden understanding had come to him. "Yes . . . I suppose it does!" he said. "I can see all sorts of . . . possibilities."

CHRISTMAS morning was bright with a wind like a whetted knife. Vespasia chose to take breakfast in her room, then joined the rest of the household to walk to the village church for the service. The fields were mantled in snow and little flurries whisked up, flying like spume on the wave. Sheep and cattle stayed on the lee side of hedges, and all the puddles and ditches were iced over.

The sound of bells filled the air, ringing far out over the white distances towards the roofs and spires of other villages whose answering peals came back. People waved and called out greetings, children's voices lifted in excitement.

The service itself was the same as always, its familiar story woven into the fabric of Christmas. They sang the same hymns, the organ swelling and thundering out until it seemed the reds and blues of the stained glass windows shivered in the sound. Then everyone poured out into the ice and the sunlight, filled with exhilaration.

Zelda walked home on Charles Doland's arm, Finnie upon her husband's, and Thelonius Quade, with a look of wry regret, engaged Harold Blantyre in conversation so Cicely might walk with Vespasia. It would be indelicate to thank him for it, but Vespasia made a note to allow him a moment's warmth in acknowledgement of her appreciation.

Immediately upon reaching the house again Cicely excused herself and went to the kitchen to make certain that everything was in order for the most important meal of the day. The dining room had been prepared and was set with the best silver, porcelain, and crystal, beautifully made tiny wreaths of holly, scarlet candles, and an arrangement of gilded pine cones, exotic nuts, and marzipan fruit.

Surprisingly, Harold's ill-temper seemed to have disappeared. The moment Cicely announced that she was going to the kitchen he appeared to be satisfied, even pleased.

Charles and Zelda went into the library, ostensibly to look for a volume on the Middle East, in order to verify some point of dispute. The Stephensons looked at each other with deep meaning, and Vespasia found herself alone with Thelonius Quade.

"Would now be an acceptable time to show me this marvellous white garden?" he asked.

She hesitated. The day was beautiful, and in spite of the snow, it had been pleasant outside. In the shelter of the hedges it would not even be cold. Her anger at the garden's destruction needed a companion and in spite of having met him only yesterday, she found in him a sensitivity that made friendship natural.

"Of course," she agreed.

Five minutes later they were on the terrace, coats on again. They walked side by side along the path and under the archway into the blank vacancy of the croquet lawn. She stopped. "It used to be here," she said softly. "I only discovered yesterday that Harold had it torn up, when Cicely was away visiting her sister."

He blinked as if not certain he had understood. "Torn up? But I thought it had trees? Roses—trellises—lilac?"

"It did," she answered, staring at the featureless snow-covered grass with its bare iron hoops.

"I see." He made no further comment, but the sadness in his voice was filled with a new understanding.

They stood side by side, looking at the emptiness, the white glare of it in the sun and shadow, for several minutes.

Then without speaking further they turned and walked back along the gravel path, across the lawn and between the herbaceous borders.

CHRISTMAS dinner was, at least on the surface, a much happier affair than the evening before. It was served early, luncheon having been very light, both to allow the servants to attend church, and because the main meal was one of the most splendid of the year. It began with soup, and then fish, and the roasted goose came with boiled, baked, and roasted vegetables, sauces, gravies, and condiments. It was cooked to perfection, and everyone said so.

There was only one possible dish to serve after it, plum pudding, with of course silver threepences inside it, a sprig of holly on top, and smothered in brandy, which was lit the moment before the butler carried it in. The air was filled with the rich odour of it and blue flames danced on top. It was set down in triumph, not before Harold, but before Cicely. She thanked the butler, and with the silver spoon set about scooping a generous portion for each person. She did it with intense concentration, as if it were a matter of importance that each should receive exactly the right piece, threepences included.

Thick, whipped brandy butter was ladled on and the flavour, the richness hung in the air as one after another they tasted it and smiled, Harold Blantyre most of all.

They retired, not separately as after most dinners, but since it was Christmas, all together to the withdrawing room, to sit beside the roaring fire and tell ghost stories. They were all shivering with pleasure as Thelonius launched into his second tale when Harold gasped and let out a cry of distress. At first they all assumed it was a reaction to the latest twist in the story, but when he clutched at his throat, and even in the firelight they could see his eyes rolling, and a look of wild fear in his face, first Vespasia, then Thelonius, realized that something was very seriously wrong.

Vespasia rose to her feet and went to him, kneeling down so she could see him more clearly as he turned and twisted in his chair, his limbs jerking.

"Poison!" he gasped, his voice half strangled. "Poison!" he looked around, his frantic gaze resting on Cicely. "White garden!"

Vespasia felt a sick misery clutch at her. Her will refused to believe it, but her brain would not obey her. Cold reason told her it could be true. Harold had subtly tortured Cicely for years. Perhaps Vespasia's own reaction to the ruin of the white garden had been the last straw which had broken her ability to endure. That shame in front of a friend had driven her beyond sanity.

She looked up at Cicely and saw the black fear in her eyes, and hope died.

The Stephensons seemed paralyzed. Finnie was sobbing, clutching her hands to her face. Robert sat staring at Harold, but unable to think of anything remotely useful to do. Doland put his arm around Zelda, but she brushed him away and lurched forward to fall on her knees beside her brother.

"Harold!" she said, aghast. "Who? Who poisoned you?" She reached out and touched his face. "He's burning up!" she said wildly. "He's pouring with . . . with sweat!" There was no time to look for euphemistic words. And indeed Harold did look very red in the face, although in the light of candles and fire it was not easy to judge a difference in his normally ruddy complexion.

Vespasia felt for his pulse, but he would not keep still long enough to allow her to count the beats. He flung himself away from her, groaning and gasping, twitching all his limbs.

"His heart is racing!" Zelda cried out, her own face white, eyes blazing. "We've got to calm him! What can we do? Think of something!" She looked at Cicely with bitter accusation. "What did you give him?" she shouted. "Before it's too late!"

Cicely looked ashen, and Vespasia realized she was truly

afraid. She began to stammer, tears running down her cheeks.

"Cicely! You didn't!" Finnie said, aghast.

"Do something!" Zelda screamed. "Laudanum! Don't just stand there, you . . . you . . . for God's sake get some laudanum to calm him down, slow his heart until we can get him upstairs to his bed!"

Cicely stood motionless, staring at Zelda's passionate face.

Half on the floor now, Harold writhed and thrashed about.

Cicely leapt into life, picking up her skirts, and running out of the room, leaving the door swinging behind her, and they heard her footsteps clattering across the hall floor and up the stairs.

Vespasia did what she could to ease the desperate man and assure him that help was coming, although in truth she had no idea if any help were possible. All that filled her mind was horror that Cicely should finally yield to such fearful temptation. It grieved her almost more than she could bear. Her mind raced over crazy possibilities of trying to defend her, even somehow conceal what she had done. If he died a jury would call it murder. They would not see the years of petty cruelty and the pain which had finally destroyed her judgement between good and evil.

Zelda was rocking herself back and forth, repeating Harold's name over and over. The others were still sitting or standing uselessly. Thelonius Quade drew Vespasia's attention by touching her on the shoulder.

"Do you know where the village doctor lives?" he asked. "We should despatch a servant to fetch him, or I can go for him myself."

"I have no idea," Vespasia replied. "Zelda?"

"I don't know!" she waved her arms. "I'll send a servant, before it's too late. No! Judge Quade, you should stay here . . . please! Anyone can fetch the doctor, only you can see that . . . that justice is done . . . if . . . ." She covered her face with her hands. "Where is Cicely?" she howled. "He's getting worse! Lady Vespasia, for God's sake, go and get her to hurry!"

As if he had heard her, Harold thrashed into a new spasm of agonized movement, gasping and groaning.

Cicely came back into the room, a glass of liquid in her hand, and pushing past the others she knelt on the floor, her skirts billowing around her, and almost forced Harold to drink. He gulped and swallowed, gagging, then taking the whole draft, emptying the glass. He sank back, shuddered, and lay still.

There was intense, ghastly silence except for the whickering of the flames in the hearth.

"Oh God!" Zelda howled. "What have you done?"

"It was laudanum!" Cicely said hoarsely. "Just laudanum, as you said!"

Finnie continued to cry.

Vespasia felt for Harold's pulse, and his body was now perfectly relaxed and still, so she had no difficulty finding it. "He is very much alive," she said firmly. "Perhaps we could ask the footman and the valet to carry him upstairs to his bed. If he has indeed eaten something harmful, a dose of salt and mustard might be beneficial."

"That would make him extremely sick!" Zelda protested.

"Precisely," Vespasia agreed, rising to her feet. "That is the purpose."

The footman and the valet were summoned and duly, with great difficulty, carried Harold Blantyre up the stairs to his room.

"I shall sit with him, until the doctor comes," Zelda said, very pointedly looking at Cicely.

Cicely was ashen-faced. Vespasia took her by the arm. "Come with me," she ordered. Cicely obeyed, her eyes hollow, her body shaking. In the library Vespasia faced her. "What did you give him?" she demanded. "Tell me the truth, before it is too late."

"Curry powder," Cicely answered. "The special very hot powder sent us from India, that's all. I wrapped it with his threepence, in a golden brown piece of muslin. Have I killed him? I didn't mean to, I swear! I just wanted to frighten him . . . ."

Vespasia was startled. "I don't see how it could do," she said in confusion. "And even wolfing down his food as he does, how did he not taste it?"

"I put it in at the last moment, so it wouldn't dissolve into the pudding," Cicely admitted. "I know how he eats. I'm sometimes surprised he tastes anything at all. But curry powder shouldn't do that to him, should it?" Her eyes begged for a denial.

"No . . . unless he has something else wrong with him," Vespasia considered any possibility within her limited knowledge. "He did drink a good deal of port after dinner, and brandy before."

"Vespasia! What am I going to do?" Cicely whispered.

"For the moment, nothing," Vespasia said decisively. "We shall go back and join the others. I hope Charles Doland will be some comfort to Zelda. I had no idea she was so close to Harold. It was my belief she was not fond of him."

"She isn't!" Cicely said with a gulp. "He has refused to give his permission for her to marry Doland, and she is furious with him. I think he is doing it from spite. Doland is perfectly respectable, and as good an offer as she is likely to get, but Harold refuses them all. It is the third offer she has had that I am aware of, and she is very attracted to him."

"Really!" An idea, quite ridiculous, stirred in the back of Vespasia's mind, but it was too absurd to consider.

They returned to the withdrawing room and sat in terrified and wretched silence around the fire. Minutes ticked by, until at last the dusk and candlelight was shattered by a fearful scream. Stephenson and Doland shot to their feet, but Thelonius Quade was at the door before them, Vespasia at his heels.

All eyes turned to the landing at the top of the stairs where Harold Blantyre was reeling towards the first step, staggering blindly like a man fighting in his sleep. Behind him Zelda was screaming again, "Stop! Harold, stop!" Just as he reached the top she lunged after him, grasping at his shirt, but she was too late. He pitched forward and with a series of sickening thuds he crashed step after step all the way to the bottom, and lay motionless, blood on his face and oozing slowly out of his mouth.

Zelda crumpled into a heap on the floor, sobbing.

Vespasia went over towards Harold, but Thelonius stopped her. He bent instead, touching his fingers to Harold's neck.

"I am afraid this time he is dead," he said quietly. "I'm very sorry."

Zelda lifted up her head. "You did it!" she accused Cicely. "You murdered him!"

"It was only curry powder!" Cicely whispered. "Just curry powder! I only wished to frighten him!"

"Liar!" Zelda retorted. "Liar!"

Vespasia had nothing left to turn to but her absurd idea, but it was gaining strength in her mind. She left the tragic tableau at the bottom of the stairs, walking straight through the green baize door to the kitchen.

The servants were startled to see her and embarrassed. Ladies of her standing never visited the kitchen. No guest should see the array of pots and pans and the dirty dishes sitting around in stacks until they should all be washed, after the servants, too, had dined. After all, it was Christmas.

"Excuse me," Vespasia said hastily, making her way to the pudding dishes. In front of the shocked scullery maid she unstacked them until she found the one with the pool of brandy butter and the two plums on the piece of golden brown muslin, in which was still left the silver threepenny bit, and a yellow-brown mess of curry powder. He had known. He had not eaten any of it. He had pretended the writhing and the heat. In the reflected firelight the burning face was easy enough. It was his revenge upon Cicely for trying to frighten him. He would terrify her, make her think she had succeeded beyond her dreams.

What had he died of? Alcohol and laudanum, making him so dazed in his senses that it was not a difficult thing for a sister who hated him to lure him to the top of the stairs, and, in appearing to rescue him, actually push him?

But how would she prove it? She took the plate, carrying it into the hall, where now only Thelonius and Zelda remained. Vindicating Cicely mattered above all.

They stared at her in amazement. "Harold's plate," she said simply. "It does look like curry powder, but it really hardly matters, since he didn't eat it anyway."

"Then what caused his convulsions?" Zelda demanded, rising to her feet and coming down the stairs slowly. Her voice trembled and she clung to the banister as if she might fall.

"Revenge," Vespasia said simply.

"He was burning up!" Zelda retorted.

"He was drunk, and sitting next to the fire."

"He wasn't! He just had two glasses of port! I know, because I was sitting next to him!"

"And you were watching him?" Thelonius asked softly.

"Yes!" She swivelled to glare at him, and realized too late that he had a deeper, and more dangerous reason for asking. "I didn't give him anything!" she defended herself. "You all know that! She did!" She pointed to Cicely.

"She gave him laudanum," Thelonius said. "As you begged her to. On top of a goodly amount of alcohol."

Zelda started to say something, and then stopped. "I thought . . ." she began again.

"You saw an excellent opportunity to rid yourself of a cruel and domineering brother who had already twice blighted your life," Vespasia told her. "And you took it. You knew he hadn't swallowed whatever was with the threepenny piece. You knew he was deceiving Cicely, and the rest of us, so you added your own deceit to his. And then when he was so fuddled with brandy and laudanum that he couldn't stand up straight or keep his balance, in pretending to save him, you pushed him down the stairs."

Zelda's look was cold-eyed and perfectly honest. "You might believe that," she said huskily. "But you'll never prove it."

"Probably not," Vespasia agreed. "Public opinion will say that Harold Blantyre drank too much and fell down the stairs, but Charles Doland will know what really happened, and that will ruin your chances of marriage more effectively than Harold Blantyre could, had he lived another thirty years."

Zelda turned to Charles Doland, and saw in his face that it was true. Perhaps it was not her hatred for Harold that disturbed him so much as the fact that she would have allowed Cicely to take the blame.

"What is to be done?" Vespasia asked Theloneus Quade later, when they were alone in the withdrawing room. The doctor had been and the rest of the household had retired to bed.

"Nothing," he answered. "Only Zelda knows what she really intended, others will believe whatever her behaviour from now on dictates. I hope Cicely creates another white garden, and no one will ever destroy it. In future years perhaps you and I will be here again, and you can share it with me then."

"I look forward to it," she answered him gently.

DEAN ASKS ANNE:

Q: *Your first novel was published twenty-five years ago, and you've since become one of the world's best-loved writers of historical fiction. Have you ever felt limited, in your choice of period, by the success of two very popular series?*

A: Yes, but I am thrilled to be starting a new series set in World War I, as well as the Victorian ones in the new year.

Q: *You will soon be publishing the first book in a new historical series. What would you like to tell your fans about the new character and the new setting?*

A: Delighted. Joseph Reavley is the oldest of four adult children. He will become a chaplain in the trenches.

Q: *Do you think reader expectations of historical crime fiction have changed in the years since you published your first novel?*

A: Yes, they expect more detail, more characters, more of a novel.

AND HERE IS A RECIPE FROM THE 19ᵗʰ CENTURY:

VICTORIAN ENGLISH BUTTER SCOTCH

3 pounds sugar
1 pound butter
1/2 teaspoon cream of tartar
8 drops lemon extract

Mix three pounds sugar, one pound of butter, half a teaspoon cream of tartar, and eight drops extract of lemon.

Add as much cold water as will dissolve the sugar; boil it without stirring until it will easily break when dropped into cold water. (We call this the 'hard candy' stage.)

When done, add the lemon.

Have a dripping pan well buttered and pour in one-fourth-inch thick and, when partly cold, mark it off in squares. If pulled, when partly cold, until very white, it will be like ice-cream candy.

Copyrights and Permissions